DISCARD

Belshazzar's Daughter

Belshazzar's Daughter

Barbara Nadel

FELONY & MAYHEM PRESS • NEW YORK

All the characters and events portrayed in this work are fictitious.

BELSHAZZAR'S DAUGHTER

A Felony & Mayhem mystery

PRINTING HISTORY
First UK edition (Headline): 1999
First U.S. edition (St. Martin's Minotaur): 2004
Felony & Mayhem edition: 2006

Published by arrangement with St. Martin's Press

ISBN 978-1-933397-49-8

Manufactured in the United States of America

Printed on 100% recycled paper

Library of Congress Cataloging-in-Publication Data

Nadel, Barbara.
  Belshazzar's daughter / Barbara Nadel.
    p. cm.
  ISBN 978-1-933397-49-8 (alk. paper)
  1. Ikmen, Çetin (Fictitious character)--Fiction. 2. Police--Turkey--Istanbul-
-Fiction. 3. Jews--Crimes against--Fiction. 4. Istanbul (Turkey)--Fiction. I.
Title.
  PR6114.A34B45 2011
  823'.92--dc23
                          2011035619

To Malcolm and Alexis
with all my love

The icon above says you're holding a copy of a book in the Felony & Mayhem "Foreign" category. These books may be offered in translation or may originally have been written in English, but always they will feature an intricately observed, richly atmospheric setting in a part of the world that is neither England nor the U.S.A. If you enjoy this book, you may well like other "Foreign" titles from Felony & Mayhem Press.

⬩◦●◦⬩

For more about these books, and other Felony & Mayhem titles, or to place an order, please visit our website at:

www.FelonyAndMayhem.com

or contact us at:

Felony and Mayhem Press
156 Waverly Place
New York, NY 10014

Other "Foreign" titles from

FELONY&MAYHEM

PAUL ADAM
The Rainaldi Quartet
Paganini's Ghost

KARIN ALVTEGEN
Missing
Betrayal
Shame

ROSEMARY AUBERT
Free Reign

ANNA BLUNDY
The Bad News Bible
Vodka Neat
Breaking Faith

ROBERT CULLEN
Soviet Sources
Cover Story
Dispatch from a Cold Country

NICHOLAS FREELING
Love in Amsterdam
Because of the Cats
Gun Before Butter

TIMOTHY HOLME
The Neapolitan Streak
A Funeral of Gondolas

ELIZABETH IRONSIDE
A Good Death

PAUL MANN
Season of the Monsoon
The Ganja Coast

BARBARA NADEL
Belshazzar's Daughter
The Ottoman Cage
Arabesk

CLAIRE TASCHDJIAN
The Peking Man is Missing

ESTHER VERHOEF
Close-Up

NURY VITTACHI
The Feng Shui Detective

L. R. WRIGHT
The Suspect
A Chill Rain in January
Fall from Grace

Belshazzar's Daughter

Chapter One

A ROOM. FOUR FLAT, tar- and nicotine-stained walls.
A window: filthy, caked with viscous, black dust. Not that it
matters. Some windows don't have views. Some windows just
reflect, like mirrors.

Chairs and a table. Rough-hewn, this stuff, like the poor
sticks country peasants might have in their hot little sun-baked
hovels. But this is not the country. The air is thick—almost solid.
The city chokes upon its love affair with the internal combustion
engine. Not a sound, save the roar of the traffic. The shrieking
silence of the inner city.

There's a bed too. A small, narrow cot. It has an iron headboard, a series of hard, cold tubes. Functional, it recalls hospital
wards, prisons, institutions for the sad, the bad, the less than
whole.

Recently there was fierce activity; the bedclothes are
rumpled like old skin. One stained pillow lies burst open on the
floor. Its guts flutter about on the tiny floor-level breeze. Small

1

grey and white feathers, curled forever into short, permanent waves.

And yet there is not the smell of sex here, that faintly sweet odour, the one that not even bathing can erase.

Turning away from the bed it is possible to look at what lies upon it via the reflection in the mirror that hangs on the opposite wall. A sharp movement causes the flies that lie across the bed like a rug to stir and take flight. There's a lot of blood. That which hasn't oozed into the mattress drips lazily down an arm, along one outstretched finger on to the floor. In the wide, pinned-back eyes lies the still, silent reflection of the open doorway. A reflection within a reflection—the fascination of the infinite.

An empty bottle rolls over the exhausted carpet underneath the table and encounters an empty cigarette packet. The door creaks very gently on its ancient, rusted hinges and a sickness, unexpected, rises rapidly. Too rapidly to be controlled.

The door swings open a little wider and light footsteps sprint almost soundlessly down and out into the street below.

The door remains open and after a while the flies regroup. They cannot be seduced away for very long. The sound of the feet is not even a memory before the insects get back to the business of feeding. The thing on the bed has spread its goodness far beyond its own cracked shell. The flies make a large, mobile pattern on the wall, slipping and sliding with the movement of the thick liquid. They must be quick. The hot sun will dry it soon and then it will be useless. The flies know this and bloat themselves.

The final class of the afternoon, eight wealthy, spoilt and sulky boys between the ages of fifteen and seventeen, had been difficult. It had been a pure grammar session too. Probably not a good idea for a hot afternoon in August, but what choice did he have? The tests were coming up in just over a week and none of the students was ready, not even the painfully devout headscarf brigade, the girls from Bursa. And who could blame them? Few of them possessed even the most elementary grasp of the English language, and to be shut up in a stuffy room for hours on end during the hottest month of the year...He didn't want to be there himself! But he didn't really have a choice. He never did.

But now he was going home. The best part of the day had finally arrived. Though still breathlessly hot, there was that slight feeling of relief in the air which comes as afternoon slips imperceptibly over into early evening: the promise of night and a slight drop in temperature becoming a reality. It wasn't an unpleasant walk either, his route to the bus stop. Unless of course one had to live in this run-down and commercially defunct quarter of the city.

Balat. He tramped its filthy streets, its winding labyrinthine alleys, six days a week, but it never bored him. Dickensian charm was what this district possessed. David Copperfield, Pip, Mr. Jingle, Fagin: none of them would have been out of place within Balat's ambience of poverty, petty crime and picturesque filth. Fagin, especially, would have fitted in perfectly. Jews, old Jews, were the one and only commodity that Balat could boast of having in anything approaching abundance.

Not that they were obvious, these ancient, winter-clad, shy little Jews, muttering gently in some language they kept exclusive, secret, like themselves. If others had not told him of their existence it is doubtful whether he would even have known they were there. They blended. Suspicious of strangers and a perceived outside world that largely hated them, they would turn their faces to the wall as he approached and disappear into the brickwork, the concrete, the stone. For centuries the Ottoman Empire, now the Turkish Republic, had provided a safe haven for Jews. It was famed for its humane attitude towards the Hebrews. But old, suspicious habits, learnt in the hard schools of Western Europe, die hard. It wasn't personal.

Of course, at its root it was all economic. In 'better' parts of the city there were thousands of middle-class and wealthy Jews who lived lives identical in almost every way to the Turkish majority. But in Balat things were different. When money and comfort are absent, other more fundamental aspects take on greater importance. Traditions, rules, taboos.

Robert turned the corner into the nameless, snakelike back street that ultimately gave on to the main road and the bus stop beyond. It was exceptionally sultry. Even putting one foot in front of the other was an effort. He stopped and delved deep into his shirt pocket for his cigarettes and lighter. It was, for him, one of the luxuries of living in a city like Istanbul, this freedom to smoke in the street without attracting reproving glances. How different it all was from London. In so many ways. He lit a cigarette and took a long, deep, luxurious drag.

As he stood smoking, looking towards the thick distant traffic of his destination, a door creaked open behind him. He turned to look. There was nothing there save the blankness of a very shut, very old apartment building. Shut, that is, with the exception of a small wooden door on the ground floor that swung and creaked rustily upon its ornate iron hinges. There was nobody about. Like a ghost-town scene from an old Western movie, late-afternoon Balat was silent and, on the face of it, uninhabited. But Robert knew that it was only an illusion. Thousands of people lived in Balat. As soon as the outsider was gone, hundreds of old Jews would disengage themselves from the walls, pass from stone into flesh, from silence into rapid unintelligible chatter. At six-foot-three, with hair the colour of varnished pine, Robert knew what they thought. Knew what type of foreigner they would, quite naturally, assume him to be.

He turned back again, but, as he did, a movement just on the periphery of his field of vision caught his attention. He did a double-take and found himself face to face with what looked remarkably like a small gnome or elf framed in the doorway, its hand upon one rusty hinge. It was a woman, tiny, dressed all in black, her eyes momentarily caught in his, filled with fear and distrust. Then she dropped her gaze, her eyes sinking to the floor beneath her feet as she moved slowly backwards, dissolving into the deep shadows of the tenement that was, with her shyness, her prison. A sharp needle of pity pierced his consciousness as he watched her go. There was no way he could make her understand that he was safe, that he meant her no harm. Few of these people could speak Turkish, much less English, and for all he knew she might be one of the real unfortunates, the ones with numbers tattooed on their wrists, forearms or buttocks. Some Jews from Eastern Europe and Germany had settled in the comparative safety of Turkey just after the War; the names Belsen, Auschwitz and Ravensbrück still rang in their ears forty-seven years on. She disappeared.

Robert finished his cigarette and ground the smoking butt beneath his heel, pushing it deep down into the thick dust of the road surface. He felt better for his short rest and was just about to continue on his way home when a second figure appeared, this time in the doorway of the apartment block directly in front of him. At first, although the figure was familiar, he was so surprised that he almost ignored it. But the face, if not the tattered black jeans and unfashionable baggy shirt, was unmistakable, wasn't it? He moved his head forward a little, the better to see it. Could it be, possibly? Natalia? In Balat? The figure moved. It looked once up the street and then, sweeping its gaze down towards him, froze.

It all happened very quickly. He smiled and went to raise his hand to wave in greeting. She flinched, dropped her gaze and then, like the natives of the quarter, turned her back as if trying to blend herself with the wall. Robert took one pace forward and was just opening his mouth to speak when, visibly trembling, she sprang to one side and started running down the street in the direction of the main road.

Without really thinking about what he was doing, Robert followed. Now oblivious to everything else around him, he ran. Before him, running more swiftly on almost silent feet, was Natalia, slim, raven-haired, exquisite. Running away, frightened. Of him? If he had time he would have felt hurt, affronted even. But there wasn't and she was fast, faster than he had imagined.

Just before Natalia reached the bottom of the winding back street, she turned off sharply to the left. Robert was nearly upon her now. As she veered to the side he briefly, just for a moment, caught her. Long strong fingers grabbed at, but could not grasp, one bony shoulder blade. His arm recoiled as if burnt. It was thin, that shoulder blade, through the cheap cotton. Not round and luxurious and sexy like he remembered. Could he be wrong? Could this be someone else? She gasped, panicking under his touch, and increased the speed and thrust of her legs. Robert stopped.

He was in a courtyard, windows and squat green doors on all sides. As usual, not a soul in sight. Before him, so narrow it was more like a tunnel than a street, stretched an alleyway down which Natalia had disappeared. As he stood panting heavily, hands braced against his knees for support, he looked down into the depths of the warren-like thoroughfare. All he saw was the absence of things. Light, movement, colour, Natalia's fleeing figure...

For a few seconds he gathered himself thus, then he stood straight. She had gone. Not so much as a breath disturbed the pollution-coated afternoon air. Dazed, he made his way out of the courtyard and stopped in the street beyond. He looked up and down three or four times, but to no avail. The street, like the courtyard from which he had just emerged, was silent save for the roar of the traffic booming from the main road at its now nearby northern end. He moved towards the comforting sound of people and machines in motion, his mind a dark pit full of anxiety and a nagging distrust of what his eyes and his hands had just revealed to him. Perhaps he'd just had too much sun. Maybe the heat had fuddled his senses. And yet it had been her face! There could be no doubt with a face like that, surely! So fine and yet so sensual, well bred and yet somehow wild. Christ, he had to get home! If he started thinking about her now and moved in the direction of that shop...

He walked unsteadily towards the bus stop, the noises of people and vehicles growing around him with every step.

Dreamlike, that had been the quality of the experience, and yet he knew he was awake. The world of Main Street, Istanbul was too loud and intrusive to leave him in any doubt. Eighteen months ago he would have put it down to the medication and that would have been that. But...

He looked behind him to the exit from which he had just come. From his angle of sight the buildings on either side of the tiny thoroughfare looked very close together now, as if they were sealing, closing for business. The temperature was over thirty degrees, but Robert Cornelius's blood felt cold.

'Fucking bastard!' she said out loud, holding a hand encrusted with paste jewels up to the rose-coloured swelling above her right eye. She couldn't believe it. Again! That was twice she had been beaten and denied her fee in as many days. What on earth made these men think they had the right? It was a service, like any other. Would they take bread from the bakery and then beat up the baker to avoid paying him? Of course not! But tarts? Tarts, especially of the old and very used variety, were another matter. She knew the risks, she'd always known them, but that still didn't answer the vexed question of why. Men wanted sex, tarts provided sex. So why wave a twenty-thousand lira note in her face and then give her a black eye? Why not just take and have done with it? Guilt? A sudden vision of the broken-down wife with her prolapsed womb and ten children back home? Memories of youth when sex was free and life not quite so cheap?

But knowledge didn't make it any better. Nothing except money assuaged the growling hunger pangs in her stomach and the urgent desire for a drink with more of a kick than tea.

'Twenty thousand fucking lira!' she announced to the silent, midnight streets of Balat. Thirty-one years on the streets, pandering to the basest of men's desires, had done no favours for Leah Delmonte. Prostitution was no soft option. Like the movies, all couches, high-class madams and sherbet, it was not.

Of course, it had not been quite as hard when she was a girl as it was now. She had called herself Dolores in those days, and officially she had been employed as a dancer. 'Madame Lilli proudly presents, direct from Madrid, Spain, Dolores, wild and passionate gypsy flamenco dancer!' Just the memory of it made her want to cry. And they had known no different, all those soldiers, marines, young rich boys out for kicks, passing through her hands. Her ancestors had come from Seville, Toledo, some God-forsaken hole like that, and the Ladino language she had grown up speaking was supposed to be similar to Spanish. It was close enough for them. And she *had* been Dolores: she was exotic, she was beautiful, and at that time, undoubtedly, she could dance. But no more. Turning forty had sounded the death-knell for Dolores. That was five years back. Five years of being just Leah again. Plain Leah, good enough only for quick bunk-ups against walls.

And she was broke. She and Lilli, Madame Lilli as she had been in her youth, owed three months' back rent on their shabby one-room apartment. Leah at least tried to get work, but Lilli— six years older than Leah, fat, blotchy, and tortured by appalling varicose veins—Lilli was not enthusiastic about working the streets any more. She sat in most evenings, eating, smoking, and listening to morbid Arabesque songs on the radio.

Leah turned the corner and found herself facing the entrance to her run-down apartment block. What a place to end up! A dirty doss-house not five minutes' walk from the dirty doss-house where she had been born. Whatever had happened to all those dreams she had nursed so carefully as a child? Whatever had happened to her mother's great ambitions for her daughter? Mistress to the President of the Republic by the time she reached twenty! What crap!

Leah looked towards the window of the tiny ground-floor room she shared with her ex-madam. The light was on, and through the thin nicotine-stained curtains she could clearly see Lilli. Back already. If, that is, she had even been out. Leah's heart sank. She couldn't face it. Lilli and her endless moaning about money, the awful scenes whenever she looked in the mirror. What Leah needed was a drink. A stiff vodka would help, or raki, even just the one would do. But where the hell was she going to get money for alcohol? She forced herself on towards the dimly lit entrance hall, her eyes stinging with barely restrained tears. It was the boredom of it that was so bad. The hunger, the lack of nice things, the sordidness she could take; but the dullness! The never-changing, stupefying boredom...

And then she remembered. She stopped. Of course! Old Meyer, the Russian on the top floor. 'Shouting' Meyer. Lonely, anti-social, mad, some people said. But he always had booze, lots of it. Odd really. Why someone with the economic power not only to pay the rent, but to smoke and buy at least one bottle of vodka a day, should choose to live in a filthy rat-hole like Balat was a mystery to her. But Leah was not one to question. She pushed those thoughts away from her and imagined the delicious taste of neat spirit on her tongue. Provided you kept quiet, tolerated his unintelligible raving, and could close your mind to the smell of his room, Meyer was a safe bet. His filthy bottle could be your filthy bottle, and there were always plenty of cigarettes in his place, scattered like sticks of chalk all across his floor and over his bed. It was a last resort, drinking with a lunatic, but she was desperate.

She crept past her own door on the ground floor, careful to avoid the all-too numerous creaking floorboards, and ascended the stairs. Naturally, nosy Lilli would want in on the party if she knew, and Leah was determined that if any drink were going, she, and she alone, was going to have it. She, at least, had tried to find some work. Lilli didn't deserve a drink. Braving Meyer's shit-hole was Leah's treat. She licked her lips and moved forward.

It was heavy going for her unfit body, up three flights of stairs to the top floor. It was with great relief that she finally emerged on to the uppermost balcony and into the outside air again. She stood, hands on hips, panting for a few seconds. There were three doors giving off from this balcony. Cell-like hovels existed behind them. The first two were occupied by the Abrahams and their ever-increasing brood. The last one, at the far end, was Meyer's.

When she had composed herself a little, Leah turned her attention to her appearance. The old man was a complete crazy, but that gave her no excuse for turning up looking a mess. He was old, but he was still a man. And she was a woman, a professional woman. She still had a certain pride. A little powder on her sore and blackened eye, a dab of lipstick here, eye-shadow there...

She patted her elaborate hennaed wig with her hands, making sure it was firmly in position. A relic of happier, more solvent times, that wig. When she originally purchased it, she hadn't actually needed it. Perhaps she'd had a vision of the future all those years ago. She replaced the make-up in her cheap mock-leopard-skin bag, drew herself up to her full height, and sashayed past the filth-encrusted doors of the Abrahams' quarters.

Meyer's door was open. This was not unusual; the old man rarely shut it during the summer months. His tiny cell caught the sun nearly all day and a source of ventilation was absolutely vital for both his comfort and his health. His light, however, was off. This did not augur well. It indicated that he had probably drunk all his liquor and was now sleeping it off. Leah didn't know what to do. She had been looking forward to this drink, and to be thwarted like this...

She turned the possibilities over in her mind. She could wake the old man and ask him for a drink, thus risking a justifiably angry outburst on his part. She could go away boozeless and depressed. Or...

Or, if Meyer were dead drunk, she could switch on his light, go in and scour his room for dregs in discarded bottles. There was unlikely to be much, but even a drop would do. It was doubtful that he would wake unless shaken, and she was desperate.

She pushed the door gently with her foot, letting just enough light into the room to discern the bottom of his bed. A smell of sour vomit—or was it rotten vegetables?—assaulted her nostrils. No. Burnt food—meat. Filthy old bastard! God, but she needed this drink! She knew that the light switch was on the wall just beside the door, but she couldn't see it. She searched. Her roving hand skittered noisily over the cheap plasterboard wall as her deep-red fingernails sought out the telltale protrusion. She found it. The switch clicked and suddenly the room was bathed in a jaundiced light from the single grimy bulb. For a second she didn't really know what she was looking at. At first, and to her confusion, it appeared that someone had thrown a heap of old clothes and a large lump of meat on to the bed. But then she saw the eyes, crusted with blood but open, forced apart by the action of rigor, staring right at her. From the mouth downwards, right to the tops of his legs, Meyer was just a mass of blood and weeping organs. So ravaged was he that even some of the rib bones were exposed, white, stark, covered only by thin streamers of raw, shredded flesh. As she looked on, horribly fascinated, what was left of the liver detached itself and fell glutinously on to the blood-soaked bedclothes that surrounded the body. Leah felt a bitter sickness rise in her throat, but she couldn't stop looking. And the smell! Leah put her hand to her mouth and gagged. She had not eaten that day and the hot bile from her stomach, its only contents, seared her throat.

Her gaze travelled up his body once more, his entrails, his eyes, his hair, the wall behind the bed...the wall...

It was there. Drawn in what appeared to be blood. Huge, its hard edges feathered by dried drips and smears of red: a swastika.

Every brittle, Jewish bone in her body screamed in recognition. Sour yellow bile bubbled between the fingers clenched around her mouth and then she screamed. She didn't move. Even when Mr Abrahams from next door came in to see what was wrong, still she didn't move. She just screamed.

And twenty minutes later, when the first of the policemen and the doctor arrived, Leah, her legs wet with her own urine, was still screaming. She knew what the swastika meant all right.

'Inspector Ikmen?'

The little man half lying on the couch was holding the telephone to his left ear, but his eyes were closed. It was dark. Still obviously an unhallowed hour of the night. Not the sort of time to be talking on the telephone, not the time to be doing anything apart from sleeping.

'Suleyman?' he growled. 'What do you want?'

The voice at the other end of the line took one very deep breath and sighed. 'There's been an incident, sir. A very unpleasant business. In Balat.'

Chapter Two

THE VOICE WAS GRAVE and, for the normally cool Suleyman, unusually querulous, almost as if he were trembling. Çetin Ikmen half opened his eyes and observed with some irritation that he was still wearing his clothes from the day before. It was not easy living with Fatma when she was pregnant, consigned to the couch for three months at a stretch. Ikmen took a packet of cigarettes from his crumpled jacket pocket and lit up.

'So who's dead then?' He sounded resigned.

'An old man, sir. One of the old Balat Jews. A neighbour, Mr Abrahams, said the victim's name was Leonid Meyer. That is, as far as he could identify—'

'Where and how did he die?'

'In his apartment, sir.' Suleyman paused. It was a tense, troubled silence. 'As for how he died, Inspector...well, I think you'd better come and see for yourself. The doctor's already here, but...I've never seen anything like it before. Never.'

Ikmen started to wake up. He had not been imagining things. Suleyman was upset and it took a lot to rattle his cool exterior. It was bad, then. A nasty one. Shit.

'All right. Where are you?'

'Bottom of Fevzi Pa,sa, turn off towards the Kariye. You'll see the cars and I've got men posted outside the entrance to the block. Top floor.'

'Any witnesses?'

'There's the woman who found the body, another neighbour; but she's still in shock, sir.'

'All right, I'm on my way.'

'I'm sorry, sir, to wake you...' Suleyman's voice broke into something that sounded almost like a sob. 'I think you'll need to bring—'

'I never work without it, Suleyman, you know that.'

'Of course, sir. I'll see you—'

'I'll be as quick as I can.'

Çetin replaced the receiver on its cradle and stubbed his cigarette out in one of the numerous nearby ashtrays. He rubbed his face with his hands and, rising wearily to his feet, moved unsteadily across the room to the light switch. With a flick of his finger the room was bathed in white, cold, slightly pulsating neon. The effect upon his tired night-time eyes was like having sand thrown into his face. It was at times like this that Çetin wished he had an ordinary job: in a bank, driving taxis, hotelier—anything except police inspector.

But then, realistically, what else could he do? After twenty-two years on the force, it was no longer just a job. Like smoking or drinking, it was a habit, an addiction, an essential part of him. Giving up would mean painful withdrawal symptoms. He moved, blinking painfully, into the kitchen.

As he passed the sink he caught sight of himself in the small, cracked mirror above the draining board. Lit from behind by the merciless neon from the living room, his face stared back, an education in shadows, pits, lines and, where his cheeks should have been, deep skull-like depressions. Although the force could never be described as boring, it did little for a person's looks. Stress, erratic hours, long meetings in smoke-filled rooms, dead bodies...

He opened the door of the battered cupboard beneath the sink and took, from a long line of identical bottles, an unopened one. The English, he recalled from his language lessons at college, considered the dog to be man's best friend. But Çetin disagreed. Brandy was, in his opinion, far superior. It helped him think, gave his ulcer something to do, meant he could cope with the inhumanity of his chosen field of police work. Murder. How and why had he got into that? He had never got used to it, inured to the ugliness of its consequences. But then perhaps that was the reason in itself. If he ever did he would quit.

He put his bottle on the kitchen table and scribbled a short note to Fatma on the back of an envelope. She wouldn't be pleased. She'd never really got used to the job, or the drinking. He thought of her angry fat cheeks in the morning, her pudgy hand screwing his note up into a ball and hurling it petulantly down on to the floor. It wasn't fair. A devout Muslim wife and mother saddled for all eternity with a drunken, largely absent policeman. But it wasn't all bad. Çetin picked up his bottle again and smiled. There were eight Ikmen children—so far—with another due in a few weeks' time. Philosophical differences aside, this was a good marriage, characterized by both love and passion.

He checked his pockets for cigarettes, lighter and car keys, and made his way quietly towards the front door of the apart-ment. He looked around at the dim, dingy corridor and listened for the gentle breathing of his sleeping children. The unpleasant thought occurred to him that he would not be standing thus in his own home for many hours to come.

When he reached the third floor of the building he found Suleyman waiting for him at the top of the stairs. Tall and slim, his face looked drawn in the watery light of the single bulb above the stairwell. His eyes, large and sensual, looked even bigger now, widened by shock, stilled by the lateness of the hour. He tried a smile as Ikmen mounted the top step and drew level with him, but it was an effort which resulted in only a slight movement of his mouth.

'Where is it then?' Ikmen gasped. Fifty cigarettes a day did little to enhance his stair-climbing abilities. He took the wrapper off the top of the brandy bottle and tossed it away.

'The one at the end, sir.' Suleyman pointed to the third door down. 'Dr Sarkissian's still in there.'

Ikmen uncorked his bottle and took a large fiery swig from its neck. When he had finished he wiped the top with his sleeve and offered the liquor to Suleyman. His deputy shook his head. Ikmen smiled. 'Damned religious maniac!'

They walked in silence along the balcony. The immediate neighbours, like most of the other inhabitants of the block, were awake, nervously awaiting developments, clustered around doorways in their night-clothes. As they reached the second door a small, middle-aged man in a dressing gown came out to meet them. Suleyman turned to his boss.

'Ah, Inspector, this is Mr Abrahams, the deceased's neighbour.' Ikmen stretched out his hand in greeting. The small man took it warmly and bowed slightly over his outstretched arm. 'Mr Abrahams,' Suleyman continued, 'this is Inspector Ikmen. Perhaps you could tell him what you told me.'

'Of course.' The little Jew smiled sadly. Looking into the Abrahams' doorway Ikmen became aware of what seemed like hundreds of pairs of eyes watching him. Children, lots of children. Eight? Ten? No, more! It reminded him of home, the comfort of the couch, the endless litter of toys in the little ones' bedrooms. The same, but different. Here there was squalor, hunger in the eyes of these children, the awful stench of too many bodies crowded together in a tiny space.

'It was about midnight,' Mr Abrahams continued, his voice heavily accented and obviously unused to long expositions in the Turkish language. 'We, all persons, are sleeping. And then it comes, screaming, terrible, from Meyer apartment. All waking now. Rivka, my wife, very frightened. She say me "go look". So I go.' He paused, his bottom lip beginning to tremble, pain, great pain crossing and then settling into his eyes.

Ikmen put a hand on his shoulder. 'Please go on, Mr Abrahams.'

'The door is open and first I see Leah Delmonte. She live downstairs. Leah screaming, screaming like, like...crazy! She sick on dress too. I go her and then I see. Leonid on bed, Inspector, but not Leonid.' Mr Abrahams cast his eyes down towards the ground beneath his feet. 'Like someone cut and pull him body with swords. Terrible. Blood and, and smell too. Like meat. Leah screaming, but not look at Leonid, Mr Meyer. She look at wall. Because on wall...'

Shaking violently now, overcome by the horror of his recent experience, Mr Abrahams broke down in tears.

'There was a large swastika drawn on the wall, sir,' Suleyman whispered softly into Ikmen's ear. 'Looks like it might have been drawn in the victim's own blood.'

The night was hot, but Ikmen suddenly felt a chill ripple through his body. He turned again to the little weeping Jew. 'Thank you, Mr Abrahams. I realise it must have been hard.' His words seemed so trite under the circumstances. 'You've been most helpful.'

The two policemen pushed gently past the traumatised little man. From the apartment a dozen necks craned to watch them go.

'You catch him, yes, Inspector!'

Ikmen turned. Abrahams was ramrod stiff now, pulled up to his full height, his face trembling with fury.

'I will do everything I can, Mr Abrahams.'

Avcı was barring the door to the Meyer apartment, his arms crossed over his barrel chest. It was difficult for Ikmen to believe that this giant of a man was only twenty-one years old, younger even than his own eldest son. Though alert, Avcı was not on this occasion looking his usual cheerful Neanderthal self.

'Hello, Inspector,' he said as Ikmen and his deputy approached. Both men nodded briefly in reply and Avcı moved smartly to the left to allow them admittance. As he did so a short, fat man wearing pebble spectacles emerged from behind him.

'Hello, Çetin!' His voice was spirited, jolly even. He looked down at the bottle in Ikmen's hand and smiled broadly. 'I'm glad to see your habits are still as disgusting as ever,' he said, holding his hand out in the direction of the brandy. 'May I?'

Ikmen placed the bottle in the man's sweaty palm and lit a cigarette. 'Hello, Doctor. What's all this about then?'

Dr Arto Sarkissian uncorked Ikmen's bottle and took a long, satisfying draught from its depths. 'Wonderful!' He recorked the bottle, wiped his wet mouth upon the sleeve of his shirt, and returned the brandy to its rightful owner. 'Well,' he continued, 'it's all very fascinating actually, Çetin. Horrible, but fascinating. In fifteen years I've never seen anything like it.' He clapped his fat hands up to his fat cheeks. 'You'll see in a minute, but, just to summarise…'

There was an awful stench somewhere on the air. Even through the thickness of his cigarette smoke Ikmen could smell it. Burning mixed with blood.

'The victim received blows to the head. Some sort of blunt instrument, I should imagine. Considerable force was used, breaking the skull and exposing sections of the brain tissue. After that came the acid.'

'Acid?'

'Yes. Sulphuric would be my guess. Poured over the body and, interestingly, down the victim's gullet. It's possible he was still alive when that occurred.'

'I told you it was unpleasant, sir,' Suleyman muttered as the doctor related his findings. Avcı fanned his livid face with his left hand. Trying to push the nauseating smell away, Ikmen supposed.

'What about this swastika?'

'Drawn in the victim's blood, I should say.' Sarkissian crossed his strong arms across his chest. 'The murderer used a cloth, rag, something like that. From the condition of the corpse, its rigor, I'd put time of death at around four, five, maybe five-thirty yesterday afternoon. Come and have a look.'

Suleyman visibly whitened at the invitation. He looked at the doctor and smiled weakly. 'Dr Sarkissian, if you don't mind...'

The doctor laughed loudly and punched one gross palm with his other fisted hand. 'No, not you, Suleyman, I know you've seen it already,' he said. 'Come on, Çetin.' He turned and bustled merrily back into the apartment.

Ikmen took one last swig from his bottle and issued his orders to his deputy. 'All right, Suleyman, while I'm in there there's some things you can be getting on with. First, I want a complete press blackout on the acid and the swastika, understand? We don't want panic or this city's lunatic fringe getting new and interesting ideas. That means silencing the neighbours, everything. Give no details to anybody, do you understand?'

'Yes, sir.'

'Also, speaking of the neighbours—in this block and across the street—I want our men talking to them. I want to know where they all were and what they were doing around the time of the murder. I want to know if they saw anything, heard anything, any odd people about the place. And I want background. Anything and everything that they know about Meyer.'

'Yes, sir.' Suleyman turned and made his way back down the stairs.

The swastika was larger than he had imagined. Really quite huge. It dominated the tiny, litter-strewn apartment, making it look even more like a cell or one of those awful concentration camp barrack rooms in old documentaries about World War II. 'Bit of a shock, isn't it?' chirped Sarkissian as he removed a bloodstained sheet from the ancient iron bedstead. 'Here's your victim. He was in bed when he was attacked.' Ikmen could see that it had once been human. It had arms, legs, eyes, hair. But from the mouth to the groin it was like looking in a butcher's shop window. Blood, offal, misshapen lumps of meat, even at places bones sticking through torn and twisted ribbons of flesh. Now he was actually next to the thing the smell was overpowering. And those eyes! The horror in them! Was that why Sarkissian reckoned that Meyer was still alive when the acid was poured down his throat?

He couldn't speak, and silently indicated to the doctor that he should re-cover the corpse. He'd seen enough. As Sarkissian replaced the sheet over Meyer, Ikmen tried to come to terms with what he had just seen. He felt sick. Not enough to vomit, but distinctly unwell. Suleyman had been right. It was impossible to put that thing, an obscenity on that scale, into words. And the swastika—it was so personal somehow. As if it justified the act.

'Your man Suleyman's a very professional officer,' the doctor said lightly. 'There were two others with him when he arrived on the scene. Youngsters, younger than him. You can imagine how they were when they saw all this. Poor Suleyman admitted to going quite green himself. But he took charge, got them out, assigned tasks to them straight away. Tried to take their minds off it.'

Ikmen found his voice. 'I wish someone would take my mind off it.' His shaking hand brought the bottle of brandy up to his lips.

'Like I say,' the doctor continued, suddenly grave and devoid of his usual chirpy lightness, 'I've never seen anything like this before. The acid was obviously used as an instrument of torture. The killer didn't apply enough to consume or conceal the victim's identity. I can't really let myself think about the kind of agonies this poor old man went through before he died.'

Ikmen wiped the top of the bottle with his sleeve and passed it silently to the doctor. He was going to have to be careful now. Looks, he knew from long hard experience, could be deceptive. He gazed up again at the swastika. Meyer was—had been—a Jew. A racist murder, on the face of it at least. Until he had more information at his disposal perhaps. But for now it was the only lead that he had to go on. It was awesome! So blatant! It was hard to believe that even they—Nazis, Hitlerphiles, whatever—would be quite so brazen. Such people existed, he knew. But now, at this vast distance in time? Unless it was a crank, a sick mind working alone, killing for thrills.

'Do you think it's anti-Semitic, Arto?'

'Looks like it. The way the world is these days, it wouldn't surprise me. Hate is endemic to the human race, I thought you knew that.'

'But here?'

'Why not? It's happening all over Europe, Çetin. Germany, France; there's even been a Mussolini revival in Italy. Communism, Fascism, it's cyclic: Reds for a few years, then Nazis for a few more, then Reds again. It's why neither of us gets involved in politics.'

'Or religion.'

'Or religion. We're individualists and individualists don't join. That way we don't get sucked into ideologies that lead to things like this.' He tilted his head sourly in the direction of the body on the bed.

Ikmen sighed. 'I wonder why him, why Meyer in particular?'

'That's your job to find out,' the doctor replied, giving the policeman back his bottle, 'unless of course you subscribe to the concept you Turks call "kismet".'

'That it was his fate? No, I don't believe that. I don't believe that anything this horrible could be...ordained, if you like.' He paused. 'What's Armenian thinking on it, Arto?'

The little doctor's many chins wobbled as he laughed. 'What, kismet? I don't think we have any thinking as such. We're Armenians, hated infidels, outsiders, there's never been enough time to philosophise. Too many people trying to kill us, just like the Jews in fact. Grab your wife's jewellery, hope for the best, and run like the Devil's on your tail!'

Ikmen took one more look at the sheet-covered remains of Leonid Meyer and put his hand lightly on the doctor's shoulder. Levity, even Arto's well-meaning variety, was out of place here. It was like whistling in a cemetery. 'Come on, Arto, let's get out of here.'

'All right.' The doctor rolled down his sleeves and picked up his attaché case from the rickety chair by the side of the bed. 'There's a body bag and transport on the way. If any relatives turn up you'll have to tell them that I've got to do some more tests before I can release the body. It'll be quite a long job.'

The two men moved towards the door.

'What about the woman who found the body?'

'Leah Delmonte? I sent her to hospital. She was in deep shock. I'd give it a good twelve hours before you contact her, Çetin. And when you do, be gentle, OK? When she's had enough, you stop.'

'Of course.'

Sarkissian looked almost tearful. 'She's an old prostitute, you know. Lot of them round here. But then that's in the nature of poverty, isn't it? The degradation of the self.'

Ikmen often wondered what went on behind the merry eyes of his old childhood friend at times like this. He was always so cheerful, so light, so disrespectful. The Inspector knew it was simply Sarkissian's way of coping. His humour was a breastplate shielding the softness of the heart within. 'Come on, Arto,' he said, 'you're getting maudlin.' He strode purposefully out of the room and stopped by the door to speak briefly to Avcı. 'All right, Constable?'

'Yes, sir.'

'Good boy.' He patted him gently on the cheek with under-standing. 'We're going to dust for prints now. I'll send forensic up as soon as I get downstairs. Give the lads any help they need and try to keep the neighbours away, OK?'

'Yes, sir.'

Ikmen turned to Sarkissian. 'Ready, Arto?'

They walked along the balcony towards the stairs. The Abrahams had disappeared back into their apartment now, but they could still be heard. The father weeping; the children, their voices angry, disgruntled by lack of sleep, each trying to find some small area of floor on which to rest their ill-nourished little bodies. Ikmen sighed deeply. What hope was there for such people?

The two men descended the filthy stairwell.

'I'll let you have my report as soon as I can, Çetin.'

'Good.' Ikmen lit a cigarette. 'How is Maryam?'

A small but discernible cloud passed across the Armenian's features. 'As ever. And Fatma?'

'Staggeringly huge.'

Sarkissian smiled. 'And how is Timür? Still fighting Allah?'

Ikmen laughed. His mirth echoed and bounced like a ball, up and down the gloomy stairwell. 'Oh yes. Some things, and my father is one of them, never change.'

'When he dies he's either going to get a dreadful shock, or he's going to be unbelievably smug for all eternity.'

'I would think the latter, wouldn't you?'

Sarkissian grunted in agreement.

They reached the bottom of the stairs and stepped out into the noise and glare that always seemed to surround police cars *en masse*. Sarkissian held out his hand and smiled. 'I'm going to get down to the mortuary now. I want to have everything ready when they bring the body in.'

Ikmen took his hand and smiled back. 'See you later, Arto.'

As Sarkissian left, Suleyman returned. He was looking pleased with himself. Ikmen turned aside and hailed a tall man leaning sullenly against the wall of the apartment building. 'Demir!'

The tall man straightened up and came to attention. 'Yes, sir.'

'You and your men can go up now. The doctor and I have finished.'

'Right.'

'Oh, and Demir?'

'Yes, sir?'

'The usual. Anything of interest, papers, anything at all, back to the station.'

'Right, sir.'

Suleyman, now standing directly in front of his boss, was patiently waiting his turn. He had news.

'All right, Suleyman, what have you got?'

'A woman across the street, sir. A Mrs...' He consulted his notebook. 'Yahya. Said she saw a man, a stranger, hanging around the corner here at about four, four-thirty yesterday afternoon.'

'Any description?'

Suleyman smiled. 'Quite good, actually, sir. Tall, about my height, very blond, fair-skinned. Could be Western European or Scandinavian. Apparently he was smoking a cigarette, just standing in the road.'

Ikmen threw his cigarette butt on to the pavement and ground it out with his foot. 'Well done, Suleyman. It might mean nothing at all, but get a statement anyway.'

He looked up and across the road towards the dark, silent bulk of the Byzantine Kariye Museum. He thought back to his last trip to the site. Marvellous thirteenth-century mosaics: the Birth of Christ, the Death of the Virgin Mary; holy pictures glittering through the thin light of a late autumn afternoon. Fatma, outside, too pious to enter; the children running riot around the narthex and annoying the foreign tourists. The hundreds of foreign tourists, he recalled, even then, in October.

Suleyman hadn't moved. He was watching Ikmen. 'I know what you're thinking, sir, but it doesn't apply.'

'What?'

'The Kariye was closed. Been closed for weeks, sir. Emergency repair work.'

Ikmen sighed. 'Well, I suppose that cuts it down a bit. Any thoughts on why a foreigner might come here if the Museum's closed?'

Suleyman looked around at the district with undisguised distaste. 'I can't imagine, sir.' He turned and made his way back to the opposite apartment block.

Ikmen took a large pull from his bottle and watched as two stout orderlies carried a blue body bag across the street and up the stairs. He was starting to feel weary. He leant against the side of a waiting squad car and briefly closed his eyes, but Meyer's burnt and smashed face reared up in his mind and he snapped them open again.

'Sir?' A short, very swarthy individual was standing at his elbow, his once-smart blue uniform hanging limply from his spare frame.

'Yes, Cohen, what is it?'

'Sir, I couldn't help overhearing your conversation with Sergeant Suleyman…'

'Yes?'

Cohen shrugged. 'Well, it's just that I know this area. I was born here and one of my uncles still lives here. I just thought you'd like to know that there are some Europeans who work here, sir. Just a few streets away in Ayvansaray. The Londra Language School. Teaches English, French, stuff like that. Been there years.'

Ikmen pursed his lips, thinking. 'Mmm…'

'Well, it's a possibility, what with the Museum being closed. There's no other reason for tall blond men to come down here. I mean, even the tarts are a bit—'

Ikmen smiled. 'Yes. Thank you, Cohen, very useful. Do you know where this place is?'

'Oh yes, sir, I can take you there if you want.'

Ikmen took another swig and lit another cigarette. 'Perhaps tomorrow, if nothing better turns up. We'll see what Sergeant Suleyman gets from this Yahya woman, see if anyone else saw this man. Could just have been some disappointed tourist who didn't realise the Museum was closed.' Ikmen waved his constable off about his business.

Robert Cornelius didn't like late starts. His first class began at eleven o'clock; two hours later than usual. Tuesdays! He hated them. What could you possibly do with two extra hours at the beginning of the day?

But he recognised that he was particularly tetchy on this occasion. The events of the previous afternoon had unsettled him. A whole night of questioning and requestioning his own senses and memory had resulted in no firm conviction. Whom had he seen in Balat? He had seen Natalia. Well, he had seen her face. And that was the problem. If he had seen her face then why had she not acknowledged him? What was it about that fleeting touch that had so unnerved him? Why had she run away? Oh, she could be obtuse, even cruel at times. But it was just her way, her charm even. Didn't he like women like that? Well, obviously! His own history bore his preferences out time and time again.

He sighed heavily, sat down on one of the cheap plastic chairs on the balcony of his apartment and sipped his coffee. Of course this worrying and agonising was pointless. He either asked Natalia what she had been doing in Balat, or he didn't. He knew already he would choose the latter option. Ignorant bliss. Except that it wouldn't be; he would worry, he would fantasise, he would look at her with jealous, suspicious eyes.

Being in love with someone is not easy. In the early stages of a relationship there is a lot of uncertainty, a lot of nervous tension. Will your lover meet you? Will she phone? Is the attraction mutual or are you just a meal ticket? Unfortunately, even when the relationship matures, the problems do not go away. They take on new and, if one is not too careful, even more destructive forms. Familiarity can often breed suspicion.

Robert had been seeing Natalia Gulcu for just over a year. Seven years his junior and dramatically beautiful in a dark, full-lipped way, she had stunned him at first sight. He had been buying a bracelet for his mother in the Gold Bazaar. Natalia was both the merchant's assistant and his translator. She could speak two languages in addition to Turkish—brains as well as beauty. She had helped him a great deal on that occasion, his Turkish being quite ropy in those early days. She had persuaded him to purchase a gorgeous and expensive piece of jewellery and then she had teased herself into his bed. He had never had sex like it. He was hooked.

To his surprise, this sensual creature wanted to continue their relationship. On her terms, but he didn't mind. And, like it or not, that aspect at least was familiar. In a way it was comforting. As the months passed, lust became love and he showered her with presents to prove it. But this love of his was no easy taskmistress. In a whole year he had learnt little about Natalia. Her family, her history, even the location of her home, they were all still mysteries to him. While he prattled merrily on about his friends, his parents, his brother, her personal details remained a closed book. He had to make do with vague hints and riddles. Some of her family members were Russian, hence her first name, but that was as far as he could get. And he didn't push it.

He also didn't push the infrequency of their meetings. At least they were regular. Once at the weekend, and then again on Thursday afternoons, when they both worked short days. He wanted more, always had, right from the start, but that didn't suit Natalia; she had other, unnamed things to do during the remainder of the week. So Robert was alone for most of his leisure time; alone, resentful and suspicious. That wasn't unfamiliar ground either. And to make matters worse, he had to suffer all this in silence. She was dominant, unchallengeable, very like his ex-wife in that way. And, he felt, quite capable of walking out of his life without a thought should she be crossed. It was not a happy arrangement. But since when had that been a feature of his personal relationships? Sometimes Robert would even consider finishing the thing himself. But then they would have sex again and he would realise that he could no more live without her than he could fly.

He put his empty cup down by his chair and lit a cigarette. It had crossed his mind that perhaps Natalia and her family lived in Balat, but that was absurd. It was a poor Jewish district and Natalia was neither of those things. She dripped jewellery in a manner that he found almost vulgar, dressing like the wife of a plutocrat, and a crucifix or two always adorned the long golden ropes around her neck. Unless, of course, she was married?

With tremendous self-control Robert stopped his racing mind dead in its tracks. The 'married' theory was not one that he would entertain. Whatever her reasons for behaving as she did, marriage could not be one of them, for no better reason than the fact that he refused to believe it. There was a limit, even to his paranoia and fretting—on the surface, anyway.

He looked at his watch and decided that the time had come to make a move. He had a job to do; a thankless, largely point-less job, but gainful employment none the less. He would have to push away these thoughts about Natalia for the time being. He could once again rejoin his internal agonising when school was over at five-thirty, when he was free from the rigours imposed upon him by uninterested students, greedy school directors and demoralised fellow teachers.

Out on the street, Robert resumed his usual dreary daytime routine. On his way down to the Beşiktaş Iskele bus stop he bought a morning paper from the man outside the grocery shop and scanned the first two pages. He was proud of the way that, over the past two years, he had managed to master the Turkish language, with its endless suffixes and prefixes, not to mention the nightmare of vowel harmony. It had not been an easy task. But Robert had persisted. Being effectively deaf and dumb in most situations had irked him. Admittedly, with no close friends, and seeing Natalia only twice a week, he'd had plenty of time for study. But it was still an achievement.

A small article at the bottom of page two caught his eye. The name *Balat* appeared in the title of the piece, so it was only natural he should notice it in view of recent events. But it wasn't about Natalia. Why should it be? An old man had been battered to death in one of the seedier apartment blocks. There were no details, just that the police were investigating.

He closed the paper, folded it in half and continued on his way to the bus stop. The air was hot and dusty. The pollution left an acrid taste across his lips and in his mouth.

When he arrived at the Londra Language School, Robert found the place in a state of some confusion. The first thing he noticed was the police car parked in front of the entrance. Two rather disreputable-looking officers were sitting in the front, smoking and failing to answer their blaring radio. They ignored him as he passed and made his way towards his classroom. Typical police! he thought as he turned into the main entrance hall. It was then that he saw the students.

There seemed to be hundreds of them. Leaning against walls, squatting on the floor, eating, smoking, an endless babble of loud chatter coming from their throats. Why the hell weren't they in their classrooms?

'Robert!' A fair woman of about fifty ran towards him from the direction of the toilets, waving.

'Rosemary? What's going on?'

She came to a stop in front of him, breathing heavily. Her head was a good twelve inches below his own. She craned her face upwards and back to see better, her features breaking into a mass of crinkles, bags and lines as she greeted him with a smile. 'We've got the cops in, Robert.'

'Yeah, I noticed the car outside. Why?'

She took his arm and drew him conspiratorially away from the students. 'They're questioning the staff about our movements yesterday. I don't know whether you've seen, but there was a report in the paper today about a murder in Balat. It's to do with that.'

'Why us?'

Rosemary shrugged. 'I couldn't tell you. It's only the male

staff they want to interview. They've made camp, as it were, in the Director's office. They've already seen Colin and I think Lindsay's in there now.'

'Is it just the Brits or are they seeing everyone?'

'I think it's everyone.' She thought hard for a second or two. Rosemary was vague at the best of times, but under stress... 'Dieter's certainly been seen. As for the Turks, I don't know.'

He pointed at the students. 'Don't you think somebody ought to be teaching this lot, Rosemary?'

A collection of light and delicate fingers tapped him on the left shoulder. Robert deflated at their touch. Turning round quickly he found himself staring into the plump, self-satisfied face of Mr Edib, the School Director.

'Good morning, Robert!' he beamed from beneath his moustache.

'Good morning, Mr Edib!' Robert replied.

'Has Miss Hillman'—he indicated Rosemary with a sweep of one manicured hand—'told you about our guests?'

'Yes, Director, I know the police are here.'

'Good, Robert. Is just a few questions, that's all. The Inspector is in my office. He will see you now.'

'Now? I've only just arrived!'

The Director shrugged. 'You are next on the list. I have been sent to get you.'

Robert sighed and got a good grip on his briefcase before making his way towards the wide sweep of the staircase leading to the upper storey.

He was the oddest policeman Robert had ever seen, in the flesh at least. Dishevelled, red-eyed, reeking of both booze and cigarettes, he was like some sort of crime novel character, a refugee from the 1950s. Thin almost to the point of emaciation, he shifted constantly in his seat as if desperately trying to find a position that suited him. Between frequent swigs from a large brandy bottle on the desk, he would clutch his stomach with his left hand, as if trying to massage away a pain. Robert speculated that he must have an ulcer the size of a grapefruit.

He smiled when Robert entered, but he didn't get up. A hand crowned with yellow and splitting fingernails indicated to the Englishman where he should sit. Robert sat. The policeman lit up a long brown cigarette and cleared his throat. There was a large map of the Balat district on the Director's desk before him underneath the bottle which, Robert noticed, was only half full.

The policeman consulted a small, shabby piece of paper in his right hand. 'Mr Robert Cornelius?'

It was a deep, amazingly sober and cultured voice. Robert could not help wondering whether some strange act of ventriloquism was at work. The President of Turkey's voice relayed through the body of a dockside wino.

'Yes, I'm Robert Cornelius.'

The policeman's face broke into a wide and surprisingly white smile. 'Good morning, sir,' he said. 'My name is Inspector Ikmen and I work for the Istanbul Police Department. I apologise for taking your time like this, but a very serious crime was committed near here yesterday and I must ask you some questions. It is only routine, I assure you.'

His English was perfect. So much so that after a while Robert found that it irritated him. There was a feeling of being bettered and outshone. It reminded him of the time his best friend at school won the year prize for English. He had congratulated him, but what he had really wanted to do to him was much more primal and violent.

The policeman shuffled in his chair and clutched at his stomach again. He took a long pull from his bottle and slammed it down noisily on to the outspread map.

'Now,' he gasped through this latest onslaught of neat spirit, 'let me give you some details. Yesterday a murder was committed in Balat, the district bordering Ayvansaray. The victim was an old man called Leonid Meyer. It was a vicious attack.' He rubbed his eyes with his fingers, hard, almost as if he wanted to push them through to the back of his head. 'The victim was battered repeatedly about the head with a blunt instrument of some sort. It is imperative we apprehend the murderer as soon as possible.'

'Of course.'

'Our doctor has fixed the time of death at between four and five-thirty yesterday afternoon. In a moment I will show you where it occurred. In the meantime let me explain why we are intruding upon the lives of yourself and your colleagues.'

He ground his cigarette out in the Director's blue glass ashtray and immediately lit another. With a big friendly smile he offered the packet to Robert, but the latter declined. Although a hardened smoker, even Robert was beginning to feel that the shuttered little office was becoming too fuggy for comfort. It reminded him of every Accounts Department of every office he had ever visited.

'We don't have any witnesses.' A smoke-enveloped hand flew through the air in a large and expansive gesture. 'But at about half past four a woman in the block opposite remembers seeing a tall fair man standing outside the victim's apartment, here.'

He leant over the map and indicated an intersection of two streets that were all too familiar to Robert. The disturbing sight of Natalia reared large in his mind once more. There was only one apartment block on that corner; it was the one from which he had seen her emerge. He felt the blood drain from his face; his hair shifted and straightened on the top of his head.

'Now, the Kariye Museum was closed yesterday. The usual coachloads of tourists were not, therefore, present. As you know, apart from the Museum, the district has little to interest visitors. This school being the only other source of significant numbers of foreign men in the area, it was only natural—'

'It was me.' His voice contained an iron certainty. But his eyes shifted nervously. It had come out very quickly. It had caught him unawares.

'Pardon?'

Robert attempted a smile. The little man craned forward.

'It was me,' he repeated. 'I was on that corner yesterday afternoon. I go that way most afternoons. It's on my route home. I remember stopping there at about four-fifteen, four-thirty. It was so hot, I had to stop and rest for a while. I had a smoke.'

It was done. His voice had trembled slightly as he said it, for no good reason, but it was out. And why not? He'd done nothing wrong, he had nothing to hide. The Inspector took a small notebook from the pocket of his raincoat and started writing.

'So for how long did you stop, sir?'

'About five minutes. Long enough to get a bit rested and finish my cigarette.'

The little man scribbled furiously. 'What did you see or hear, if anything, while you paused?'

Robert thought. What had he seen? One little old woman in a doorway and then...It was a dilemma. It also sounded, to his internal ear, ridiculous and stupidly complicated. There were too many 'maybes'.

Maybe it had been Natalia. Maybe she had been running away from that apartment block for some reason. Maybe she had seen something, maybe she had done...Maybe? His heart jolted. Maybe not. He had no way of knowing. He couldn't make a judgement—any judgement. He didn't want to know. Did he? But the truth! His old schoolboy values of honesty and decency shrieked for release. He knew that he was pausing just that little bit too long, but he had to make a decision. He didn't know where a long exposition of the facts would lead, but he felt certain that it would bring anxiety.

'Well, Mr Cornelius?' The alcohol-misted eyes were turned full upon his face like the beams of tiny searchlights.

When Robert finally spoke, the lie seemed to come easily. 'I only saw an old woman in a doorway.' He laughed nervously. 'If you know anything about Balat, Inspector, you'll realise that they're rather a shy and retiring lot.'

'Are you certain?' The eyes bored steadily into his face once more.

Robert had a fleeting doubt; he felt it become visible on his

face, but only for a second. 'I'm certain,' he said gravely, drop-
ping his earlier light and good-humoured manner.

The policeman grinned. 'Good. That at least has cleared
up one mystery. Thank you for being so frank and open, Mr
Cornelius.' He pushed his notebook and a rather chewed pen
in Robert's direction and took yet another long swig of brandy.
'Perhaps if you could just write that down for me, together with
your full name and address...'

'Like a statement?'

'Yes. Just a few lines setting out the facts. It's just for the
records, sir. I don't think we'll be needing you again after today.'

It sounded innocent enough, committing half the truth to
paper. Robert picked up the pen and started writing. Another
waft of smoke swept from the policeman's mouth in his direction, stale and acrid. But it was less bitter than the feeling Robert
had in the pit of his stomach as the great gap where he should
have recounted seeing Natalia yawned large on the paper before
his face.

He signed, dated and added his address to the bottom of his
account, then passed it back to the policeman who read it and
put the notebook back on the desk with a smile.

'You write in Turkish, Mr Cornelius! He was obviously
impressed.

'I try,' Robert said, 'although my Turkish is nowhere near
as good as your English.'

The Inspector threw back his head and laughed. The
resultant sound was brittle and tubercular. 'I wish my father
could hear you say that, sir! Oh yes, that would give him a lot of
amusement!'

Robert was at a loss as to how to respond. He just wanted
to be out of that stuffy room as soon as possible. Perhaps then
he could put what he had just done behind him. Robert leant
forward. 'Can I go now, Inspector?'

'Oh, I'm sorry.' He stopped laughing and wiped his eyes
with the cuff of his raincoat. 'Of course you can. Forgive me, sir.
I have been awake nearly all night working on this case.'

Robert got up from his chair and bent across the desk, extending his hand towards the policeman. 'Goodbye, Inspector.'

They shook hands. The little Turk's hand, Robert observed, was like the rest of his body. Dry, warm and grimy.

'Goodbye, sir, and thank you. We will be in touch should we need you again.' Robert winced, a reaction not lost on the policeman. 'But I don't think we will.'

The Englishman's face relaxed and he walked towards the door. He was free. Now he could forget.

As Robert pulled the door shut behind him the policeman's smile vanished and he looked down at the short statement the Englishman had just given him. His expression said nothing about what he thought of the document, but there was a distinct sense of unease in the smoke-sodden air around him.

Chapter Three

SERGEANT SULEYMAN LOOKED down at the meagre collection of papers, books and documents on the table and sighed. Each item neatly packaged in individual plastic bags, every one labelled in a fine and cautious hand. It wasn't much to show for a long lifetime. A passport, a couple of photos, a few bills, books of various sizes.

Ahmet Demir entered the office and placed another bag down upon the table. 'Is that everything?' Suleyman asked.

'Just about, sir,' replied Demir. 'We've a few scraps of paper left, torn bits, rubbish, you know. Then that's it.'

'Good.'

'When's the Inspector due back?'

'I don't know really. He's been interviewing up at that language school all morning. I suppose it depends how he gets on.'

Suleyman bit his lower lip nervously. It was nearly midday, Ikmen had been working for a very long time. He would be tired now; tired and irritable. Of course at the school he would conduct himself with characteristic professionalism. When he returned to the station, however...

'How did you get on at the Museum, sir?' Demir's voice cut across Suleyman's musings.

'Nothing much. Two women were turned away at about lunchtime. There's been a "Closed" notice outside for weeks. Balat has little to interest tourists when the Museum is closed.'

Demir shrugged. 'I'll just go and finish off then, sir.'

'Oh, Demir...'

'Yes, sir?'

'Any luck with the fingerprints yet?'

Demir yawned and rubbed his eyes. He was shattered. 'No, not really, only the victim's. No sign of forced entry. Looks like the murderer just walked in through the door, did what he had to and left. I don't think he can have touched anything.' He smiled weakly. 'That old man lived like a pig, you know, sir. There was even a heap of vomit over by the door.'

Suleyman pulled a face.

Somewhere deep inside, Demir sneered at his discomfort. He didn't have a lot of time for Ikmen's handsome, fastidious young sergeant. He continued with only thinly disguised glee. 'Dr Sarkissian wants to take a look at it, fish around—'

'All right, Demir!' Suleyman waved him out of the room. He'd heard quite enough.

Demir closed the door behind him as he left. Suleyman squeezed uncomfortably between the recently acquired evidence table and his desk and sat down.

Owing to lack of space, Ikmen and Suleyman were required to share an office. For men involved in such serious work it was an insult really. Tiny, cramped and airless, the whole room was dominated by Ikmen's enormous mahogany desk. He worked in total confusion, mountains of paper, files and ashtrays reared up and out from the sides of this impressive edifice. Suleyman's desk, by contrast, was small, neat and functional. His tall figure dominated the empty wastes of wood in front of him.

Suleyman's paperwork lived where Allah intended, in drawers and on the shelves above his head.

It was an unconventional partnership. Suleyman, young, unmarried, clean-living and quiet, was an odd fish to find in the same pool with Ikmen. But unlike all the other sergeants the Inspector had worked with before, Suleyman pleased him. Ikmen could trust him. There was nothing underhand, sly or competitive about the man. None of that awful trying to score points off the boss and make him look stupid that seemed to be the overriding obsession of most young sergeants in the station. Suleyman, for his part, knew that he was valued and it pleased him. His pay was low and the conditions of the job were often dreadful, but working with Ikmen more than made up for all that. Ikmen taught him about life, 'the raw material of homicide', as he put it. There were so many elements. Even a simple thing, like sex, could be so involved. Since working with Ikmen, Suleyman had come to see that life was a lot more complicated than he had originally thought.

The office door flew open and smashed against the corner of the sergeant's desk. A bony hand clutching a large bottle and an overpowering smell of stale cigarettes preceded the visitor into the room.

'Hello, sir.' Suleyman stood up.

Ikmen headed straight for the table wedged between the two desks and placed his bottle on it. He delicately fingered each small plastic bag, peering red- and watery-eyed at their contents. 'This is Meyer's stuff, I take it.'

'Yes, sir.'

Ikmen motioned for Suleyman to resume his seat and grabbed a small handful of bags. He squeezed behind the bulk of his desk and sat down. A skyscraper of cardboard files obscured Suleyman's view of Ikmen almost completely.

'I found our tall foreign witness at the school,' said a disembodied voice. 'An Englishman, a Mr Cornelius. He was having a rest and a cigarette on that corner at about four-thirty yesterday. Said he saw and heard nothing, but I wonder.'

'What makes you think that, sir?'

'Unsteady, nervous eyes. Not quite right, Mr Cornelius. Don't ask me how!' He paused. 'Hesitation too. Seemed to take him an awful long time to decide that he hadn't seen or heard anything.'

'Perhaps he was just considering. Searching through his mind to make sure he didn't miss some minor detail that might be of use to us.'

'You're too trusting.' Ikmen sighed deeply. 'Come over here will you, Suleyman. Help me look through this lot.'

Suleyman got up from his seat and, squeezing round the evidence table, made his way to the 'business' side of Ikmen's desk.

'One Turkish passport.' Ikmen held a small, flat, green thing up to the light. He screwed his eyes up against the hot glare from outside the window and grunted impatiently. 'Suleyman, do you think we can have that window shut, please? There's dust blowing all over me and it's not helping.'

The dust which in the summer billowed up continually from the road below was indeed unpleasant. Suleyman, however, found it infinitely preferable to Ikmen's cigarette smoke. The window and its degree of openness was a constant bone of contention between them.

'But, sir!'

'Just do it, will you? If you die from passive smoking I promise to support your aged parents.'

Suleyman stretched behind Ikmen's back and pulled the edge of the rotted window-frame downwards. Dust and grit already in the room fell and settled on every surface as the gentle breeze that kept it aloft was extinguished. The smoke from Ikmen's cigarette wafted straight into his face. He grimaced and fanned it timorously with his hand.

'What's this?' said Ikmen, holding up a small plastic-covered volume. 'Address book.'

He unwrapped the item and started carefully flicking through its yellowing pages. Suleyman craned his head down over Ikmen's shoulder to get a better view. At first glance the book appeared to be empty. Page after page of blank sheets appeared before the policemen's eyes.

'Not exactly a socialite, was he, sir?'

Ikmen ignored, on principle, all and any of his sergeant's rudimentary attempts at wit and so continued to work his way methodically towards the end of the volume. It was only when he reached the very last page that his efforts were rewarded. Suleyman looked at the four separate blocks of black, spidery script and frowned.

'What kind of writing is that?'

Ikmen held the page very close to his face. The effort of trying to decipher the characters caused him to screw his face up and squint.

'Cyrillic,' he said after a pause. He rubbed his unshaven chin with his hand. 'I think so anyway.'

'Cyrillic?'

Ikmen twisted his head around and looked hard into Suleyman's face. Whatever the state was teaching young people in schools and colleges obviously did not extend to providing them with enough pointless trivia.

'Cyrillic script,' he expounded with great patience, 'is that used by people belonging to the Slavic ethnic group. Russians, Poles, Bulgarians...'

'Ah.'

'Logical really. Neighbours seemed to think he was a Russian émigré, didn't they?' He stared down at the strange characters. 'By the way, Suleyman, what happened at the Museum?'

'Nothing. Saw nothing, heard nothing.'

'Like my Mr Cornelius. Did you contact the hospital?' He took his eyes away from the address book and looked into his cigarette packet. His face whitened. He looked up sharply. 'Oh no, I'm out of cigarettes!'

It was a violent, but at the same time plaintive outburst. A cry for help. Suleyman chose to ignore it. A small revenge for the closure of the window.

'Miss Delmonte is still too traumatised to be interviewed, sir. You can take it up with her doctor if you like, but...'

Ikmen wasn't listening. A real crisis had occurred. The worst. He threw the empty cigarette packet down on the floor and put his head in his hands. The sort of tantrum Suleyman had feared earlier threatened. Ikmen was overtired and something like this, a lack of cigarettes, was all that was needed to set him off. The young man knew that he had to be very careful.

'I can't function like this!' Ikmen raised his head again and snapped out an order. 'Go and ask Cohen for some cigarettes.'

Suleyman clambered his way towards the door. No progress could be made while Ikmen was craving nicotine.

'Oh, and while you're at it, ask that lot if any of them can read Cyrillic script. It's unlikely, half of them have trouble with Turkish, but you may as well ask.'

'Yes, sir.'

Suleyman left, pulling the door shut behind him as he went. Ikmen looked down at the little address book again. If the Department was, as he had always suspected, full of half-educated morons, it didn't really matter. He knew a man who could decipher strange and exotic alphabets of almost any sort with no problem. The cigarette crisis, however, was quite another matter. If that one wasn't resolved in the very near future there was going to be a tantrum of catastrophic proportions. He had been without nicotine for more than five minutes. Ikmen's Law clearly stated that the maximum time between each cigarette should be no greater than three minutes, barring sleep and death. His fingers twitched nervously, aching for something carcinogenic to hang on to.

Ikmen's telephone rang. He scrabbled wildly amid the confusion heaped upon his desk as he attempted to locate it. Pens, paper, ash and dust flew everywhere. He narrowly missed tipping an ashtray into his own lap. Then with a creak, a groan and a loud slap as cardboard hit linoleum, a great pile of files avalanched to the floor and revealed, at last, the offending article. Ikmen picked up the receiver and scowled. The fingers of his left hand ached. He hoped that Suleyman wouldn't be long. He spoke into the phone.

'Ikmen.' What now? he thought gloomily.

The tumultuous silence at the other end of the line left Ikmen in no doubt as to the identity of his caller. Only one person ever really made him sweat for an answer.

He groaned. 'Hello, Fatma.'

Her voice was deep, soft and tired rather than angry. 'Just one question, Çetin. How do you expect me to feed us all on two hundred lira?'

Ikmen shut his eyes for a second and ground his teeth angrily. Stupid! He could have left a few notes for her on the kitchen table, but he hadn't. He checked quickly inside his jacket pocket for the bulging wallet he knew already was there, and groaned again. 'Oh, no! I'm sorry, Fatma. I got called late last night and in the rush—'

She remained frighteningly calm. 'It's all right. We've all had bread for lunch. Just...' It wasn't all right and her voice broke. Fatma's battle with her anger was over. Her composure snapped. 'Just don't bother to come home at all!'

'I—'

'There is not so much as a tomato in the refrigerator! Of course we have enough brandy for the combined armed forces of NATO...'

Suleyman came back into the office and threw a full packet of cigarettes on to Ikmen's desk. The Inspector was on them like a starved hyena. He even smiled, weakly.

'...have eight children and yet you still behave as if you were a single...'

Fatma's voice was getting even louder. But Ikmen was on his way to personal sanity again. He excused himself to her.

'Just a minute, Fatma.' He put his hand over the shouting receiver and lit up immediately. 'Thanks, Suleyman. Any Russian speakers on the force?'

'Not one, sir.'

He took his hand away from the telephone and spoke to his

wife once again. This time he was more collected, less afraid, as if tar and nicotine had invested him with courage.

'Sorry, Fatma. Look, I'll send a man round with some money right now. Is Timür there?'

'Unfortunately.'

'Can I speak to him?'

'If you want. Just get that money to me!'

She banged the receiver down and he heard the sound of her slow, heavy footsteps, padding laboriously down the apartment hall. He looked across at Suleyman. 'There's something I want you to do.'

'Sir?'

He put his hand in the pocket of his jacket and drew out a bunch of keys. 'Here are my car keys. Drive round to my apartment and'—he pulled a large wad of notes out of his wallet and placed them in Suleyman's hand—'give my wife this.'

'Your car, sir?'

'Yes!'

Suleyman made as if to go but Ikmen held up a hand to stop him. 'And that's not all. Pick my father up while you're there.'

'Sir?'

'My father can speak Russian.' He gestured towards Meyer's tiny address book lying open on his desk. 'He can decipher this for us.'

'Bring him here, sir?'

'What do you think!'

The silence at the other end of the phone ended with the arrival of a dry and querulous voice. 'Çetin?'

Suleyman put Ikmen's keys and money into his trouser pocket and left the office. 'Hello, Timür. Sorry to bother you, but...I've got something here I don't understand and I need your help...'

Robert Cornelius had reckoned without his conscience. He

didn't like lying. It made him feel bad. There was that previous experience of course, which had, against his expectations, been resolved in his favour. But this he felt was different. This was, somewhere along the line, going to rebound upon him when he least expected it. He was convinced. Perhaps it was a function of having attended public school that made him think like this? Seven very impressionable years of being told you cannot expect to get away with anything has a lasting effect. His masters had in the main been right too. Robert had rarely got away with anything. Barring that one exception. Or rather two? Those out-ofcharacter explosions of violence that had led to so many lies, so much guilt.

It made him feel quite bitter sometimes—often. Child and man he had always, like it or not, paid his dues. It was the whole reason why he was so nice, so easy to get on with. Unpleasant acts came back upon a person. Pleasantness and honesty, however insincere, were merely tools, aids to self-preservation. Common sense.

He looked at the faces of the students sitting before him. Two were diligently working their way through the exercise on page nine. A minor but nevertheless satisfying victory for academia. There were ten in this set and the usual form was for him to set work and then watch the whole class stare out of the window for the next half-hour. The two who were working, Turkish boys, had obviously either taken fright at the notion of the impending exams, or been bullied into it by their parents. There could be no other reason. Robert knew how the minds of adolescents worked better than most.

Eight years teaching at an inner-London comprehensive had given him tremendous insight. He shuddered. Even five years on, the merest thought of Rosebury Downs School made him cold, his mouth dry and parched. He could still see their faces: Billy Smith, the Norris twins, that little blond bastard who always sat by the radiator. Robert pulled his mind away quickly.

He looked at his watch. Thank God! Only five more minutes of this class and then break time. Coffee, fags, the comparative safety of the staff room. There were other people to talk to in there. Fellow teachers—inane, boring, often downright annoying, but they provided what he desperately needed. Distraction from his own thoughts. That nagging and persistent desire to do something very unwise. And pointless. What good would questioning Natalia do? The damage, the concealment was done. Whether or not she was in Balat was surely academic now? Anyway, maybe she had gone there in connection with her work? It was unlikely, but then anything was possible, wasn't it?

But still his mind refused to let him rest. Natalia had always emphasised the fact that their relationship had to be built upon mutual trust. How would it look if now, after just over a year of (admittedly uneasy) peace, he started putting her through the third degree? Knowing Natalia as he did it would almost certainly mean the termination of their affair. But the doubts remained. That she had nothing to do with the murder, he was certain. But what had she been doing there? That afternoon stroll had a definite dreamlike quality, both at the time and in retrospect. Perhaps it was the archaic nature of the quarter? A district of the city that had got caught up and detained somewhere halfway along its journey towards the present. A place of ghosts. It had been hot too, very, very hot. His head bare; the heat haze; dizziness; a recovering but nevertheless untreated gippy stomach...

But really such excuses were puny. Close investigation would no doubt reveal—what? Names and faces from many and various points in time became confused, missorted, like jumbled cards in his head. He had to stick with the bad stomach! That was a fact, all the rest was—he made himself look at his wrist.

The class was over. Thank Christ! His musing subsided into the deep feeling of relief that swept across him.

'All right, everybody,' he said. 'Books away now.'

There was a frantic scraping of chair legs against the floor as ten suddenly animated teenagers leapt from their seats and made towards the door of the classroom, their faces smiling, voices chattering merrily as they pushed past him. Robert was reminded of the Bible story about Jesus raising Lazarus from the dead. He didn't understand. Surely learning was supposed to be a pleasurable and mind-expanding experience?

'Complete the exercise on page nine at home!' he shouted above the general multilingual babble. Then added in a barely audible voice, 'If any of you can be arsed.'

The students left the classroom. The more academically inclined would probably return for one or two of the afternoon sessions. The rest, Robert knew, would repair to Taksim Square and the exotic delights of McDonald's. There they could do what they did best: spend money, imbibe plastic Americana of the worst kind and show each other their jewellery. Very like their English counterparts in fact, although probably minus the flick knives. Just like teenagers all over the world.

Robert gathered his papers, pens and textbooks together and put them into his briefcase. There had been very little point taking them out in the first place, but…He locked his case with its small brass key and leant heavily on the top of his desk. Even if he did go and see Natalia, how the hell was he going to broach the subject of Balat? Even to him it sounded ridiculous. What business was it of his anyway? The decision to lie to the police about Natalia's presence had been his and his alone. She had seen him. She must have done. Logically, if there had been anything, well, dodgy, she would have contacted him. He was after all her lover, and weren't lovers supposed to share the bad as well as the good?

Robert Cornelius picked up his briefcase, checked his pockets for cigarettes and made his way purposefully towards the staff room. Perhaps half an hour of undiluted cricket scores and the relative merits of Turkish manhood would cure his ridiculous internal wrangling.

Timür Ikmen was less a person and more a total experience. If Mehmet Suleyman thought Çetin Ikmen was a larger-than-life character, the Inspector's father had to rank amongst the immortals.

The drive back to the station was interesting and not just because Ikmen's old Mercedes handled like a dead cow. Like his son, Ikmen senior existed in his own private smoke cloud. Tiny, bent double and cruelly twisted by arthritis, Timür Ikmen reminded Suleyman of the old, gnarled olive tree that stood at the bottom of his grandparents' garden. Ikmen senior, however, unlike the tree, talked continuously. It wasn't just idle chatter either. Much of it was prurient and, at times, downright offensive.

The questions started as soon as Fatma Ikmen eased him, his teeth gritted against pain, into the car.

'So what do you do with yourself when you're not on duty then, young man?'

The old, generally, liked to hear that the young were behaving themselves. Suleyman's reply was quite truthful too. Reading, the occasional visit to the opera, accompanying his father and grandfather to the mosque whenever duty permitted. He might have guessed that the old man would not react in the normal manner; after all, he was an Ikmen. Suleyman was to regret his own rash and foolhardy honesty.

'Good-looking young man like you! It's a waste!'

'Pardon?'

'A waste! It's boring! How old are you?'

'Twenty-eight, sir.'

'Virgin?'

'I beg your pardon, sir?'

'I said, are you a virgin?'

'Well, I, er...'

Sex was not the only subject upon which the old man expressed strong views during their short journey to the police station. Religion ('don't understand it') and contemporary Turkish politics ('an aberration') also got an airing. By the end of the journey, Mehmet Suleyman was left in no doubt as to the character and opinions of his passenger. He was an atheist, an anarchist, an intellectual snob and a libertine. He also possessed marvellous spirit in the face of his 'bastard illness'. He still wanted to do things: travel, learn new skills, meet women. Not women his own age—only young and pretty ones. It occurred to Suleyman that Timür Ikmen did not so much live life as intimidate it. When they arrived at the police station, they found Çetin Ikmen waiting for them on the pavement. As the car came to a halt he opened the door and peered inside. Suleyman's pale face spoke eloquently about his recent experiences.

'Ah, I see he's been talking at you,' said Ikmen as he lifted the old man from his seat.

'Can I help, sir?' Suleyman offered.

Ikmen was just about to reply in the affirmative, but the old man pre-empted him. 'I'm not a filing cabinet!'

Ikmen sighed deeply. 'It's all right, Suleyman, I can manage.' He moved his head close to his sergeant's ear and dropped his voice to a whisper. 'The best thing you can do is make sure there's a glass of tea ready up there for the old bastard.'

The very confused young policeman, somewhat thankfully, left the Ikmens to their own devices.

The old man looked at the shakily executed script in the address book and frowned. Slowly he inserted one twisted claw into the top pocket of his jacket and withdrew an ancient pair of spectacles. Rather than put them on, he simply held them up to his eyes and peered.

'All right, Çetin?' he said.

Ikmen took a pen from the middle of the mess on his desk and opened his notebook. 'Yes, OK.'

'Right, the first one is Rabbi Şimon, 33, Draman Caddesi, Balat. Then, er...' He peered very closely, moving his spectacles down until they almost touched the paper below. 'Maria Gulcu, 12, Karadeniz Sokak, Beyoğlu. Um, Sara Blatsky, 25/6, Gürsel Sokak, Balat, and finally, Şeker Textiles, Celaleddin Rumi Caddesi, Üsküdar.'

'Telephone numbers?'

The old man looked down at the page again. 'For the Rabbi and the textile company, yes. Look here.'

Ikmen peered at the top set of figures and carefully copied them down on to the back of his hand. He then picked up the telephone receiver and jammed it hard against the side of his head.

'I'll ring this Rabbi Şimon right now,' he said and then, waving his hand in the general direction of his two companions, added, 'You two amuse yourselves in whatever foul way your hearts desire.'

Timür Ikmen raised one eyebrow and said something that Suleyman couldn't quite catch—although the chances of the word not being an oath of some sort, he knew, were quite slim. For a few moments silence reigned as the old man and the young policeman both tried to decide what might and what might not be suitable topics for conversation.

As soon as Ikmen received a reply on the telephone, he turned away from the others in order to obtain some privacy.

One long, nicotine-stained finger tapped down hard against the cover of the little address book, waking the hot and slightly soporific Suleyman from his reverie.

'That's a curious combination,' he said, 'that foreign first name, "Maria", coupled with the Turkish surname.'

'I suppose so.' Suleyman hadn't really thought about it until now. 'But then there are a lot of mixed marriages these days. Could even be one of the victim's relatives. He was, apparently, Russian by birth and considering that no relatives have come forward so far—'

'How old was this person?' asked Timür.

'The neighbours seemed to think that he was about ninety.'

The old man smiled sadly. 'Old enough to be my father.'

'Yes.' It was a curious, if not, in view of Timür Ikmen's extremely raddled appearance, a disturbing thought. 'Yes, I suppose he would have been.'

'Makes you wonder, doesn't it?'

Suleyman frowned questioningly. 'Mr Ikmen?'

'Why anyone would want to kill anything that old. I'm nearly seventy-three and I'm totally fucking useless. But somebody of my father's vintage...' He shrugged his shoulders helplessly as his son replaced the telephone receiver with a satisfied grunt.

'Rabbi Şimon will see us at nine-thirty tomorrow morning, Suleyman.'

'Good.'

Ikmen turned to face his father and smiled. 'Well, thank you for coming in and helping us with that bit of translation, Timür. It's saved me a lot of time and aggravation.'

Timür looked at the grubby floor beneath his feet and sighed. 'I suppose you want me to go now, don't you?'

'Well, I've got things to do. Check up on the other three names. Then, after that, I must contact Arto...' He looked at his watch. 'Can't afford to sit about at the start of an investigation. Your clues are like women, you have to grab them quickly before they cool down. Suleyman will drive you home again—'

'How is Arto Sarkissian?'

Ikmen lit a cigarette and wordlessly passed it to his father. 'Oh, same as ever. Fat, overworked...you know.'

Timür smiled. His two sons had grown up with the Sarkissian children, Arto and Krikor. Every summer for fifteen years the two families had gone on holiday together. Wonderful holidays. There had been other benefits too. The Sarkissian boys had always been studious. Their diligence had rubbed off on Timür's elder son, Halil, the accountant. Çetin, on the other hand...'

Timür stretched to the side and tapped Suleyman on the elbow. 'Do you know Arto Sarkissian?'

'Yes, sir.'

'A fine doctor. My son grew up with him. Inseparable, they were, as children.' He became gloomy and he showed it. 'Pity he didn't follow his example when it came to choosing a career!'

'Timür!'

Suleyman cleared his throat. He didn't know what to say really. One could never be sure when the old man was joking and when he wasn't. Cruel jest, it seemed to Suleyman, was the principal form of communication between this father and son. He didn't begin to understand and had the feeling that he wasn't really meant to either.

Ikmen interrupted his sergeant's musings by handing him the car keys once again. 'Here, you drive him back. I'll help you down the stairs with him and then I must get on!' He slipped his arms gently around his father's waist and hauled him slowly to his feet. 'Come on, Timür, time to go.'

'Oh, wonderful!' said the old man, his voice dripping with what sounded very much like resentment. 'Back to your lovely wife and beautiful children!'

'You love it!'

Suleyman followed the Ikmens out of the office and down towards the stairs. He watched the two men descend, locked in an embrace, both swearing loudly and copiously at each other.

He saw her, but she didn't see him. The window, although only dimly and inadequately lit, threw back a yellow, glittering glow into the tiny cubby-hole shop behind. It was well stocked. Mr Avedissian, her employer, made sure of that. The stock wasn't just anything either. All was gold without exception and the workmanship was of the finest, from the tiniest signet ring right up to the great Egyptian-style collar that took centre stage in the latest display. The patrons of Avedissian's were, with few exceptions, wealthy and powerful. Only the best was good enough. Not surprising that this minute cupboard-like shop had attracted Robert's attention all those months ago when he had been searching for some jewellery for his mother. Not for tourists, Avedissian's; there was not even the slightest whiff of popular influence upon its glittering, high-class shelves. It had been just what he wanted, and so had the assistant who had served him. Just what he had, and still, wanted.

He looked at her dark, delicately sculptured profile, her smooth skin lit and warmed by the soft iridescent gleam bouncing off the precious items around her. A princess in her treasury, bathing her beauty in the warm fires of great wealth. A thick black curl flopped forward on to her broad forehead. One long, perfectly manicured hand pushed it away, back over on to the crown of her head. The movement was lazy, sensual, typically her. She was arranging a display of rings, her face set, intent upon the task in hand. Absorbed, and yet he knew that at least part of her mind would be elsewhere. Maintaining that perfect profile, sustaining the most alluring stance possible, took concentration. A very high degree of self-absorption, self-love.

He pushed the door open. Glowing colours assailed his eyes. Before he found Avedissian's it had not occurred to him that gold could be so variable. White gold, cold and hard as silver; red gold, warm, fiery, sexual; yellow workaday, familiar gold; and then, most mysterious of all, green gold, unnatural to the eye, jealous, evil. Green gold was Natalia's favourite.

The bell above the door clanked rustily as he entered and she looked up. Enormous, round, brown eyes, ringed with black kohl, protected by lashes so thick they were almost feathers. Her mouth opened slightly, but she did not smile. He had not expected her to. He was a trespasser, poaching upon her time, the space in which she did 'other things'. The unknown country of her life without him.

'Hello.'

'Hello,' she replied, her heavily accented English stiff, devoid of emotion. 'What you do here, Robert?'

'I came to see you.'

Her face didn't change. Beautiful, severe, a little nervous even, he thought. She put the ring display on to a shelf behind the counter.

'I wondered if you wanted to come for a quick drink.'

The ring display fastened to the shelf with a sharp click. She turned back and looked at him again, her neck held high, elongated and arrogant.

'Is Tuesday.'

As usual when faced with her displeasure, he fumbled his words clumsily. It irritated her, he knew. She hated him in apologetic, doormat mode, and yet what did she expect? Her eyes were ice, they offered no help or support to their lowly struggling victim.

'Well, I was just, er, you know, passing, and…er, it's very hot and I thought, um…Well, it's, er…'

'You come to spy on me.' It was direct rather than cruel. A statement made between friends rather than lovers. Consequently it wounded him heavily.

'Er…No! No!'

She walked over to the shop window and started switching off the display lights. The warm glow of precious metal dimmed as the life-giving illumination was withdrawn. She didn't take her eyes from his face for a second.

'I have other things I must do.'

Robert remained silent, nervously holding his peace, his mind concentrating fully upon blocking out what the 'other things' to which she was referring might be.

'I am busy. I will see you Thursday.'

She turned and slid one graceful hand into a drawer beneath the counter. There was the sound of keys jangling impatiently in her hands. Keys to the front door of the shop, his cue to leave. His dismissal until his appointed time returned once again. Bitterness rose in his throat, the taste of jealousy and suspicion. Emotions he knew could only be expressed at his peril.

'I saw you in Balat yesterday.' His voice had an edge. The running, frightened figure thrust itself through the alleyways of his mind once more. Her face was blank, haughty and without movement. Suddenly, he felt foolish.

The jangling stopped. She fisted her hand firmly around the keys and looked down at the Rolex upon her slim, tanned wrist.

Robert hadn't seen that watch before. It wasn't one of his gifts. But then neither was the solitaire diamond that hung around her neck. He didn't know where that came from either. *Other things!* The expression on her face had still not moved a millimetre.

'I am here yesterday, all day.'

'Mmm.'

It was a weak and bad-tempered little reply on his part. It reflected how he felt. Diminished.

'You don't believe?'

'I don't know. I thought I saw you—'

'You thought!' Her lips pulled back over her teeth in an ugly sneer. She might just as well have slapped him.

Believe or not; it wasn't really the issue any more, not for Robert. He had upset her. He looked into her face. It quivered just a fraction, but the sneer remained static. He knew that look; he'd seen it before. It usually came just before she told him to get out of her life. She did that occasionally. Numerous and very elaborate presents had to follow in order to avert disaster now. Robert, not for the first time, wondered whether his bank account could bear it.

'You think you see me in Balat yesterday?'

'I thought...' His voice died in his throat. 'He thought', what the hell did that mean? What the fuck was the value of his thoughts anyway? His spirit seemed to die in his breast, turn its back, surrender.

But unbelievably she turned her most beautiful smile full beam upon his face. The sudden change of expression robbed him of his breath.

'OK,' she said brightly. 'One quick drink. You tell me about it.'

He coughed. 'Right.' His voice sounded husky, nervous, smoke-dried.

She turned the rest of the shop lights off and locked the display cabinets. As they went through the front door, he turned and stole a furtive glance at her again. Her face was anxious and there were lines, deep and hard, from the corners of her mouth down to her chin.

The Sultan Pub, a peculiar mock-Tudor establishment opposite the Blue Mosque, was a strangely ideal place for a quiet talk. Its clientele, almost without exception Western European youth in transit, did not tend to linger. One or two stomach-churning local whiskies and then out was the usual form. The internal décor was pure Hollywood Salzburg: beams, cowbells, Alpine horns and pictures of blonde girls with plaits. Cool mountain streams and snow figured quite heavily too. The Southern Europeans' insatiable hunger for the cold.

Robert and Natalia sat down at the table affording the best view of the famous mosque and were quickly joined by the teenage waiter.

After they had ordered their drinks they sat in silence for a while. Robert, at least, was not anxious to open conversation. The drinks arrived quickly and he took a generous gulp from his glass. Natalia, her glass untouched, gazed blankly out of the window, her eyes riveted to the graceful dome of the mosque.

'I'm not accusing you of anything, you know.'

She didn't answer; she didn't react in any way. Self-conscious, he took her hand. The waiter slouching arrogantly against the bar saw their hands join and smirked.

'I'm just confused, that's all. I was on my way home yesterday afternoon, not feeling a hundred per cent, and suddenly there you are. I go to say "hello", greet you, and you're gone!'

'Was not me.' Her tone was flat, matter of fact. Her earlier smile had disappeared long ago. It irked him. Of course it had been her! Who else had a face like that?

'Look, I know what I saw, Natalia. I'm not asking you to explain yourself. I just don't like mysteries. Whatever you were

there for is your own business, I just...' He paused. What he had
to say was difficult. He couldn't accuse her of lying, but he was
finding her denial very hard to reconcile with his own experience. Whatever that was. 'Look, it doesn't matter why you were
there, I just want to know if you *were* there. I need to know
whether I was seeing things or not. It's important—for me.'

She started to sip her drink. Her face was grave, but still—
defiantly, he felt—unmoved.

He tried a slightly different tack. 'I was afraid, when you
didn't acknowledge me, that perhaps I had upset or offended you
in some way.' He pressed her hand gently in his. 'You know how
I feel about you. I couldn't bear it if something that I did wrong
came between us.'

'I not you property.'

Her stilted pronunciation irritated him. He had an urge
to correct her. It was not the first time. Her foreign 'otherness'
frequently grated. She could use it as a weapon, an excuse not to
understand or be properly understood.

His voice had hardened. 'It's important.' He paused. 'Look,
I'm not saying for a second that you were involved, but there was
a murder in Balat yesterday.' She put her glass back down upon
the table with a thud. 'I have, because I was in the area at the
time, already been interviewed by the police.'

He tried to look into her face, but she dropped her eyes.

'Police?'

'Yes.'

Her features had shifted position slightly, thin lines
surrounded her mouth once more, the same lines that had
marred her face earlier when they left the shop.

'The police came to the school this morning. They interviewed all of us. The scene of the murder's only a few streets
away. As it happened, I was in the area at about the right time. I
gave them a statement.'

She looked up, her eyelids snapping apart to reveal wide,
deeply searching eyes. Her pale face, he fancied, was a shade
whiter.

'What do you say in the statement?'

He lit a cigarette. 'That I was in the area near to where the murder was committed at four-thirty yesterday and that I saw and heard nothing unusual. I saw a woman—'

She jumped. 'The one you think was me?'

He paused. Now she was scared. He'd only seen her like this once before. In Balat. That same face. He shuddered. It was almost tempting to string her along, let her believe he'd told the police, see how she would react. But Robert knew that was not in his temperament. That was her trick.

'No, I didn't tell them about...you.' Her face relaxed, just a fraction, but enough for him to notice. 'I couldn't be a hundred per cent certain it was you and if it wasn't, I didn't want to make unnecessary trouble. The woman I told them about was standing in a doorway, she was old, I doubt very much whether she could harm anybody.'

'I could not hurt people!' She folded both her hands around his and gripped tightly. 'I not there, Robert!'

She wanted him to believe her, which was precisely why he couldn't. He felt a sudden need to draw his hand away from her. He pulled his arm back sharply and her hands fell apart and rested limply on the top of the table. For the first time in their relationship he felt as if he was in control. He smelt her fear. It was an intoxicating experience.

'I want to believe you, Natalia, but, quite frankly, it's difficult. I can't very well call my own eyes liars.' He paused. That had been a stupid thing to say and she, as well as he, must know it. But he had to go on. 'I know we've been seeing each other for some time, but I still don't really know you. I don't even know where you live, for God's sake!'

She looked down at the table again. Her hands, resting on the white linen cloth, trembled very slightly. It was mention of the police that had first rattled her. Right up until then she had been her usual cool, haughty self. Of course she had been in Balat! He had seen her. Her repeated denials were ridiculous! Was what she had been doing there so terrible? He couldn't believe it. If she had been unfaithful, he would forgive her—probably—she knew that. And why was she so alarmed by police involvement in a crime that had nothing to do with either of them? Or did it?

He looked at her sad, down-turned face, her soft rounded shoulders. Oh God, but of course, that touch! The thin, wasted bone that had slipped through his fingers like an oiled fish. It didn't make any sense. And why on earth would a beautiful young girl like Natalia murder some penniless old alkie? Robert inwardly chided himself. Now he really was wandering into the realms of fantasy!

She raised her head, and, to his surprise, she smiled.

'Look, Robert, I tell you the truth about Balat, I not there, but...' She shrugged helplessly, a little nervous laugh accompanying the gesture. 'I understand what you say. We very close now and you know little of my life. Perhaps time to change that. You maybe come to my home, meet my family...'

Her words caught him off guard. An invitation to her home was the last thing he had expected. It was quite obviously a ploy to distract him from the issue. Christ, it must have been her! And yet an invitation to her home...

Greed, the kind of selfish, thoughtless longing that makes all lovers occasionally act against their better judgement, possessed him. Ever since he had realised that he was in love with Natalia, Robert had harboured secret and long-term ambitions for this relationship. The failure of his previous marriage had all but destroyed any confidence he may have had with women. To a certain extent Natalia, simply by not leaving him, had given him back some of that confidence. Although educated, Robert was simplistic in his thinking when it came to his personal life. He didn't want to be single any more. And if Natalia wasn't the right woman, then who was? There was nobody else! Meeting her family was surely a significant step! So she'd slipped from grace a little in Balat? A tawdry but probably, to her, exciting liaison with one of the local toughs. It had to be that! Was he going to let something like that, a minor indiscretion, come between them? And yet if this assumption were correct, why was she so afraid of the police? He looked at her perfect, smiling face. He couldn't think why. There were lots of seemingly irrational things he didn't understand about Turkey and the Turks. Perhaps it was one of those? Perhaps...?

Although still tense, he smiled back. 'When?'

'Tomorrow evening, for a meal?'

It seemed pointless to deny himself such an opportunity. For what tangible reason would he? 'Yes.' He felt good again. 'What time?'

She spread a paper napkin out in front of her and took a pen from the pocket of her blouse. 'At about seven?'

'Fine.'

She wrote slowly and carefully on the thin tissue paper. When she had finished she handed it to him. 'My address.'

He looked at the words on the paper. So she lived in Beyoğlu, the old diplomatic quarter, near Istiklal Caddesi, the Oxford Street of the East. Number 12, Karadeniz Sokak.

She finished her drink and rose from her seat. She looked around—nervously, he thought.

'I must go now, Robert. I have things I must do.'

He was slightly disappointed, jealous even. 'Things to do' again! But he hid his feelings behind a smile.

She bent towards him as she passed and brushed her lips lightly against his cheek. Even after a year the merest touch of that thick, fleshy mouth excited him. It had explored every part of his body, kissed, nibbled, sucked. He raised his arm up to her as she passed and gently stroked her side with the back of his hand. 'See you tomorrow.' He heard the heels of her shoes click-click against the cheap linoleum floor, then the loud clunk as she stepped down on to the pavement outside. He turned to look after her, but she had disappeared into the thick rush-hour crowds on the street. Robert picked up his drink and sipped thoughtfully. The strange events of the previous day had unexpectedly played into his hands. He smiled. Balat and its ghosts, the police, his own anxiety: he could file all these things away now. He was one step closer to possessing her. It was all that really mattered.

He paid for the drinks and left. On his way to the bus stop he bought an evening paper. He noted with interest that the Balat murder had graduated to front-page news. The article even mentioned the strange policeman who had interviewed him, Ikmen, a very high roller by the tone of the article. Robert laughed inwardly at this piece of hype and continued on his way. It was only when he reached the bus stop and read the article properly that an element of unease resurfaced in his mind. Until the murderer was caught it would be difficult to get away from the subject of Balat and the events of the previous afternoon. It made him feel like there was a loose end somewhere in his life, dragging behind him, waiting to be tied.

Chapter Four

THE FOLLOWING MORNING dawned bright, clear and, as far as Ikmen was concerned, much more promising than its predecessor. As he left his apartment for Balat he actually had a smile on his face, although this had all but disappeared by the time he had negotiated the rush-hour traffic. And when he discovered that it was impossible to park anywhere within three blocks of his destination, his customary gloom returned with a vengeance. He met Suleyman, who had already been into the station to pick up messages, on the corner of the Rabbi's street.

'Ready to meet the Supreme Ruler of the Universe's representative on earth, are you then, Suleyman?'

The younger man dealt, on this occasion, with Ikmen's irreligious flippancy by ignoring it. There were, besides, much more important moves afoot. 'Forensic found over ten million lira in Meyer's apartment you know, sir.'

Ikmen frowned. 'Ten million lira? When? How?'

'Stuffed underneath the mattress of his bed, according to

Demir.' He looked at his watch and indicated that perhaps they should start moving towards the Rabbi's house. As he walked, Ikmen took a cigarette out of his pocket and lit up. 'I wonder where somebody like Meyer got hold of money like that? Money, and by that I mean their own money, is not something alcoholics usually have any of.'

'Well, I have no answers for you on that one, sir. All Demir said was that he had found a lot of money which, on the face of it, seems to have belonged to Meyer.'

Ikmen drew hard on his cigarette and sighed. 'So. The mystery deepens, eh, Suleyman?'

'It would appear to be moving in that direction, sir.'

Rabbi Yitzak Şimon was only first generation Balat. It was unusual for one of the local clerics to be foreign but then his appointment only reflected the rather more recent, albeit small, influx of Ashkenazi Jews into the area since the beginning of the century. Apart from and yet embedded within the, to him, more dark and mysterious Sephardi majority, Şimon had grown up amongst these shy, insular people with their strange language and oriental customs. His very 'otherness' had actually assisted his understanding of them. Lonely and unpopular as a child, he had watched, listened, observed the ebb and flow, identified tensions. It was all very objective. They weren't his people, he could watch through eyes unclouded by dynastic rivalry or ancient territorial right.

Until he came into contact with other children who originated from Europe in the 1950s, Şimon had simply been known as 'that Polish boy'. The words themselves hadn't hurt but the lack of playmates had frequently depressed him. It had all seemed so unfair. He had, after all, been born in the district.

But the bitterness he had felt as a child had receded. Once he had elevated himself to the exalted position of rabbi to his small flock of foreigners they had developed a sneaking respect

for him—as he had for them. Maddening and unintelligible as
they could be, Şimon had to admit that any community that
could achieve and maintain a civilised relationship with the
host nation for five hundred years was only to be admired. The
Turks, though grudgingly at times, respected them too.

He had always hoped that that situation would remain
unchanged. The recent death of Leonid Meyer had, however,
shaken him. It had shaken the whole district. Nothing was
said but there were signs that people were afraid. Suddenly, the
streets were empty after dark and the locksmith had more work
than his one small shop could cope with. The only consolation was that the police had managed to play down the racist
element. Consequently the press hadn't, as yet, really gone for
that angle. The last thing Balat needed were gangs of morbid
sightseers and unhinged fascist sympathisers. The only visitors
the district had attracted so far were the police themselves and a
mercifully low-key appearance from the Israeli Consul.

He looked at his watch. The police were due at his door
at any minute. He cleared a pile of books and papers from one
of the chairs in front of his desk and put them on the floor.
His office was hideously untidy, but as long as his guests had
somewhere comfortable to sit the interview would not be too
unpleasant. The silver samovar over in the corner bubbled
gently. He could offer them tea as well. However distressing the
subject under discussion, provided you had a glass of tea in your
hands there was a feeling, Şimon felt, that civilisation was not
too irredeemably distant.

He heard a knock on his door followed by the sound of
someone clearing their throat. Şimon walked down the hallway
and pulled back the long iron bolt that secured the entrance to
his home.

Two men stood on his doorstep: one short, swarthy, about
his own age; the other younger, tall and very smart.

The older man spoke. 'Rabbi Şimon?' It was the same
deep, dry voice that had spoken to him over the telephone the
previous day.

'You must be Inspector Ikmen.' He smiled.

'Yes.' Ikmen tilted his head in the direction of the younger man. 'This is Sergeant Suleyman.'

Şimon acknowledged Suleyman's presence with a slight bow of the head and then ushered the two men into his office.

'Please sit down, gentlemen,' he said and moved across the room towards the samovar. 'Would you like some tea?'

As he sat, Ikmen caught sight of the ornate silver samovar in the corner. It brought a smile to his face. Old charcoal-burning ones, like the Rabbi's, had become rare in post-teabag Istanbul. 'What a wonderful old samovar!'

The Rabbi turned to look at him. 'This?'

'Yes,' said Ikmen. 'Takes me right back to my childhood. Our whole house revolved around one of those things. My mother was always fiddling with it, topping it up with water, putting on fresh charcoal. The hub of old Turkish life.' He stood up and went to have a closer look at it. The samovar hissed very slightly and the Rabbi turned to the policeman and chuckled.

'Remember that sound, Inspector?'

'I do. It's a good sound.'

They smiled at each other, enjoying the moment of a shared childhood memory. Sometimes it was difficult for Ikmen to remember that he had once been young. Twenty-five years of heavy responsibility had taken their toll. And yet it had not seemed like a long time. He even wondered sometimes how he had got to be so old so quickly.

He resumed his seat and the Rabbi filled three small tulip glasses with steaming golden liquid. Whenever he used the samovar, Şimon remembered his mother too. The way she always pushed her sleeves back just before she poured from the teapot. It was the only time she ever exposed the number tattooed on her wrist, 17564. She was dead, but that number still lived, cut into his memory like diamond on glass. It was such a big number.

Şimon gave his guests their tea and sat down behind his desk.

He sighed. 'So, gentlemen, Leonid Meyer. How can I help?'

'Background mainly, sir,' said Ikmen. 'We know very little about the gentleman. Nobody has, as yet, come forward to claim him as their own. Anything you can tell us really.'

The Rabbi took a sip from his glass and then put it down on the desk. 'Well, as you already know, Leonid was Russian. He came here in 1918, just after the Revolution. Like my own parents he found integrating into the community quite difficult. He never really got to grips with Ladino, never, to my knowledge, married, and tended, inasmuch as he communicated with anyone, to restrict his friendships to within other émigré circles. I speak Russian myself and, as the only Ashkenazi rabbi in the district, it was inevitable that I should attend to Leonid's spiritual needs.'

'Was he a religious man?'

Şimon smiled. 'No, Inspector. To be truthful I was more Leonid's psychiatrist than his rabbi. He was old, he drank heavily, he just sometimes wanted someone to talk to. It was my linguistic skills he was after, not my faith.'

'I see.'

'Leonid Meyer was not a happy man. For some peculiar reason he wanted to go back to Russia. He never settled here. I didn't manage to discover whether he still had relatives in the Soviet Union, in fact I never did and still don't know whether he had any here either. However, there appeared to be some sort of unfinished business, but quite honestly, Inspector, he was always so drunk, I often found it hard to understand what he was saying.'

Suleyman took a notebook and pencil out of his pocket and started writing. 'Can you think of anyone who particularly disliked the gentleman, sir?' he asked the Rabbi.

Şimon thought silently for a few seconds. 'No. Not really. Every so often one or other of his neighbours would complain about him to the landlord. When he was drunk he tended to shout a lot. He would throw things around, curse, sob even.'

Ikmen took his cigarettes and lighter out and put them on the Rabbi's desk. 'Do you mind if I smoke, sir?'

'No, not at all.'

'Do you have any idea what all this raving and sobbing was about?' asked Suleyman.

The Rabbi slid a dirty glass ashtray across at Ikmen. 'Well, I do and don't.' He paused. 'As far as I can tell it all stemmed from sometime before he ever came to Balat.'

Ikmen offered a cigarette to the Rabbi. 'You mean when he was still living in Russia?'

The Rabbi took the cigarette and lit up. 'I believe so, yes. There was some sort of violence involved. Strangely, when one considers that Leonid came from the background that he did, which was both impoverished and Jewish, it was not violence enacted against him, but rather violent acts perpetrated by him.'

'Oh?'

'Some people were killed. Or rather Leonid and others, I don't know who, killed some people. Given the violence inherent in those troubled times I suppose it is all quite feasible. But quite who Leonid's victims were, and why, when and how it all occurred, I really do not know.'

Ikmen, his brow furrowed, sighed shallowly. 'I don't suppose he ever said whether or not these events were connected to the wider disturbances in Russia at that time?'

'You mean the Revolution?' The Rabbi smiled. 'No, Inspector, he did not. I suppose they may have been but then, given the fact that Leonid was a poor Jew, they might equally have been connected simply with his routine, for want of a better word, struggle to survive.'

Suleyman looked up from his notebook. 'Are you aware of anyone else who might know about Mr Meyer's past, sir?'

'Only, possibly, Sara Blatsky. She's an elderly Russian lady who had an—albeit sometimes uneasy—friendship with Leonid. It might be worth your while talking to her. I'm sure she'd be most co-operative.'

'Yes, sir,' Ikmen replied, 'we plan to see Mrs Blatsky as well as a Maria Gulcu over in Beyoğlu and a company called Şeker

Textiles. All these names and addresses, as well as your own, were found in a notebook belonging to the deceased.'

'I see.'

'I don't suppose you know of either Maria Gulcu or Şeker Textiles?'

The Rabbi stubbed his cigarette out in the ashtray and leant back in his chair. 'Maria Gulcu, I don't know. I don't remember Leonid talking about such a person although that, of course, doesn't mean that he didn't. Şeker Textiles, however, I do know about.'

'Oh?'

Suleyman, pen at the ready, prepared to take down any relevant details.

'Şeker Textiles,' said the Rabbi, 'was the company that employed Leonid from the time he first came to this country until, I believe, sometime in the 1940s.'

'I don't suppose you know what his job was, Rabbi?'

Şimon frowned in an attempt to remember, but only momentarily. 'He was a cotton packer. You know, baling up fabric, putting it into sacks and boxes. Not the sort of thing I could see Leonid doing from my own experience of him. His hands were very bad, you know, sort of clawed. Perhaps arthritis. I don't really know—I never asked. But anyway, apparently he liked the job but fell out with the owner of the company over something or other. I expect it was his drinking. Although considering who the owner was, or rather is, it could have been because of something else.'

Ikmen eyed the Rabbi quizzically. 'Meaning?'

'Şeker Textiles is owned by a man called Reinhold Smits. As you can probably tell from his name he had a German father. One of those who came to this country during the 1914 - 18 war, I believe. Anyway, legend has it, and I must stress here that this is only anecdotal, that Reinhold Smits was rather vocal with regard to his support for the Nazi regime in the 1940s.'

Ikmen looked across at Suleyman who was writing everything down in minute detail. 'Was he indeed?'

'So it is said.' Rabbi Şimon reached inside his desk and took out a packet of cigarettes. 'And if that is true it could explain why Leonid was asked to leave at that time. There could be no place for a Jew in a company headed by a person with such views.' He opened up the packet of cigarettes and shook one out towards Ikmen. 'Cigarette?'

'Thank you.' Before he lit up, Ikmen tapped the little tube of tobacco gently upon the top of the desk. 'You say that Şeker Textiles is still owned by Smits?'

'As far as I know. Although I really don't think that Leonid had any contact there since he left—he never spoke of it.'

'And yet,' said Ikmen, 'he still had the company's address in his book over fifty years later.'

The Rabbi shrugged. 'I have no idea why that might be, I'm afraid. His involvement with them finished, as far as I am aware, back in the 1940s.' He smiled a little rather embarrassed and flustered smile. 'What I mean, I suppose, is that I don't think it very likely that Mr Smits had anything to do with Leonid's death. I think that is most unlikely.'

With a flick of the wrist, Ikmen threw his cigarette up into his mouth and lit up. 'Yes. I see what you're saying, Rabbi. Mmm.'

A moment of tension followed which Suleyman did not understand but which he felt compelled to curtail.

'So,' he said, 'do you know what Meyer might have done after he left Şeker Textiles, sir?'

'My understanding,' the Rabbi replied, 'is that Leonid never actually worked again.'

Ikmen and Suleyman exchanged a troubled look which Rabbi Şimon both saw and acknowledged.

'That Leonid had no observable financial problems,' he continued, 'was always a mystery to me. I suppose he could always have had some sort of pension or annuity, but I never heard him speak of such things.'

'He wasn't, as far as you know, Rabbi, behind with his rent?' Ikmen asked.

'No. In fact quite the reverse. Mr Dilaver, his landlord, was put in rather a "position" because of it. Leonid was often upset as well as being almost permanently intoxicated and his sometimes ceaseless crying and shouting gave many of his fellow tenants real cause for complaint. He was also in the habit of filling his little apartment with the most awful derelicts including, I have to say, the unfortunate Leah Delmonte. But as long as he was paying the rent on time, Mr Dilaver didn't really have any cause to evict him.' He smiled. 'Besides, around here those who pay their rent at all are few and far between and from the monetary point of view the landlord could not have wished for a better tenant.'

'The crying and shouting being almost always connected to his violent past?'

The Rabbi sighed. 'Yes. It seemed to haunt him and some-times when he was very drunk, I think he might have fancied himself back there, if you know what I mean.'

'Yes.'

Addressing both policemen, the Rabbi continued, 'What-ever one's stance may be with regard to divine retribution, I really do not believe that anyone can feel ultimately happy about taking the life of another. Had Leonid felt all right about it he would have stayed in Russia, wouldn't he? I mean, just after the Revolution things got better than they had ever been for Jews there—for a little while.'

'Yes.' Ikmen glanced quickly at Suleyman and then turned back to the Rabbi once again. 'Is there anything else you can tell us, sir?'

'No, not really. Leonid, with the exception of that one event, didn't tend to talk about himself much. It was all mainly trivia: grumbling about the price of things, his neighbours' noisy children, his aches and pains, things like that. As I've said, he never spoke about his money, so I'm afraid that I can't tell you where he got it from.' He looked down at his desk and lowered his voice. 'The people are very frightened, you know, Inspector.'

'I can imagine.'

'At the risk of causing offence, I don't think that you can.' He put his hand up to his face and scratched his beard. 'Most of the people around here have never experienced real anti-Semitism. It is a credit to your people that they haven't, but...'

'Thank you, sir.'

'Both my parents were in Dachau. How they survived I cannot imagine. But through them and their experiences and the experiences of my own sad little flock of Ashkenazim here, I do have an awareness of what anti-Semitism can be like if it is allowed to run out of control. Most of the poor little Sephardis here are frightened but unaware. I look at what is happening, rearing up in other parts of Europe, and I don't honestly know what to do for the best. Part of the reason why the Germans could do to us what they did was because we were too trusting, we were not prepared.' He looked Ikmen straight in the eye. 'To your knowledge, Inspector, is this a growing problem here? Please be frank.'

Ikmen lit another cigarette and rolled a second across to the Rabbi. 'Oh.' He paused. 'What can I say? There are, and always have been, elements who discriminate against others for no good reason. I would be doing the Jews of Balat a disservice if I told you not to be vigilant. As you've probably noticed, we've increased the frequency of our patrols in this area. But my honest opinion?' His face became very grave. 'I think one person killed Leonid Meyer. A very deeply disturbed individual with some kind of crazy reason of his own.'

'Well, the swastika—'

'Oh, yes, I grant you that whoever it was doesn't care for Jews, but I don't think that's the whole story. The method used to kill him was very specific, it had to be him and it had to be that way. Personally I think there was a definite motive. This was a personal act against Mr Meyer himself. I may yet be proved wrong, but—'

'So you're saying you don't think there's any movement or organisation behind this?'

'I can't be absolutely certain, but I don't think so. I will, nevertheless, be talking to this Smits man in the near future. I've received no information to suggest a sudden upsurge in anti-Semitism in this city. Such an eventuality is, however, being taken very seriously at a level much higher than myself. The intelligence-gathering agencies are on full alert. Looking at it from a purely selfish point of view, you must remember that Israel is one of our allies in this region.'

'Of course.'

Ikmen stood up. 'Well, we'd better not take up any more of your time, Rabbi.'

Şimon rose to his feet and offered his hand to Ikmen. 'No trouble. It's very good of you to take the time to be so reassuring.'

The two men shook hands. Suleyman put his notebook and pen away and joined his boss. 'Goodbye, Rabbi Şimon.'

'Goodbye, Sergeant.'

He led the two policemen into the hall and unlocked the door for them.

'I'll keep you informed,' said Ikmen as he walked through the doorway.

'Thank you.'

Suleyman stepped out into the sunlight, taking his sunglasses out of his pocket as he went. The Rabbi was just about to go back inside when Ikmen stopped him.

'Rabbi?' His face was quizzical, but shocked somehow, as if a frightening thought had just crossed his mind.

'Yes?' The Rabbi's voice showed concern. The little Inspector looked suddenly almost ill.

It wasn't an easy question for Ikmen to ask but he asked it. 'How do you feel when you look at a swastika?'

The Rabbi's face went pale and he sighed. 'Oh.' He tried to think of a way of describing his feelings that was logical and not too tainted by emotion. He wanted the Inspector to understand him, but nice, passionless words just wouldn't come. 'Haunted, Inspector. And trapped. It's like I'm in a cage with a ghost and I know I can never be free.'

The two men looked at each other and to the Rabbi's

surprise he realised that the Inspector had understood him. How, he couldn't say, but he was glad. He was always glad when someone else, someone Gentile, finally understood. Every time it happened it meant that number 17564 receded that little bit further into the past.

'What are you planning to cook for our visitor tonight?'

Anya Gulcu looked up from her book. A tall, bearded man had entered the drawing room and was making his way towards the chaise upon which she reclined. Despite his advanced age, he walked with great purpose, his bearing straight-backed and proud. She could not help but notice that by comparison the years had not been nearly so kind to her. Thin, wasted, her hair chewed, straggly and grey, Anya had long since given up the struggle with her decaying appearance. She frowned as he approached and put her book down on the small occasional table in front of her.

'What would you recommend, Nicholas?' she said stiffly.

He sat down in a battered wing chair at the head of the chaise and crossed his hands in his lap. 'He's an Englishman, isn't he?'

'Yes.' She smoothed the long skirt of her crisp lace dress with her hand. Her mouth moved nervously as she waited for him to speak again.

'Shouldn't be too difficult, then. Have you consulted Mama?'

Her voice quavered. 'Er, no. She is not going to attend, and in view of...circumstances, I thought it better not to bother her.'

Nicholas sighed. His face suddenly looked tired and resigned. 'Oh, yes. Of course. By the way, you know that letter she received today? You don't know what—'

'No! No!' Anya swung her legs down on to the floor and perched nervously on the edge of the chaise. Her tiny hands fluttered shakily up to her face. 'What are we going to do, Nicky?'

He leant forward. He looked at her sternly, but not without kindness. Taking both her hands in his, he pressed them gently away from her face. It was obvious that her nervousness irritated him, but he tried to hide it. He loved her.

'We are going to be calm, Anya. We are going to think clearly and carry on just like we always have. Talking of which...' He looked down at his elaborate cherry-red and gold tunic and frowned. 'I don't think these clothes are going to be very suitable for tonight, do you?'

'Why not?'

He pursed his lips. This time he let his impatience show. Why did she have to have everything explained to her! 'Think, Anya, think! Mr Robert, whatever he is, is a stranger. He won't understand. We don't want to alarm him, do we? What goes on in this house when he is not here is not his concern, is it?' He looked away from her, towards the door and the stairs beyond. 'There's no reason to worry him with trivial details.'

'Yes, of course, you're right. I'm sorry, Nicky.'

He got up from the chair and strode across to the large bay window. He looked out into the street, strong, yellow sunlight illuminating his features. He couldn't bear to look at her when she was apologetic and mousy. Even when they were children this particular mood of hers had irritated him. She always did it when she was frightened, when she wanted someone else to take the responsibility, do her thinking for her.

'I will buy some lamb, potatoes and rice,' he said firmly. 'You can roast the meat and potatoes, English people like that sort of thing.' He turned to look at her. 'Do you have some salad?'

'Yes.'

'Do that with it then.' He paused. Her eyes were downcast, miserable. 'You can *do* that, I presume, Anya?' He hadn't meant that to sound nasty, but he knew that it had. He chastised himself almost immediately.

'Yes.' She looked up suddenly, panicking. 'Nicky, I honestly don't know how I'm going to do this!' Her lips trembled; she was on the very edge of tears.

He closed his eyes and threw his arms outwards in a gesture of despair. 'You just have to, Anya. It's for Natalia, remember? Your daughter?'

'But...'

His impatience with her finally got the better of him. 'For the love of God, Anya! You know what you're supposed to do, don't you! Didn't we go over it enough times for you? The man is a visitor, no one in particular, that's all! Nothing can possibly go wrong!'

She moved her head slightly, as if agreeing, but her eyes wept and her hands clutched nervously at her bodice.

It was midday; outside the sun was at its zenith, hot, strong, debilitating. But inside it was dark. Thick, purple curtains were drawn tight across every window; the unnatural light from a single oil lamp glowed sickly in the heavy darkness.

The apartment was richly furnished in purple, gold and the deep midnight black of mahogany. Heavy furniture, seasoned by long years of usage.

In the middle of the room, and dominating it, was a bed. Its foot was long, tapered and shaped like the prow of a ship. Carved and gilded waves, captured in mid-roll, sprang from both the prow and the headboard. Reaching nearly to the ceiling, this headboard provided an anchor for the metres of lilac net curtaining that hung stiff and brittle with age down on to the pillows and across the floor. As generously wide as it was long, the bed itself was covered by a purple brocade counterpane, its edges dangling close to the floor, frayed and soiled by mice.

On top of this cover, lying on its side, rested the body of a woman. A full-length lilac gown engulfed her skinny body, and a veil of thick, grey hair covered her shoulders and the upper part of her face. Though at rest, her breath did not come easily. She wheezed, her lungs rattling and creaking with mucus every time she breathed out. Crêpy, age-spotted hands clutched at the cover beneath her, tightening and relaxing with the rhythm of her breath.

Outside, in the city beyond the purple curtains, a thousand muezzins called the Muslim faithful to midday prayer. 'There is no God but Allah, and Mohammed is his Prophet…'

The woman on the bed stirred. For a second her breathing stopped, held prisoner in her throat. Her face strained as she tried to remember what should have been reflex. She folded back the corner of life and looked at its alternative. She made a gagging sound in the back of her throat. Then her muscles relaxed and the breath flowed out of her. Her hands clutched and then released the bedclothes one more time, and she opened her eyes.

Through a lattice of dry hair, Maria Gulcu surveyed her domain. Sideboard, table, washstand, pictures on the wall— nothing had changed. Even corners of the room she could not see were unaltered. She didn't have to look, she knew. Ikon screen top left-hand corner, two gold brocade chairs over by the window, the photograph album sitting on the card table next to the door. Everything in its place, as it should be. Well, nearly everything. What was wrong?

There was something at the back of her mind. An anxiety, a dread. What was it? It was recent; that was its problem. The closer she was to an event, the quicker it faded from her mind. Ten years ago, twenty, seventy—ah, yes, seventy, or rather seventy-four was easy. She kept count. A breath away.

Every second recorded, marked, stowed safely and for ever. Faces: some brutal, some loved beyond understanding. And a girl. A girl with deep blue eyes and long chestnut hair, tiptoeing on the rim of womanhood. Like the others—but not like the others. She could see the girl, could call her up at will. Getting close to the others was becoming easier with the passing years too. Maria knew why and she welcomed it. Time was gathering pace. Brutal. Hated time. There was too much. Now when she didn't need it there was too much. Then…

But what about yesterday?

She turned slowly on to her back and stared at the ceiling. Her eyesight had deteriorated considerably over the last few years. There was a pattern on the ceiling, she remembered it well, but all she could see was a blur. She pushed the unwanted memory of the ceiling paper out of her mind and turned back on to her side once again. What was it?

And it was then that she saw the letter. Thick, stubby writing on perfumed pink paper. So very typical. Ah, yes. Ah, yes. It was someone that was out of place, not something. There was a gap in the cast-list of her life. Her eyes filled with tears. Slowly connections formed in her mind as the recent nightmare returned. She pushed her hair out of her face and reached for a handkerchief in the pocket of her gown. Tears, caught and held static in the folds and creases of her face, bitter with salt, stung her skin.

How could she have forgotten? She dabbed her eyes with a corner of the handkerchief and patted away the moisture that had gathered on her flaccid cheeks. She had turned away for a second and now he had gone.

The two men walked in silence as they made their way back to their respective cars. Although the suspicious, almost hostile nature of the stares they were attracting from the local inhabitants was partly at the root of this phenomenon, there was another reason too. Uncharacteristically, it was Suleyman who first articulated this latter, as yet unspoken point.

'I've been thinking,' he said, his far superior height forcing him to speak, as it were, to the top of Ikmen's head. 'Rabbi Şimon seemed a little nervous about mentioning that Smits man.'

Ikmen sucked hard on what was probably his fifteenth cigarette of the day. 'Well, he would be.'

'How so?'

'Well, he's a Jew, isn't he!'

'Yes.' The look of blank confusion on his deputy's face momentarily angered Ikmen to a quite unreasonable degree. 'If you gave the matter more than just a cursory thought you would know, Suleyman!' He stopped and turned to face him, his eyes intent and, Suleyman was almost tempted to think, passionate. 'That man's parents went through the full horrors of the concentration camps. He knows, better than most, what anti-Semitism has done and can do.'

'But this country had no involvement in that war, we were neutral and—'

'And because we were neutral, Suleyman, people like Reinhold Smits could express their unsavoury views without let or hindrance.' He raised his cigarette-bearing hand up towards Suleyman's face; pointing his crooked fingers almost into the young man's eyes. 'We may have been at peace with our own indigenous Jewish population for a very long time, but if a Jew brings an accusation against a Turkish citizen, albeit of German extraction, it is a very serious matter. Not because the Jew will necessarily be found wanting, but because in his own mind he will be at a disadvantage. This is something that Rabbi Şimon wants to avoid at all costs and it is why, when we go to interview Smits, we must not allude to his suspicions in any way.'

'But how—'

'All we have to say, Suleyman, is that we obtained the address of Şeker Textiles from the old man's notebook and then let Smits explain himself and his involvement to us. As I've said before, and with no disrespect to the good Rabbi's feelings, I don't think that there is much to be gained from exploring some fifty-year-old item of racial discrimination. Unless there were some other element involved...'

'Like what?'

Ikmen started walking again, hurling his finished cigarette butt as he went. 'Like a reason why Meyer still kept details about his old employer over fifty years after the event.' He shrugged, speculating. 'Maybe Meyer screwed Smits's wife in the last decade—who knows!'

Despite the fact that Ikmen was so small, Suleyman did not find that he was easy to keep up with when he was tense and agitated like this. He had almost to run to catch up with him, asking breathlessly, 'So is that what you meant when you said you thought that the murder was personal?'

'Possibly. Possibly.'

'But...'

Having reached Ikmen's car, which stood out markedly by virtue of its great age against even the humblest surrounding vehicles, they stopped once again. This time when Ikmen spoke, he rather oddly addressed the ground. Only later would Suleyman consider why this might be.

'As I've said before, Suleyman, it is at the moment my considered opinion that whoever killed Leonid Meyer did so for a personal reason. If the murderer had wanted to kill any old Jew just for the sake of doing so, he could have simply stuck a pillow over the old man's face and had done with it. All the stuff with the acid—the bringing it to the apartment, the taking it away, the risk of screams from the old man, the overall danger of the whole enterprise—leads me to the belief that the method itself was key. To my way of thinking, if we can deduce why Meyer was killed in this way and for what reason, we will be able to track down who did it with comparative ease.' He smiled. 'And to that end I want you, when you get back to the station, to start working on the problem of who these other derelicts of whom the Rabbi spoke might be. If you can also arrange for us to go over to Şeker Textiles, that would be good too.'

'I'll get on to it right away.'

'Good.' Ikmen opened the as usual unlocked door of his car and slid into the driver's seat. 'I'm going to go over to the hospital to try to speak to this Delmonte woman. I'll see you later.'

'All right.'

As Ikmen pulled out into the stream of traffic it occurred to Suleyman that the reason why his boss had been unable to look him in the eye was because he had been embarrassed. Despite all

Ikmen's protestations to the contrary, something hideous and, most importantly, racist had taken place on his patch, in his city. He was embarrassed as well as disturbed. Talking to the Rabbi, Suleyman thought, must have been quite a trial for him.

Chapter Five

BEYOĞLU IS A DISTRICT characterised by great contrast. In the days when Turkey still had her Empire it was the diplomatic and commercial centre, not only of Istanbul, but of the entire Ottoman world. The Great Powers of the Victorian era, Russia, Great Britain, France and Germany, built imposing and elegant Embassies within its confines. Hotels, churches, shops and music halls sprang up; entertainment and luxury for diplomats and advisors far from the civilised, Christian world of Western Europe.

Turkey, the bankrupt 'Sick Man', courted the whole continent but cleverly, and to the frustration of the Powers, remained unwed. Deals were struck, whole countries sold, plots were hatched in the Embassies and coffee houses around Istiklal Caddesi, the capital's centre of fashion. The Sultan's Jewish and Armenian bankers tiptoed from ambassador to ambassador making promises on the Ottoman Government's behalf, securing vast, unsecured loans for their imperial master. In this manner great alliances were forged and the Europeans were hopeful, but the Ottomans never honoured these partnerships— they'd never had any intention of doing so. Their only interest was money, which they got. Turkey, and the East generally, were fashionable. Every day more wealthy and romantic Europeans would arrive on the Orient Express; hungry for a stake in the expanding Ottoman railway system; selling arms; *en route* to Anatolia and the treasures of ancient Troy. In the Pera Palas Hotel Mata Hari plied her trade, while deposed Eastern European princes listlessly waited for death.

But when the Turkish Republic was born in the 1920s Ankara became the capital and Beyoğlu slipped into a long decline. The great unwashed moved into its once graceful apartment buildings, and small shops selling cheap food and even cheaper beer appeared. Prostitutes started roaming the streets, luring the unwary into drinking clubs and cinemas offering films that left little to the imagination.

However, in the 1960s things again started to change. There was a fresh confidence in the air and fashionable retailers moved back into the area. A new generation, this time largely Turkish, discovered the delights of Istiklal Caddesi, the quaint bars of Çiçek Pasaj and the candle-lit mysteriousness of a dozen Baroque and Gothic churches.

Soon tourists arrived, and the occupants of the old Embassies, demoted to Consulates in the wake of Atatürk's reforms, found themselves busy once again.

The mean alleyways and wide boulevards of Beyoğlu came back to life, but not exactly in the image of its previous imperial incarnation. The prostitutes, the cheap cinemas and the tawdry bars remained. Tastelessness and class side by side: the strip club and the grand Imperial Lycée, school for the sons and daughters of the rich and famous; poor peasants selling flowers on the street, the glitter of brass and gold from the windows of antique shops; packs of scavenging cats eating from dustbins outside the Armenian Orthodox High School.

Robert Cornelius loved Beyoğlu, it was his favourite part

of the city. It amused him that within the space of sometimes as little as fifty yards, you could purchase a Sachertorte or a new tyre for your car, see a pornographic movie and visit the Russian Consulate.

As he alighted from the tram at the end of Istiklal Caddesi, he experienced an overwhelming contentment. It was good that Natalia lived in Beyoğlu, good that he was finally going to meet her family, good that it was summer. The street was alive with noise, colour, the laughter of happy couples and families on their way to the picturesque little bars and restaurants. A welcome early evening breeze puffed gently up from the waters of the Golden Horn, ruffling the sleeves of his shirt and drying the thin line of perspiration down his spine. The dark fears and anxieties of the previous two days seemed now like bad dreams from an embattled and distant continent.

He walked back down the street, tracing with his steps the tram-lines along which he had just travelled. Karadeniz Sokak was not far; according to his map it was the second turning on the left. The map. He'd spent most of the day looking at it, stealing glances at the area marked *Beyoğlu* while his students laboured, or not, at their exercises. The day had flown, he'd even managed to enjoy some of it, but now the real business was about to begin.

Robert was elated, but he was nervous. Because Natalia had always been so secretive about her family, he had no idea what they might be like. He didn't even, he realised when he thought about it, know how many of them lived with her. Would it just be Natalia and one ageing relative? Or would there be dozens of names to remember: brothers, sisters, cousins, grandparents? He walked past the calorie-packed window of a pâtisserie and looked at the cakes. His sweet tooth excited, he drooled. It had been a long time since lunch and he was hungry. What sort of food had the Gulcus prepared for him? Whatever it was, he hoped there was a lot of it.

The second turning on the left was just beyond the pâtisserie. A slight gap in the endless procession of shop windows showed Robert where it was. A dark and noisy shoe-mender's kiosk stood on the left-hand corner, a ladies' underwear shop on the right. Robert paused.

Karadeniz Sokak was a long, narrow alley. It was old; tall Victorian buildings packed tightly on either side, some of them galleried, top-heavy, leaning towards each other as if attempting to kiss across the middle of the street. It sloped downwards, falling away from the main thoroughfare towards Meşrutiyet Caddesi and the green and white confection of the Pera Palas Hotel. As he made his way forward, Robert could just see the front entrance of the famous building, the Art Deco canopy suspended over the revolving doors of the front entrance. Blackened with age, the structures on either side of him looked very mournful. Some were uninhabited, their broken windows echoing to the sound of his footsteps as the other more joyful noises of life on Istiklal Caddesi receded into the distance.

Number 12, Karadeniz Sokak was halfway down on the right. Like the other buildings in the street it was tall; Robert counted four storeys plus basement. Unlike its neighbours it was not galleried and, strange in an area of solid brick and stone buildings, number 12 was made entirely of wood. It had been very badly neglected. Though in places decorated with beautiful and delicately carved panels, the house as a whole presented a ravaged face to the world. Rot had invaded every plank, green mould and even grass grew on the windowsills and around the edges of the black front door. Although barely discernible, the bottom half of the house was at a completely different angle to the top, as if the structure had twisted five degrees at the waist. It was still very hot, despite the slight breeze, but all the windows were closed and shuttered. There was not a sound on the street, or from inside the house. A knot tightened in the pit of Robert's stomach. Was this sad and neglected shell to be the scene of some cruel, deceitful joke? How could anybody live in it?

He mounted the steps up to the front door. He looked down into the litter-filled well of the basement. Two pairs of rodent eyes stared back at him. He tapped the heavy metal knocker twice and waited.

For at least thirty seconds nothing happened. The rats continued to stare; the silence closed about him like a strait-jacket and Robert Cornelius felt the first stirrings of despair, followed quickly by anger.

Then, suddenly and without the usual warning noise of approaching footsteps, the door swung open. 'Efendim?'

He was a man in late middle age, tall, bearded, very erect. His bright, almost smiling blue eyes seemed to sparkle with vigour. Dressed in what must have been an extremely hot three-piece woollen suit, he looked much more like an Englishman than a Turk.

'Er...' Robert's Turkish temporarily deserted him. Clumsily, he pointed his fingers towards his chest and tapped. 'Robert Cornelius.'

The tall man's face broke into a gracious smile and he held out his hand in greeting. 'Ah, good, you have come. I am Natalia's Uncle Nicholas.'

Robert took the proffered hand and shook it vigorously. He was relieved. The release of tension showed on his face. 'Hello. Nice to meet you.'

'Please come in, young man.' The man's voice, like Natalia's, was heavily accented, but his English was better, more free flowing and natural. 'Natalia has been waiting for you.'

Nicholas stood to one side and Robert entered a plush, lavishly decorated hall. It was all very red. Wallpaper, lamp-shades, carpet...

Suleyman sighed deeply. It had been a long day and now he wanted to go home. Very little progress had been made and he felt dissatisfied. True, he'd managed, without too much difficulty, to make an appointment to see Reinhold Smits, but tracking down Meyer's derelicts had been quite another matter.

Assuming, quite wrongly as it turned out, that the landlord, Mr Dilaver, would know who these people were had proved a waste of time—the latter only angering Suleyman by his constant questions regarding when he might be able to let the dead man's apartment again.

Frustrated by Dilaver's lack of knowledge, Suleyman had then driven back to Balat where he had performed two totally fruitless interviews: firstly with Meyer's friend Mrs Blatsky and secondly with an insane-looking old woman who lived on the ground floor. Neither woman spoke more than the most elementary Turkish and with his own complete lack of Ladino, progress had been impossible. He had, just before he left Balat, come across one possible contender for the term 'derelict' lying across the doorway of the neighbourhood hamam, but the man in question, as well as being covered in his own vomit, had been so drunk as to be unintelligible in any language. It was at this point that Suleyman had decided that searching for derelicts would be a job most usefully delegated to his Ladino-speaking colleague, Cohen. When the Jewish constable returned for duty the following morning he would now find instructions to that effect on his desk. Suleyman pulled a sour face. Cohen would no doubt hate him for that.

Ikmen had not had an easy time either. Probably, Suleyman thought as he looked at the late hour indicated on the face of his watch, he still wasn't. His interview with Leah Delmonte had indeed gone ahead although Suleyman was, as yet, ignorant of the outcome. This was because Ikmen and Suleyman's boss, the somewhat explosive Commissioner Ardiç, had summoned the Inspector as soon as he had returned from the hospital. That had been, according to Suleyman's calculations, nearly four hours ago. This did not, either by the length of time involved or by prior experience of Ardiç, bode well. And although Suleyman should really have left for home over an hour before, he didn't feel able to go until he knew what was going on. At the very least, Ikmen would need someone to rave and shout at after his ordeal. And at the very worst? Suleyman didn't even dare think about that. Ardiç, as even the humblest constable knew, could be contrary to the point of lunacy.

The office door opened slowly and Ikmen staggered through it, back bent, arms hanging limply at his sides. His weary face wore an expression of patience stretched to the limit and beyond. 'That man's lack of vision is so profound it's almost clinical.' His words were spoken automatically, almost as if he were too tired or bored to inject them with any emotion.

'Bad time with the Commissioner, sir?'

Ikmen squeezed around to the back of his desk and sat down. 'You know that bastard actually wanted to take us off this case!' He lit a cigarette.

'Why would he want to do that?'

'Because it has political overtones. The Israeli Consul is, apparently, very keen to keep an eye on developments. Ardiç, the Consul and the Mayor seem to have formed the opinion that we are dealing with a full-scale Nazi pogrom. The fact that it could just as easily be one lunatic working alone seems to elude them.'

Suleyman felt crushed. 'So, are we off the case then, sir?'

Ikmen dismissed the question with a casual flick of the wrist. 'Oh, no. It took a while, as you probably noticed, Suleyman, but I eventually managed to persuade the stupid bastard.' He sat forward in his chair and peered through the leaning towers of paper.

'He was only going to put Yalçin on it!'

Suleyman looked surprised. 'I would have thought that Inspector Yalçin was a bit old—'

'Old!' Ikmen was coming very loudly back to life again. 'Yes, he is, but it's not his age I object to. The man's a cretin: finding the lavatory taxes his small brain! Ardiç said it was because of his "considerable experience in the political field", he didn't have the guts to say that it was really about my well-known penchant for fine brandy!'

'Everybody knows that you like a drink, sir.'

'Precisely. Everybody also knows that I don't get drunk!

What did the stupid man think I was going to do? Go up to the Israeli Consul and vomit all over him?'

'So how did you manage to persuade him to let you stay on then, sir?'

Ikmen stubbed out his half-smoked cigarette and lit another. 'I told him the truth. Yalçin is an unintelligent idiot who doesn't get results. If he is given the Meyer case I will resign and so will you.'

'Sir!'

Ikmen laughed at his deputy's white-faced indignation.

'Yes, I'm sorry about that, Suleyman. I wasn't going to bring you into it, but it just sort of happened in the heat of the moment. Anyway, who cares? It worked. He saw sense in the end. He knew all along I was the only man for this job.' He smiled unpleasantly. 'I think the Mayor must have put pressure on him. A great admirer of proper behaviour, our Mayor! The sort of person the boys over in Vice frequently catch with underage hookers of indeterminate sex. Anyway'—he banged his fist on his desk—'down to business. What and what has not been happening here?'

'No luck with the derelicts, but I'm going to put Cohen onto that.'

Ikmen smiled. 'Didn't speak Turkish too well, eh?'

'No.'

'What about Şeker Textiles?'

'I've fixed up for us to see Reinhold Smits at his house in Bebek tomorrow at ten.'

'Good lad!' He paused, and then eyed Suleyman shrewdly. 'I suppose you want to go now?'

'Well, sir, if there's nothing else…'

Ikmen felt mean. The boy was a hard worker and it was already seven-fifteen, but there was something else, and it was important. Like Suleyman, Ikmen felt dissatisfied with their lack of progress. He desperately wanted to achieve something, to prove to himself that the day had not been an utter waste of time.

'How do you fancy paying the woman in Beyoğlu a visit? Maria Gulcu.'

'Now?'

'Yes.' He stood up. 'I've this nagging fear that she might be a relative. If she is it could look as if we're dragging our heels. Come on, let's do some proper work before we go home and fossilise in front of the television. Show Ardiç that we're keen.'

Suleyman sighed. 'All right, sir.' He put his car keys in his pocket and rose wearily to his feet. 'Oh, by the way, what happened at the hospital this morning?'

'Ah, yes. Leah Delmonte.' Ikmen chuckled softly, but his eyes were sad. 'She danced for me.'

Suleyman looked confused.

'I think it was supposed to be flamenco. Lots of arm-waving and suggestive looks. It was poorly executed and quite terrible. Her doctor was appalled.'

'But what did she say, sir? About Mr Meyer?'

Ikmen looked down at his badly scuffed shoes and shrugged. 'Nothing. She said nothing. Hers is a pointless line of inquiry.' He looked up sharply and changed the subject. 'Come on, Suleyman, let's go and see what Maria Gulcu can tell us.'

Robert found the food mostly pleasant, but strange. In attempting to accommodate his English palate the Gulcus had succeeded in creating a culinary confusion.

In common with most formal Turkish meals, the vegetables were served separately and prior to the meat. They started with fried courgette and roast potatoes. Leg of lamb with rice, again roasted and served with a beetroot and garlic salad followed. Dessert, the most curious course of all, consisted of fresh figs and thin, watery custard. His hosts, Robert observed, disliked the sickly yellow liquid, but they all ate it—for his sake, he supposed. It was very thoughtful of them, but he had difficulty getting it down. It was foul.

As he popped the last dark, fleshy fig into his mouth, Robert stole a glance around the table. Natalia, her mother and two uncles. They were all nice, they all smiled easily (with the exception of her mother), but they were undeniably weird.

Uncle Nicholas was a Colonel Blimp character. Bombastic and blustery, he seemed to be, as far as Robert could tell, the head of the household. He, Natalia's mother Anya and the other uncle, Sergei, were siblings. The subject of Natalia's absent father had not, as yet, been raised. Her mother, compared to Nicholas, had either aged badly or was considerably older. A small, mousy woman, she spoke little and in very halting English. Most of the time she just sipped her wine in silence, nibbling delicately on her food like a nervous rabbit.

Sergei and Natalia were, however, the most problematic and disturbing members of the family. Unaccustomed to disabled people, Robert was very conscious of a desire not to stare at Sergei. Or at least not to get caught staring. Thin and wizened, Nicholas's and Anya's brother suffered from what seemed to be a condition that twisted and distorted the limbs. His arms were grossly swollen around the elbows and wrists; the flesh was puffed, bruised and painful-looking. Raising his cutlery to his mouth was slow and difficult. But his arms were nothing compared to his useless, wheelchair-bound legs. They had been the first thing Robert had seen as Nicholas ushered him into the dining room. Sergei had introduced himself, smiling; his English was better, if anything, than his brother's. But all Robert could see was the man's legs, his knees swollen and twisted like corkscrews, his feet pointing inwards and back, limp and without purpose. His ever-present smile and cheery demeanour struck Robert as almost arrogant. Such self-possession in one so disadvantaged didn't seem right somehow. His own small memory of crippled people involved those he had seen in hospital. Silent stones, hopeless and without personality.

But Natalia was the oddest of them all. She was coy, shy even, in this, surely her natural context. Like her mother, she was quiet, perhaps even a little apprehensive. Her eyes hadn't once met his since he had arrived and she silently conceded to all of her elders' requests with a grave bow of her head. It was strange for Robert to be with her and yet not dominated by her. It was almost as if she had temporarily diminished herself. Perhaps she was silently wondering what he thought of her family? What they thought of him? As she collected the dessert bowls and disappeared into the kitchen along with her mother, Robert noticed for the first time how small she was. The simple white frock she had chosen for the evening did nothing for her. Natalia needed colours, red, gold, black, to enhance her exotic beauty. White rendered her almost invisible and somehow impotent.

Nicholas produced two thick cigars from his jacket pocket and handed one to Robert. 'Smoke?'

'Oh, yes. Thank you.'

An elaborate cutter, shaped like the head of a dragon, followed. Robert sliced off the end with surprising dexterity. Beginner's luck.

Nicholas reached into his pocket again and produced a small red-gold bangle. He gave it to Robert and then looked around the table furtively. 'The women are in the kitchen, I can show you.'

The scrollwork on the outside edges, curled and cascading like waves of the sea, was unmistakable. An exquisite product from the Avedissian workshop. It was very like the one Robert had sent to his mother just over a year ago, the bangle that had brought him and Natalia together for the first time. The red pigment in the gold glowed warmly against the palm of his hand.

'Very beautiful,' Robert said, turning the object to catch the shifting patterns of light from the silver candelabra on the table.

Nicholas drew closer to him. 'Natalia got this for her mother, for her birthday. She got it Monday evening, when she finishes work.'

'She was very tired that day,' said Sergei, as if to underscore the point. He looked at Robert. 'The Gold Bazaar is always so busy in the tourist season. Especially at the beginning of the week. Poor Natalia, she hardly has time to breathe.' Robert saw the stern twinkles in the eyes of both men and his blood ran cold.

'Yes.' His tone was flat. He hoped he had managed to crush the disapproving edge out of his reply, but he knew he hadn't. Balat reared its litter-encrusted head in his mind once again, and all the old doubts came flooding back. He wasn't here to meet Natalia's family! If Monday hadn't happened he would never have even got near number 12, Karadeniz Sokak. He was deeply offended. What kind of moron did she think he was? Who in their right mind would fall for such a transparent ploy? But he knew the answer to that and his heart sank. He'd come of his own free will, hoping…Hoping for what? The food in his stomach curdled as his muscles tightened with anxiety. Whatever Natalia had been doing in Balat on Monday was more serious than he had thought. Perhaps he had been too quick to rule her innocent of dark deeds? After all, could he say that he really knew her? Perhaps by his continued silence to the police he was aiding and abetting this stranger? The uncles watched and waited. He could see their tension. It poisoned the air around them, like a noxious cloud. Robert felt a little sick and excused himself from the table.

'Er, the bathroom?'

Nicholas smiled. 'Back into the hall and to your right, the second door.'

'Thank you.' Robert left.

Silence dominated the room until the sound of Robert's footsteps was replaced by the click of the bathroom door shutting behind him.

Sergei turned to his brother and groaned. 'Oh, God!'

Nicholas, his face grim, raised his head in agreement. 'We handled it badly, didn't we? Clumsy.'

Two short raps on the front door terminated their conversation. Nicholas looked puzzled and put his cigar down in his ashtray.

'Who can that be?'

His brother's answer was sharp, bitchy even. 'Why don't you go and look, Nicky, then you'll find out. You're the one with the working legs.'

Nicholas shot the little cripple a murderous glance and strode off briskly into the hall.

When he opened the front door, Nicholas found himself confronted by two men. The shorter and older of the two was smiling.

'Good evening, sir.' Producing what looked like a small identity badge from the top pocket of his jacket he politely introduced himself. 'Inspector Çetin Ikmen of the Istanbul Police Department.'

'Police!' What little colour resided in Nicholas's face disappeared very quickly.

'Yes, sir.' Ikmen's smile broadened. 'Nothing to worry about, Mr Gulcu, I assure you.'

'How do you know my name?'

Ikmen ignored the question and inclined his head towards his younger colleague. 'This is Sergeant Suleyman.'

Nicholas looked at the young man without smiling, observing his face sharply. 'What do you want?' he said, looking back at Ikmen.

'We understand a lady called Maria Gulcu lives in this house, sir.'

'My mother, yes. What do you want with her? She's very old, you know. She doesn't take kindly to being bothered by people.'

'I won't take up much of your mother's time, sir,' continued Ikmen smoothly. 'As you may have read in the papers, an old gentleman was murdered in Balat on Monday afternoon. Amongst the deceased's effects was an address book. It contained your mother's name and the address of this property.'

'Oh.' It was more an exhalation than a word. The breath

Belghazzair

Mys

NAD

iOOO|OlPLblP|54qq5¿

Thur 10/12, 11-12:30 p

Thur 10/12, 6-7:30 pm (

Fri 11/13, 11-12:30 pm@

Connect • Inspire • Inform

drained out of Nicholas and his face sank. For a moment he stood silent, blinking, utterly helpless—a condition not lost upon Ikmen who swiftly took the advantage.

'So you see, sir, it's very important that we speak to your mother. If she knew this man, she may be able to give us some information about him. As you can appreciate, the more we know about the victim's lifestyle, the greater chance we have of apprehending his murderer.'

'I see.' Nicholas looked down at the floor and swallowed hard.

'You have heard about this murder, sir?'

'No, no—no, Inspector.' It was a distracted denial. He ran his fingers through his hair and gazed glassily into the blank space above the policemen's heads.

'Then if she did know this gentleman, Leonid Meyer'— Nicholas's eyes flickered. Just a little, a movement he knew the policeman had seen—'she may be a little upset when I tell her that he is now dead. I will be as gentle as I can, but if you or another member of the family wish to be present, I—'

'Quite so.'

'I am right, I presume, in assuming that your mother wasn't related to—'

Ikmen's words were cut short by a laugh which was both harsh and inappropriate. 'Oh, no, oh absolutely not at all, no!'

'Oh…right.'

There was an awkward pause. Nicholas didn't know what to do next. He looked at the policemen, turned and stared back into his house, then returned his gaze to Ikmen. He bit down on his lower lip with his top teeth and scratched the side of his head.

Ikmen, for his part, carried on smiling. 'Why don't you go and get your mother ready, Mr Gulcu?

Robert splashed some water on to his face and looked in the

mirror. Drips rolled down his chin and back into the sink; a transparent globe clung fiercely to the end of his nose. He looked haggard; dark circles engulfed his lower eyelids. He traced with his finger the deep lines running from his nose down to the corners of his mouth. The first stirrings of approaching middle age. He reached for a towel and wiped his chin. His hands trembled and he clicked his tongue impatiently. He hated that.

He sighed and opened the bathroom door. He would have to leave this house, get back to his apartment and think. This relationship with Natalia had always been a strain. He should never have got involved with her in the first place: she was too difficult. This latest event was the final straw and yet...

As he pulled the door shut behind him, he saw her. She was standing in the hall with her back to him, her long dark hair hanging thickly down her spine. He groaned. It was all too easy to be strong when he wasn't actually with her. But as soon as she appeared...! Even in the plain white dress she excited him. In this house she was different: quieter, smaller, chaste even. Nicer—and he liked it. But now he really looked at the proud tilt of the head, at her muscular fingers curled against the swelling of her hips, he saw the underlying and intoxicating arrogance was still there. He reached out and twined an arm around her waist, pressing his body and his rising erection into her full firm behind. She didn't move. She was looking at something. Robert followed her gaze.

Nicholas was standing at the open front door talking to someone. It was dark outside and Nicholas's body obscured the caller from Robert's view. They talked in hushed, barely discernible tones. Robert looked down at Natalia; her face was taut, unmoving, fixed upon the action at the front door. He had the uncomfortable feeling that she didn't even know that he was there. His loving gesture, his physical response to her body, was wasted.

'Natalia?'

Robert looked up with her, their heads moving in unison.

Nicholas had come back inside now; he had two men with him. One was young, darkly handsome and unfamiliar. But the other...

'Natalia, will you please go upstairs and make sure that Grandmama is decent.' Nicholas looked very pale. 'Some gentlemen from the police wish to speak to her.'

Of course! It was the Inspector who had interviewed him at the school! Unmistakable. Small, grimy, looked like an unmade bed—he was looking right at him and he was smiling.

Natalia pushed Robert's arm gently to one side and moved forward. 'Yes, Uncle.'

'Hello, Mr Cornelius.'

Natalia froze. She looked across at the small dirty man standing next to her uncle. Nicholas was sweating heavily. 'Go on, Natalia.'

She mounted the stairs and glanced briefly at the face of her lover as she passed. For once his eyes were not upon her, but fixed on the little group of men by the door.

'Hello, Inspector Ikmen,' he replied mechanically.

Natalia pulled the door shut behind her. Maria heaved her body up into a sitting position and leant back against her pillows. She looked at the silent figure sitting in the chair over by the window, its head bowed. There was a pause and then she spoke.

'When the policemen come in you stay silent.' Her voice was commanding. It was an order, it wasn't open to negotiation.

'If you want.' The reply was flat and hollow.

'It's not what I want, it's what must be.' She took a deep breath and closed her eyes for a moment. There was a knock at the door.

'Grandmama?'

She opened her eyes and reached under the bed-covers for her cigarettes and lighter. 'Come in.'

Natalia Gulcu ushered the policemen into a large, dimly lit apartment at the top of the house. For several seconds they could see little as their eyes adjusted to the gloom. Ikmen felt one of Suleyman's hands brush against his back. The young man always touched, reached out, when he was nervous. It was a curious habit for someone like Suleyman.

In this case, however, Ikmen could understand completely his sergeant's need for a little comfort. As his eyes grew accustomed to the weak viscous light from the single oil lamp in the middle of the room, he began to make out detail. Dark, heavy furniture, cupboards, chests and cabinets loomed against the walls. Pictures, dozens of them, hung in black weighty frames from a rail close to the ceiling. As the inadequate light touched them a purple glow rose up from the curtains, wall hangings, carpet. A large violet mass glittered in the centre of the apartment: an enormous gilded bed shaped like a boat, its tall headboard touching the ceiling. Waves of thin netting shrouded the bed, giving the impression that it was somehow enclosed and contained within a pale violet cloud. The lamp flickered, lending substance to Ikmen's feeling that the room was eerie. For a few seconds nothing moved. There was a faint smell of incense, like in a church.

Then Natalia moved forward and pushed the netting over the bed to one side. A waft of smoke escaped as the violet mist was dismantled and Ikmen became aware of a small figure lying beneath the covers. It wasn't short, more long and thin, its head crowned by a thick tangled mass of grey hair.

The girl then said something in a language he could not understand and the figure answered, its voice deep, dry and scarred by time. The portraits on the wall looked down on Ikmen without humour. Long-dead men and women in military uniforms, bustles and tea gowns. It was like being in a tomb or a crypt that hadn't been opened for many years. There was an aura of redundancy, a smell behind the incense of stale vitiated breath.

Natalia returned. 'Grandmama is not very fluent in Turkish. Do either of you speak Russian?'

She was an arrogant creature, Ikmen felt. Not by her words but her gaze. When she looked at him her top lip curled upwards slightly, as if she had a bad smell under her nose.

'No,' he replied flatly and then looked away from the girl towards that great gilded bed once again. That someone could have lived in his country for so long without learning his language struck Ikmen as most peculiar. But then, given the reclusive atmosphere of the apartment...

'English?' she inquired, looking over the top of his head and smiling, doe-eyed, Ikmen thought, in Suleyman's direction.

'Yes, we can both speak English—miss.' He couldn't help snapping.

The girl ignored his temporary lapse into spitefulness and spoke again, presumably in Russian, to her grandmother.

As the old woman answered Natalia stood aside to allow the policemen to pass. 'Grandmama will see you now.' As he moved past her, Natalia smiled sensuously at Suleyman once again. The young man's cheeks flushed hot.

The girl left the room, closing the door behind her.

'Come on then, Mel Gibson!' hissed Ikmen. The two men walked towards the golden and violet barge.

Robert took a deep swig from his wineglass and tried to smile at Sergei.

'You are shaking,' observed the cripple, without concern.

'I've—had a bit of stomach trouble lately.'

'Nothing you ate at this table, I hope.'

'No.' He took another big gulp and then refilled his glass from the decanter.

Ikmen! What the hell was he doing here? Robert felt as

if he should bend, throw his arms about his body, curl up against the constriction of events that were closing in around him. There was something awfully wrong in the Gulcu house, he'd noticed it as soon as he saw the place. Outward decay and internal opulence, strong jarring colours, the strangeness of the people. Until Nicholas and Sergei had tried to treat him like a fool, he'd ignored it. But now he couldn't do that any more, Ikmen had arrived and had seen him. It could only be about the Balat murder! Wherever the Gulcus were in Ikmen's mental assessment of his case, Robert was now right alongside them. He felt trapped, caught in a net, and with some very curious fellow prisoners.

Natalia came back into the room and smiled at him. She said something in a foreign language to Sergei and he answered her with a nod.

'When Uncle Nicky and Mama are finished in the kitchen we can play bezique or maybe tavla if you like.' She was so calm, so relaxed.

'But the police—' Robert started.

'Mama has a very old tavla board, it belonged to my grandfather. Would you like to see it, Robert?'

He stood with his mouth open like a fish. She took his arm and led him over to a chair by the fireplace.

'I'll bring it to you.'

She left the room again. Sergei poured a little splash of red wine from his glass on to the pure white tablecloth. He rubbed it into the material with his finger, frowning.

She looked even older close up. Her pale, withered face was almost completely brown with age spots; her blue eyes, clearly defined and bright but rimmed with red, regarded them coldly from beneath crêpy lids. An arm like a stick brought a fat black cigarette up to her mouth and a frosting of diamonds on her knuckles sparkled slowly into Ikmen's eyes. Considering she was so old and skeletal, her jaw was surprisingly firm; strong evidence that she still retained at least some of her teeth. She was, nevertheless, unpleasant. There was something crocodilian about the way her skin flaked around her fingers and elbows, leaving patches of cracked, leathery hide.

'Bend close, both of you, I want to see your faces.' Though desiccated and scarred by age her voice was cultured. Her accent was perfection: the clipped, commanding tones of the English upper classes. For a second Ikmen was quite lost in admiration.

'Come along!' She tapped the side of her cigarette impatiently on her ashtray.

Ikmen bent towards her. She reached out her hand and grabbed him roughly by the chin. 'Mmm.' Her hands were dry, her nails sharp. Ikmen felt suddenly vulnerable, as if he had inadvertently entered a room of strangers naked.

The walls of the house creaked slightly as the breeze outside strengthened.

She released her grip and Ikmen instinctively backed away from her. He wiped his chin with his hand as if trying to eradicate the touch of something tainted.

Suleyman nervously stepped forward and the old woman smiled. She didn't grab at him, but stroked his cheek gently with her thumb as if caressing fine porcelain.

'Mmm,' she murmured again, but softly.

Suleyman straightened up and turned sheepishly to Ikmen.

'You are becoming a liability!' whispered Ikmen with some passion.

'Oh, don't scold the boy!' said the old woman, stubbing her cigarette out. 'He can't help being beautiful.'

'I thought you couldn't speak Turkish, madam,' countered Ikmen.

'The parameters of my understanding are of no importance to anyone but myself. But Turkish or no Turkish, your tone was clear. I am familiar with jealousy. I was once beautiful myself.' Her voice became cold again. 'Anyway, what are your names, I can't just call you "Officer", it's too degrading.'

'I am Inspector Ikmen and this is Sergeant Suleyman.'

The old woman cleared her smoking requisites away from the side of the bed and smoothed the counterpane. 'You can sit on my bed if you like. I don't mind.'

Ikmen took her at her word, but Suleyman remained standing. Reaching into his pocket, Ikmen took out a notebook and pen.

'My granddaughter tells me that you've come for some information about the late Leonid Meyer.' Her face was like stone, it showed no emotion. A flash of light from a corner of the room caught Ikmen's attention: illumination from the lamp bouncing off the golden faces of saints on an antique ikon screen. He turned back and looked at the woman again.

Here is someone, Ikmen thought, who always likes to be one step ahead.

'Your son wasn't sure whether you knew of the tragedy, madam.'

She waved her hand impatiently at him. 'Nicholas knows nothing! He thinks I'm losing my mind. He's a fool.'

Ikmen tended to agree with Mrs Gulcu's assessment of her son. The old woman's mind was as sharp as his own, perhaps sharper. 'You did know Mr Meyer then, madam?'

She lit a cigarette and pushed the packet towards Ikmen. 'Help yourself.' He nodded in thanks and gratefully took a thick black Sobranie from the packet.

'Yes, I knew him. We first met back in Russia.'

Ikmen lit the cigarette and savoured its cool smoothness. A rich man's smoke. 'I imagine you must have been very young at the time, madam?'

'Teenagers, both of us.'

She leant her head back upon the pillows and observed him with still, piercing eyes. Her succinct replies gave Ikmen the impression that she was not going to volunteer any more information than was absolutely necessary.

'How did you meet Mr Meyer?'

'Surely that is not relevant—'

Her almost regal dismissiveness annoyed him. Ikmen held up his cigarette to silence her. 'Madam, with respect, everything is relevant. The more we know about a murder victim, the more, by extension, we know about his killer. Very few people are murdered by complete strangers. Most murders are committed by relatives, friends or acquaintances. The victim's biography is essential.'

She looked at the rings on her fingers, moving her hand to and fro across her face, catching the light upon the stones. She appeared completely unmoved by his outburst. Ikmen looked at Suleyman, but the young man's head was turned away from him in the direction of the curtains. Ikmen peered into the gloom to see what his colleague was observing. In a large brocade chair just in front of the curtains sat a figure, hunched up, its legs off the floor, drawn up underneath its chin. Whether it was male or female he couldn't tell, but its eyes glittered through the darkness like a cat's, its stare fixed upon Suleyman.

'Leonid Meyer was from a town called Perm.'

Ikmen turned away from the mystery in the corner and back to the old woman. That sounded familiar. 'Perm? In the Ural Mountains?'

His answer surprised her. 'Very good, Inspector!' She smiled a little. A very little. 'After the Revolution in 1918 my family went to Perm. I met Leonid there. We ran away together.'

Ikmen stubbed his cigarette out in her ashtray. It was at times like this that he silently blessed his father for those long ago and, at times, boring lectures on the subject of European history. He narrowed his eyes thoughtfully. 'I would not have thought that Perm was a good place to be in 1918.'

She was temporarily taken aback. 'Why?'

'The Bolsheviks were extremely powerful in that area then. Your family, surely, could not have been safe in such a place?'

'What leads you to that conclusion, Inspector?'

'You did not, madam, learn English from a book. You learnt from an English speaker, a governess or nanny. This is obvious from your, I must say, amazing fluency. It follows that your family must have been wealthy and therefore at consider-able risk in the Urals.'

She smiled. 'You are a clever man, Inspector. And where did you learn your excellent English?'

'My father taught European Languages at the university for most of his working life. He taught me English. Unfortunately he did not share his knowledge of Russian with me. But I know a little of Russian history. Our house was always full of books on all kinds of different subjects.' Ikmen smiled. He took his cigarettes out of his jacket and placed them on the bed. 'Why did you run away with Meyer? Why did he run away with you for that matter? He was a poor Jew, wasn't he, and you...'

'We were in love.'

'But you didn't marry him?'

'No.' She laughed. It was a deep, rasping sound, like a cough. 'As you have quite rightly surmised, the relationship could not last. Whatever people say class will always and inevi-tably intervene in these matters. Leonid was a peasant. Imagine your daughter, if you have one, marrying that pretty sergeant of yours.' She waved her hand in Suleyman's direction. 'She would soon tire of him. He's a peasant. Breeding, as the English say, and they are the experts, always shows. However soiled the clothing.'

Ikmen smiled and offered her a cigarette; she declined with a wave of her hand. 'You came to Istanbul together, you and Meyer?'

'Yes. We parted and I met my husband, Mr Gulcu.'

'Why Istanbul?'

'Why not?' Suddenly her eyes became misty as she stared beyond him into the darkness. Her expression soft now, almost tender. 'I cannot tell you how it was in Russia. Everyone was dead, or dying. I would have willingly gone to hell to get away from it. There were so many dead. They lay in piles by the roadside. It was impossible to breathe for the smell. Everything was poisoned. Even your ruined country was a paradise by comparison.'

Ikmen had the feeling that she wasn't quite with him

anymore. Her mind was staked to a memory that was both horrific and very current to her. He instinctively lowered his voice, almost as if in prayer. 'And your families, yours and Meyer's?'

Tears welled up in her eyes, the pupils moving as if watching a scene being played out on the opposite wall. She mumbled something to herself in Russian. Then her eyes drifted slowly back towards him. He watched them move. Saw how difficult it was for her to tear them away. 'They all died, Inspector, all of them.'

Ikmen heard Suleyman shuffle his feet on the carpet. He had given the young man little thought since the strange old woman had started speaking. He wondered in passing what his sergeant felt about being described as a peasant.

'Madam, from your experience, and presuming that you kept in contact with him, is there anyone you can think of who might have wanted to kill Mr Meyer?'

'Leonid and I did not see one another often, especially after my marriage. Leonid drank.'

'Do you have any idea why?'

'Presumably because he liked it, Inspector. Addiction to alcohol is a very common vice amongst my compatriots.' She paused. A faint whimpering sound from the chair by the curtains filled the silence.

Suleyman leant forward and pointed behind him to the source of the sound. 'Madam, this person—'

The clouds disappeared as quickly as they had come and she laughed again. 'You really are a peasant, aren't you, my darling!' Although continuing to stare at Suleyman, she addressed Ikmen. 'You must teach the boy to ignore servants, Inspector. People will think he has no class.'

Ikmen cleared his throat in a very obvious fashion. He didn't want to go down the social-class road again. 'Quite. Well, madam?'

She shrugged. 'I can think of no one. Among his own kind, in that awful place where he lived, perhaps...'

'Other Jews?'

What she seemed to be suggesting had not occurred to him before. An enemy from within the community?

She looked him steadily in the eyes again. That piercing, reptilian stare of hers. 'Jews or enemies of Jews.'

Ikmen looked back into her eyes and had the strangest feeling. It was like an understanding passed between them, the knowledge of a shared experience. Of course it was absurd—he had only just met the woman! But the feeling persisted. It was like *déjà vu*. And he knew that she was experiencing it too. He felt unnerved and shook his head slightly as if trying to loosen something distasteful from his mind.

'Mr Meyer had a considerable amount of money. Did you know that?'

'No.' But she didn't sound surprised. 'Perhaps therein lies your motive, Inspector.'

'The nature of the killing would suggest not, madam.'

She raised an eyebrow, questioningly. 'Oh?'

It was an effort not to be drawn by that ravaged but intelligent face. Ikmen had always been susceptible to high intellect. The urge to share knowledge with an equal was strong. Perhaps if he told her the details of the killing, Maria Gulcu could shed some light onto the murkier corners of the case. He was almost certain that she could. He didn't know why. He wanted to tell her even though she—she seemed to know. The squalid, bloody apartment in Balat, she—but he held back. She coiled her arms around each other, slowly, like courting snakes. Despite her age the movement was sensual, almost suggestive. Ikmen felt suddenly repelled. He cleared his throat and became very businesslike again.

'The intimate details are confidential, madam.'

She gave a little shrug and cleared her throat. 'As you wish.' It was a light dismissal, as if the subject didn't matter to her. But it did.

Ikmen looked at his watch. It was getting late and the room and its occupant were beginning to oppress him. He needed to get out. Only then could he think his own thoughts again. While in that room it was impossible not to be affected, invaded, by her presence. There was, however, one more question that he had to ask.

'Do you know anything about Mr Meyer's involvement with a company called Şeker Textiles, madam?'

She looked away as she spoke, but Ikmen could just see out of the corner of his eye that her turned face was smiling. 'Yes, he worked for them when he first came to this country. Until, that is, he had that falling out with his superior.'

'I don't suppose you know what that was about, do you?'

She turned back to face him, the smile now gone from her wasted lips. 'It was in 1940 or thereabouts and the owner of the company, a Mr Smits, was a very patriotic German. Need I say more?'

'No.' Ikmen sighed. 'No, I think that speaks for itself.'

He then changed tack slightly, wanting despite the interest this whole situation held for him to be out and on his way now as soon as possible. 'Is there anything else you can tell us about Mr Meyer, madam?'

She looked down at her covers, picking idly at them with her fingers. 'He drank, he lived in poverty, he had nothing and nobody. What can I say?'

'But you loved him at one time?'

Her face hardened into a scowl. 'Yes, I did. There are sometimes reasons for loving someone that have nothing to do with the intellect or even the body. But I do not expect that you can understand that, Inspector.'

'I might if I knew what those reasons were.'

She put her cigarettes and lighter back under her covers and closed her eyes. 'I am tired of this. Your curiosity is becoming prurient. Please go.'

She was not unpleasant, but Ikmen knew that, for the time being, further questioning was useless. She had spoken and that was that.

Ikmen put his cigarettes back in his pocket and stood up.

'Very well. Thank you for your co-operation, madam.'

She laughed, but without mirth. 'Goodnight, gentlemen.'

The two officers moved towards the door. As Suleyman drew level with him, Ikmen felt the young man's hand upon his shoulder.

Çiçek Pasaj is a small neon-lit alleyway. It extends from Istiklal Caddesi and, proceeding westwards, fizzles out as it joins Balık Pazar, the fish market behind. It is lined with bars and small restaurants called *lokantalar*. It has, for as long as anyone can remember, been a magnet for both the working classes and the intelligentsia of the city. Hard, dedicated drinking and an air of down-at-heel eccentricity have always characterised this small area of insobriety. Now, of course, tourists make up a large part of its clientele, a new phenomenon reflected in the more sanitary appearance of the place. It was completely redecorated at the end of the eighties. Before that time, however, the word 'raffish' would probably have been a most apt description.

Çetin Ikmen well remembered the old days of riotous fighting, of granite-hard and insistent prostitutes, of dirt, grime and cheap liquor. He mourned their passing bitterly. Not that he was concentrating on his surroundings at this time. Suleyman was very excited and he'd never seen him like this before. It came as a bit of a shock.

'I kept expecting Dracula to appear from under the bed or out of a cupboard!'

Ikmen refilled his glass and leant towards his colleague. The accumulated drunken babble of Çiçek Pasaj was fairly loud, but he didn't want the whole world to overhear their conversation. 'Keep your voice down, Suleyman! I wish you'd have a drink. It would make you feel better!'

'And that person in the corner!'

'Let me give you a little advice about the world and your place in it, Suleyman.' He lit a cigarette. 'The world is infinitely variable and as a police officer you, more than most people, will be exposed to its extreme quirks.' He looked down gravely into the depths of his glass. 'The old Gulcu woman was unnerving though. I had the strangest sensation—'

'At least she didn't want to drag you into that horrible bed!'

Ikmen roused himself from his reverie and chuckled. It was pointless trying to explain what he had felt in that peculiar apartment. He did not yet understand it sufficiently himself. 'Oh yes, you were quite popular, weren't you?'

Suleyman leant heavily across the table. 'I felt, well, like an object, a thing in front of that ghastly old woman and her dreadful granddaughter—'

'I thought the girl was quite attractive.'

'She kept looking at my—'

'Well, yes. The Lady Chatterley syndrome.'

"What?'

Ikmen laughed. 'Nothing.' They fell silent. Suleyman's excitement seemed to have temporarily blown itself out.

Ikmen took a gulp from his glass and rolled the liquor briefly around his mouth before swallowing. In the bar opposite, the old Lebanese accordionist struck up the 'Marseillaise'. 'Putting the house aside for a minute, the weird set-up et cetera, there were a lot of things that troubled me about that interview.'

'Like what?'

'All that stuff about her family moving to the Urals just after the Revolution. It doesn't make any sense. Rich people like that, they would have been torn to pieces. And how did she, a wealthy Russian, get to meet an ordinary Jew like Meyer? Even after the Revolution, the different classes rarely mixed—apart from anything else they were on quite opposing sides during the ensuing civil war. And why would they, especially him, leave the country?'

'She said it was dreadful there. They were afraid. And they were in love.'

Ikmen stared steadily into space. 'Or were they?' He shifted his gaze and looked at Suleyman. 'I can't imagine that woman

loving anything. I know that's a terrible thing to say about a
person, but I can't imagine it. I felt quite exhausted when I came
out of that room. It was like I'd been leeched.'

'How do you mean, sir?'

Ikmen smiled gently. 'Nothing.' Again, it wasn't possible for
him to explain how he felt. It was such a deep knowledge, almost
inaccessible. On the face of it the Gulcus were just a rather
eccentric Russian émigré family who were nervous of the police.
But that old woman! When she had mentioned the enemies of
the Jews it had struck him. The words could have been said by
anybody and he would not have turned a hair, but from her...
it was the obvious relish with which she used the words, that
reptile look she had given him. Was she planting thoughts in his
mind and, if so, why? What had produced that feeling of shared
experience? Why had he got the impression that what he had
seen in that dingy Balat apartment was no mystery to her? Ah,
this was an old feeling, but it was one that over the years he had
come to trust. He wasn't done with Mrs Gulcu yet—or indeed,
with the as yet unseen Reinhold Smits.

'So what did you think about the old woman's version of
the Şeker Textiles story, Suleyman?'

'She seemed to be suggesting a similar scenario to the one
that the Rabbi outlined.'

'Yes.' Ikmen smiled, but rather grimly, or so Suleyman
thought. 'I'm looking forward to meeting Smits. It isn't every
day that you meet someone who agrees with the late Adolf
Hitler.'

'Not that we know that for certain.'

Ikmen raised his glass in agreement. 'Not, as you say, that
we know that for certain.'

He then swigged a long and satisfying draught from his
glass and turned his attentions towards something he imagined
his colleague had missed. 'Suleyman, did you notice that man in
the hall with the granddaughter?'

'Yes. You spoke to him, didn't you?'

'Yes. That was Robert Cornelius, one of the Englishmen I

interviewed at the language school yesterday. He was the one who was in the area at about the right time. The one I felt uncertain about.'

'Could just be coincidence?'

'It could.' Ikmen poured more liquor into his glass. 'I'd like you to check him out though. We've got all his details back at the office. Send them through to London, will you? I'd like to know a bit more about Mr Cornelius.'

'To Inspector Lloyd?'

Ikmen smiled, he always did when something made him recall his all too brief visit to London's Scotland Yard some fifteen years before. John Lloyd and his colleagues had certainly shown his little band of Turkish detectives a good time during that crazy, faraway fortnight. Not that Ikmen and his fellows had learnt a tremendous amount about policing, but the English beer had been excellent and Lloyd, at least, had over the years proved to be a most valuable link with the English police system. However, there were also other more domestic things that needed attention too. Ikmen cleared his throat. 'Yes. I'd like a bit more on the Gulcus too. Get Cohen to do it. That and interviewing various derelicts should keep him away from drink and women for a bit.'

'Yes, sir.' Suleyman sipped his lemonade quietly, but his face was troubled.

'What is it, Suleyman?'

'Well, sir…Look, don't you think we should be picking up a few people with form? Mr Meyer had money and that district is crawling with thieves, drug-pushers and all kinds of other crazies. I can think of six who live within a kilometre of the apartment just off the top of my head.'

'I don't seriously think it was robbery. What thief goes armed with a canister of sulphuric acid? The murder weapon and the acid were taken away by the murderer after the killing. The room was not turned over as if someone were searching for something. No, I still maintain this was personal. Meyer was meant to die and he was meant to die in that particular fashion.

We're not looking for some sick junkie who kills for the price of a fix, we're looking for either someone who hates Jews or someone who hated Meyer. The more I think about this case, the more convinced I become that whoever killed Meyer had a motive. A very strong, even perhaps a justifiable motive.'

'Well—'

'I know I look as if I just scramble about drinking all day, but I have given this a lot of thought. There was no trace of our murderer, apart from his deed, in that apartment. Not so much as one print, so far. Even the body itself has not, according to Arto Sarkissian, yielded up anything of any use. And look at the act itself! On and off I've been thinking about it all day. The ghastly look of that corpse. The absolute terror in its eyes—' He broke off and stared into space, gently shaking his head as if he didn't or couldn't understand.

Suleyman finished his drink and put his glass down on the rough wooden table. He wasn't convinced, but he was making the best of it. 'Well, I'll trust you, sir.'

Ikmen smiled. He knew Suleyman had reservations, but he appreciated his confidence. 'Good. I suppose you want to go off home now?'

'I think so.' Suleyman reached behind him and put on his jacket. 'By the way, sir?'

'Mmm?'

'What was all that stuff about peasants?'

'Oh, you understood all that, did you?'

Suleyman stood up. 'I understood the individual words.'

'Mrs Gulcu is an appalling snob. She equates intelligence with class. She thought that because I am educated I must be aristocratic.'

'She thought I was a peasant though, didn't she?'

Ikmen smiled again. 'As I said before, the Lady Chatterley complex, the desire to have power over handsome young workers. A common fantasy among the upper classes, like their notion that all the peasants must by definition be stupid.

Opinions, young man, that helped to bring Imperial Russia to her knees. Don't let it bother you.'

Suleyman shrugged. 'It doesn't. She was wrong. It made her look stupid.'

Ikmen's interest was aroused. 'Oh?'

'Until Atatürk my family were very powerful on the Black Sea coast. Provincial Governors for centuries.'

Ikmen looked amazed. 'You never told me?'

Suleyman's face darkened slightly. 'What's the point?' But his mood changed quickly and he laughed. 'Anyway, maybe one of my ancestors had one of yours put to death. They did a lot of that. Embarrassing, eh?'

Ikmen raised his glass to him. 'History coming back to haunt us!' But his voice faded as he spoke and he started to feel odd again. 'Goodnight, Suleyman,' he said, softly.

'Goodnight, sir. I'll pick you up at about nine if that's OK.'

'That's fine.'

The young man left and the cheery noises of the drinking classes closed in around Ikmen. It was a fitting end to an evening drenched in ghosts that Suleyman's ancestors should enter the conversation. The rich, the privileged and the cruel.

It was ten-thirty when Robert arrived at Rosemary's apartment. How he got there he couldn't remember. Or why. It was as if he had patched into that curious automatic device that takes over when you are very, very drunk. The one that gets you home but flatly refuses to let you know how.

Robert was a little tipsy, but by no means drunk. Mostly he was confused. In the hour or so since he'd left Natalia's house, he'd been through many emotions. Fear had been uppermost, of course, fear that he had committed a grave error. That he had totally misjudged Natalia, indeed that he now knew even less about her than he did before. Fear that she wasn't just quirky, but something terrible, her and her peculiar set of relations. It had made him feel bad, soiled somehow, a willing party to something both unclean and beyond his understanding. The arrival of the familiar policeman had simply served to underscore this feeling. He felt caught out, watched and deeply paranoid. He wondered what Natalia's invisible grandmother had told them. He wondered what the woman was like and why she had not joined the rest of the family for dinner.

And yet he had been unable to say anything to Natalia or her family. When the policemen had gone—even in fact, now he thought about it, while they were still in the house—a sort of normality had been maintained. Nothing to do with either the events of Monday or the police had been so much as touched on. They'd played cards, talked about nothing; he'd stared at Natalia's body, almost, but not quite, obscured by the thickness of her plain white dress. Overriding everything, the demon of lust still wouldn't leave him in peace. Perhaps Natalia possessed some magic, maybe she was skilled in the use of subtle aphrodisiacs...

He pressed the bell on Rosemary's front door and tried to work out what he was going to say when she answered. What he wanted from his colleague was ill formed in his mind. Basically, he supposed, it came down to comfort. He didn't want to tell her anything, he wanted a cup of English tea with milk and some mindless platitudes; he didn't want to be alone.

The door opened. 'Hello, Robert!'

She had her hair in curlers and was dressed for bed. The BBC World Service on the radio whined in the background, the sound scarred and pitted by static.

'Hello, Rosemary, can I come in for a minute?'

He'd only been to her apartment once before. It had been for her fiftieth birthday party the previous November. Then it had been very cold. She had worn a blue velvet evening dress and had been escorted by her then beau, a twenty-five-year-old Kurdish boy. Since then there had been two Turkish boys and a Sudanese. Rosemary's thirst for true love was dimmed by neither time nor difference in age. Robert found himself hoping that she wouldn't get the wrong idea about his somewhat late appearance on her doorstep.

She smiled. 'Of course, come in.' Her smile was easy, but Robert could see that she was concerned. He looked briefly at his face in the small mirror by the door and realised why. His face was white, his eyes black and staring. He looked like he had just wandered away from a nightmare.

She stood aside to let him pass and then ushered him into a very comfortable and tastefully arranged sitting room. Robert sat down uneasily on the edge of a large brown sofa while Rosemary turned off the blaring radio.

'So,' she said, turning round to face him and smiling once again. 'What can I do you for?'

For one horrible moment Robert felt that all his worst fears about Rosemary were about to be confirmed. But as she moved to sit in the armchair opposite him, he noticed that her smile was motherly, her movements a little coy and retiring.

'Oh, just a chat really.' He laughed nervously and brushed an imaginary speck of dust from his trousers. He had to say more than that! It was hardly justification for interrupting an ageing spinster's comfortable night-time routine. But he couldn't think of anything. He grinned instead and became silently irritated with himself. A good-natured but nevertheless tense quiet hung across the room.

'That wind's getting up,' said Rosemary, nodding her head towards the window, apropos of nothing. She was as embarrassed as he. It was ridiculous. He had to say something. He had to say what was on his mind. Disguise it a bit, dress it up, but do it. It was, after all, why he had come. Not to talk about Natalia would be a waste. Rosemary was older, experienced; she knew about love.

'Love life's a bit on the skids,' he blurted finally. He chuckled slightly as he said it, his stiff upper lip planted firmly on his sleeve for all the world to see. 'Don't think I'll ever get it right.'

'Oh dear.' She looked very old in her curlers, sitting with her hands clasped firmly together in her lap. She wasn't relaxed either. It occurred to Robert that perhaps she was just as afraid of his unwanted sexual attentions as he was of hers. After all, he was hardly her type. It was not only for the weather that Rosemary had spent most of her working life in the Middle East.

'Would you like a cup of tea?' she said after a pause.

'Do you have milk?'

'Lots. And sugar. Would you like one?'

Robert nodded. 'Two sugars, please.'

'The cup that cheers.' She patted his hand and went out into the kitchen.

Several minutes later she returned with two large mugs of steaming tea and a rather serious question.

She gave one mug to her guest. 'Look, Robert, I'm not prying, but is this lover of yours a local girl?'

'Yes.'

'Ah.' She eyed him critically. 'I take it you're quite serious about her?'

Robert took his cigarettes and lighter out of his pocket and lit up. 'Yes I am. I only have serious relationships. Screwing around isn't really my style.' It sounded smug even to him; he hated himself for saying it. 'Not that I've anything against people who do, you understand...'

'It's all right, Robert!' She was smiling again. 'Some of us want to settle down and some of us don't. Horses for courses and all that. But—'

'Rosemary?' He felt a sudden and overwhelming urge to tell her things. Not the lot, of course, just generalities. He sat forward and licked his lips nervously.

'Yes, dear?' She put her mug down on the coffee table, her face serious and concerned.

'Rosemary, what would you do if you found out your lover might have done something terrible?'

'Like what?'

'Stealing, drugs, prostitution...' He carefully avoided the actual crime that was on his mind. 'Not in the past, I don't mean. I mean if he was doing it now, whilst going out with you?'

She looked thoughtful for a few seconds and then sighed deeply and picked up her mug once again. 'I suppose it would depend upon how strongly I felt about my lover. If I weren't that involved, of course, it would be easy—just ditch him. If I were involved, however...'

'Would you inform the police?' He was sitting on the edge of the sofa again, his fingers trembling slightly around the filter of his cigarette.

Rosemary sighed again. 'If I were deeply involved, I don't know. I like to think I'd do the right and morally correct thing, but I can't be sure, Robert. At the risk of sounding awfully crude, I think it would largely depend on sex. I had one lover, a Turk he was, who made me tremble every time he came near me. It would have been very difficult to give him up to the authorities. It was hard enough giving him back to his wife!' She paused. 'I just don't know is the short answer.'

Robert drank his tea in silence. When Rosemary spoke again she sounded helpless and lost. 'You know this cultural difference between ourselves and the Levantines is a sod. Knowing what's really going on is often well-nigh impossible. It's so easy to get involved in things that you don't really understand. On the one hand you could jump to an erroneous conclusion that could wreck your relationship. On the other, you could get yourself into a lot of trouble.'

Robert ground his cigarette out in the ashtray and finished his tea. 'I just want to be married again, Rosemary. I know I'm at risk of making a mistake simply because my desire for a settled life is so strong, but...Honestly, if I lose this girl, I don't know what I shall do. She's got to me somehow, I don't know what it is—'

'Sex,' said Rosemary flatly, a sad half-smile playing about her lips. 'It's always sex, dear. Bloody dangerous, it is! If your partner is good it can obsess you.' She looked down at the floor. 'Especially if you've had a bad time in the past. Lust and love can get very confused sometimes, I know, believe me.'

'She's all I think about!' He spoke very softly, almost to himself. 'Even now.'

Rosemary clasped her hands in front of her chin and suddenly looked very determined. 'You know, in my opinion, and you won't like this, you should start seeing other people a bit more. Inject some fresh air into your life, dear. I'm sure this girl is wonderful, she must be or you wouldn't be so...Stop being the mystery man of the Londra Language School and get about like the rest of us! You're divorced, of course you want to marry again and I'm sure that one day you will, but take it slowly, Robert. "Marry in haste, repent at leisure", remember?'

Robert smiled, put his cigarettes back in his pocket and stood up. 'I know, Rosemary. Anyway, I think I ought to go now, I've bothered you enough with my nonsense.'

'It's all right, I don't mind.' She stood and put her hands in the pockets of her dressing gown. 'Don't feel you have to go. Talk more if you want to. I'm manless at the moment. It's been really rather nice having a little male company for a change, albeit of the platonic variety.'

They both laughed. It had been very nice spending time with a woman who wanted nothing from him. As Robert left he thought how pleasant it would be to do it again sometime. But not yet. At a point in the future when he didn't have so much on his mind, when she, Natalia, was either out of his life or properly in it—cooking his meals, going on holiday with him, sleeping in his bed. The notion flashed briefly across Robert's mind that he was 'sad'. A 'sad man' hung up on marriage and domesticity. But from his perspective, outside, that kind of life had always looked so safe. When it worked. Even back then, even through a haze created by drugs, despite the divorce, he had never stopped dreaming about it. Hoping.

'Goodnight, Robert,' said Rosemary as they reached the front door. She stood on tiptoes and kissed him lightly on the cheek. 'I'm sure that if you use a little judgement, you'll be all right.' But her bright face changed in an instant and she became very grave. A final thought had just occurred to her. A horrible one. 'If the police are involved you know she's not worth it, don't you?'

'I know,' he replied, and walked briskly through the doorway and on to the landing. 'Goodnight, Rosemary, and thanks.'

Rosemary shut the door behind him and returned to the sitting room. From a tiny box on the windowsill she took a pinch of marijuana resin and crumbled it between her fingers. She looked around for her pipe, but couldn't locate it. She sighed and emptied the crumbled narcotic into her mouth. It was the only way she could get to sleep without the comfort of a man in her bed. She understood her recently departed guest more than he knew.

Chapter Six

FATMA IKMEN STIRRED the customary 'poor man's breakfast' of soup slowly and with some malice. Four small children sat at the big scrubbed table in the centre of the room and slurped noisily from metal bowls. Four down, four to go: the breakfast madness wasn't over yet.

It annoyed her. The older children were so bad at getting up during the holidays. Lazing in bed all morning listening to their radios was all very well, but it stretched breakfast out so. It was just a mercy that neither of the two men bothered to eat in the morning. That would have been intolerable.

Fatma put a slow hand deep into the small of her back and rubbed. This pregnancy was not as easy as the others had been. She was more weary this time. She looked at her face in the small mirror above the sink. It wasn't a particularly lined face, but it was nevertheless obviously the face of a woman who would not see forty again. It irked her a little. Perhaps it was the onset of middle age that made her feel so negative about this new baby?

In retrospect it had not been one of her better ideas, and yet she had no one to blame but herself. It was the old, familiar story. As soon as the last baby had started walking Fatma had wanted to be pregnant again. Most of her children had been conceived out of broodiness. Poor Çetin! She actually felt sorry for him sometimes, although she would have rather died than told him so.

But he was good really. All she had to do was drop the appropriate hint and she was pregnant again. No lectures about lack of money, no grumbles about the restrictions placed upon his sex life when another one was on the way. Sometimes she wondered if he went elsewhere...*Stupid, stupid woman!* She pulled herself together. Çetin, with his wretched job, barely had enough time for the family, let alone mistresses! And he was loving, both to her and the children. True, he couldn't always remember all of the little ones' names and his caresses were sometimes a little vague and distracted...

She heard him close the bedroom door behind him and imagined him, tatty briefcase in hand, tearing down towards the front door. She also heard another door open, slowly, a little tentatively—his father. Fatma allowed herself an infrequent scowl. It wasn't that she actually disliked the old man and it was a fact that without the money Çetin's elder brother gave them towards Timür's upkeep, life would be tough, but...It wasn't worth thinking about. After all, they weren't exactly young lovers, were they? The group of small children around the table attested to that. Not to mention the others who were still in their rooms. Nevertheless...

The old man put his head around the side of the door and called out to his son's rapidly retreating back. 'Çetin!'

His son turned to look at him, an unlit cigarette hanging at a crazy angle from his lips. He looked as if he was in a hurry, flustered and annoyed.

'I'm leaving for work, Timür! What is it?'

The old man beckoned him over with his hand. 'You were very late home last night.'

He wanted details. It was difficult for Timür Ikmen to keep himself from meddling in his son's work. Çetin's cases were often a source of excitement, an emotion the old man still craved with a passion. And anyway, he'd actually helped him with this one. He was owed something.

Çetin looked angrily at his watch. 'Suleyman's going to be picking me up in about two minutes! I've an old German to see at ten!'

'What have you found out?'

The younger man sighed impatiently. His father's eyes were eager, greedy for information. Oh, well, it was one of his few remaining pleasures! 'I've spoken to both the Rabbi and that Maria Gulcu woman,' he said. 'The latter was a very exotic experience!'

'Why? What was she like?' Timür was almost breathless with anticipation.

'Weird. She's probably older than Allah and she lives in a sort of shrine to Old Russia.' He cast his mind back to the events of the previous evening and tried not to shudder. 'She said she used to be the dead man's lover when they were both young. There was a terrible...oh, malevolence about her. It's hard to explain. One of my—you know.'

The old man stared glassily into space. 'A malevolent old Russian.'

'Yes.' Çetin picked up his briefcase from the floor and tried to pull his mind away from the unpleasant picture his father had just painted. 'She rather fancied my pretty little sergeant.' Suddenly and horribly, he realised that he was using Maria Gulcu's own rather spiteful description of his colleague.

Timür's dry burnt laugh rattled towards him down the hall. 'I'm not surprised!'

'Çetin!' Fatma's voice wound its deep and sonorous way out of her kitchen and zeroed in upon its target.

Çetin squared his jaw and marched purposefully towards the front door. 'I am gone!'

The old man watched his son close the door behind him and stumbled back into his room again. 'A malevolent old Russian!' he repeated to himself. 'How exotic!'

The house was much more beautiful and a great deal less sinister than he had expected. In the car, his eyes narrowed against the glare from the road, Suleyman had imagined that Smits would live in a very dark, Gothic sort of place. But logically there was no real reason why he should. Some Nazis, if indeed Smits were one of their number, presumably enjoyed classic elegance just as other people did. The enormous marble entrance hall and the immaculate English butler who showed them in did, however, strike him as a little excessive. There was rich, but there was also rich and vulgar, and Smits's set-up definitely smacked of the latter.

'Would you come this way please, gentlemen?' the butler said.

Ikmen and Suleyman followed him across the hall and through a door which the menial held open for them. Like the hall, the room they found themselves in was enormous, but unlike the hall it was dark. Books, thousands of them—some black, some dark green, a few wine-red—lined and described the contours of every wall. The bright sunlight from outside seemed to be absorbed by their spines, thinned by their no doubt yellowing pages. An old and venerable library. The den of some impractical and absorbed academic.

'Inspector Ikmen and Sergeant Suleyman, sir.' The butler smiled at them both, bowed politely and then left. The man the policemen found themselves facing struggled painfully to get out of his elegant wing chair and smiled.

'Please forgive me, gentlemen, getting to my feet is not the

easy operation it once was.' It was a deep, beautiful, almost oper-
atic voice. He motioned them gracefully towards some chairs
opposite his own. 'Sit down, please.'

They moved forward. As he passed the old man, Suleyman
took a good look at him. Reinhold Smits had been very handsome once. His hair, though grey, was still luxuriant and the
bones of his face had that chiselled look that was almost stereo-
typically German in its hardness. He dressed well too. Given
that he had at least to be somewhere in his eighties, Reinhold
Smits wore stylish clothes. He dressed like a young busi-
nessman, rather like Suleyman himself, and it suited him. A
pale grey double-breasted suit with matching shirt and tie flat-
tered his thin, languid form. As he reseated himself his bony legs
jutted out in front of him like tall silver birch trees.

Ikmen sat down and Suleyman seated himself beside him.

'Well,' said Smits, lacing his fingers underneath his chin.
'How can I help you gentlemen?'

Ikmen smiled in that slightly sad way that people do when
they wish to be both friendly but also convey bad news of some
sort. 'We've come about one of your ex-employees, sir.'

Smits smiled also, although his was patient rather than
sad. 'That much I gathered from my secretary. I have had many
employees over the years. Might I ask who you wish to inquire
about?'

'I'm afraid it's someone who worked for you many years ago
in the packing department,' Ikmen said. 'One Leonid Meyer.'

Knowing how vitally important Smits's reaction to this
information would be, Suleyman was not surprised to see that
Ikmen leant forward a little in order to observe the old man
more closely. Not that there was anything, not even a flicker of
recognition to see.

'I'm afraid,' Smits replied, 'the name is not immediately
familiar.'

'Oh,' said Ikmen, 'that surprises me.'

'How so?'

'Our interest in Mr Meyer stems from the fact that he was

recently found murdered in his Balat apartment. He was named in the newspapers and so I assumed...'

'Ah.' Smits held up one long, thin, silencing finger. 'Ah yes, the old gentleman battered to death. Yes, I am aware of that. But as for his being one of my people...' He shrugged. 'I mean he may well have been, but if as you say it was many years ago...'

'Yes,' said Ikmen. 'I'm sorry sir. I realise that it must be difficult when one employs so very many people.'

'Quite.' Smits twirled one delicate wrist through the air like a magician and changed the subject. 'May I interest you gentlemen in a cup of tea?'

The rapid change of direction caught both policemen unawares.

'Er, yes, thanks,' said Ikmen. 'That would be nice.'

Smits then turned to Suleyman. 'And you, young man?'

'Oh, thank you, yes.'

'Good!' Smits took a small silver bell from the table beside him and rang it. He then leant forward and raised his eyebrows as if he were imparting some great and scandalous secret. 'Of course the tea will be *au lait*, to the English taste, but Wilkinson cannot make it after any other fashion. I hope that is acceptable?'

Suleyman hated English tea, but it seemed churlish having accepted now to refuse. 'Fine.'

Ikmen was obviously of the same mind. 'Yes, yes,' he said, but Suleyman could see from his face that he didn't relish the prospect either.

For several minutes after this exchange they all sat in silence, until the butler appeared and Smits gave him his orders. Suleyman noticed that Smits's tone was quite different with the servant. It was harsh and without warmth. Perhaps, he speculated, Smits was one of those who believed the 'lower orders' undeserving of common politeness.

As the butler left, Ikmen opened up the conversation once again. 'Getting back to Mr Meyer...'

'Yes?'

'And acknowledging that this was all a very long time ago...'

'Your point being?'

'Two quite independent sources have led us to believe, sir, that you actually dismissed Mr Meyer from your employ sometime in the early 1940s.'

'Really? Might I know who or what these sources might be?'

'I'm afraid I cannot divulge that information.'

'No, no of course you can't. Stupid me!'

Ikmen looked across at Suleyman who nodded very slightly, well aware of what was now expected of him. He took over. 'What we can tell you however, Mr Smits,' he said, 'is that Leonid Meyer still had the name and address of your Üsküdar plant in his address book at the time of his death.'

'Did he really?' A look that was almost impossible to interpret passed across his features. 'How very odd.'

Ikmen, who had now silently slid back into the depths of his chair was, Suleyman observed, watching closely.

'Er...' Smits paused briefly as if trying to gather his thoughts in the right order. 'Did either of these sources of yours say why I might have dismissed this man?'

'Not really—'

'Unless,' Ikmen, suddenly animated again, interjected, 'unless you include idle speculation under the heading of reason.'

Smits raised his eyebrows. 'I might.'

'Well,' Ikmen continued, 'there is one theory that you may have dismissed him for drunkenness at work.'

'Yes?'

'And there is another'—here Ikmen smiled, rather too pointedly for Suleyman's nerves—'that you dismissed Mr Meyer because he was a Jew.'

It was at this point that the butler returned with the tea, which was just as well considering that Smits's deep tan had now turned an alarming shade of grey. Not for the first time, Suleyman wondered whether his boss had gone too far too soon.

As the butler placed the tray down on to the coffee table he asked his master whether he should pour and received an affirmative reply. As the menial performed his task, Smits reminded him that he should make it 'Au lait, after your usual fashion, Wilkinson.'

The china was, as would have been expected, of the finest quality. A delicate, almost transparent cup and saucer were handed to Suleyman; the cup's little handle was so small that it was impossible for him to slot his finger through it with any degree of comfort. But then that wasn't its purpose. Suleyman observed how Smits drank, keeping his little finger aloft as he tilted the cup to his mouth. Unnatural, affected and obviously quite correct. Amid great discomfort he attempted to copy Smits's method, the foul taste of the beverage only adding to his misery. Smits, who had been keenly observing Suleyman's struggles, acknowledged the young man with a small nod.

But when the butler had gone, the atmosphere changed quickly. Smits turned to Ikmen and, with all vestiges of politeness gone, made his position quite clear. 'You can't imagine how thoroughly sick one becomes of slights upon one's character due to no fault of one's own. Your assumption that I dismissed this Meyer character because he was a Jew can only be connected to the fact that my father was German—a leap of so-called "logic" that I resent deeply!'

'The assumption is not mine, sir,' Ikmen put in, 'it is—'

'The idea that the words "German" and "Nazi" are somehow synonymous is wounding in the extreme! I neither recall nor do I currently have any interest in this Meyer fellow and the fact that he was a Jew is, I believe, immaterial to anyone but him!'

'I—'

'I don't know where you received your information from, but I would suggest that you put those persons right about the fact that my involvement with the deceased was, if indeed it happened at all, of a totally benign nature. Furthermore, if any more stories of this nature were to come to my attention I could, as you can imagine, access enough legal expertise to both exonerate myself and destroy those who speak against me!'

His anger temporarily spent, Smits retreated, trembling, behind his now shaking cup and saucer. Ikmen, for his part, took a little time out too, time during which he also drank (with revulsion) and thought.

Strangely, or so Suleyman thought at the time, when Ikmen did speak, his tone was both gentle and conciliatory. 'I do apologise if my words have offended you, Mr Smits,' he said, 'but with this being a murder investigation you can, I hope, appreciate that I have to explore every angle.'

Smits, rather than reply, simply sulked further back down behind his cup.

'I would not,' Ikmen continued smoothly, 'for one moment suggest that you possess anti-Semitic views. I know very little about you and, anyway, I would not simply take the unsubstantiated word of others against you.'

'Well...'

'If, however, you could check through your past records and see whether this man did ever work for you, I would be grateful. I realise that it was all a very long time ago, but...'

Smits shrugged. 'I will do as you ask, although I hold out little hope of success. As you said, Inspector'—and here he paused for just a moment, his eyes twinkling in the reflected glow from the gold-rimmed cup—'it was a very long time ago.'

Ikmen smiled and then put his not even half-finished teacup down upon the table. 'Very well then, Mr Smits, I will leave that with you.'

He looked across at Suleyman who was attempting to pour the last of the liquid down his unwilling throat. 'Sergeant Suleyman and I have things to do, as, I am sure, do you.'

'Yes.' Smits moved to ring the bell to summon the butler, but Ikmen stopped him.

'We'll see ourselves out, sir, thank you.' He bowed slightly as he stood. 'Goodbye, Mr Smits.'

'Goodbye, Inspector.' His face, which until that moment had been set and grave, suddenly broke out into an uncontrollable, wide sun-ray smile. 'And goodbye to you too, Sergeant. You take care out there now, won't you?'

'Goodbye, sir,' Suleyman replied, bowing very slightly prior to exiting.

It wasn't until the two men had left that Smits allowed the smile to drop from his face. As he heard the front door close behind them, he rang the bell to summon the butler once again. In the minute that it took Wilkinson to return, Smits wiped his hands across his brow several times and shuffled in his chair as if seeking, but not finding, some sort of comfort.

When Wilkinson did finally knock and gain admittance, Smits's tone told him all he needed to know about his master's mood.

'Get my address book and look up the number for Demidova.'

'Yes, sir.' He made a move to walk further into the room— an action that was quickly cut short by Smits's voice.

'I mean now, Wilkinson!'

'Yes, sir, but the tea—'

'Just leave the bastard tea things and do as I have asked!'

'Er, yes, sir, er...' He scuttled out far more rapidly than he had arrived. This type of mood that his master was exhibiting, though uncommon, was not unknown to the butler.

Smits, now alone once more, looked into the middle distance, an expression of blind fury playing upon his taut, aged features.

Under Ikmen's direction, Suleyman brought the car to a halt just outside the entrance to Reinhold Smits's drive. As soon as the engine had been switched off, Ikmen began to speak. 'So what did you make of Mr Smits, Suleyman?'

'Well, I suppose his reactions to the questions were under-standable. Whatever his connections may or may not have been with Meyer, they happened a long time ago. And the contention that he dismissed Meyer because he was a Jew came rather rapidly and—'

'You think I handled that part ineptly?' It was said with a twinkle in his eye which Suleyman, nevertheless, missed entirely.

'Oh, no, I don't think that you—'

Ikmen laughed. 'It's all right, Suleyman, you can criticise me—provided'—here he scowled in a most overt and theatrical manner—'you don't do it too often.'

Suleyman smiled, if a little weakly. 'I just thought that you launched into that particular subject a little hastily. I wasn't sure about forcing his antagonism at that point.'

'Oh, but I was, you see.' Ikmen raised a finger in order to stress his point. 'My reasoning being that if Smits did know Meyer, whose name originally you may have noticed elicited absolutely no reaction, and if he did indeed dismiss him because he was a Jew, he is probably quite a worried man now.'

'Which of course we want him to be?'

'Absolutely. How Smits behaves from now on and whether or not he "discovers" whether Meyer worked for him all those years ago could give us some useful pointers to his alleged anti-Semitism.'

'Without, of course,' Suleyman added, 'giving us any clues as to whether Smits may have murdered Meyer.'

'No.' Ikmen's face dropped slightly again and he sighed. 'No, even if Smits did dismiss him for that reason there is still nothing, as yet, to connect him to the murder. And even if Smits is involved there has to be more to it than simply Jew-baiting. I mean, if he'd wanted to kill Meyer because of what may or may not have occurred in the 1940s, he would have done it long ago, wouldn't he?'

'Yes.'

'And besides'—he paused briefly to light up a cigarette—'I don't think that Mr Smits is the only person in the frame.'

'No?'

'No. I can't tell you why, but I feel that those Gulcu people could be involved too. It may be that I am being led astray by the appearance of Mr Cornelius in their home, but—'

'Ah!' Suleyman, suddenly remembering, turned quickly towards Ikmen. 'Yes. I telephoned London about him. Inspector Lloyd said he'd get back when he had some news.'

'Good.' Not that Ikmen had really heard, in the fullest sense, what his deputy had just said. His mind, as had happened before when he thought about the Gulcus, was fully on that family and their strangeness. 'You don't think I'm being a bit irrational about those people, do you, Suleyman?'

'Well…' He did and he didn't, it was hard. 'Well, yes and no, I…They were very strange and it was odd that Cornelius should be with them at the time of our visit. But from what the old woman said it would seem that she had at least some affection for Meyer. I mean, to kill him would be—well, really rather nonsensical. It…'

'A bit like Smits killing him after all this time, I suppose. Yes, I see what you mean, Suleyman.'

The younger man eyed the older one narrowly. 'You're not convinced though, are you, sir?'

Ikmen smiled. 'Oh, I don't know, Suleyman. Mind you, whichever way you look at it, it's doubtful whether any of the extraordinarily elderly people we've seen so far could actually have perpetrated the crime themselves.'

'No,' Suleyman agreed, 'I think they would have to have had some help.'

'Oh, yes indeed. Someone young and fit. Perhaps, in Smits's case, someone typically Aryan too…'

Suleyman smiled. 'Someone like Cornelius?'

Ikmen laughed, a short, sharp retort. 'Perhaps. Although I think that that particular mixture might just be a little too rich for my stomach.'

'Meaning?'

'Meaning that it is quite exotic enough having the Englishman "involved" with the lovely Gulcu girl without throwing the disturbing Mr Smits into the equation too. Let's not get too carried away, eh?'

'No.'

'Anyway'—Ikmen, laughing, banged his hand down hard against the dashboard—'let's get back to the station. I must find Cohen and then get out to see the Blatsky woman and some of those derelicts. She has, in my opinion, waited quite long enough for a slice of our attention.'

Chapter Seven

THEY MET, AS THEY usually did on their shared short day, at the bus-stands on Taksim Square. In spite of the fact that he had left his school at twelve and she her shop just thirty minutes later, both of them looked and indeed were quite tired. Although very little had happened to either of them since their last meeting, internally they had both been very busy with their own thoughts. Robert, in particular, looked pale and strained— not, of course, that his beautiful companion seemed to notice. When the bus arrived she simply got on board and sat down without either proffering a ticket to the driver or speaking so much as a word. Gallantly, but typically, Robert found himself paying for her transport. Then, as if to compound his burgeoning isolation, Natalia didn't speak a word to him during the entire course of their journey across the city. In an attempt to distract himself from her coldness, Robert looked out of the window and tried to enjoy the view. The route back to his apartment took them right along the edge of the Bosporus. The broad seaway sparkled in the sunlight; ferries ploughing and criss-crossing their way between Europe and Asia left glittering trails of thick white foam in their wake, like great, fast-moving snails.

Although next to Natalia, he wasn't happy. His hands clenched and unclenched nervously as he desperately tried to think of something to say. But nothing would come. Not even the kind of mindless trivia the English are supposed to be so good at. Talk of the weather, the iniquities of politicians, the price of food.

Looking at her was bad. It made him want to fall on her, bury himself between her hair and her massive breasts. But if he turned away from her it allowed his mind to think. Here was a person he loved without understanding, a woman at whose capabilities and motives he could only guess. Logically the object of a person's desire was no less prone to unspeakable acts than any other mortal. But logic had never been Robert's strong suit. Some things defied it and yet still seemed to make perfect sense. Like Billy Smith, his bane, his *bête noir*, the wicked boy. London. He could see the child. Twelve years old, thin, red hair and freckles. He looked mischievous and self-satisfied, every child with red hair seemed to. It had been stupid to dislike him just because of his appearance. Unfortunately he had made no secret of it either. His colleagues had criticised him. But he had been right. It was Billy who extorted money from the smaller children, Billy who disrupted his class and called him 'Blondie' to his face, Billy and the Norris twins who were caught with the cat in the playground. The poor cat. Its fur, black, silky, caked with its own thick blood. The memory even two thousand miles away in Turkey made the acid in his stomach rise. Little bastards! What he hadn't wanted to do to them! And yet, despite the poor cat's pain, the incident had given him some satisfaction. It had vindicated him. For a short while afterwards the other teachers had understood. But only for a short while, just until Billy and the twins got going again. Then things had changed. Robert looked down at his hands and sighed deeply. It was so hot. That was the worst thing about Istanbul really, the awful, stifling, humid heat.

He turned to look at Natalia again. Her face was still cold, as cold as it had been when they had met. She hadn't wanted to go with him. It was 'their' Thursday afternoon, a regular and, on his part, much treasured weekly event in their lives. But this time she hadn't wanted to go. Perhaps she thought that the little pantomime he had witnessed at her house was enough? That now he would just go away, dissolve silently into the background? But all this was based upon the assumption that she didn't care for him and he knew that that was just not true. If he meant nothing to her, why had she stayed with him for so long? How could she have loved him with such perfect passion? Oh, she cared. Something was very wrong, but she still cared.

Her mouth was straight-set and her beautiful eyes were dead in their sockets. Robert's heart sank and all the old doubts returned. She didn't want to be with him now.

He made up his mind that as soon as they reached the apartment he would ask her straight out about what had been going on the previous evening. He didn't expect a coherent answer, but he would have at least to try. While he still had no answers he couldn't help but be constantly anxious. He tried hard not to make comparisons, but it wasn't easy. He'd felt like this before. Wired. He knew when. It wasn't hard to remember, but it was unwise. He'd left all that behind him, back in England: the sweats, the crippling worry, that feeling of haziness, lack of control. Robert brought his hand up to his brow and wiped away the perspiration that had gathered just under his hairline.

When she got inside the apartment she went straight to the bathroom and took off all her clothes. It was so hot and the heavy waistband of her skirt had chafed as it rubbed her sweat into the soft skin of her belly. Besides, wasn't that, after all, what

Robert wanted? He didn't want to talk. He'd made that quite obvious during their silent and boring journey. Robert always wanted sex. What man didn't? And yet in this case perhaps it was a blessing, a distraction. Yes, a distraction. His 'little presents' were always good too, usually expensive. He was so open-handed she didn't have just to take as she did with the others. Robert had always been so generous. Desperate. She looked at herself in the mirror. Slim hips, flat stomach, rich, full breasts that dropped only a fraction as she loosed them from her brassière. Normally her body was a pleasing sight, but this time the look of it irked her. Her beautiful body was trapped. Her mind clouded with misery again. She'd felt like it all day; she'd felt like it all her life. One coincidence, that's all it had been. A chance in a million. But that chance had built a chain and it was one that she could feel strangling her. Robert was at its head, a link. One she couldn't afford to break—yet.

She felt sure that he would press her for the information again. He was out there beyond the bathroom door, waiting. Perhaps she should tell him. But then would he understand? Could he? She thought about his stupid, doglike face, besotted, and she felt sick. If only Monday hadn't happened!

She closed her eyes and tried to steady her nerves. Sex would stall him for a little while. He was so simple it might even shut him up completely—for the moment. There was no choice anyway! For now, while panic and fear still sullied the air around her, she was stuck with this man, a man she had been trying to offload for weeks, months even. It hadn't always been so. There had been a time when that very English reserve, which she now found so tedious, had excited her. But that was way back when she still imagined that she could persuade him to take her to London. Escape! One great big cosmopolitan city all to herself, no mothers, no grandmothers, no uncles…lots of exciting foreign men. Such a pity that Robert had been so intractable on that subject. Such a weakness of his always to let the past colour his present. She briefly laughed at her own hypocrisy and then fell silent. London was a dead dream now. Buried, like all the others. Her anger flared once more and she stamped her foot impatiently. Ah, how she was bored! To death! God knew she'd dropped enough hints! But perhaps it was better this way. Perhaps, seeing what he'd seen and being her enemy would have been worse. For the moment it was safe, all she had to do was keep him happy. It wasn't difficult. Unpleasant, but not difficult.

She put her hands around her breasts and pinched her nipples with her fingers. Who was she going to fantasise about today? There had to be someone. She couldn't just go in there and concentrate on him. How unadventurous he was sexually! And this time could prove even worse than usual! The stupid heavy-handed uncles had really screwed up. She could tell by the way he had been to her afterwards. And then the police had arrived. That had not improved things. Natalia had a nasty feeling that she might not receive her usual present when the sexual deed was done. No valuable little trinket to make it run just that little bit smoother. That Robert loved her, she was certain, but he was becoming uneasy. Unfortunately she knew why. She also knew that in his place she would be uneasy too.

She increased the pressure on the sides of her nipples and closed her eyes. Today it would have to be good. Today she was going to have to give him a very good time. Just thinking about him made her nipples go limp, her mouth clench into a hard unsexy line. She felt herself start to panic. This wouldn't do! Not at all!

She put her mind to concentrating. As usual, those of a martial nature were the first to come to mind. The Guards outside the Dolmabahçe Palace! Tall, big, handsome, the power of the submachine-gun resting between their feet, primed, safety catch off, ready. Guns! Ah, that was something! Hard, cold, delicious to the mouth, heavy and painful in her vagina. Ecstatic pain; agony from heaven. She remembered the marine and his games. The awakening. The day upon which it had all suddenly made sense. What had she been? Seventeen? Rising and falling, enveloping and then releasing him with her body. His eyes closed, pushing, pushing the pistol deep into her mouth. The click of the trigger as one by one the empty chambers were eliminated. Fellating cold metal, her body high, counting, waiting for the last click that would detonate and explode inside her head. Four, five...The metal wrenched itself from between her lips and a shot rang out somewhere to the side of her head. She'd heard herself scream, almost dead with pleasure.

She felt her nipples harden in her fingers and her breathing came sharply in gasps. Gunmetal! How she'd wanted him to... And then there were the others that followed. The Kurd; the rich Armenian with his gold chains and Armani suits; the raddled police officer in Üsküdar; and then boys. Lots of them. Boys in uniform, boys with guns, boys willing and unwilling to play. But they always played in the end, of course. Ah yes. There were only two ways out of the game and so they always chose 'play'. Play...

She stopped herself. At last she was ready. No good wasting the moment now! She opened the door and saw him lying back against the sofa, his long legs spread wide. As long as she remained safe inside the fantasy, the memory of the game, her revulsion wouldn't show. It never had done before.

She stood in front of him, her nipples dark, painfully sensitive, engorged with blood. He looked up at her and she reached down to unzip the fly of his trousers. Her mouth ached and drooled for the bitterness of steel. But she found only his soft tongue. Her fingers wound themselves sensuously around his stiffening penis. At least he was big. At least she had that. She lowered herself on to him and prayed that it would hurt.

His telephone rang. Sergeant Suleyman, in one smooth movement, both picked up the receiver and knocked one of Ikmen's overflowing ashtrays on to the floor.

'Damn!' Ash swirling about his feet, he spoke into the instrument somewhat tetchily. 'Suleyman.'

'Hello, Sergeant Suleyman?' The voice was English, cheery and, thankfully, familiar.

'Oh, hello, Inspector Lloyd. How are you?' Although he had never actually met the English policeman himself, Suleyman instinctively felt sorry for him.

'Oh, you know.' He sounded tired. Police work was the same the world over, long, often boring shifts, meagre pay, even more meagre sleep. And London, he'd heard, was a tough city: bombs, an exploding population, ethnic tension. 'I've got something on this Robert Cornelius chap for you.'

'Oh.' Suleyman picked up a pen and took the lid off with his teeth. The dead cigarette butts on the floor stared up at him with, he felt, almost gleeful intent. "What is this, Inspector Lloyd?'

'I've got no details, just bare facts, I'm afraid.'

'Yes?'

'In June of 1987, Robert Cornelius was arrested in connection with an assault upon the person of a barrister, a Mr Simon Sheldon, that's SHELDON...'

Suleyman wrote it down quickly.

'Barrister is lawyer, yes?'

'Yes, that's right. Cornelius admitted the charge but Mr Sheldon dropped it for some reason and your man was let off with a warning. It happened in Islington, that's North London. Cornelius was living up there at the time.'

'Thank you, is very useful.' He continued taking notes, the pen-lid sticking out sideways from his mouth giving his face an unexpectedly rakish look.

'Oh, I haven't finished yet!' said the cheery voice from London. 'Just before he allegedly assaulted Sheldon, in April 1987, Cornelius was accused of striking a child at the school where he worked, Rosebury Downs, that's Hackney, East London.' He laughed grimly. 'One of the most violent parts of the city, Hackney. A right shit hole. Anyway, his accuser was a Miss...' He broke off briefly to consult his notes.

'Yes?'

'A Miss Sandra Smith. Cornelius was supposed to have struck her son William across the face. In school.'

Suleyman struggled to get it all down on paper. Mr Cornelius had quite a past for a quiet English teacher, or so it seemed. He just hoped he'd got it all down properly and that Hackney really was spelt HAKNI.

'So what happen with the child, Inspector?'

He heard Lloyd chuckle lightly at the other end of the line. 'Well, believe it or not the lucky bastard got off again! Insufficient evidence.' He paused for a second, consulting his notes once again. 'Mind you, he resigned from his job shortly after. Although whether out of guilt or because young William Smith and his cronies gave him a rough time in class, I can't say.' He sighed deeply. 'Anyway, that's it.'

'OK.'

'Oh, except that...'

Suleyman frowned. There was something in Lloyd's voice, a certain hesitation that he felt was of significance. 'Yes, Inspector?'

'Well, it may not mean anything, Sergeant, but Sheldon's statement regarding the attack did also include an accusation of racism against Cornelius.'

'Racism?' The word was not immediately familiar to Suleyman, although what he felt upon hearing it unaccountably alarmed him.

Lloyd was, however, all too ready to explain. 'Racism means making remarks or doing things to mock or denigrate another's race or religion. Simon Sheldon was Jewish, you see, and apparently your Mr Cornelius was not very polite about that.'

'Oh.' Suleyman, writing as fast and furiously as he could, struggled to stop his shaking hand rendering his words illegible. 'Oh, thank you! Thank you!'

The cheerful voice at the other end of the telephone grunted knowingly. 'That's quite significant, I feel, Sergeant.'

'Yes, well, is very good, Inspector. Of great use to Inspector Ikmen, I think.'

'Good. Good, I'm glad.' Lloyd sighed heavily. 'Anyway, have you made any progress yet?'

'Little. Small ones. Inspector Ikmen looks to er...' He groped for the right word and he didn't find it. 'Psychological explain, you understand?'

The voice at the other end of the line roared with laughter. 'Oh, Çetin! Tearing around building biographies, getting to know the victim. I don't know!' He paused. 'Trouble is, he's so often bloody well right!'

'Inspector Ikmen is very clever.'

Lloyd laughed again. 'I know, the bastard! Anyway, look, Sergeant, give him my regards and if there's any more help I can give you, just say the word.'

'Thank you, Inspector. You have been very help. It's good.'

'All right, Sergeant, speak to you soon.'

'Goodbye, sir.'

'Bye.'

Suleyman pushed himself back against his chair and looked at the note he had just written. Sheldon. A Jewish lawyer. It would get Ikmen going all right. More strange connections, if tenuous. And the child. Hitting a child! Suleyman wondered what Sheldon and this Smith child had done to Cornelius, if anything. He wondered whether Smith was a name that English Jews used. He wondered, more immediately, how he might sweep up the upturned contents of Ikmen's ashtray without soiling his hands. He had just decided that two pieces of old card provided the answer when Ikmen's telephone rang.

He went over to his desk and picked up the receiver. 'Hello, Inspector Ikmen's extension?'

'Where's Ikmen?' It was Commissioner Ardiç's voice and he was not sounding best pleased.

'Oh, Commissioner, I'm sorry, the Inspector isn't here at the moment, he's out with Cohen.'

'What's he doing? Who's Cohen?'

'Well, sir, he's interviewing. One of our victim's friends, an old Jewish lady and some old drinking...'

'Arsing around with life histories.'

'Biography-building, yes, sir. Can I help at all...?' His voice faded out and he felt annoyed with himself. Why did he always sound so weak!

The Commissioner sighed. 'I've got a meeting with the Israeli Consul in fifteen minutes. I've only just been told myself! You know what diplomats are like! He wants a progress report, of all things, on this Meyer case.'

'Oh.' Weak again!

The Commissioner sounded like he was pulling himself together. 'Look, Suleyman, if Ikmen isn't back in time you'll have to do it. It'll look terrible for the Department, but it can't be helped. Just be here in fifteen minutes and bring all your papers and stuff. Do you have Sarkissian's lab report yet?'

'Yes.'

'Well, bring that along too. If any of us can understand it, it will be a miracle, but...Oh, and Suleyman...'

'Yes, sir?'

There was a long pause followed by a deep sigh. He obviously meant to say something of great importance, but decided against it. Suleyman imagined, bitterly, that it was probably something Ardiç didn't consider him bright enough to understand. It would be typical of the man. 'Oh, nothing!'

The line went dead and Suleyman gently replaced the receiver. A briefing with the Israeli Consul was not a regular occurrence. The great and the good coming to listen to him! He moved around the side of Ikmen's desk and wondered where he should start to look for Dr Sarkissian's report. In the tower block of files or perhaps within the depths of an overflowing drawer. And what about the upturned, stinking ashtray? He quickly grabbed two used envelopes and hunkered down in order to get to grips with the job at hand. He had just managed to balance the stinking load delicately on to one of the envelope flaps, when suddenly the full portent of what he was about to do struck him. A diplomat, the Commissioner, the as yet complete lack of progress! He felt his hand twitch but it wasn't until he saw the whole reeking mass hit the floor again that he gave vent to his feelings.

'Oh, fuck it!' he cried, not caring that probably the whole floor could hear him.

Despite the fact that Ikmen and Cohen had already spent rather more time in that tiny, cabbage-tinctured apartment than either of them would have liked, Ikmen at least felt he had to get some semblance of a clear story before he could even think about leaving.

Mrs Blatsky had proved to be a very pleasant, if rather alarmingly whiskery old lady and had been only too willing to answer any questions that the officers put to her. That she spoke very rapidly and that her grasp of neither Turkish nor Ladino was very secure was not her fault, Ikmen knew. It did not, however, do a great deal for his patience.

Just before he spoke once again, he smiled. Mrs Blatsky duly smiled back, exhibiting an extremely large and varied selection of broken teeth.

'All right, madam,' Ikmen said, 'let's get this straight, shall we? Leonid Meyer was, so he told you, a Bolshevik during the course of the Revolution. Is that right?'

Small, pudgy hands moved several times in front of his face before she actually started speaking. They reminded Ikmen of a pair of fat love-birds.

'Leonid moves with the Bolsheviki, yes!' She smiled sweetly. 'It was ever so with the men in that times.'

'I see.'

'Like some boys from the *shtetl*, Leonid moves to the armies of the Commissars. You see?'

Ikmen, his eyebrows raised, turned to Cohen for clarification. '*Shtetl?*'

'It's a settlement of Jews, sir. Sort of a ghetto.'

'Right.' He turned back towards the smiling little woman again. 'So, what you are saying, Mrs Blatsky, is that Leonid Meyer was actually a communist who, if I understand you correctly, also fought with the Bolsheviks during the Revolution.'

'Exactly, yes.'

'Right.' Here he paused for just a second in order to collect his thoughts. It was most important now that she understand him fully. 'OK, Mrs Blatsky, now I want you to think very carefully about what I am going to say and then give me as honest an answer as you can.'

Her smile remained static as she nodded enthusiastically.

'Now, Mrs Blatsky, did Leonid Meyer ever tell you anything about how he killed people back in Russia?'

'Oh, yes!'

Considering the morbidity inherent in the subject it seemed somewhat incongruous that the old woman appeared so cheerful about it all. But then, Ikmen reasoned, that was obviously just how Mrs Blatsky was.

Gently, but persistently, Ikmen pushed the thing forward. 'Could you then perhaps tell us about that, Mrs Blatsky?'

'Oh, yes!'

He leant forward slightly and, although this movement was almost entirely involuntary, motioned her onward with his hands. 'And?'

'Pigs of the bourgeoisie is what they say. Leonid and other boys shooting, bang! bang! Lots of money, pigs of the bourgeoisie, as they say.'

'So he killed some people, people with money?'

'As I say, yes.'

'And then?'

Here for the first time her face dropped, and Ikmen suddenly saw just how very ancient this woman was. 'Leonid is afraid.'

'Afraid?' Ikmen sighed and sat back slightly in his small grease-stained chair. 'What was he afraid of, Mrs Blatsky? It sounds to me as if he had done his duty as a good Bolshevik. What do you mean?'

She shrugged. 'Maybe this, maybe that. But Leonid is always afraid since then, I see.'

'But you don't know why, is that right?'

'As I say, yes. Leonid don't speak proper when he is in drink.'

Although addressing Cohen, Ikmen let his head fall back, gazing at the smut-smeared ceiling as he spoke. 'So now we have got Meyer the Bolshevik, have we? How interesting. Meyer the Bolshevik who, in addition, did his duty and then promptly ran away to live in a country that was still officially at war with his own.'

'The 1914–18 war that would be, sir?'

'Yes, Cohen, as you say. The war during which the old Ottoman Empire finally died and Leonid Meyer and Maria Gulcu left their respective Slavic homes and came to live with us. The war during which, also I should imagine, our friend Meyer developed his taste for strong liquor.'

'Oh, liquor, yes!'

Ikmen lowered his head to look at the old woman again. Once more, she was smiling. 'Yes, Mrs Blatsky? Is there something else?'

'Oh, yes, liquor, yes!'

'Yes, liquor, we've both said the word several times now, what about it?'

'Well, for Leonid, it makes sleep when fears of the other come to him.'

Ikmen looked at Cohen who shrugged his own lack of understanding. 'The other, madam?'

'The one who knows he bang! bang! at the rich pigs. The one who sees.' Her smile then broadened considerably before she concluded. 'The one that still lives.'

'Lives? Lives where?'

The old woman, still smiling, pointed to the ground beneath her feet.

She disengaged herself from him and wandered naked towards

the wide-open balcony doors. Robert marvelled at how sublimely unselfconscious she was about her body. The whole district of Beşiktaş was going about its business under those huge round breasts of hers. That she could be seen was certain, but she didn't give a damn. Natalia liked herself. She knew that the sight of her body could only provoke two emotions. Desire or envy. Either way it was OK with her.

Robert did up his shirt and pulled himself back into his trousers and pants. He felt exhausted.

Sex with Natalia was a puzzle. It was like she was playing with a doll. She did everything, all he was required to do was lie, sit or stand as the case may be, and enjoy. He had never actually 'taken' her once. And yet she always seemed satisfied. She was! It was just that orgasm had a different effect upon her. It seemed to invigorate her. As if she took the strength from his climax, incorporated it into her own body and recycled it. The process shattered him. He loved it, of course, but he felt very wasted afterwards, as if he'd just had a bad case of flu and needed building up.

Despite the heat, Robert felt cold and bloodless. She'd kept him going for a long time, her skilful fingers, mouth and genitals bringing him just so far and then stopping. A teasing look into his eyes and then another part of his body would be attacked for a while: an ear, his throat, a single nipple. Then back again, lowering herself on to his penis, so sensitive he cried out in pain. She liked vocal sex; words, cries, excited her. As he came up to his climax, she would shout encouragement. 'Tell me to fuck, Robert! Fuck!'

He screamed, pain and pleasure finally coming together, and she was off. She always got off immediately. No post-coital kissing and caressing, just a lot of rather active parading about the room. Looking at her exaggerated profile in window-panes, mirrors, the shine on the coffee table. Pleased with her performance. It made him feel hollow and cheap, as if he were spying on her. Maybe if she cuddled him afterwards, he would not feel so bad, so jaded.

Robert lit a cigarette. 'Would you like some coffee, Natalia?' He knew better than to talk of love to her just after sex.

She walked out on to the small balcony and smiled down into the busy street below.

'No.'

Robert got up from the sofa and staggered into the kitchen. His legs felt weak and he was still seeing stars—the fallout from heightened blood-pressure. He poured some thick, dark coffee from the percolator into a cup and leant against the side of the fridge to drink. His icy veins responded well to the hot liquid, and as he drank, he started to feel at least some life returning to his body.

He watched her through the open kitchen door. She was pointing down into the street and laughing. Some passer-by had seen her. She liked to shock. A favourite diversion was to walk the streets in a dress slashed almost to the waist, parading yards of breast before the general public. He would have needed to carry a submachine-gun to protect her against the jeers, the leers and the groping that went on every time that particular demon entered her soul. He hated that incarnation. The whore.

But Robert had other business with Natalia apart from her sexuality. She was so cocksure! Did she really think that he had forgotten? Did she honestly believe that even her brand of sex could wrench his mind away from the events of the previous evening? Now he had to talk to her. Now they were alone. The perfect opportunity.

He went back into the living room and collapsed on the sofa. Natalia came in from the balcony and stood, statuesque, hands on slim hips, smiling at him.

'Do you enjoy that fucking, Robert?' It was arrogant. Not a question at all. She knew he'd enjoyed it. He always did.

But for the first time he ignored her haughty inquiry. His voice even but cold, he went straight to the heart of the matter. 'What was going on last night, Natalia?'

Her face clouded slightly and she moved forward as if making to leave the room. She made no attempt to answer and, as she sashayed past, she looked at him like he was nothing, her face devoid of any tenderness. She made it quite obvious that one such as Robert did not deserve a reply. Robert felt a sudden angry heat take him. He loved this woman. He'd just given his all to her, for Christ's sake, and she couldn't even give him a straight answer to a straight question! He looked at her big, livid breasts jiggling arrogantly in front of his face and his temper and his passion flared.

As she passed him he grabbed her wrist, hard. She cried out in pain and a look of fury whipped across her face like a slap. 'You hurt me!'

But this time she wasn't going to get away! Not like in Balat. He ignored her claim to pain and tightened his grip. He lowered his voice to almost a whisper. 'I'm asking you about the game you and your family were playing last night.' He looked into her face. 'The one the police interrupted.'

For a second it was just as if she had been turned to stone. Not a muscle moved on her, not so much as a twitch. There was no warning as she brought her free hand back as if to strike him. But he was too quick for her and caught it in mid-air. Amid her angry screams of protest he pulled her roughly down next to him on the couch.

'All that clumsy shit from your uncles about you being at work on Monday. It must have been really galling for you when the police turned up. The fucking Murder Squad!' His voice rose, ugly and rasping. He flinched from it. His vehemence, his violence was alarming. But he couldn't stop now. 'What did they want Natalia? You?'

She squirmed. 'Robert!'

'What happened, Natalia? You and one of your boyfriends decide to get a few extra kicks with some poor half-dead old pensioner! What did you do? Rip off his money? Well!'

She screamed and tried to kick him, but he pushed her flying leg roughly aside with his foot. The bitch wasn't going to hurt him! The slag, the whore, the bloody Istanbul bike! The words in his mind excited him.

His anger was making him hard again. He swung a leg across her lap and ground his genitals against her writhing pubis. The rough cloth of his trousers grazed her naked body and made her cry out. This wasn't what was supposed to happen! A man on her? No, wrong, it was wrong!

He pinned her arms against the wall behind and kissed her roughly on the mouth. He was going to take her! For the first time ever, he was going to take her! His head swam with excitement—the anticipation of rape.

'I bloody saw you, Natalia! I lied for you, you whore!'

She screamed again, her eyes filled with tears and what looked like terror. Robert felt powerful. He bit her hard on the shoulder as his aching erection battered against her, bruising her flesh. He took one hand away from her and unzipped his fly. His penis felt hot and angry in his trembling hand. He pushed it hard up against her, loving the feel of her shaking flesh against his. He was going to fuck her! Oh yes, he was!

'Don't play with me, Natalia!' He shook her hard by the wrists. 'Tell me the truth!' He pulled her legs apart and prepared to enter her body.

Her eyes went hard for a second, almost sexual, but then she was crying, deep and plaintive sobs, like a child's. She dropped her head on to her chest and her face screwed up into a crumple of lines and soft folds. She said a few words in a language Robert didn't understand and then she moved her pelvis towards him. Surrendering.

The heat within him had not gone, but as he looked at her Robert knew that he couldn't take her. Not willingly passive. Not broken. That wasn't what he'd wanted. Robert released his grip upon her arms very slightly and pulled his pelvis away from her body. He felt a slight softening in his penis. 'Well?'

It ripped from her throat, a torn, bleeding thing. 'You do see me in Balat! It was me!'

The relief washed over him like a hot shower and he felt his whole body relax and go limp. He hadn't been seeing things, he hadn't! Thank God! He released her hands and pushed himself away from her lap. She put her face in her hands and gave way to what looked like grief. Copious tears ran between her fingers and splashed down on to her thighs. Robert's breathing eased. He felt like he'd just woken up. But if she had been in Balat... He felt sick. What had he woken up to? He raked his fingers through his damp, thick hair and waited for her to stop crying.

Chapter Eight

'IKMEN!'

He turned and saw the Commissioner's familiar angry face sticking out from behind his door. He smiled and sauntered casually over to him, a long-dead cigarette end hanging from his lip.

'I've just been talking to the Israeli Consul about the Meyer case.' Ardiç's tone was accusatory rather than informative.

'That must have been pleasant for you, sir.' It wasn't down-right impertinence, but almost.

The Commissioner, puce to the ears, ushered Ikmen into his office. He sat down at his desk and relit a thick cigar sitting in his ashtray. Then he twirled his moustache nervously. 'It was hideously embarrassing! I had to make up excuses for you.'

Ikmen sat down and flicked the end of his cigarette on to the floor. Ardiç didn't deserve good manners, he was too stupid. 'I should have thought the Consul would have been pleased that I was out working on a case in which he has so much interest.'

'It's not the point!' Ardiç roared. 'You're supposed to be in charge of this case! It's you everybody wants to see: the Israelis, those bastards from the press—'

'I'm sure you handled it, sir.'

The Commissioner took off his glasses and threw them petulantly on to his desk. 'Look, Ikmen, like it or not, you have a certain—I won't say fame, but notoriety. I didn't want you on this case as it is, but while you are on it, you should play by the rules!' He flung his hand out in the direction of the corridor. 'I've given you men to do the job with! You've a sergeant sits about on his arse all day looking like some sort of male model! You are based here, Ikmen, and you should be here. Get them to do the work! You're the fucking boss, or supposed to be.'

Ikmen lit a cigarette and turned a hard eye on his superior. If Ardiç was going to go straight in with heavy boots on, then so was he! He'd had enough of this fat, strutting little desk rider! What did he know about the job? 'Now look here, sir, it's the way I work. You know that! Second-hand reports from pimply constables may be good enough for people like Yalçin, but I earn my money! A case in point'—he stood up and started pacing, lionlike, in front of the Commissioner's desk—'yesterday evening I interviewed an acquaintance of the murdered man. Now what the woman in question had to say was, on the face of it, of scant importance. If I had not been possessed of a little knowledge about her country and its history, her conversation would not have meant much to me. Also, how she answered me, what her mood was like, what her body did were'—he struggled for the right word—'interesting. If I hadn't been there I would have experienced none of this! Her ambience, if you like, alerted me to something, I still don't know what it is, but what I have learnt from other sources today has only proved to underscore my unease about this woman!'

'What *things?*' Ardiç emphasised the last word with a coating of pure contempt.

'Meyer was involved in some sort of purge against the bourgeoisie back in his own country, Russia. He killed people.

The subsequent guilt tortured him all his life. Guilt or fear, I don't know which. Now this woman I met last night claimed that in Russia she was his lover and that she and Meyer, at some point, left the country together.'

'So?'

'Meyer murdered people like her! May even have killed people in front of her! And if she did know anything about that, it could well mean that she had considerable power over him. She, or if not her, then someone else obviously had to have had some influence in order to persuade Meyer to leave Russia. Nice little Jewish Bolsheviks like him had the world at their feet. It was people like this Maria Gulcu who had to leave the country then, not Meyer. Even given the guilt attendant upon his act, he would have to have been absolutely mad to leave. I mean, guilt is one thing, but to jeopardise your new, powerful life in the Jew-favouring Soviet Republic is quite another. It makes no sense historically. It was 1918! The beginning of the new dawn! The slaves will always turn and when they do—'

'Oh, for the love of Allah, Ikmen, will you shut up about this nonsense before I really lose my temper!'

Ikmen passed a shaking hand across his forehead and sat down.

Ardiç pointed an accusatory finger towards him. 'Now listen, Ikmen, from what your little girly-boy sergeant tells me you've got something of a lead with this Smits character.'

'As yet we've no proof that he—'

'If this Smits is or was a Nazi sympathiser, I want to know about it and so does the Consul. And if he was, I want him in here giving a fucking account of himself!'

'Well, yes, I agree, sir. But I will need time in order to see what Smits does from now on and—'

The Commissioner screamed, 'With one dead Jew lying under a fucking two-metre swastika, time is not what we have, Ikmen! We all know about your famous intuition, but forget it. Throw your confounded biographies into the waste bin and put some real pressure on this Smits man before anything like this happens again. I do not want this city crawling with Mossad agents. What I do want, however, is to please the Israeli Consul who, unless you've been in an alternate reality for the last few days, you will know is a very important man!'

Ikmen looked down at the floor in silence. Knowing that Ardiç was under intense pressure to secure an arrest, any arrest, as soon as possible was of little comfort to him.

Ardiç took a deep breath and calmed himself. Ikmen was, at least temporarily, brought to heel. 'Now,' he said, 'the press don't know the more revolting details of this case and that is to your credit, but they still want to see you. The man was a Jew and there's a lot of panic about Moslem fundamentalism in this country at the moment. So I want you to see representatives from the press tomorrow and reassure them. Make certain that the bastards don't go crawling around Balat. Tell them we're preparing to make an arrest, pursuing fertile lines of inquiry—'

'Lie.'

Ardiç flared once again. 'Yes, lie! What do you want our wealthy Jews in Yeniköy and Bebek to do? Pack up all their money and fuck off to Israel?'

Ikmen regarded him steadily. 'And the poor ones in Balat? They know, remember.'

'Ah, but they're not telling, are they, Ikmen?'

'No, sir, they're too afraid. Closed communities are like that, sir. Vulnerable.'

Ardiç growled. Little people with little money were not exactly his thing.

Ikmen got up out of his chair and made towards the door. He didn't want to be in the same place as this man for any longer.

'If that's all, sir?'

Ardiç put his cigar back in his mouth and leant back in his chair. 'Only one thing.'

Ikmen turned. 'Yes?'

'I had your sergeant with me when I was talking to the Consul. Even if he is a rather effeminate young man, he's articulate.' He dropped his eyes. 'I wouldn't give him too much autonomy if I were you, Ikmen. I think he might just be able to handle it.' He sniggered, childishly.

Ikmen's face whitened and he marched smartly out of the office, slamming the door behind him. Ardiç's laughter followed him all the way down the corridor and halfway up the stairs.

'So, you and the Consul are best friends now, is that right, Mehmet?' Cohen lit up a cigarette and smiled.

Suleyman scowled. 'Hah, hah, very funny.'

'Well, you must admit that it's a bit of a plus point for you.' Cohen perched himself on the edge of Suleyman's desk and crossed his legs. 'Could be the start of your rapid rise through the ranks.'

'I don't think so.'

Cohen laughed. 'Oh, excuse me! Bright, articulate and good-looking? If I were you I'd push and scratch my way to the top and let no bastard stand in my way. I mean, just think what sort of effect the sight of a handsome inspector under thirty would have upon the females around here.'

'Oh, give it a rest, will you!'

But Cohen was in his stride now. 'Power excites women.' His face dissolved into a leer. 'I knew this girl once, had a thing about power and guns—'

'I thought you were married,' cut in Suleyman, sourly.

'So?' Cohen leant down across the desk and put his face close to Suleyman's. 'Doesn't mean I can't have a little bit of variety once in a while. They like the uniform too.'

Suleyman snorted. Cohen was so shallow it was almost a talent.

'You always looked good in the uniform, Mehmet.' He winked lasciviously. 'You're not telling me you used to iron your whole kit every day just for the benefit of the public!'

Suleyman nervously fingered his tie. Cohen put him on

edge. He always had done, ever since they were constables together. Cohen was so...direct!

He changed the subject. 'What happened with Mrs Blatsky anyway?'

'Not a lot. I didn't do much really, she spoke just enough Turkish. The Old Man did most of the talking. She was ancient and had a bit of a beard coming.'

Suleyman removed his jacket. 'I don't suppose you listened, did you?'

'I did, as a matter of fact,' replied Cohen archly. 'She said Meyer had killed some people back in Russia.'

Suleyman replied in kind. 'Well, we know that!'

Cohen leant across the desk again and waved his finger in Suleyman's face. He looked like a young child telling his best friend a naughty secret. 'Ah, but did you know that he was a fully paid-up commie when he did it?'

'No!'

'Oh, yes. Went about killing the rich for the glory of Marx, he did. And what is more, someone who is still alive now knew all about it too!'

Suleyman frowned. 'What, someone back in Russia, or—'

'No, here,' said Cohen. 'In the city.'

Suleyman suddenly felt his blood curdle in his veins. He knew a prime candidate for that role and so did Ikmen. The Inspector was, according to Cohen, now in with the Commissioner. He imagined the man's impatience. Sitting there just itching to get over to the Gulcu house. And when he told him about Cornelius and his attack upon a lawyer. A Jewish lawyer...

'Not that the old Jew's drinking cronies were any good.' Cohen had changed the subject. 'All they could do was try to ponce money off us. Although one of them did say that he saw a big black car behind the apartment block but he couldn't remember whether it was last week or yesterday.'

'Mmm.' Suleyman wasn't listening. His brain was too busy trying to cope with the range of possibilities this new piece of information had thrown up.

The door banged open and performed its customary smashing operation against the side of his desk. Suleyman jumped. Cohen slid lazily to his feet and stood facing the door with his hands in his pockets.

'Hello, Inspector.'

Ikmen stepped forward, grabbed Cohen by the elbow and threw him roughly through the doorway. 'Get out of my office, Cohen, you perverted animal!'

As the constable dived into the corridor, Ikmen slammed the door shut behind him and stood in the middle of the room, fuming.

'Cohen wasn't doing anything wrong, sir!' said Suleyman in an effort to protect his junior colleague.

Ikmen shot him a glance he was fortunate to survive. 'I know that, but I'm angry and I need to take that out on someone! Would you rather I took it out on you?'

The sergeant looked down and mumbled in the negative.

'Oh, don't worry, Sergeant!' Ikmen said wearily. 'I'll make it up to Cohen some other time. When I don't want to kill everybody and myself and you and—'

Suleyman remained calm. 'Bad time with the Commissioner, sir?'

The two men looked at each other. The younger one was secretly amused and the older one knew it. He could vent his spleen on Suleyman as much as he liked, the shock value of his rages had ceased to have an effect many years ago. A grim smile caught the corners of his mouth and he sighed. 'Oh, Suleyman, what are we going to do?'

'Sir?'

Ikmen walked around his desk and sat down in his chair. 'Ardiç wants this case wrapped up as soon as possible.' He sneered. 'The political dimension! The way I see it I'm supposed to produce some mindless Nazi, preferably the very convenient Reinhold Smits, on demand. Sorry, *you're* supposed to produce some mindless—'

'Me!'

'Yes.' His voice was flat and grim. 'Ardiç wants me here for the benefit of the press. I believe he wants to turn me into some sort of media personality. You and the boys have got to do all the work from now on. I'm just supposed to sit about giving orders. I won't, of course. He can stuff it!' He wiped the sweat from his brow with the back of his hand. 'I hear you did a good job with our friend the Consul?'

'Did the Commissioner tell you that?'

'Yes.'

Suleyman laughed. 'I told him what he wanted to hear basically. I simply said that we were pursuing several lines of inquiry, including a possible Nazi connection, which is where I suppose I stupidly mentioned Reinhold Smits.'

'Well, he was bound to find out sometime. Anyway, I'm glad you did well.' And he meant it. His young protégé was learning fast. Faster than he had, that was for sure. 'Of course Ardiç latched on to the Smits thing like a leech, but that's not your fault. However...' Only then did his face drop. He looked sad for a moment. He was pleased for Suleyman, but Ikmen knew that he was treading on very shaky ground with his superior. He knew how quickly a sergeant could be promoted, an inspector sent back into the wilderness.

Suleyman sensed his unease and changed the subject. 'London called about Robert Cornelius.'

'Ah.' Ikmen looked up. Back to the case. It was what he needed. 'Well?'

'He has a record. Assault upon a lawyer in 1987. A Jewish lawyer called Sheldon.'

Ikmen nodded. 'Interesting. Political?'

'There were no details. Apparently Sheldon didn't press charges.' He paused. 'There was an alleged assault upon a child too, in the same year. That didn't go any further either. Lack of evidence. Mr Cornelius seems to have something of a past. Do you want him brought in, sir?'

Ikmen considered. It was a very tenuous connection, but given Cornelius's presence at the scene plus his surprise appearance at the Gulcu house, it wasn't totally ridiculous. If the child were Jewish too...'Ye-es,' he said slowly. 'Have one of the men pick him up first thing tomorrow. He's not going anywhere, is he?'

'OK. Cohen told me that Mrs Blatsky was quite useful.'

Ikmen brightened considerably. If only he had been able to talk like this to Ardiç. 'Our Leonid was a Bolshevik, according to Mrs Blatsky. Active, murderous and committed.'

'And so the people he murdered were...?'

'Oh, quality, Suleyman, quality. Bourgeois pigs, as the old woman had it.' He smiled grimly. 'Typical fodder for the times.'

'And Mrs Blatsky does know this for certain, does she, sir?'

Ikmen sighed. 'Inasmuch as anyone could make out Leonid's drunken ramblings, yes. She was, however, rather unsatisfactorily unclear on this witness to Meyer's crime business. I presume the delightful Cohen has enlightened you about this?'

'Yes, sir.'

'Someone, the "other" she called him or her, still living in this city, knew about Meyer's killings. The old woman didn't know who, said Meyer never told her who or at least she doesn't think that he did. She did register his fear of this "other" though, said that only the liquor could make him feel OK about it, actually believed it may have kept him going. The "other"...' He sighed again, this time far more desperately and deeply than before. 'You can imagine who crossed my mind, can't you?'

Suleyman shuddered at the thought of her. 'It doesn't prove anything though, does it, sir? I mean, there are still so many questions. Did the incident happen at all or was Meyer just making up alcohol-soaked stories? And if it did happen and Maria Gulcu was a witness, why was a woman like her there witnessing the thing and why did she then leave the country with him? At the risk of putting a block upon your enthusiasm, it doesn't seem to make a lot of sense.'

Ikmen sighed a third time. No, it didn't make much sense. Even he had to admit that. 'I don't know. Perhaps the people

Meyer killed were connected to her in some way.' He shrugged helplessly.

But Suleyman was shocked. 'You can't mean revenge? Why wait'—he worked the mathematics out in his head—'seventy-four years to do it? Why watch him do it and then leave the country with him? It's madness!'

'I know that!' blustered Ikmen. 'But it keeps on worrying away at me. I can't get it out of my head that Meyer's death was an execution. Personal, targeted.' He reached into his drawer and pulled out a large unopened brandy bottle. 'If anti-Jewish crazy people were declaring war on the Jews there would have been more of a build-up. Nothing has happened in Balat for years, not a thing! And yet I must admit that I do feel that Smits is connected to it all in some way and there can be no hiding either from the fact of the huge swastika on Meyer's bedroom wall.'

'But we don't know for certain whether Smits was a Nazi or not.'

Ikmen took the top off the bottle and flung it down on his desk. 'No, no we don't.' He took two big gulps from the bottle and wiped the neck on his sleeve. 'As far as we know Meyer did nothing but sit on his arse and get pissed for the last seventy years of his life. Where the hell Reinhold Smits, Maria Gulcu, Robert Cornelius and Meyer's large amounts of money fit into the picture, we really don't know.'

He offered the bottle to Suleyman, who declined.

'And then there's the fact that the wretched man was a Russian as well as a Jew!' Ikmen put his hand up to his head in despair. 'The fucking Russian psyche! Talk about out of your depth!'

At that point, there was a knock at the door and Cohen entered. 'Would either of you two sirs like some tea?'

Ikmen raised his head. 'Provided you don't accompany the drink with lewd references to your recent dealings with breasts and bottoms, yes, Cohen,' he said.

'Right.' The constable left the room.

Suleyman gave way to an uncharacteristic bout of hilarious laughter.

Natalia had been gone for nearly an hour, but Robert had still not moved from his place on the sofa. His eyes frozen to the forest of television aerials on top of the opposite apartment block, he watched as the evening sun slowly dipped behind the buildings. A streak of smoky copper, thrown across the blue sky like a ribbon, marked its progress towards the west. The dying of the light.

The heat of the day and the frantic afternoon activity, both sexual and violent, had left him feeling limp and wasted. But it was not an unpleasant feeling and in a way he was grateful for it. His supine, undemanding body placed no strain upon his depleted energy levels. He needed what few calories he possessed in order to think. What Natalia had told him, although explaining much, had left him thoughtful. He was anxious still. No, he hadn't 'seen things'. Yes, he was still in his right mind—but...

That she hadn't wanted to tell him was evident. He hadn't used violence of that order for many years. It had shaken him. He had nursed a hope that perhaps he was no longer capable of such acts, but that was obviously not yet the case. It was her lack of regard, the way she assumed she could just ignore his question and sweep out of the room, that had inflamed him. It had been exactly the same with the earlier incidents. Didn't these people realise, Natalia, that awful barrister, that bastard Billy Smith, that if he asked a question he expected an answer? Ignoring him, pretending that he didn't exist, was an insult. It made him feel diminished, persecuted even. Violence really was the only way out when others decided you were a non-person. Or when you deep down and secretly saw yourself in that role. It was scant justification for littering her beautiful body with bruises, however, and Robert knew it.

He turned his mind to what she had told him. That he had wrested her story from her by force gave it a certain credibility. But it had—he couldn't quite think of the right word—Ruritanian aspects to it. Aspects that were hard to believe.

Gulcu was not, according to Natalia, the family's real surname. When her grandmother came to Turkey as a refugee from Russia in 1918, she had met a man called Gulcu and had three children by him. She neither legally married him, nor did she apply for Turkish nationality. Quite why she omitted to do this or how in fact the family managed to live without any legal status was not explained. Likewise, where Natalia's own apparently Turkish and again dead father fitted in was also a mystery.

The murdered man in Balat had been a friend of her grandmother. Like her he was Russian, another refugee from the violence that tore apart and destroyed Tsarist Russia in 1917. In the past they would get together frequently and share memories of their homeland. On these occasions, Natalia's grandmother would always provide a meal for the impecunious Meyer. He was given to hard liquor and frequently forgot to feed himself properly. But time passed and Meyer and Maria, the grandmother, became too old to socialise. The Gulcus' provision of food to their less fortunate old friend, however, continued.

Every week one of the younger members of the family would journey across the Golden Horn to Balat and present the old man with a parcel of food. He was rarely sober, but always grateful. Maria apparently maintained that it was only by virtue of her parcels that the old man survived.

On Monday it had been Natalia's turn to make the journey. She took a long, late lunch break from work and arrived at Meyer's apartment at about three-thirty. She gave the old man his provisions and talked with him for a while. But more time passed than she realised and she was appalled when she looked at her watch to discover that it was already four-thirty. She was due back at the shop. She left Meyer, very much alive, and ran down the stairs and into the street. Emerging into the sunlight her own and Robert's paths briefly crossed.

The lead-up to this point in her story had been strange and outside his own experience, but Robert could neither prove nor disprove any part of it. The final section, her rendition of their encounter, was a different matter.

According to Natalia she ran because she had to get back to work. She was not aware of anybody else on the street and just headed straight towards Fevzi Paşa Caddesi and the buses. The reason she gave for not acknowledging Robert was a) she was in a panic and b) because of her short-sightedness she couldn't actually see him.

Things had calmed down considerably between them by that time. She was apologetic and, once again, loving towards him. She was like she used to be just after they first met: tenderness and caring lending substance to her sensuality. His own guilt at handling her so roughly had also intervened. She had kissed him and slipped her hand into his trousers, gently massaging his penis. What he had to understand was that contact with the police could be very dangerous for her and her family. It was bad enough the authorities knew her grandmother was friendly with Meyer, but if they knew that she, Natalia, had been in the vicinity when the old man was murdered things could get very difficult. The police would almost certainly require a statement, they would run a check on her, she may even be required to appear in court. The check would reveal her true status; the court would take a dim view of evidence supplied by an illegal alien. The family could be deported. Back to Russia, penniless, standing for ever in an endless queue for bread...It was an unappealing image but it dissolved when she lowered her open mouth down upon him and he released himself into a warm stream of erotic pleasure.

It was only as she raised her head up from him that the small tears in her story started to open up and become holes. The bellow that accompanied his climax had faded and given way to a smile as she had turned to look at him. Grateful, he had stroked her strong, fleshy back. But his fingers tensed as they explored a softness that had not been there only three days before. He remembered the clothes she had been wearing: hard, thick jeans, that coarse and unflattering shirt. Clothes he had never seen before—or since. Clothes she would have deemed unfit to clean the house in. Clothes that could easily be burnt. Perhaps had to be. As he came down from his sexual rush, his mind began working again.

She left and his mind continued to work. In order not to be able to see a tall, rather striking man across a narrow alleyway, a person would have to be very short-sighted indeed. Without recourse to either glasses or contact lenses, that person would be rendered almost blind. Natalia wore neither.

He wished that his guilt and his lust had not silenced him. She had gone, but in her wake the ghosts of unanswered questions reverberated and echoed around him. And yet what could he do? Just before she had left he had, at her request, sworn everything she had told him to secrecy. She had given him no choice; she wanted it that way and, besides, he had been weak. The violent man, in the wrong. She'd caught him at his most vulnerable. But would the Turks really deport the family if they found out the truth? A family who had not only lived in their country for over seventy years, but had children by their men? And besides, surely if Natalia were to explain the situation to the authorities they could not in all conscience refuse an application for citizenship? She was, after all, Turkish in every practical respect. It didn't make any sense!

Robert shook his head impatiently. There was something else, there had to be. Something he had not managed to threaten and slap out of her. Something to do with that bony shoulder blade perhaps? A thing he would have to torture out of her. Except that he wouldn't. He wouldn't hurt her again—ever. But what were she and her family about, really?

A deeper, darker truth. Robert knew this existed, some-where. In retrospect he'd known for a long time. The inky, hidden heart at the centre of her tale. But he was tired of all this thinking. He'd come back to it later when he felt stronger. He got up suddenly from the sofa and switched on the television.

❀ ❀ ❀

Çetin Ikmen's visit to the Gulcu house that night was more a whimsical than a planned act. That he found himself there was almost as much of a surprise to him as it was to them. Maria was sitting in a chair in the middle of the room when he arrived. Although she looked composed, he could however feel her anger and knew that he was far from welcome.

'Alone?' she said. Her voice rang as if she were declaiming something of great importance. 'Where is your pretty friend?'

Ikmen stopped directly in front of her chair. 'Sergeant Suleyman has another life away from this case, madam.'

The reptile eyes smiled unpleasantly at him. Ikmen changed the subject.

'Mrs Gulcu, I've some more questions about Leonid Meyer.'

She lit one of her Sobranie cigarettes and sighed. 'A subject that holds much fascination for you, Inspector.'

'I imagine the death of such an old and close friend would not be completely without interest to you either, Mrs Gulcu.' *Touché*, Ikmen thought with some satisfaction.

She shot him one of her clammy glances. 'I cared for Leonid when he was alive, Inspector. His empty corpse is no concern of mine.' She patted the footstool beside her. 'Sit.'

Ikmen walked around her chair and placed himself down next to her heavily jewelled hand. Over by the window somebody coughed. Maria Gulcu turned her head slightly and said something in Russian. A young man's voice answered her, also, Ikmen assumed, in Russian.

In time with the voice he saw the shut curtains move slightly, and, as his eyes grew accustomed to the light, Ikmen saw a pair of eyes and a pale face staring at him through the darkness.

When the voice spoke again Ikmen noticed that the accent was quite precise, but the tone, he felt, lacked something. It was like listening to a young child who is unused to and a little afraid of adult company. And yet the voice was clearly that of a man, as was the body. Ikmen could see the feet and the head. Slim, but well formed. The old woman followed the line of his gaze and spoke.

'You must forgive Misha,' she said, waving one hand in the general direction of the window. 'The child of a maid we once had here. She is sadly dead now, but I continue to care for the boy. He is a little simple, but useful for the more mundane household tasks.' She laughed hoarsely. 'His mindless conversation sometimes amuses. When I am particularly bored.'

Her blatant cruelty caught Ikmen unawares, but only for a moment. He might have expected it. But the notion of this young person locked away for maybe years with the reptilian Mrs Gulcu, providing her with some sort of sick amusement, appalled him. He remembered her penchant for his young sergeant and shuddered.

'I want to ask you about an incident that is alleged to have happened in 1918, madam.' Ikmen took his cigarettes out of his pocket and lit up.

He saw her stiffen and shift in her chair. She turned her head slightly, away from him.

'Meyer may possibly have been involved in political violence.'

She leant forward to stub her cigarette out in the ashtray. The effort of moving, or maybe, Ikmen thought, something else made her suddenly labour to catch her breath. 'I see.'

'According to his rabbi, Mr Meyer's alcoholism was related to guilt over a violent incident he had been involved in.' Ikmen paused on purpose, for effect. 'I was wondering if you could tell us anything about it, Mrs Gulcu?'

Her head snapped round savagely and she looked down her long nose at him. 'What could I possibly know about some shabby Bolshevik outrage?'

'I was hoping that you could tell me, madam.'

'Well I cannot.'

Ikmen smiled. 'I find that very hard to believe, madam.'

'Oh?'

'Yes.'

He paused for a moment, trying unbeknown to her to work out whether she knew what she had just said or not.

'Well?' she said impatiently. 'What?'

'In view of the fact that you knew Mr Meyer was a Bolshevik without my actually telling you so, I find your avowed lack of information on the subject quite unintelligible. You can, I hope, see my problem?'

She sucked unpleasantly and noisily on her teeth for a second. 'I thought you people were supposed to catch criminals, Inspector. I did not realise that the Istanbul police were also professional historians!'

'The past is simply today with better skin, Mrs Gulcu.'

Even beneath the rouge and powder he could see that her face had drained of blood. She knew exactly what he meant. He had hit a nerve, a raw thing. 'The Revolution is a very painful subject for all Russians in exile, Inspector Ikmen.' She spat his name like a curse. 'You are a Turk, you cannot understand. When you deposed your masters you sent them all abroad and allowed them the luxury of a frustrated exile. We were never given that option. We were—'

The man in the corner cried out, the unintelligible Rus-sian word ripping from his throat like a sob.

She pointed towards the curtain and her anger towered across the room like a giant. 'You see!' she shouted. 'All of us, not just me! Even our children. We all, all émigrés, die a little more when we remember...' Her voice trailed off and she trembled, staring into the distance as if trying to pierce the darkness with her eyes. She was seeing things, scenes played out against the sensual black background. She was living elsewhere again. Back there.

Ikmen remained calm in the face of this graphic exposi-tion of the great Russian soul and doggedly pursued his course. 'The incident I have described may be of importance in deter-mining whether or not Mr Meyer had any enemies, madam. This subject, by your own admission, arouses great passions.

Perhaps even now there are still those who would be prepared to act upon them.'

Her reply was a spit. 'I know nothing about Leonid's activities before we met! All right, I knew he had been, was, whatever, a Bolshevik at some point. But love is very blind, Inspector Ikmen, and when I fell in love with Leonid and we left our country together nothing like that mattered any more. That is all that I know!'

'Then I take it you were not present during the violence in which Meyer was involved?'

'Present? As in watching, you mean?' Her face, for all its great age, its massive scarring by time, betrayed genuine outrage. 'Who on earth do you think I am? What kind of person do you imagine me to be? I...'

Ikmen dropped his gaze, the old woman's reaction temporarily shaming him. 'I am sorry, madam, it is just that we have recently come into possession of certain information that would seem to suggest that someone else, someone now living in this city, knew in detail about—'

'Well, I can assure you that it was not me!'

'Very well, madam.' He raised his head, daring now to meet her still furious eyes. 'I'm sorry, I'm afraid I had to ask. I imagine that you can understand—'

'Oh, I can understand, Inspector. But that doesn't mean that I have to like it.'

'No.'

'No.'

A moment of pure silence followed—a moment during which a question that had been troubling Ikmen distilled within his mind. That she answered it at all was a tribute to his audacity.

'But did you really love Leonid Meyer, Mrs Gulcu? I mean honestly, seriously love a poor little Jew like him?'

She smiled. Unexpectedly, considering what Ikmen was really doing was calling her a liar, she smiled. 'Well now, Inspector, you are a clever little man. I think you know the answer to that question.'

'So you didn't?'

She shrugged. 'It was an arrangement. I was a young, educated, beautiful girl and he was a poor ugly little Jew. But I needed to get out of Russia, Inspector. Giving Leonid my body in return for his protection was a small price to pay for the chance to avoid the multiple beatings and raping that I would have had to endure without him. I gave him the one and only chance he would ever have to possess a—' She stopped short, pulled herself back and away from something and tried to regain her composure.

'A what, madam?'

She looked suddenly exhausted and stared down at the floor, her eyes glazed. 'A woman who didn't smell of the gutter.'

It was not what she had been about to say, Ikmen felt certain. He changed tack slightly. 'So, just to clarify, they weren't your family, Mr Meyer's victims?'

'My family were shot by the secret police, the Cheka.'

'Who were Bolsheviks.'

She leant across and put her face close up to his. She was so close he could see, beneath the make-up, a long scar that ran from her left eye down to her chin. 'Would you give yourself to a person who killed your family? Even to save your own life, Inspector?'

'That would depend how I felt about death, madam. If I felt that death was truly the end, then I believe I might do anything to survive. I would hate, but I would probably go on. Perhaps even because of the hate.'

The side of that cunning, crêpy face touched his cheek. Her rank breath played against his ear. 'And what do you believe, Inspector Ikmen?'

He fell silent for a moment. He didn't know. Others believed or didn't believe as the case may be. That was their business. He was interested, but only insofar as it aided his understanding of other people's psychology and motives.

'I don't know what I believe. That is the truth, madam. But if someone murdered my family I would find my life after that point very hollow and purposeless. Although perhaps the thought of revenge would give me some direction. I mean, what use are success, principles, social position if nobody loves you?'

'It depends.' She narrowed her eyes and smiled at the corners of her mouth. 'It depends upon who one is, how valuable one's life may be to oneself and to others.'

'And was your life "valuable" enough to allow you to give yourself to your family's killer?'

She laughed. It was an unexpected reaction to his question and caught Ikmen unawares. 'I am an Orthodox Christian, Inspector. Death to us is merely a door to a happier and more fulfilling life. If Leonid had killed my parents, what did I stand to gain by not joining them?' She shrugged. 'But all you need to know, my dear Inspector, is that I did not kill Leonid. I can say that with my hand on my heart. My conscience is clear.'

Ikmen smiled. 'I didn't ever think, madam, that—'

'Somebody of my advanced years could physically perform such a task?' She laughed again. 'No, you are right—in my case.'

Ikmen narrowed his eyes. 'By which you mean?'

'I mean, Inspector, that there might be other elderly people capable of such an act.'

He looked at her questioningly.

'There are plenty of old men in places like South America who still, occasionally, make trouble for people like Leonid and his kind.'

'You mean like old Nazis?' He eyed her steadily. 'Rather a long way away from here, aren't they?'

She met his gaze squarely and without blinking. 'Some are, some aren't.'

He feigned his surprise to perfection. 'Oh, you mean like the director of Şeker Textiles, Mr Smits?'

'Oh.' She smiled again, this time revealing cracked and yellowing teeth. 'Did I say that?'

'No.'

'No, I didn't, did I.'

Ikmen sighed deeply, a little unnerved to have been so easily and quickly outwitted. 'There is not, as yet, any reason to suppose that Mr Smits had any motive with regard to the death of Leonid Meyer, madam.'

'No?'

'No. But'—and here Ikmen smiled, slowly and with some pleasure—'but if I find one I will be sure and come back to let you know.'

Chapter Nine

THERE WAS A DOWNSIDE to living in Istanbul. The sunshine, the friendliness of the people, the exotic excitement of the place were things that Robert loved and would not have changed. The heavy and often irritating presence of the authorities, however, was another matter. The last of many military coups had taken place in 1980. It had left its mark. Armed police and even more heavily armed troops were never far away: stalking the streets with young grim faces, looking for signs of dissent and insurrection, stopping and questioning people for, as Robert perceived it, completely pointless reasons. Horrific stories circulated about what happened to people should they have the misfortune to be taken into police or military custody: stories of medieval torture and mind-bendingly protracted interrogation.

When he had first arrived in the country, Robert had been to visit the British Consulate. Among the pieces of advice dispensed by that office was one about 'keeping your nose clean' with the police. Turkey was a friendly nation and in the event of any 'misbehaviour' by a British national it was made quite plain that Turkish justice, albeit amid some protest, would be allowed to take its course. In other words, Her Majesty's Government was quite prepared to let you sweat it out on your own.

Through his albeit brief contact with Ikmen, however, Robert was almost tempted to believe that he had seen the human face of Turkish bureaucracy. But he was not convinced. The odd smile and an undeniably charming demeanour cost little. The shrewd, dark eyes had hardened as Robert had struggled to answer his questions and the Englishman wondered what more drastic methods were at the Inspector's disposal should he decide to get really tough with a suspect. Why he was thinking about this again he didn't exactly know. He had done nothing wrong! Well...But he'd woken with it on his mind and now it just wouldn't go. He got a twinge, just a suggestion, of wanting to be back in London.

He put his books and papers into his briefcase and tried to forget about it all.

Until, that is, the knock at the door. Robert stopped what he was doing and went to answer it. It was probably only old Ali, the *kapıcı*, with his drinking water. He usually called before Robert left for work, checking that everything in the block was fine, dispensing water and elaborate, religiously inspired good wishes.

But when Robert opened the door and saw a tall, young man wearing a blue police uniform, he felt his face blanch. It was as if his earlier thoughts had taken on the guise of eerie premonitions.

'Yes?'

'Mr Robert Cornelius?'

'Yes.' He knew his voice had started trembling but there was nothing he could do about it. He looked at the large gun holster on the officer's hip. Thick leather and cold, hard metal.

The young man smiled. He had nice teeth, but rather too many for Robert's liking. A lot of the younger Turks were like that. The officer spoke. 'You please come to police station. Inspector Ikmen need to talk with you.'

'Natalia?'

'Grandmama?' She walked over to the bed and pulled aside the purple netting.

'We have a problem, don't we? Need to talk.'

'We?' The girl pulled away from her grandmother's caress and averted her face.

Maria Gulcu hauled herself painfully up on her pillows and reached across for her cigarettes. 'Something needs to be done about these policemen. They are becoming very tiresome.'

Oh, it was easy for her to say, but what? Natalia flung herself down into the chair beside Maria's bed. 'And what do you suggest that might be, Grandmama?' Her voice was calm, but it definitely had an edge.

'I don't know, Natalia.' Maria's hands dropped into her lap and she cast her eyes downwards. The innocent. 'I haven't been out of this house since before you were born.'

'But you nevertheless want a convenient solution.' The sentence snapped out of Natalia like a bullet. Already it was all too obvious to her who exactly was supposed to provide this solution.

Maria rose to her unpleasant attitude. Her eyes fixed on the younger woman's face and turned to ice. 'Oh, yes!'

'So what do you suggest I do then, Grandmama?' She returned the old woman's basilisk gaze and coughed a little in the back of her throat. Maria's incense had recently started to affect her chest. Like the old woman herself, it was beginning to cloy. When Maria didn't answer, Natalia continued. Her tone was one of heavy mockery. 'Bribe the Inspector? Buy him lunch? Sleep with him?'

'No.' Maria lit her cigarette and then blew large, expertly rounded rings of smoke at the ceiling. 'No, I was thinking of approaching the problem from a more oblique angle.'

'What do you mean?'

'What I mean, Natalia, is that although the Inspector is aware of the fact that Uncle Leonid had enemies in this city, he is not, at present, in any position to verify that.'

Natalia eyed her grandmother through veils of pure jaundice. 'And this concerns me how?'

'Although the police know of the existence of someone who may very well have killed Uncle Leonid...'

'Yes, yes, but he—'

'Although they know, they have little evidence upon which to draw. However, that does not mean that that particular situation might not change sometime in the future.'

'Ah.' Natalia raised her eyebrows out of sudden realisation of what was being said rather than surprise. 'And you want me to...'

'No.' Maria's smile was sweet, almost as if it had not emanated from her. 'No, Natalia, I just want you to listen for a moment—listen and learn about a grave injustice that was done to Uncle Leonid by a very unpleasant man many years ago. The incident affected me also, very badly. This awful man who wanted me, absolutely persecuted...'

But Natalia knew her grandmother too well and although she smiled as Maria spoke, her heart was already hardened to whatever she had to say. 'No, I don't think so, Grandmama. I don't think I want to hear it.'

'Then you must be forced to!' Maria suddenly leant forward and grabbed Natalia by the chin. The younger woman pulled away as the older one's rancid breath puffed violently into her eyes. 'I am not asking you, Natalia!'

The girl groaned. Not for the first time she felt trapped, caught on the end of one of Maria's talons like a worm. It had happened to all of them at one time or another. But of late it was always Natalia. 'Why me?' And then, rather more acidly, 'Again.'

'Because you live in the world, my darling.' It was said with spite, laced with jealousy. 'You chose to be a little bit free. You were also, and please believe that I am so grateful for this, very willing to go out to Uncle Leonid when—'

'Don't!'

Natalia was not inclined to cry easily but on this occasion, quite suddenly, her eyes were brimful with moisture. This did not go unnoticed by her grandmother and although the latter did not go so far as to attempt to comfort her granddaughter she did soften her tone somewhat.

'Look, I know that you have suffered most horribly already, Natalia, and I am sorry for that. But what we have started we must now finish. There is so much at stake here and—'

'Yes, I know. I know.'

'And so I, we, need you to do something more in order to complete this work. Do you understand?'

'Yes, I...'

'And so now. This boyfriend of yours, this Mr Cornelius...'

The sudden change of direction and the renewed firmness in her grandmother's tone made Natalia's head swim. 'Yes, er, what of him?'

'He was around and about at the time the police say Leonid was killed.'

'Yes, he—'

'And he has been interviewed by them, has he not?'

'Yes.'

'Well.' Maria smiled as she ground her cigarette out in her ashtray. 'Strange as it may sound, that could work to our advantage, inasmuch as I believe Mr Cornelius may well be very interested in this old injustice perpetrated against Uncle Leonid. By your own admission, he is very interested in the whole affair. He is troubled, looking for answers...'

'Oh, my God, you mean...'

Natalia sat back heavily in her chair and stared at the wall. The old woman's smoke drifted across her face and stung her eyes. There was nowhere for it to go. Open windows were not permitted in Maria's apartment. The smoke and her perfume and the sickly reek of her incense were not allowed to escape. She bathed in them, embalming her live body in their mixture of sweet and sour odours.

'I mean,' said Maria, 'that I think you should listen to my story and then make up your own mind about how you might use it. After all, if Mr Cornelius is actively seeking answers, and if he is as disturbed by recent events as you say...'

She didn't want to stay, much less listen, but then if Natalia wanted to get away from the dreamy, soporific darkness of Maria's presence, she would have at least to consider...As a child, listening to Grandmama's stories day in and day out had excited the young Natalia, made her feel special, loved, superior. It still did, despite the fact that with adulthood had come difficulties, the psychological realignment she knew she had never achieved. And the family as a whole had so very much to lose: the material things, the safety, the gift of the past...

She felt herself weaken even before she spoke—almost before her thoughts had organised themselves. 'All right,' she said with a sigh, 'all right, tell me if you must.'

Suleyman mustered all of his schoolboy English and made a start.

'Thank you for coming, Mr Cornelius.'

'I didn't have much of a fucking choice, did I!'

Suleyman shot a rather alarmed glance at Ikmen. The older man motioned for him to continue.

Suleyman cleared his throat. 'My apology, sir. But there is one thing, I am sorry, we must ask.' He moved a small piece of paper across the desk and placed it in front of him. 'Is about two things which happen in 1987.'

Cornelius laughed sourly. 'I was in London then, for God's sake!'

'Yes.' Suleyman consulted his paper. 'Is about a Mr Simon Sheldon, sir, and—'

'What the—!' Cornelius whipped round in his chair and looked at Ikmen. He was furious. 'Have you been checking up on me?'

'Routine, sir. We check everyone out in cases like this. Just part of the investigation. You are not alone.'

'Routine! What my past has to do with—'

'Please listen to Sergeant Suleyman, sir.' Ikmen was tired. He didn't have either the time or the stomach for outbursts. He hadn't had his first drink yet.

Cornelius fell furiously silent and turned back towards his young interrogator. He didn't like this young policeman, with his smooth hands and perfect features.

Suleyman cleared his throat again. 'First in 1987 you were assaulting Mr Sheldon in Islington, North London. Mr Sheldon did not make charges.'

'So?' It was said with some arrogance, but Cornelius crossed his arms and hunched his legs back closer to his body.

'Could you please maybe tell us about that, sir?'

'Why?'

Suleyman swallowed hard. 'We must know sir, be-cause...' Quite without warning his command of English failed completely. Knowing what he wanted to say wasn't enough. How to say it, that was the problem! He opened his mouth and made a few faltering noises, but he couldn't speak.

Cornelius looked at him like he was an idiot. Suleyman's failure seemed to please the Englishman. 'Well!'

Ikmen jumped into the breach with an easy and erudite grace. 'The murder of our Mr Meyer may, and I must stress that this is only a theory, sir, possess a racist or, more specifically, anti-Semitic dimension. Mr Meyer, like most of the residents of the Balat district, was a Jewish gentleman.'

Cornelius was silent for a moment as the realisation of what Ikmen had said dawned upon him. His face became very white and he had to lick his suddenly dry lips in order to make them work. When he did finally speak his voice quavered slightly as if his throat were partially blocked. 'So you think that because I had a fight with Sheldon in 1987, I am some kind of Jew-baiting—'

'We do not think anything of the sort, Mr Cornelius.' Ikmen took his feet off the waste-paper bin and lit a cigarette. He made sure he kept his voice light and pleasant. 'It is a line of inquiry, that is all. But we must check. Your motive for attacking Mr Sheldon may be quite justified. It may also be ugly and political. I do not know until you tell me.'

For a moment, Cornelius seemed mollified, but it was a lull that did not last. 'Why me? Why are you checking up on me?'

'We check up on everybody who was at or around the scene of the crime, sir. As I told you, it is routine. You are simply assisting—'

'You with your inquiries!' Cornelius shouted.

'Yes, sir.' Ikmen smiled very warmly. It was important not to get worked up at times like this. Calm usually gave one the edge.

Cornelius raked his fingers through his hair and then fumbled in his pockets for his cigarettes. 'In my country, Inspector, "assisting the police with their inquiries" usually means that one is under suspicion.'

'I can assure you—'

'And if a confession is not forthcoming, then they take you down to the cells and beat one out of you!'

The office went very quiet. Ikmen looked at Suleyman and then back at the livid Cornelius once again. He sighed. Foreigners were never easy. It was annoying, but he decided to bow to the inevitable. 'Would you prefer to have a representative from your Consulate present, sir?'

But rather than defuse the situation, Ikmen's suggestion seemed to alarm the Englishman still further. It was not a reaction he had anticipated.

'No! No, I don't want that! No!' His unlit cigarette quavered dangerously between his fingers.

Very odd! But Ikmen kept calm. 'Very well, sir.' He paused. 'Perhaps you would like to tell us about Mr Sheldon.'

As Cornelius lit his cigarette, Ikmen noticed that the man's hands were shaking.

'Simon Sheldon QC was my now ex-wife's lover. I caught him in my bed with my wife and I broke the bastard's jaw. I don't hate Jews, only Sheldon. I think even you can appreciate why.'

Ikmen leant back in his chair and looked at the bowed fair head before him. The man looked ashamed, but not, Ikmen suspected, of his criminal act. No, Cornelius was ashamed that his wife had taken a lover. Tall, blond and attractive, it must, Ikmen thought, have reflected badly upon his virility.

'I am sorry, Mr Cornelius,' he said and crossed his arms across his chest.

The Englishman lifted his head. 'Are you?'

'Yes. But I think you can appreciate why I had to ask.'

Cornelius didn't answer.

Ikmen breathed in deeply and consulted his notes. 'And the child, William Smith, Mr Cornelius? Rosebury Downs School in Hackney?'

'Oh come on, for Christ's sake!'

'I am sorry, sir.' Ikmen's tone hardened. 'But I need to clear these matters up.'

'Billy Smith was a little bastard!' Cornelius sighed. 'The child lied. Lots of them do it. Claim that "sir" hit you and get him into trouble. It was a game, for Christ's sake! I never touched the little swine! I never touched any of them! God, I wanted to, juvenile barbarians! But I didn't and the court upheld my innocence.' He looked up at Ikmen and sneered. 'Oh, and before you ask, Smith wasn't Jewish. I doubt he was actually human!'

'I see.'

Cornelius laughed mirthlessly. 'No you don't! Unless of course you've been a teacher too. Inner London schools are fucking hell, Inspector Ikmen. Animal houses! As you no doubt know, I resigned soon after that incident. But not because of it. I resigned because I'd had enough of children, because my wife was leaving me and because I could feel my life falling to bits around me. It isn't nice, Inspector, strain like that...' He stopped and stared up at the ceiling. His eyes glistened with bulging tears, but he did not allow them to fall. He swallowed hard to contain them and breathed deeply for a few seconds.

Ikmen bit his lip. It had not been pleasant interviewing this man. If what he had just told him was true, then 1987 had been one hell of a year for him. But there was one more thing he had to ask him before he could let him go. Cornelius looked so broken that he was loath to do so. On further consideration, however, perhaps it was better to hit him with it now. Perhaps it would have more effect. Kicking people already down wasn't nice, but it had its place and he had a job to do.

'What do you know about the Gulcu family, Mr Cornelius?'

Ikmen couldn't see his face, it was turned away from him, but Suleyman could. Cornelius's face reddened in a moment.

'Why?' His tone was measured, but taut.

'I saw you at their house on Wednesday evening. I just wondered if you knew them well.'

'Are they under suspicion too?' Still he didn't look at Ikmen. He was trying not to look at Suleyman, but the young sergeant had caught his eye and he was not letting go.

'No,' replied Ikmen levelly. 'I just wondered what your connection was, that is all.'

'Natalia Gulcu is a…friend.' He hesitated slightly before the last word.

'A friend.' It was a statement, not a question, but Cornelius reacted violently to it.

'Yes, a bloody friend!' He raised his head and looked defiantly at Ikmen. 'What the hell is this?'

Ikmen was silently asking himself the same question. From his albeit brief experience of Cornelius and Miss Gulcu it had appeared that they were more than friends. Whatever her ancestry, the girl was Turkish and it seemed to Ikmen strange that a middle-class Turkish girl should allow such physical intimacy with a man who was only a friend. The man had rubbed his body up against her, pawed at her hips! He wondered if he was being unnecessarily narrow minded but then decided that he probably wasn't. Not that any of this adequately explained the way Cornelius was now behaving. He must, at the very least, desire the girl. And she in her turn had behaved as if she were accustomed to his caresses.

Ikmen looked Cornelius straight in the face for a second. The man's defiant expression told him that it was unlikely he would learn much more about this relationship. But there were other ways of finding out.

Ikmen smiled broadly and stood up. 'Thank you, Mr Cornelius, you may go now.'

There was a pause. 'You mean that's it?'

'Yes.'

For an instant he looked confused. Relief and confusion mixed. He collected his briefcase from under his chair and rose to his feet. 'Will you be—requiring me again, Inspector?' It was not said pleasantly.

Ikmen offered him his hand. 'Not unless you have anything else to tell us about Monday afternoon, sir.'

Cornelius smarted. He ignored the outstretched hand and made his way towards the door. Something had angered him again. Perhaps the reference to Monday afternoon. 'If I discover that my father was Heinrich Himmler I will be sure and let you know, Inspector!'

Ikmen did not rise to the bait but he did use the Germanic reference in order to ask one final question. 'Oh, talking of which, you don't happen to know a man called Reinhold Smits do you, Mr Cornelius?'

The Englishman's face was now completely blank and without expression. 'No, why?'

Ikmen smiled. 'Oh, no reason. Thank you.'

Cornelius was just about to open the door when a thought seemed to strike him and he stopped. Without turning he spoke in a low, suddenly very calm voice. 'One question for you, Inspector Ikmen.'

'Yes, sir?'

'When you catch this murderer, what will happen to him?'

Ikmen shrugged and lit a cigarette. 'There will be a trial and if found guilty he—will be sentenced.'

'To what? Sentenced to what?'

Ikmen watched Cornelius very closely, and as his words flowed he saw the lines deepen around the Englishman's mouth. It was like watching fabric rumple and fold. 'Often a prison term. Twenty, thirty years. However the Republic does retain the death penalty for certain offences, Mr Cornelius. Murder, like this one, with malice aforethought, would come into that category.'

'I see.' Cornelius played a little with the handle of the open door before continuing and then said, 'Is that the case for everyone? The death penalty, I mean?'

'Everyone?'

'Yes. I mean all categories and types of people?' Because this elicited absolutely no response from Ikmen that he could see, Cornelius elucidated a little further. 'Like, are there any exceptions dependent upon a person's status or...'

'Possibly. For those already terminally ill, for instance, or some females, the mentally incapacitated...'

'Oh.' He brightened just enough for a keen eye to notice. 'Oh right. Thank you.'

Ikmen bowed his head slightly and smiled. 'You are very welcome, sir.'

Just before Cornelius left, however, the policeman's eyes connected with his and for just a moment both men remained quite frozen in each other's gaze. Then with a short cough Cornelius turned away and stepped out into the corridor beyond.

As he closed the door behind him and Ikmen and Suleyman listened to the sound of his retreating footsteps, Ikmen turned to his young deputy and smiled. 'Did you catch most of that, Suleyman?'

'Most of it, sir. I'm sorry I messed my questioning up, I—'

'It's all right.' He walked over to the window and looked out into the street. For a few seconds he watched to see whether

or not Cornelius passed by. But he didn't and Ikmen gave up
and turned back into the room again. 'What are your thoughts,
Suleyman?'

'About Cornelius? He was very afraid, wasn't he, sir?' He
thought for a moment. 'But then even the most innocent behave
irrationally when they come in here.'

Ikmen scratched his head. 'Yes, true. Although I don't
think that he was really terrified until the end of the interview.'

'Sir?'

Ikmen smiled grimly. 'I find close interest in the techni-
calities of the death penalty rather unhealthy, don't you?'

'Oh,' Suleyman replied.

'Oh indeed,' said Ikmen, relishing every short syllable.

Ahmet Demir flung himself down in Cohen's chair and hooked
his long feet under the bottom of the desk.

Cohen, laboriously working his way through the top
drawer of a filing cabinet, mumbled through a cigarette, 'Get
out of my chair, Demir.'

His words fell upon deaf ears. Demir pushed himself
deeper into the chair and got comfortable. 'What are you doing
after work tonight, Cohen?'

'Is it your business?'

'If it involves attractive Swedish women, yes.'

Cohen turned away from the filing cabinet and gave Demir
one of his world-weary and bloodshot stares. Sometimes he
hated his own reputation. Every sex-starved little constable in
the place came to him for advice or wanted to go out on the
pick-up with him. Demir, with his long, lanky body and face like
a goat, was a particular irritation. For some bizarre reason the
man thought he was attractive, at least he tried to behave as if he
did. But then working for forensics perhaps sharpened a person's
talent for self-deception. After all, every day of the week the boys

down there had to pretend that the dreadful smells that accompanied their work didn't exist. It was vital for survival.

But forensics aside they were all an ugly bunch, all of Cohen's 'fans'. He wouldn't have minded so much if at least one of them were still young, for at forty he was beginning to have difficulty attracting women himself and relying on charm and exquisite sexual technique only worked if he operated alone or in concert with a younger and more attractive man. But Demir, at any age, had never stood a prayer.

'Well, Cohen?'

The door to the office swung open and Suleyman entered. He smiled at them both and Cohen smiled back. Ah, his favourite person, *the* man to go out on the pull with—if only he would come. Cohen looked down at Demir. The Goat was scowling. He knew it! Cohen laughed inwardly to himself. Jealousy! What a fool Demir made of himself every time Suleyman crossed his path—and the whole station knew it!

'What can I do for you, Sergeant?' He walked over to his desk and shoved Demir out of his seat. 'Let the Sergeant sit down, you!'

Suleyman was a little embarrassed by this display of naked preference and started to protest. 'Oh, Demir, please, no...'

But Demir got to his feet and tucked his shirt into his trousers. If Mehmet Suleyman was in the room, it was time for him to leave. 'It's all right—Sir,' he said, flinging a very unpleasant glance at Cohen. 'I was just leaving.' He stomped heavily towards the open door and left. He did not do his colleagues the courtesy of closing it behind him.

'Ugly bastard!' muttered Cohen under his breath.

'Yes, well...' said Suleyman, slipping into the recently vacated seat. 'Cohen, it's about that information the Inspector wanted you to get on the Gulcu family.'

Cohen pulled up an empty waste-paper bin, inverted it and sat down on it opposite his colleague. His face looked tired, bored and defeated. Suleyman knew the signs. Cohen didn't hide much. His mobile, almost comic little face was used to expressing exactly what it felt, whenever it felt it.

'We're looking at very little progress here, aren't we, Cohen?'

'You could say that.'

'Oh, no!' Suleyman groaned. 'The Inspector will go crazy. You knew it was important! What have you been doing?'

Cohen lit a cigarette and waved it at Suleyman between two very yellow and oily-looking fingers. 'Oh, I've been working on it, Mehmet! I have! It's just that I can't find much. Well, nothing. Really.'

'Nothing?' Suleyman narrowed his eyes. 'What do you mean?'

Cohen pulled a notebook from beneath his telephone and opened it on the desk in front of him. 'This is what I mean, right. The house, number 12, Karadeniz Sokak, is registered as belonging to Mr Mehmet Gulcu. All the services, with the exception of one I'll tell you about in a minute, are registered to him also. He, apparently, pays the bills.' He paused, seemingly for some sort of dramatic effect.

'Yes? Well?'

'Unfortunately Mehmet Gulcu, bachelor, died in September 1935. He apparently had no children and left behind him only a strong and irrational desire to continue to pay his bills and taxes from beyond the grave.'

Suleyman rubbed his chin thoughtfully. Mehmet he supposed had to have been the old woman's sort-of husband. 'What about Maria, Natalia and Nicholas Gulcu?'

Cohen gave him a tired smile. 'Well if they do exist they don't work, don't live anywhere, don't have passports and have never paid taxes. I've looked for them everywhere!'

He knew Cohen, knew how sloppy he could sometimes be. 'Are you sure about this?'

Cohen cast his eyes heavenwards. 'They're not registered in Turkey, Mehmet, I've told you!'

Suleyman's face creased into a frown.

'And then there's the telephone,' said Cohen.

'What about the telephone?'

'Their number is registered under the name of Mrs Demidova. And guess what?'

It wasn't a giant leap. 'Mrs Demidova doesn't exist either?'

'Correct.' Cohen smiled. 'I was just having a final triple check, knowing what old Ikmen's like, when you came in.'

Suleyman sighed. 'So let me get this straight. We've a non-existent family headed by a dead man who possess a telephone registered in the name of someone else who also doesn't exist.'

Cohen clapped his hands.

'The Inspector isn't going to like this at all.' Suleyman bit his lip nervously. Ikmen was going to think he was mad when he told him this lot. He didn't relish the prospect. 'How can they not exist, Cohen? It's not possible! Everybody has to have papers, get a passport, visit the doctor, do a job—'

'You don't need papers to get a job in this city,' observed Cohen. 'In fact, you must know as well as I do that the black economy all but runs the bazaars. I mean, if you arrested everyone in retail who didn't have any papers we probably wouldn't be able to buy anything. I do take your point, Mehmet, but jobs do not come into it if you ask me.'

'True enough. But what about all the other things—bank accounts, military service, just going about the daily round of things? It's very odd, but then...' He sighed. 'Then again I suppose if her name were once Demidova—like a maiden name—and she came into the country as Demidova, she may very well have had papers way back which could I suppose have got lost over time. If she and her children maybe even registered as Demidova. But that doesn't exist either, does it? I...'

Cohen sniffed. 'Seems to me they must've lived on old Mehmet's money.'

'Yes, they could, but what about paying for services and things. I mean unless they've always paid in cash...'

Cohen laughed. 'Perhaps Mehmet Gulcu does all that for them too!'

The look Suleyman gave him was not kind. 'This is serious, Cohen! This is, this is—weird!' He put his hands up to his face. He spoke softly, to himself. 'Who are they?'

Cohen shrugged. 'Immigrants. You know what they're like!'

'Yes, well, Maria Gulcu was at one time, or is, whatever it is. But the others?' He pulled Cohen's notebook towards him. 'How did Mehmet Gulcu die, do you know?'

'No. I must be able to find out though.'

'All right, do so then please, Cohen. I'd better go and tell the Inspector right away.'

'OK.' Cohen started to make his way back over to the filing cabinet. Halfway there, however, he stopped and turned to Suleyman again. 'Oh, Mehmet?'

'Yes?'

'If you like we could go out and pick up some women tonight. Have a few beers, laugh, might even score if we're really lucky—well, *you* might.'

Suleyman gave him a look of complete exasperation, said, 'I think not,' and left the office. Cohen sorted through a stack of papers in the cabinet and pulled those relevant to the top. It was a pity Mehmet wouldn't go out with him, but then he never went out with anyone. Bit of a mystery man really. He wondered vaguely whether perhaps he preferred boys. It wasn't a judgemental thought because Cohen really didn't care. Women, men, items of furniture—it was all the same really. They could still go out on the pick-up, him for the girls and Suleyman for the boys. The young man's body would still bring them over, but there wouldn't be any competition. Perfect really. He would have to ask him about it at a later date. Cohen smiled.

Chapter Ten

IT WAS WITH GREAT RELIEF that Robert Cornelius climbed down from the bus that evening.

As he started to walk up the hill towards his apartment, he felt the beginning of the cool of the night and he could see the relief at its coming written on the faces of the people that he passed. There was almost a carnival atmosphere during the evenings following these long, jungle-humid summer days. Men and women sat in the streets and on their balconies fanning themselves with just about anything that came to hand, drinking from long, cool glasses, their children playing noisily around the shops and in the gutters. All waiting to switch on their lights, shower, and retreat to their bedrooms. There, gasping like beached fish, they would lie grateful and naked on top of their bed-covers. Aching for sleep.

Robert knew how they felt, but he couldn't wait that long. There was a whole bottle of gin in his bedside cabinet and he had every intention of drinking as much of it as he could. He wanted oblivion for a few short hours. Sober it wouldn't leave him alone. Everything that had happened before his visit to the police station had been as nothing compared to that event. That Ikmen was quizzing him both about his past and about Natalia and her family could only mean that the whole lot of them, somewhere along the line, were or could be 'in the frame'. And on top of that he was now starting to wonder whether the answers he had given the policeman had been indeed the 'right' answers. If only he could remember the conversation in detail! If only he could be certain that he hadn't said anything that revealed his own inner insecurities regarding Natalia.

He drew his hand across his sweating brow and turned into the small street that led to his apartment block. Of course he would have to tell Natalia about his interview with the police. Perhaps in a way it was a good thing; it might alert her to the urgency of the situation and force her to tell him what they both really knew was the truth. Overreaction cut in sharply. Of course they would have to leave the country. He didn't want to but it was essential now and his job didn't matter, he was bored with it anyway. Yes, they would go away and he would look after her. It was...

He pulled himself suddenly up short. But why had she done it? Why? She must have had a reason, but what if she refused to tell him? What if there was no reason? What if...? What? Surely no reason could be good enough to excuse murder? Lots of misdemeanours could be brushed aside, but not this. This was a human life! Taking that away from somebody was wrong! In all cases, without exception, wrong!

And then he saw her. She was standing on the steps leading up to the front entrance of his block. His heart jumped. She looked stained and weary and a bead of sweat was running down her neck and between the swellings of her thinly concealed breasts. She did not smile as he approached. He drew level with her and looked down into her face. She returned his gaze coldly, but there was a vulnerability there now that he had rarely seen before. He liked that. It turned him on.

He took her roughly by the elbow and kissed her mouth so hard it was almost a bite.

Arto Sarkissian put the folder down on the metal draining board and pulled on a pair of surgical gloves. The report from the laboratory was bald, factual and very confusing. It had been a day or so since he had seen those peculiar marks on the cadaver's right hand and forearm and he wanted to take another look. That the scientists at the lab would lie about such a thing was impossible, but Arto wanted to be sure. Not of course that his own naked eye could tell him much. But he felt an urge to confirm the facts, his own observations and the data from the tissue samples sent to the laboratory.

He looked across the bleak tile and chrome wastes of the windowless little room and moved towards one of the three marble slabs in the centre. A small hump covered with a white sheet and an unkempt and pathetic foot sticking out at an angle lay on the largest table. Everything was ready, except perhaps Arto himself. He wanted to rub his face vigorously with his hands, to try and pump some life-giving blood into his tired brain, but his surgical gloves both repelled and thwarted his attempt. It was late and he was tired.

Arto Sarkissian had been a police surgeon for fifteen years. In that time he had seen a lot of dead people. Women, men, children, babies. At least one example of every stage of decomposition of the human form had passed through his gentle hands. He tried, every time he pulled the covering sheet away and looked into what remained of another human face, to at least attempt to operate with some semblance of dignity. He knew he always failed. Death was ugly, it was naked, it had no control over its bodily functions and it always stank. He stank too. Even after a shower he could still smell himself—their smell on him.

He drew the sheet up on either side of the corpse and folded it over on to its chest. He wanted to see the arms. He had no desire to see the torso and the head again. He knew what was there, the blood, the acrid sulphuric acid—car battery acid. His stomach turned at the thought, but the lab's analysis couldn't be wrong. Someone had actually taken the trouble to drain a car battery. It took time, effort, the persistence of a driven and malicious psyche. He felt his face burn with anger and he was glad, for once, that he was alone with his 'subject'.

He pulled the body's right arm from under the sheet and held it, knuckles uppermost, to the light. There it was, patch of scar tissue one. Down the right-hand edge of the forearm, extending up the hand and stopping just short of the knuckles. He could even see the place where he had excised the tiny piece of tissue to send off to the lab. He turned the arm over and examined the palm of the hand. Patch of scar tissue two, palm of the hand, extending to the tips of the fingers and the thumb. That he had missed such obvious blemishes during his first examination seemed strange to him now. The massive scarring leapt out at him, throwing itself into relief. Perhaps the appalling acid injuries had distracted his attention, perhaps he just wasn't much good any more. He allowed himself a little laugh and pulled the heavy, cold arm up level with his eyes. 'Severe burns, probably consistent with the handling or use of gunpowder' was how the lab had described them. They were old too, sustained when the victim was a very young man, sixty or maybe seventy years ago. Arto looked at the deep discoloration and traced the edges with his finger. Where the damaged tissue met the healthy skin, ridges of hard, callused flesh had formed like small mountain ranges. It was obvious that no attempt had ever been made to repair the damage with grafts. Meyer had probably just bound the affected areas in bandage and hoped that infection wouldn't set in, a not unusual way of dealing with a wound in the early part of the century. Arto wondered how his subject would have managed with the pain in the weeks or even months that it must have taken for his burns to heal. He could clearly see evidence of puckering, the painful fusing of pieces of burnt tissue. On the palm this was so bad that he doubted whether splaying of the hand had been possible since.

Arto replaced the arm and leant his back against the opposite slab. It was intriguing to speculate how the injuries had been sustained. Of course it was hardly germane to the current investigation, but then Arto wasn't really concerned directly with that. Finding who had murdered Leonid Meyer was Çetin Ikmen's job and one that Arto didn't envy him. Rumour had it that the authorities wanted the Meyer case brought to a successful conclusion as soon as possible. He could imagine the pressure and it made him glad that he was an academic and not a man of action.

He walked back to the sink, removed his surgical gloves and threw them into a waste bin. Lolling down on the draining board, he pored once again over the results of the laboratory report. At the bottom of the second page, Dr Belge, the author of the document, suggested that a consultation with Faud Ismail in ballistics might prove instructive should Arto wish to know how the burns were sustained. He did want to know, it had piqued his interest and he was certain that Çetin would be curious too.

Arto took off his lab coat and flung it into the laundry basket. He looked at his watch and saw that it was already nearly eight o'clock. He shrugged. His day was not finished, but it didn't matter. His wife, God rot her, wouldn't miss him. Arto scowled briefly and then turned his mind to other, more professional things. He had to telephone Çetin Ikmen, pass on his latest findings, and give him the rather surprising news about the regurgitated food found near the entrance to Meyer's apartment. It wasn't the old man's, and its main constituent was not usual, and yet it had been expelled on the day of Meyer's death. Unless evidence turned up to the contrary it would seem very likely that it had belonged to the murderer. An odd thing which painted a curious picture. A torturer with a weak stomach, someone not cut out for killing. A calculated, brutal, but nevertheless amateur murder.

Arto walked through into his small adjoining office and picked up the telephone.

'You went to police!' Her voice was a screech, ugly.

'I didn't really have much of a choice, Natalia! They came and got me!'

She slapped the palm of her hand against her forehead and muttered a familiar Turkish oath.

'They didn't want to know anything about you!' Robert lied. It seemed pointless at this stage to increase her anxiety, if that were possible. 'They wanted to know about me, some incidents in my past. Back in London, years ago.'

She hopped nervously, almost pawing the ground with her feet, and yet despite her agitation she had, he felt, that look in her eye, that teasing sensual expression that never failed to arouse him. He felt his flesh stir. Hardly appropriate, given her distress, but he couldn't help himself. Without thinking he put his hand out towards her and slipped it between the thin material of her blouse and her flesh.

'No!' She turned her head and pulled his hand away. Eyes ablaze she punched him roughly from her with one hard, clenched fist.

Even under such fraught circumstances, it came as a shock. Robert gasped. He staggered a little from the blow, but managed to retain his balance, if not his dignity.

He knew he'd behaved badly, made a play for sex at the wrong time, but he still wanted her. For a few seconds they stood perfectly still, staring like two gladiators across the arena of Robert's lounge, both, for different reasons, breathing with difficulty. Although unable to think straight, Robert was hit by the distasteful notion that since the murder and his deepening suspicion about his lover, he had actually wanted her more. It was not the first time that thought had occurred. Even as they stood facing each other out, she twisted, spiky with anger like a weasel, he ached to get inside her body, to take her.

Robert knew that if he wanted to, he could rape her. In this mood she would fight, but it didn't stop him wanting to do it. He was stronger than her, he'd proved it before. He moved just a fraction of an inch towards her, but then he stopped. This was the bestial side, that side he'd wanted to leave behind, but hadn't. Oh, if only she would come to him willingly! If only she loved him the way he loved her! But he knew now that she didn't. He'd always really known. And yet that seemed to make him want her even more, if that were possible. He couldn't, daren't, touch her. His erection hurt and he crumpled down on to the sofa with a groan. 'For Christ's sake, Natalia!'

'What?' She looked at him with disgust, her lip curled; she knew what he wanted. Her head was very high and there was an icy light in her eyes. Cruel. 'What you want, Robert?'

He groaned and leant forward as if trying to cover and protect his aching genitals. 'I want you!'

'You want fucking with me!' she screamed.

It was so loud that Robert put his fingers up to his lips and went 'Sssh!' He didn't want the neighbours, if they were in, to hear her language, or old Ali the *kapıcı* for that matter. Especially old Ali. But she ignored him.

'You want stinking piss inside my beautiful body!' Hot tears flew from her eyes and splashed like rain in the air around her face. It was such an excessive, insane display that for a few moments Robert found himself incapable of either movement or thought. Only the faintly unpleasant sensation of his penis softening penetrated his absorption in her madness. She screamed again. 'What I do, Robert! You fucking go to police!'

Beautiful, tapered hands flew convulsively up to her face and long red fingernails clawed deeply into her cheeks. Robert came to with a jolt. *Christ, she's going to tear her own eyes out!*

In an instant he was up. He rushed across the room and caught her wrists in his hands before she drew blood. As he touched her, she screamed as if burnt, but he held on. Just gently, but nevertheless firmly, he shook her as if trying to vibrate some sense into her hysterical head. Her mouth opened, but no sound came out. Then her eyes closed and her lips curled and stretched back as if she were in physical agony. Robert pulled her still closer and stroked her face softly with one finger. Natalia gave in. She toppled forward, crushing her head into his shoulder and he felt the wetness of her tears through his thin shirt. She cried bitterly for several minutes. Her sobs were long and heartbreaking, like those of a small, distressed child. Robert, of course, knew why she was so shaken by his visit to the police and he knew that he should hate her, even perhaps fear her, but he couldn't. It was too late for that. He stared steadily ahead, rocking her. The thick heat pressed hard upon his sweat-soaked body and despite her presence he felt very alone. He'd slipped into this thing via the long corridor of love and now he couldn't get out.

When he felt sure that she would do herself no further damage, Robert released her hands and put his arms around her shoulders. The force of his dark passion, that old, uncontrollable friend, had evaporated, and it was with a brother's rather than a lover's hand that he eventually led her over to the sofa and helped dry her sodden face with a tissue. Christ, she actually thought he had betrayed her! How could she think that? Was she so afraid, was she so guilty? Did she place so little trust in him? Could she really not tell that it didn't matter to him what she did or had done?

As her breathing regained a regular and steady rhythm once more, Robert slipped into his bedroom and returned a few seconds later with a bottle of gin and two glasses. However she felt, he, at least, needed a drink. He sat down beside her and poured them both large measures. She drank without thanks or expression, giving him no cause to apologise for lack of mixers.

Robert, a veteran of numerous lonely sessions with neat gin, gulped his down in one and then poured himself another. For what he was about to say, he needed some fortification. Over the last few days the truth had dawned almost without him noticing and although he had tried to fight it, he had an admission to make to her and he had to make it quickly before his courage died. He hoped that it would change things. Perhaps it would even make her love him, really love him.

He took a deep breath. 'Natalia, if you did kill that old man it won't make the slightest bit of difference to the way I feel about you. I love you.'

He heard her take a last gulp of gin and swallow. She stared blankly into her now empty glass and then poured herself another large measure of spirit.

For a second Robert wondered whether she had actually heard him. But she had. He knew she just didn't know what to say. What he actually wanted himself was a mystery too. An admission of guilt? Perhaps—although he shuddered away from the thought. He told her again. 'I love you and I will do anything and everything I have to to help and protect you. I...'

It was a terrible admission and his voice failed him, his throat closing against revealing further evidence of the depths to which his infatuation had made him sink. He tipped his glass to his lips and then rested his head back against the wall behind. He stared fixedly at the ceiling and wondered what sort of thing he was becoming. He didn't know. In love he became unpredictable, even to himself. Events happened; things, maybe parts of him, got broken or went missing—or so it seemed. It had never been any different. Even before Betty, even with 'casual' girls in pubs and at discos, it had always been the same. Take them home, possess them, put them in an apron and never let them go. A woman was comfort, warmth, a wall of breasts and belly against the blackness 'out there', against the cold and inevitable loneliness of life. Sometimes he got hurt or he hurt one of his lovers—that was inevitable, especially in view of the fact that there was only ever really room for one important lover in his life at any given moment. Quick screws, to which he did sometimes succumb, amidst much self-loathing, were one thing, but it was always the main lover that was important. In the end not much mattered, only her—whoever she happened to be at the time. And Natalia was the greatest of them all. He had realised that very early on, despite all the difficulties. She was beauty, his kind; he could lose himself in her flesh, her belly and breasts.

He felt the pressure of fingers on his leg and looked down.

'I don't kill anyone, Robert.' Her words were slow, calm and deliberate. 'Not me.'

Her eyes were so clear and lovely that he almost believed her. But Robert knew what little snakes they all were—women. His wife had lied too, consistently. Women's weakness, they couldn't help it. But he was disappointed. If she would only share it with him, he could wrap her guilt up in his love and take her away.

'Mr Meyer was a very good man.' Her words broke his train of thought and he looked down at her questioningly. Was she just deceiving herself with this show of affection for the murder victim or what? If she was, it was a good performance. 'Mr Meyer, the dead man. He help Grandmother out from Russia.'

'Oh?'

'Yes. They come to Turkey together after Revolution. For little time they were lovers.'

Robert recharged his glass and leant back into the depths of his sofa. 'Go on.'

'Leonid Meyer then take job in a cotton factory. He work for the German man called Mr Smits. He was not a good man, this Mr Smits.'

Robert had the distinct impression that something very important was being said here. But whether its importance stemmed from the truth or from some darker motive, he couldn't tell. In addition, he was almost certain that he had heard the name Smits somewhere before. 'And so?' he said.

'This man Smits one day see Grandmama and say to Leonid Meyer that he want her for himself.' Her eyes widened as her story unfolded, making her once again animated and even more beautiful. 'Leonid Meyer argue with Smits about this and Smits then put him on a very bad job at the factory.'

'So what happened then?'

'When the war begin in Europe, lot of people here agree with the Germans. So Mr Smits get rid of Leonid Meyer from his job, say to him, "You go from here now, you dirty Jew," and—'

'Oh, what!' Of course! Now he remembered. Ikmen had mentioned someone called Smits, almost in passing, but...

Natalia looked at him questioningly. 'What is it, Robert?'

'I'll tell you in a moment. Go on.'

She shrugged. 'There is little more to tell. From that day Smits hate Leonid Meyer. Make certain he never get other job again. Leonid Meyer very unhappy always.' She looked up at him. 'What is wrong, Robert?'

'The police asked me about this Smits man, I'm sure of it. Whether I knew him—I said that I didn't. It was only a brief mention, but...I suppose it may indicate that they are seriously considering his part in—'

'Grandmama,' she put in, as if the old woman were the only authority on the matter of any merit, 'believe that they do not take seriously this Smits.'

Although his eyes were, as ever, filled with love for her, Robert also now viewed Natalia with some caution. 'Oh?'

'Also,' she continued, 'it may be that this man has some place in this problem that they do not yet know.'

Robert felt part of his mind harden as he considered what her words might mean.

But Natalia, as she so often did, pre-empted him before he could speak. 'We cannot, as I tell you before, because of trouble with immigration, make any more conversation with police. Who can say what will happen if they know I am with Leonid Meyer on that day? But if some other person were to tell them about this man...'

'You mean like me?'

'Yes.'

He stood up and rubbed his head with his hands. Both her strange and troubling mood swings and her disturbing words were, together with the enormous midsummer heat, fuddling his brain. 'But I can't say anything about this Smits to the police,' he said, 'I've told them I don't know him. I mean they'll want to know where I got my information from. And that's apart from the fact that this man may well be entirely innocent.' He turned to face her. 'What do you want me to do?'

'I do not know,' she said simply, 'but if you can think of something to help us in this situation then I would be grateful. And this man Smits...well, Grandmama say he was a Nazi person, so...'

'You know that for a fact?' He so wanted to do as she asked, so wanted for her to be grateful.

She smiled. 'Oh yes. Smits was a Nazi, that is sure.'

He took her hands in his. 'All I can say, Natalia, is that I will try and—'

'You are clever man, you will do.' She kissed him, silencing any further protest or doubt. And as her embrace took effect upon his body, as he once again slid his hand between the thinness of her blouse and the thickness of her breast, Robert surrendered entirely to his feelings. If Natalia said that she had nothing to do with the murder then why not just believe her? And if someone who was, or had been, a Nazi could possibly be implicated then why not nudge things along in that direction? Quite how, he did not know yet, however...

And yet...

And yet what if she were...

He felt one of her hands slip quickly, like a small dextrous fish, inside the waistband of his trousers. And for the rest of their time together his internal wrangling stopped completely.

Chapter Eleven

ÇETIN IKMEN ROLLED OVER on to his back and peered myopically at the face of his watch. Ten to six. Just too late to try and get some more sleep (although that was a joke) and too early to start moving around. He cursed and then hit the back of the couch with murderous intent. Many more nights like this and he would go insane.

It wasn't that he actually resented Fatma for consigning him to the couch. It wasn't even that he would have actually preferred to sleep with her in her current condition. Pregnant, she was both huge and restless and, if he were honest, he would have to admit that being with her would be almost as bad as being where he was now. If only he could find some way to stop almost smothering himself against the back of the confounded thing every time he turned over, he could cope. He had tried just about every position and technique he could think of, but to no avail. The couch, Allah damn it to hell, was far too cunning to allow itself to be outwitted by a mere policeman. It wanted him sleeping down on that awful smelly floor and if he wasn't really, really dedicated to defeating it, that was where he was going to end up.

He cursed again, murmuring the word 'bastard!' under his breath, lest he wake his sleeping family. That done, he sat up and instead of performing his usual morning ritual of reviewing the horrors of another sleepless night, he turned his mind towards the more productive subject of his current case. Just before he and sleep had entered into their familiar nightly battle for supremacy, Ikmen had written down a few notes regarding possible routes through the maze of evidence that had accrued in the Meyer case so far. With one lazy but deft movement he picked a cigarette up off the floor, threw it into his mouth and lit up. Thus fortified, he then lurched across to the light switch, pressed it and flooded the lounge with ghastly neon brilliance. As he shuffled back to the couch from hell, rubbing his eyes as he went, he picked up the notebook from the place where he had dropped it so many agonising hours before—on top of a heap of laundry. Amid a welter of cigarette smoke, he then sat down and reviewed his handiwork. Basically there were three main bodies of information.

Firstly there was the strictly factual evidence. Leonid Meyer, an elderly Jewish man, had been first battered with some sort of blunt instrument and then subjected to torture by sulphuric car battery acid. His death had been protracted and agonising and, having witnessed its course, his assailant had then drawn a large swastika in Meyer's blood on the wall above his head. At some time either before, during or after the event, someone—possibly the assailant—had been sick over by the door. Forensic analysis had since revealed that the main constituent of said mass was principally beetroot. The Englishman, Robert Cornelius, had by his own admission been in the vicinity of Meyer's apartment at the time, as had, rather more tenuously, a large black car— although this latter piece of evidence, it had to be admitted, had come from an old alcoholic who couldn't even remember his own name. In addition, further investigation of the corpse by

Arto Sarkissian had revealed some extremely old but nevertheless deep burn scars on Meyer's hand and arm—scars caused, possibly, by gunpowder. Ikmen, looking at this veritable rag-bag of disconnected evidence, sighed deeply, put his cigarette out and then immediately lit another.

Around these somewhat bizarre facts revolved, so he believed, the two other bodies of information, which he had labelled 'Two Routes to Resolution', as he saw it so far.

The first one concerned the original and most immediately obvious explanation for Meyer's death, which was that of anti-Semitism. Supporting evidence for this included, of course, the swastika, plus the testimonies of both Rabbi Şimon and Maria Gulcu—both of which had included reference to the notion that Meyer had suffered from anti-Semitism before. Against this was the fact that there was not, apart from one address in Meyer's notebook, any hard evidence to suggest that the man who had been named as Meyer's anti-Semitic persecutor had ever known the victim or held such unsavoury views. In any event, their supposed liaison had happened so long ago that it was almost irrelevant. In addition, there was no reason to suppose that anti-Semitism was a growing movement within the city, either amongst the young or, like Smits, the older generation. The only really concrete act of violence against Jews that had come out so far was that which had been perpetrated by Robert Cornelius. And that had happened in England for reasons, if Cornelius were to be believed, which stemmed not from anti-Semitism, but from rather more personal motives.

The second, and perhaps most esoteric, route concerned issues surrounding Meyer's past. One source had expressed the opinion that Meyer had been a member of the Bolshevik party when a young man back in Russia, and Maria Gulcu's reaction had seemed to confirm this. Quite naturally, for those troubled times, he had killed people in the course of his duties. Unusually, however, he had then traded his new life of working-class glory for a life of poverty in a foreign country, firstly with a woman who only ever tolerated him and secondly with his only true love—the bottle. Tortured by guilt and, possibly, fearful lest some, as yet unknown, witness to his old crime should come forward and reveal this horror to the world, Leonid Meyer died without any of the honours the old Soviet Government would have, no doubt, bestowed upon him had he stayed where he was. Those who mourned him included the widow Blatsky and the Gulcu family who, he now knew, possessed absolutely no legal status in Turkey. A group of ghosts headed by the oldest spectre of them all, Maria Gulcu—the woman who could never love or be loved—unlike her granddaughter. And here, once again, was Mr Robert Cornelius, teacher of English, lover of Natalia Gulcu, destroyer of Jews—the only person in the right place at the right time.

And yet, although Cornelius seemed to pop up in each and every body of evidence or route to resolution that was contemplated, what on earth could his motive for killing Meyer be? So he knew the Gulcu family and had once hit out at a Jewish lawyer—that amounted to very little really. Even the fact that he had admitted being in the vicinity of the crime and had been identified didn't mean that he had been involved with it. Although the fact that he had exhibited more than just a passing interest in the mechanics of the death penalty—or rather those people who might be excepted from that process—did strike Ikmen as odd. Unless Cornelius actually had someone in mind with regard to this, his interest would appear to be quite unintelligible.

That Cornelius was close to Meyer's apartment at the time of his death, and that he was also involved with a family who knew the dead man and possibly also knew about that man's guilty past, seemed like more than mere coincidence. However, this did beg the question of why the Englishman had so willingly admitted to being in Balat on that fateful afternoon. Surely if he had known what was happening, he would have at least tried to distance himself from the event?

Ikmen got up, went over to the window and opened the curtains. The full, fierce heat of the day was still several hours away, but already the shopkeepers were washing down the pavements with water. By lunchtime everyone would be well and truly frazzled in the heat and the dust and the ever-present swarm of flies. By then, he knew, thinking would be next to impossible. By then he, like everybody else, would be simply going through the motions. He put the light out, returned to the couch and sat down again.

What his boss, Commissioner Ardiç, wanted was, of course, a neat and quick solution. He'd even told the press that they were indeed on the brink of a major breakthrough. Not that Ikmen had done so in person, of course. He'd made very sure that he was well and truly out of the way when that press conference had started. Ardiç had nearly gone berserk. What he wanted was Smits and, furthermore, Ikmen's backing for the Nazi connection theory. And, to be honest, Ikmen had to agree that if Smits's past or present allegiances could be proved as well as a rather more current connection with Meyer, this probably was the most fruitful direction in which to move. Of all the people that Ikmen had interviewed so far, Rabbi Şimon had seemed to be the most reliable and he had been of the opinion that Smits could be involved at some level. The big black car as reported by the raving alcoholic was a tenuous link but Ikmen had seen such vehicles on Smits's drive.

What really puzzled Ikmen most was not, however, something that was, or seemed to be, central to the case. It was how and indeed why the Gulcu family appeared to live in the country without any official status. There had to be a reason, although he could not fathom what that might be. But that it was connected in some way to Leonid Meyer was, irrationally but pervasively, on his mind. He was just pondering how, now that he was in possession of this fact, he might effectively hide this information from the heavy-handed clutches of immigration until after his investigations were concluded, when the lounge door burst open and his father staggered in.

'Good morning, son,' Timür said as he moved painfully over towards the couch. 'Got a cigarette?'

'Yes, thank you.'

The old man positioned himself next to his son on the edge of the couch and then peered at the notebook in the younger man's hands. 'Well, let's have one then!'

'What?'

'A cigarette!'

'Oh.'

Ikmen picked one up out of his packet, placed it in the old man's mouth and then lit it. Once his coughing had subsided, Timür Ikmen pointed down at the book and cackled. 'Now there's something I haven't seen for a very long time.'

Ikmen, unable to work out what his father was referring to, frowned. 'What?'

'The name Reinhold Smits.'

'You know him?'

'I know of him,' the old man replied. 'What's your interest in him, Çetin?'

'He owns Şeker Textiles, that company that our murder victim once worked for.'

'Oh, Smits owns that, does he?'

'Yes, I think he always has. I told you about it the other day when...'

The old man made a dismissive gesture with his cigarette. 'Oh well, it passed me by then, you know how it is. And besides, with all the companies Smits owns it would be difficult to recall each and every one.'

'So he owns more than just Şeker Textiles, then?' Ikmen asked.

His father shot him a jaundiced glare. 'Marvellous detective you are! Smits owns cotton mills and fields, coal mines, white-goods plants—you name it, he has it. Like most Germans he's very good with money.'

'So, er, how do you know of him then, Timür?'

The old man dragged contentedly on his cigarette before replying. 'When I was a young lecturer I was involved in a demonstration outside one of his places. All his workers went on strike and we went out in support of them.'

'Went on strike? Why?'

'Because Smits had unfairly dismissed a couple of his people. I was very political in those days and—'

'Unfairly dismissed? How?' Ikmen was having a feeling about this, a very bad feeling.

'Well, the 1939 – 45 war had just started and so Smits got rid of these men because they were Jews. He was right behind Adolf Hitler and all that Nazi business, just like his father. It was, I believe, early autumn and...'

But Ikmen wasn't listening any more. Ikmen, in his mind, was very far away. Back with another old man who couldn't or rather, so it appeared, didn't want to address his past.

Robert Cornelius was angry with himself. His last lesson had been a complete disaster. It was one thing having little real interest in your students, but it was quite another actually showing it for all the world to see. If he wasn't careful he was going to lose his job and if he lost his job he lost his apartment too. If only he could focus on something other than Natalia. But he was wasting his time even trying. She had shown him something the previous night, something he had never seen before—a tenderness. Her hands had cradled his pain. Like a small child healing a wounded bird, she had stroked him back to life. Then, just before she left, he'd told her all about Betty. About the hurt. But now he had to help her. He wanted to help her; she was his now, she'd said so. Promised. If only he could think of something!

He'd been back over the problem a dozen times, but he was still no nearer to a solution. What he had to do, somehow, was inform the police that this old Nazi, if indeed he was such, had once had a personal grudge against Leonid Meyer—if indeed he had. All this was based upon pure hearsay which emanated from a source that was, at best, he had to admit, dubious. To further compound the problem, there was also the issue of how he was, if he was, going to tell the police. He neither wanted nor felt that it was wise to tell them directly. If he did, they would probably question his motivation. They would certainly want to know where he, a man by his own admission totally unacquainted with Smits, had got his information from. There was, however, yet another issue that was even more deeply troubling than any of that: why had Natalia asked him to perform this task?

If it had merely been a case of, as she had said, protecting the Gulcu family from further investigation because of their illegal status, that would have been acceptable—just. If only she hadn't been at Meyer's apartment on the day of the murder! If only he hadn't seen her! If only he could believe that she had not been involved in the old man's death!

But he couldn't believe her even though he wanted to more than almost anything else in the world. Even though what she was putting him through now was bad, very bad, for him.

Great curling waves of self-loathing crashed across his tortured mind. What kind of person even contemplated feeding false information to the police? Even if this Smits man were a Nazi that was still a million miles away from the assumption that he was a killer too! Putting aside his politics he might even be quite a nice man with grandchildren and charitable interests and all sorts of good things. Because Robert didn't know him he couldn't possibly hazard a guess about what he was like!

But all that was, unfortunately, he knew, the rational, lighter side of the argument. The irrational, but to Robert, far weightier and more important side related to Natalia and what she wanted. And because he wanted her, what she wanted had to take precedence. What a foolish, weak, unpleasant little man he was! Complying with the demands of an evil, manipulative girl!

It made him laugh—not because he was happy but because there was nothing else to do in the face of such an abomination. Every mistake he had ever made he could trace back to some woman, or rather his desire to possess some woman. But then unless he wanted to change now, what on earth was the use of pursuing such fruitless lines of thought? And he didn't want to change.

No.

What he wanted was Natalia and in order to get her he had to do this thing—one way or another. If only his mind would work upon the problem. If only he could think without feeling sick!

Think! Think!

Chapter Twelve

'**A**NYONE WOULD THINK that I was asking you to murder somebody!'

Suleyman replaced his car keys in his pocket and sighed. 'Mother...'

'I mean, I think I am being really quite flexible. If you tell me a time I will work with that and—'

'But, Mother, as I have told you several times now, I can't tell you what time I'm going to be home tonight because I don't know what that is going to be myself.'

Nur Suleyman pouted—an expression that was not terribly appropriate either to her age or her position in life. 'But if you can't give me a time then I can't possibly go ahead with tonight's meal. I'll have to tell Auntie and Zuli not to come...'

'But if you hadn't invited them without asking me this wouldn't have happened!'

'I wanted it to be a surprise!'

'What kind of surprise is that!'

She looked for just a moment as if she had been slapped. Suleyman leant against the side of his car and put his hand up to his head, instantly regretting what had just been said.

Recovering herself, Nur Suleyman's face now took on an expression of anger. 'What do you mean by that?'

'I didn't mean anything. I'm sorry, Mother...'

'Do you want to be single and lonely for the rest of your life?'

'No. Look—'

'Well, you're behaving as if that is exactly what you do want. I can't understand you! Your cousin will make an excellent wife—'

'Mother!' He took his car keys out of his pocket again and rattled them in front of her face. 'Not now. I have to go!'

'Oh well, if your job is more important...' Nur turned quickly on her heel and then marched, straight-backed, into the house.

Suleyman sighed and then, pushing himself away from the side of the car, walked around to the driver's side.

'Could I speak to Mr Smits, please?'

'Who is calling?'

'It's Inspector Ikmen.'

The butler paused, although only briefly, before replying, 'I am afraid that Mr Smits has already gone out for the day, sir.'

'Oh.'

'Can I take a message, or...'

'No, no, that's all right. I'll ring back later. Thank you.'

'Thank you, sir.'

Wilkinson replaced the receiver in its cradle and turned to face his master. 'That was Inspector Ikmen, sir. I hope I—'

'Yes, yes,' Smits replied, 'you did absolutely the right thing.' For just a moment he fiddled with a pair of tiny calfskin gloves and then put them, with some determination, on his hands.

'And now I really am going out, Wilkinson,' he said. 'I may be some time.'

As he turned to leave the butler noticed that his face was white.

Suleyman hardly noticed what his fellow road-users were doing as he sat within the grip of heavy traffic along the coast road. Consequently, he was subject to several furious horn-beepings as those behind him attempted to gain those vital extra few metres. Not that such behaviour, on this occasion, bothered him unduly. His mind was far too occupied with replaying the recent altercation with his mother for it to be troubled by a little irate traffic. When one is facing what amounts to in all but name an arranged marriage, most other aspects of one's life pale into insignificance. Not, of course, that Mehmet Suleyman had anyone else but himself to blame for his current situation. The match, which was with his first cousin Zuleika, had been both suggested and set up by his mother and his aunt. Theoretically, at least, he could have said 'no' to this at any time, and considering the fact that the whole idea of his cousin appalled him, it would have been in his own interests to do just that. But, in practice, like a lot of things, it wasn't that simple.

What Nur Suleyman wanted, she tended to get. Both Suleyman and his father had always let her have her own way. The only exception to this rule was his elder brother, Murad, who despite wild protestations from Nur had married a Greek. That he was now, as far as Nur was concerned, a non-person within the family group was quite chilling and, furthermore, demanded the kind of rebelliousness Mehmet Suleyman knew he didn't possess. As a member of the once ruling classes, albeit one with neither money nor social position, Suleyman was aware that he had certain duties and to marry well was one of these. To either deny or attempt to circumvent such a duty went against everything he had been trained to be. That it was making him unhappy was simply a price he had always suspected he would one day have to pay.

Obsessed as he was with these morbid and uncomfortable thoughts he hardly noticed the passing scenery as he battled his way towards the centre of the city. This condition only held, however, until he was obliged to stop the car to allow a large limousine to exit from between a pair of tall iron gates. Not that the place itself was instantly familiar—there were many such large entrances to old mansions along this stretch of road— but Smits's drawn little face in the back of the limousine was unmistakable.

It was a terrible thought. Robert had first noticed it growing towards the end of the last lesson. It had started slowly at first, but then, suddenly and unaccountably, it had accelerated, weaving its way into his brain like a maggot. He'd been appalled, but it lodged there looking at him. For a while he fought it and, to his credit, it was a brave fight. But this thought had allies: panic, fear, the needs of his own body. He should have silenced it earlier, he knew that now.

Because it wouldn't let go, Robert cried off his next class, pleading a sick headache. It pleased the students, he could tell. When he announced the cancellation, they didn't exactly cheer, but he could see the relief on their faces, the sweet anticipation of time spent munching burgers and discussing their unwanted virginity. If he had cared, it would have been an insult.

Although claiming to be sick, he didn't go home. The idea of his silent, empty apartment appalled him. Instead he sat in a corner of the staff room and smoked. At least there he was on the periphery of reality; people coming and going; the sound of ridiculous or boring chatter. It didn't drown the voice of the thought, but it prevented it from completely overwhelming him. He knew this stuff. These things were all basically the same. With others around it could nag rather than scream. Alone, he would be entirely at its mercy. Robert didn't want to be alone, because that way he knew he didn't stand a chance. It was just too bloody good.

He stubbed one cigarette out and immediately lit another. He didn't really like chain-smoking, it made him feel sick, but he had to do something. If he did absolutely nothing people would become concerned. But closing his eyes and pretending to be asleep wasn't a solution—he'd tried that. As soon as his lids had drooped, he'd felt the thought hook its icy fingers round his testicles.

Robert didn't want to do it. It was good, but he didn't want to do it. The thought constantly showed him the advantages, but the disadvantages were immense. They far outweighed the benefits, but only, and unfortunately, on the rational plane. In the domain of the emotions, Robert's real home, where logic is useless and the rational mind a joke, there was nothing to be done but follow the long finger of the thought. And yet he could see, despite the fluffy and appealing images that littered this path of the heart, exactly where it led. Brief sweetness gave rapidly over into a space that contained nothing. An echoing, doorless room, waiting to be filled.

'Do you want a paracetamol?'

He hadn't noticed Rosemary slip into the chair beside him. She could have been there for hours for all he knew. Looking inward with such intensity blinds the eyes. His answer was stupefied and sounded drugged, even to his own ears. 'What?'

'A paracetamol. Helena said you had a headache...'

'Oh.' He looked at her eyes and was shocked by the level of concern he found there. Perhaps he looked terrible? Robert made an attempt at a slight smile. 'No, no thanks.'

She moved her powdery face close to his. 'Are you all right, dear?'

Robert felt himself start to panic. Rosemary, though notoriously vague, was no fool. Again he wondered how he looked. He put his hand to his chin and heard a faint rasping sound as his fingers dragged across his unshaven flesh. He moved his hand up; his cheeks were still unmistakably flushed from the previous night's gin. He didn't need a mirror to tell him that he looked a fright. His appearance was probably the reason why Rosemary persisted. It was unlike him. Robert was always at least clean and tidy, well, he had been until—When had it all started? How many awful days now?

'Robert...' Rosemary frowned. 'Don't you think you should go home?'

'Oh, no! No! It's OK—really.'

But Rosemary wasn't convinced. She touched his knee lightly with her fingers. Robert froze.

'If this girl is giving you this much grief, I'd get out if I were you.'

As he turned to face her, Robert felt pain as the taut muscles in his neck unwillingly moved. He could see by the expression on her face that he was answering her advice with hard and contemptuous eyes.

She looked sadly down at the floor and sighed. 'Just a thought, Robert.'

He felt ashamed. Poor Rosemary, she hadn't deserved a killing look, she was only trying to be kind. But it was too late. She rose from her chair and smoothed her skirt down towards her knees. Robert didn't follow her with his eyes. She'd momentarily drowned out the voice of the thought and perhaps that had been wrong. Perhaps he shouldn't have spoken to her at all. Speaking was sometimes bad. He'd spoken to the headmaster about the Norris twins and Billy on numerous occasions, but it had never done any good. Betty likewise. Best to keep silent, like back at school when he was a child. The thought was good in that it gave structure, direction. Just like school really—good old Christ's Hospital. The other way there was too much freedom, too many paths. Some could be right, but he knew that he would choose the wrong one, he knew it! Then he would be alone again, single, without her. People like Rosemary just couldn't understand.

Rebuffed, Rosemary walked away from him and joined the

small cluster of people around the coffee machine. She looked back at him once, but as she became more involved in the trite niceties of break time she soon stopped paying him attention. Briefly, but without real concern, he wondered whether her conversation was about him, but he decided that it wasn't. They were all laughing, so it couldn't possibly be. It was about sex, the latest staff conquests. He felt sorry for them. The fleeting ego-building one-nighters with foreigners young enough to be their sons or daughters. The last resort of the desperate middle-aged ex-pat.

The thought resurfaced.

In order to make the thing work, he had to go over to this Smits's textile plant which was, she had said, somewhere in Üsküdar. Location was important and actually doing it there would lend the thing the credence that he felt it needed. In addition, he had to think himself into the role of a racist of death-dealing magnitude in which the police had cast him. That was not easy because it was so dreadful, so utterly unlike the person that he really was. But then for the purposes of the thought, which was to be the instrument of his continuance with Natalia, he had to put things like that to one side.

He bent his mind to discovering what kind of words and beliefs someone associated with Smits might express. Silently, at first, he mouthed the word 'Jew'. The strangeness of its resonance appalled him. Was it perhaps because they were such an ancient race or maybe because hatred of them, on account of the 'death' of Christ, was so ingrained inside the European psyche that the word, now attended, made him feel so odd? Despite the already stifling heat, Robert shuddered. If just simply thinking of a word in a particular context could elicit such deep, if repellent, reactions, how much more might saying or writing or acting upon these feelings achieve? He thought about people, thin like sticks, starved beyond sanity. And then of others, their long medieval robes flapping in the crisp, Northern European wind as grave-faced men in black pushed them roughly into huge, devouring bonfires. Even playing around with such images appalled him, and yet…and yet he had to do it because she wanted and needed him to and what if the old man were guilty and…and…

'Jew.' He said it this time. Not loudly, but audibly enough for a few heads to turn in his direction. For some reason, it made him laugh, although not for long because several other of his colleagues were watching now, their faces both puzzled and concerned.

Under normal circumstances, whatever they were, he knew that he should have been grateful in some way for their concern. But he wasn't. They were nothing, nobodies to him. His mind was filled only with her now and, emboldened by his obsession and in order to place the idea firmly in his mind, he said it again.

'Jew.'

Now they were all looking at him; looking and wondering and not knowing in any sense what he knew. Robert smiled. This secret was his and hers—this awful, repellent, death-defying deed.

When he did finally rise from his seat, he did so slowly and without a word. I'm going to do it now, he said to himself, right now. Many eyes watched as he made his way to his little cupboard-like office and closed the door behind him.

Despite the gravity, not to mention the unpleasantness that underlined the occasion, Reinhold Smits did smile when he saw her. He couldn't help it. Though so very much older than the woman that he remembered from all those years ago, she was still, unmistakably, herself. Still arrogant, still unsmiling, still marvellously regal.

'Hello, Maria,' he said.

She held her hand out to him, the knuckles glittering with diamonds. 'Reinhold.'

He took it and, bowing over the outstretched claw, brushed his lips lightly against the crumpled skin. 'I don't have to tell you why I have come.'

'No,' she replied, 'you do not. Please sit down.'

He took the chair beside her bed, smoothing the legs of his trousers as he sat. 'Whatever you may think,' he said, 'I didn't kill Leonid.'

'You had ample reason to do so.'

He nodded his head in assent. 'Yes. But then he had reason to want me dead also.'

Her short laugh came out like a cough. 'I don't think so! You took his job, which was nothing. As for me and my relationship with Leonid...'

'Yes?'

'You never got me, Reinhold, in either the romantic or the political sense. Leonid had no reason to want your death.'

He smiled a small but none the less acknowledging smile. 'Yes, I see.' Whether he did or not only Smits would know, but now he changed the subject. 'And so how are you, Maria? How is what is left of your life?'

'I am who I always was, Reinhold, and I remain, in that sense, as it were at your mercy. But for you, being in thrall to Leonid must have been extremely galling.'

He sighed. 'It was at first. But as the years passed...'

'You must have given him a fortune during that time. Most of which he poured down his throat.' She slid her eyes upwards to meet his. 'Was it all worth it?'

'In the beginning, yes.'

'And later?'

Unable or unwilling to meet her gaze for any longer, Reinhold Smits shifted his attention to the floor. 'As far as I am aware, all those who could or would substantiate Leonid's stories either disappeared or died many years ago.'

'But you kept on paying?'

He shrugged. 'What else could I do? He still possessed the photographs and besides he couldn't work again after I dismissed him. I provided him with no references and his escalating drunkenness precluded even illegitimate work. We were both, if you like, in thrall to each other, a situation which suited us, and anyway, without the paltry little amounts from my ample coffers, he would have starved.'

'How very humane of you.'

He turned back to face her, but this time his expression was filled with disgust. 'Well, somebody had to do it! And even though it wasn't me who put him in that position in the first place and even though he hurt and frightened me beyond—'

'You have only yourself to blame!' She stabbed one hard, unforgiving finger dangerously close to his eyes. 'If you hadn't been such a monstrous pervert, Leonid would not have had cause to do what he did!'

'In order to protect you!'

'Yes.' Although seated she pulled her neck up to its full height and raised her eyebrows so that she was looking down upon him. 'Back then my life was at stake, Reinhold. My life! What you wanted to do would have exposed me to all manner of dangers, not from one, but from many quarters. That my use of Leonid to prevent you from doing that caused you both so much discomfort is very sad, but I'm afraid that from my point of view, it was very well worth doing!'

A long silence followed her outburst. Time during which both of them reflected, for their own reasons, upon things that had been, things that were far from edifying. But when the conversation did resume the subject, for the time being, was changed.

'You look very well,' she said.

He smiled. 'Chemotherapy is a marvellous preservative.'

'Oh.' For the first time during their meeting she looked both confused and at a disadvantage. 'I'm sorry.'

'There's really no need,' he said. 'I've done everything that I ever wanted to do, plus more. I have no complaints—bar one, of course.'

'And what is that?'

He looked up at her, but this time he did not smile. 'I should like to be left alone by the police. Should like to die with my reputation intact.'

'I see.' She reached across to her bedside table, took a cigarette out of one of her packets and lit up.

'In part,' he continued, 'I suppose that it was my own fault really. Had I not written to offer my condolences to you on the death of Leonid, you might have quite forgotten about me altogether—'

'I doubt that!'

'But then to mention my name to the police was, even for you, Madam Maria, a little spiteful, don't you think?'

'If, as you say, Reinhold, you had nothing to do with Leonid's death, then surely whatever information I may or may not have given to the police is irrelevant.'

It was so like her to push the argument back on to his shoulders. She was, and always had been, so dreadfully sly. How little the years had changed her. Quite suddenly, Reinhold Smits lost all patience with niceties and became, for such an old man, fiercely animated. 'As I believe I said to you on the telephone, I will not tolerate your groundless and, to my mind, unbalanced spite!'

She laughed at him. 'This, from a Nazi! Really, Reinhold, I—'

'My beliefs have nothing to do with it! There—'

'Listen, Reinhold, the police already knew that Leonid had worked for you at some time. And, to be fair, your opinions were not unknown at the time. Besides...' Here she paused. She took a long deep-lunged drag upon her cigarette and looked him straight in the eyes.

'Besides what?' he said, his eyes still flaming with too long pent-up rage.

'Besides, whether you killed Leonid or not, you were in his apartment on the day that he died, weren't you?'

'No, I...' His words denied it, but his face, which was now the colour of ashes, told a different story.

Maria Gulcu smiled. 'Remember when you telephoned me just after the police had been to visit you?'

'Yes, it was—'

'Remember what was said? The conversation we had about when and how Leonid died?'

Something, maybe even, he thought, his poor, tired old heart, tightened in his chest. 'Yes?'

'Remember how we wondered how someone could batter an old man so savagely and how you said that even despite your beliefs you thought it was absolutely dreadful that the murderer had then drawn a large swastika in Leonid's blood just above his head?'

'I do recall it, yes. What is your point?'

'The point, Reinhold'—she smiled again, this time revealing all of her yellowing teeth—'is that, try as I might, I cannot find any reference to such an occurrence in any of the newspaper reports I have read about the incident.'

Without moving his head, he slid his eyes away from hers. 'Well, then, I suppose...Well, the police must have told me it...'

'Oh, I don't think so, Reinhold.' Her voice was soft now, honeyed, almost seductive. 'They certainly didn't tell me about it. And if you consider the thing logically, that does make sense.'

'How?'

'Well, if you were a policeman who was confronted with a bizarre and possibly racially motivated crime, would you want to let every madman in the vicinity know about such a thing? Crazy people have been known to copy such acts. I'm not saying that you are lying, Reinhold, but I think that the likelihood of Inspector Ikmen furnishing you with such information is very slight.'

He wrapped his arms protectively about his thin body and put his head down. 'But he must have! He did! How could he not have?'

'I don't know,' she said and then, grinding her cigarette out in her ashtray, she posed him a question. 'You tell me, Reinhold. You tell me?'

'So what time, approximately, was it when you saw old Smits?'

'It must have been about nine.'

'Are you sure?'

Suleyman shrugged. 'Fairly.'

Ikmen smiled, one of his evil I-know-something-that-you-don't grins. 'His butler told me he'd already gone when I called at eight-fifteen.' He sat down and put his feet up on the top of the desk. 'I get the impression that Mr Smits doesn't want to talk to us any more. I don't suppose you saw where he went?'

'He turned off at Dolmabahçe, towards Taksim.'

'Mmm.' Ikmen took time out to light up a cigarette and then look at, if not attend to, a rather large lump of dirt beneath his fingernails. 'I need to do a bit of historical research concerning Mr Smits today, Suleyman.'

The younger man moved just fractionally in the direction of the ever-closed window, but came to a somewhat embarrassed halt when he saw the expression on his superior's face.

Rather more diplomatically than usual, Ikmen made no reference to what had occurred and continued smoothly along his train of thought. 'My dear father informed me in the early hours of this morning that he remembers Smits and, further-more, recalls him as a known Nazi sympathiser.'

Suleyman sat down. 'Interesting.'

'Yes, I thought so too, although confronting Smits with information received from my elderly father is hardly profes-sional, even though I happen to believe every word of it.'

'So what are you going to do?' Suleyman asked.

Ikmen took a small notebook out of his trouser pocket and thumbed through its pages until he reached the relevant place. 'I'm going to see a Professor Mazmoulian, modern history expert up at the university. He has, so Timür tells me, encyclopaedic knowledge of the social history of this city. It is something of a passion with him.'

'So when are you doing this then, sir?'

'The good professor said that he'd see me at midday. If my luck really has deserted me, he may even treat me to lunch in the canteen which, if memory serves me right, is to good food what impotence is to good sex.'

Suleyman smiled. 'I see.'

'But then if the professor has any information on old Smits it will all have been worth it—I suppose.'

'Yes.' Suleyman, for want of anything else to do, briefly fiddled with the few neat items on his desk. 'So am I coming with you, or...'

'No. No, I'd like you to do something else today, Suleyman.' Ikmen looked up and smiled before speaking again. It was, he had always thought, important to accompany unpleasant news with a cheerful countenance. 'I'd like you to do a bit of surveillance today.'

'Oh.' Suleyman felt his face fall, even though he didn't really want to show his feelings in this way. Surveillance was notoriously stressful, time-consuming and dull.

But Ikmen chose to ignore his feelings anyway. 'Yes, Robert Cornelius, the Englishman. I'd like you, at a discreet distance of course, to see where he goes, what he does, who he talks to.'

'All right, but...'

'But what?'

'But I didn't think we had a lot on him and—'

'We don't,' Ikmen said, 'not really. But that he seems to figure in just about all of the possible scenarios we've identified so far I can't help thinking is of significance.'

'He does?'

Ikmen looked at him quizzically and then, identifying his mistake, he apologised. 'Oh yes, of course, I haven't let you in on my recent musings, have I? Right, well, look, Suleyman, I think I'm going to be pretty tied up today, as are you. What do you think about having a case conference at my apartment tomorrow? I mean, I know it's our day off and—'

'That would not be a problem, sir.'

'Oh, good. We should also, hopefully, be able to review Dr Sarkissian's latest findings by then.'

Suleyman stood up, took his car keys off his desk and put them in his pocket. 'I thought Dr Sarkissian had completed his work on this case.'

'He had, but then he found something else that...Look, I'll tell you all about it tomorrow. Get over to the Londra Language School now and see what you can see. Chart his whole day and don't let him see you. Be aware too that if he decides to go off to a club or something, you'll be on until the small hours...'

'That's perfectly all right with me, sir.'

Strangely for Suleyman, or so Ikmen thought, he appeared to be almost relishing the prospect of being out all night. But then if that was what he wanted to do...

'All right then, Suleyman, I'll see you tomorrow then— unless, of course, something dramatic happens.'

'See you tomorrow, sir.'

After Suleyman had gone, Ikmen closed his eyes for a few moments and tried to imagine what Mr Smits might be thinking at that moment in time. The images this conjured up were rather strange.

Chapter Thirteen

A TALL, THIN INDIVIDUAL sauntered into the reception area and smiled very expansively at the man who was his visitor. 'Hello, Arto, how are you?'

'Faud!' Arto got up and took the man's hand warmly. 'I hope I wasn't—'

'No! I was just having a break, as it happens.' Faud Ismail smiled. His was a handsome face in a casual, vaguely dissolute sort of way. He patted Arto's broad back warmly. 'What can I do for you?'

Arto picked up his briefcase. 'I want you to have a look at some photographs for me, Faud. I want your professional opinion. It's Çetin Ikmen's Balat murder victim.'

Ismail looked confused and put his hand up to his head. 'I wasn't aware there was ballistic involvement in that case?'

'There's not, at least not as regards the murder itself.' Arto clicked his tongue impatiently. It wasn't easy to explain. 'Look, Faud, can we go through to your office?'

'Of course.'

Ismail turned and led the way out into a long, cigarette-butt-strewn corridor.

At the end of the corridor he pushed open the door directly ahead of them and went into his office. It was a strange place, to Arto's way of thinking. Large colour posters of handguns lined the walls, some complete, others in section, showing their inner chambers and mechanisms. Gun manuals the size of computer instruction books littered the desk, sitting on portions of probably unread newspaper. Faud didn't have time for current affairs, what with his job and, so it was rumoured, a very demanding elderly mother. As he sat down, Arto noticed that a rifle was propped up against the wall behind him. He hadn't been to Ballistics for a while. He'd forgotten what an unnerving experience it could be.

Ismail saw his eyes skim the surface of the weapon and laughed. 'Don't worry, my Kalashnikov isn't loaded today!' He sat down. 'Come on then, get your gruesome photographs out!'

Arto reached into his briefcase and removed two large colour pictures. They showed the right arm and hand of Leonid Meyer in close-up. He spread them out on the desk. Ismail bent low and examined them closely. He whistled sharply. 'Nasty!'

'The Pathology Lab says that they are probably gunpowder burns. They're old too, sixty or seventy years. Very severe, must have been extremely painful at the time.' He pointed to one of the shots. 'As you can see, as they healed, they puckered considerably. This seems to suggest that no treatment was given after the injury, probably just bandaged, wrapped in rags, something like that.'

'Mmm.' Ismail put on his spectacles and held one of the photographs up to the light.

'Now, Faud, we know what did this. However, what I need to know now is how. How would somebody sustain gunpowder burns like this, under what circumstances?'

'Well...' Ismail put the photographs down and then sat back in his chair and laced his fingers together under his chin.

He didn't take his eyes from the pictures in front of him. For a few moments he thought in silence. 'Any reason to believe that this man worked in the ballistics industry?'

'Not that I know of.'

'Mmm.' He went back to his thoughts and sucked hard on his top lip. 'Soldier?'

'Yes. He was Russian. We think he may have fought on the Red side in the 1917 Revolution—well, Çetin does. He's trying to piece together some details about his past. His military history could, apparently, be pertinent.'

'Right.' Ismail took a pencil from his drawer and pointed it towards the livid image of Leonid Meyer's right hand. 'Now this...' He paused for thought again. '1917, you say? Russia?'

'Well, 1918, actually, the wound.'

'OK.' He took in a deep breath. 'This here, on the hand, this could be the result of a faulty weapon. People like the, oh, you know, the Russian Revolutionaries—'

'Bolsheviks.'

'Yes. People like that weren't always professional soldiers. Any old firearm would do, however decrepit. You can get nasty burns from old, unmaintained pieces. You can't just pick up a gun and fire—well, not if you want to be safe.'

'So an old, possibly faulty gun, you think?'

'Maybe, maybe.' He rubbed his chin with his hands and sucked in his already slim cheeks. 'Then again he could have had an accident—oh, fireworks? Some industrial process? 1918 to 1992, it's a long time. A lot of things can happen in, what, seventy years?'

'Yes, right. What about the arm?'

'Ooh.' He looked at the photograph and sighed. 'Again, I can only speculate. Ruling out fireworks and industrial causes, which I assume you want me to do...'

'Yes—at least I think so.'

He stared at the ceiling for a moment, marshalling his thoughts. His hands moved very slightly as he worked the spacing out in his head. 'Possibly being in the vicinity of an old cannon. Unlikely, but…well.' He shrugged. 'Someone standing very close beside him letting off a great number of rounds very fast. It would have to have been in a confined space of some sort. He must have been unable to move away. If you could, you'd shift long before you got this badly burnt.'

'Caused by somebody else's firearm?'

'Yes. Could be. Possible scenario is a left-handed person standing on his right, slightly behind…If Çetin's victim were close enough, and especially if he used both hands to hold his weapon, the trajectory of a large number of bullets passing could have caused this. It's—'

Ismail's telephone rang. 'Excuse me, Arto.' He picked it up and spoke into the receiver. 'Ismail.'

Arto looked at the photographs again. The kind of scenario Ismail seemed to be suggesting struck him as being not unlike a firing squad. Two or more people firing at something, side by side, letting off a large number of rounds. And yet there were differences. In a firing squad where there were two ranks the front rank usually knelt down or squatted, while those behind stood and fired over their heads. And of course this type of execution was nearly always performed in a courtyard, outside— in some sort of open space at least. It had to be, confined spaces presumably increased the risk of ricochet. Of course it wasn't strictly Arto's problem, but ever since he'd first noticed the burns on Meyer's arm and hand he had been gripped by an unmistakable feeling that they were important. Why, he didn't know, but Çetin had been very interested when he'd told him and Çetin was not accustomed to getting worked up about nothing.

If Faud Ismail was right then it was quite possible that the murdered man had been a murderer himself. And if that were so it moved Meyer from his current position as oppressed Jewish victim into quite a new and more sinister role.

It felt so good to be out in the open. Natalia ran her fingers through her hair and delighted in the feel of the gentle early evening breeze as it played between the strands and massaged her scalp. In an hour the park would be closing, she would have to be quick. Lucky and quick.

But then luck didn't come into it unless you were fussy. Natalia wasn't. As she started the long climb up the hill towards the Palace, she felt her body tense. Her eyes darted from side to side as she ascended. What she sought had to be there. It always had been before; beside a tree, to the edge of the path, standing on one of the bridges that spanned the ornamental pond...

All day she had waited. Cooped up in that tiny box of a shop with only doddery old Avedissian for company. Endless puerile chatter, all it did was provide a background to her anxious thoughts. What she needed was release, a few moments to be her, unencumbered and undiluted Natalia. There was only one way that she had ever, could ever do this. And it was going to happen—it had to! She'd broken a date for this, her need had been so desperate, a date with a Kurdish silversmith.

A young couple, arm in arm and laughing at some recently shared joke, passed her as they made their way back to the gates. Whatever they had come to do in Yıldız Park they had obviously done it. The young man was very handsome and Natalia, just for a moment, felt jealous. The young man would have suited her very nicely. Well, partially suited her anyway. There was one thing, one important thing missing.

She pushed onwards and upwards. So far, nothing, but Natalia did not lose hope. Looking deep in amongst the trees she undid two more of her blouse buttons and smiled as her rich cleavage came into view. She was breathless, both the climb and the anticipation were beginning to get to her. All she hoped was that he was young, that he'd do exactly as she said. But then he would because she'd do anything in return, anything. At least, that's what she'd tell him.

Natalia fanned her hot face with her hand. She could see people moving about, laughing and running around amongst the trees, but they were all couples. A twinge of anxiety started to pull at the pit of her stomach, but she squashed it down. This was Yıldız Park on a Saturday evening! Yıldız Park, old abode of the Sultan's, playground for Istanbul's lovers and adulterers. She paused for a moment to catch her breath and skimmed her eyes across the horizon.

He was leaning against a tree, his long legs crossed casually, his arms folded across his chest. His dark green uniform was a little tight which was good because it meant that she could see the outline of his muscles. She liked muscles. Also, he had— something. Yes, he'd do. He'd be fine.

Natalia swept her hair back from her face and walked towards him. As she approached he turned his head away, as if trying to avoid her eyes, but she knew that he'd seen her. He was young. Nineteen? Twenty? He had to want what she wanted, but his youthfulness probably made him shy. It wasn't the first time she'd encountered this phenomenon. It only meant that a slightly slower, maybe less crude approach was required. Initially.

As she drew level with him, she smiled, even though he still wasn't looking at her. 'Your Commander let you out for the day?'

He turned his head. His soft young face was pink; long dark lashes hid his slanted Anatolian eyes. 'Hello...miss.'

Natalia laughed and the boy's thick lashes parted and flicked upwards revealing a pair of frightened soft brown eyes. He looked like a young bear, lost and scared in an unfamiliar forest.

Now she was up close, Natalia ran her eyes over him in detail. She wanted to be sure this was a good choice. There were bound to be more men, soldiers, further up the path she had just left. She needed to convince herself that this boy was about the best she could do. She smiled at him.

He was good, she had to admit it. Dark, muscular, young. His large hands augured well, and there was a pistol on his hip. It sat in a leather holster, the handle gleaming in the dying rays of the sun. A thing of great beauty and excellent craftsmanship.

As she looked at the weapon Natalia felt her heartbeat

quicken. She was full up, almost in pain. She opened her mouth and ran her tongue slowly around every millimetre of her lips. He gazed at her questioningly at first; he obviously had no or little experience. But as her hands loosened the remaining buttons of her blouse, the corners of his mouth turned upwards and he smiled. She pierced his eyes with hers and, without looking downwards, she unfastened her brassière.

Natalia felt her breasts lurch forward, the delicious sensation of the cool breeze touching their skin. The boy's eyes widened and he put a tentative hand out towards her. She walked towards him and slotted one big, dark nipple between his outstretched fingers. He let out a little gasp as he felt the heavy weight of her in his hand.

'Come on,' she said, her voice thick with sex. 'Let's get a bit further away from the path.'

She disengaged her breast and took his hand. They didn't have to go far. The undergrowth became dense and almost impenetrable only about twenty metres away.

But the place had to be right: a tree with smooth bark or a flat and bramble-free piece of ground. Standing or lying, she didn't mind as long as she didn't tear her skin. Pain was all right, pain was great, but she didn't want marks on her body.

'Er, miss, er...'

She turned. 'What!' She hoped he wasn't going to talk.

'Um?' His shaking hand offered her two crisp twenty-thousand lira notes.

Natalia snorted and pushed his hand away. 'I don't want your damn money! Just do what I tell you, OK?'

It was obvious from his expression that he could hardly believe his luck. 'Oh, th—'

'Shut up!' She moved some tangled weeds aside with her foot and looked about her. 'This will do.'

As she sank to the ground Natalia slipped off the remainder of her clothing. The soldier stood and watched her, mesmerised. If he was worried or offended by her brusque manner he certainly didn't show it. He just looked at her, his eyes wide, lips wet.

Natalia bundled her clothes into a small heap and put them on the ground beside her. She stretched out one long, tanned leg and caught some of the material of his trousers between her toes. She threw her head back and looked up into his livid, sweating face. His chest heaved as his breath came in unsteady laboured gasps.

For a few seconds they just stared at each other. Natalia, impatient, even started to get bored. She didn't want to savour the moment, the boy wasn't important enough! But then slowly and with trembling fingers he unzipped his fly and his dark penis sprang, erect and painful, into his hand.

Natalia felt her skin tingle. The boy was huge; he'd hurt. She hadn't been really wounded for a while. She wanted to be.

'If you do what I say this time, you can have as much as you want,' she said coldly. She opened her legs wide and rubbed her breasts with her fingers.

'Oh.' But he didn't move, just stood stupidly with his penis jutting out from his trousers like a stiff, dead snake.

Now she was losing patience. An idiot boy from the country in all probability. She'd just have to take control. Well, it was what she did best.

'Sit on the ground and take your pistol out.'

'Pistol?'

'Look, do you want me to fuck you or not!' she snapped.

For a moment he looked confused, but then he undid his belt buckle and pulled his pistol from its holster. Natalia felt her whole body flush and open as he held it out towards her.

The boy sank to the ground and stretched his legs out in front of him. Natalia sprang forward and took his penis between her fingers. It was very hot and she could feel the pulse of his blood tearing through the engorged veins.

'Now,' she said as if she were issuing instructions to a particularly dim servant, 'when I get on top of you I want you to put that pistol in my mouth.'

He looked from Natalia to the pistol and then back at Natalia again. He didn't seem to understand. With a grunt of irritation she pushed his torso back and straddled him. She had to raise her body up quite high in order to clear his penis. 'Like this,' she said.

She thrust herself down his length and he groaned.

As she rose and fell on him, she took the gun from his hand and put it, barrel first, into her mouth.

At first he tried to take it away from her, but she slapped his hand to one side. The stiff metal tasted good, bitter and acidic. That, and his great bulk inside her, heightened Natalia's senses and she felt a rapturous loss of control sweep across her body. But she wanted more. She grabbed his hands and clamped them hard on to her swaying breasts. Although so recently broken, he knew what to do and he pinched her nipples hard. She cried out—it was so good.

But his face was agonised now; he wouldn't last long. Too young. She closed her eyes to shut out the vision of his stupid, grateful face and increased her pace. He was tearing her apart and she loved it.

Arms like bands of steel wrapped themselves around her and she pushed the gun deep into the back of her throat. This was what she thought of their history. This was what she would have done if the hard-eyed men had turned their weapons upon her! She felt like crying; it always had that effect. If only she had been there—it would have all been so different. They'd be home, in the right place, not grubbing around with these filthy, these disgusting foreigners. Fucking thick, musky Turks on dirt floors!

The man beneath her bellowed and bucked like a bull. She opened her eyes and taking the pistol from between her lips, she turned it towards him and rested the barrel against the bridge of his nose.

He stopped moving almost immediately and his eyes became very still, frozen in fear. His chest heaved as he tried to contain his post-coital panting.

She, on the other hand, was quite calm.

Natalia smiled as her finger clicked the safety catch off. She felt him crumple and shrink inside her. His face lost all its colour and took on the appearance of ashes. Grey and shrivelled.

'Mmm...'

She laughed at his faltering attempts to speak and jammed the barrel so hard against him that he cried out.

Terror was a good game. It was the only one she really liked to play. Of course it could only be played with scum like this boy, but then she liked scum too. She took the cheap watch off his wrist and flung it on to her heaped-up clothes. Terror fulfilled all her needs.

He was sweating heavily now and she knew that very soon he would start begging for his life. That was always amusing. She looked down at his big, shaking body and ground her hips against his groin. With one finger she spitefully flicked the base of his penis.

Very slowly, so there could be no possible chance that the dullard wouldn't understand her, Natalia spoke. 'If you don't get that thing of yours up and do it to me again I'm going to blow your head off.'

By the time Robert Cornelius reached Celaleddin Rumi Caddesi, he was totally and utterly exhausted. What, of course, he should have done was ask Natalia what the name of the company was first—before he took off into the back of beyond. But so anxious had he been to get into the area and do what had to be done that all thought of the practicalities had, at the time, escaped him. As a consequence he had stalked the streets for hours, asking probably unwise questions of suspicious local residents, until finally he had arrived where he was now: a place that had been variously described by some as the only and by others as one of many textile plants within the Üsküdar district.

Not that being on the exact site of the actual textile plant owned by this Smits character really mattered that much. He'd thought originally that it would, but upon reflection, surely it would be enough if he were simply in Üsküdar. Besides, if someone connected with the old Nazi were really to do something nefarious, would he do it precisely on his own doorstep? No, he wouldn't. He'd be more intelligent than that.

But now he, Robert Cornelius, was where he needed to be and it was at this point, when all the excuses had effectively run out, that the full portent of what he was about to do hit him. Carefully wrapping a handkerchief around his fingers, he took the letter out of his pocket and stared down at it. This had to be madness! He recalled, with a sad but knowing smile, that during the course of all the awfulness back in Britain people had told him he was mad for many months. They hadn't known the half! Not even the most pessimistic consultant could have even dreamed of the still deeper depths to which he would sink: the ultimate insanity that he was about to perpetrate now. Deception, perverting the course of justice, impersonation, libel.

As he looked at the neat, typewritten address on the front of the envelope, he imagined how the other words—the mad, twisted, hate-filled words inside—now looked. In his mind they were mobile, dripping with the spite of ages the modern world hoped it had forgotten. But then if they secured her for him, were they too high a price to pay? If they kept her safe even at the expense of some old Nazi's life, then surely that had to be a good and right thing?

But finding or inventing justifications for something was not the same as approving of one's foul actions at the very core of one's soul. Discomforted by these thoughts, Robert turned away towards the more practical aspects of the operation. What he needed now was a post-box. Not as numerous or as easily identifiable as its British counterpart, Robert knew that tracking down the elusive Turkish post-box could be problematic. In more 'touristy' parts of the city it was easy, as most of the hotels

would gladly take in cards or letters for foreigners. But here—
here what he needed was a post office and he certainly hadn't
seen one of those yet.

Wearily he started walking again, stopping every few metres
to peer into some unobtrusive place that just might be the lair
of the shy and retiring Turkish post office. And for a short time
this rather humorous pursuit both filled and entertained his
tired mind. It recalled several once well-loved surrealist comedy
shows from his youth: shows where ill-assorted people routinely
hunted down haggis or worked ceaselessly in clothing mines. It
was nice being in that old childhood comedy place again—it was
safe, completely devoid of any semblance of the adult creature
that he was now. For one tiny moment, he even smiled—properly, fully, just like he had done when he had been a child.

But then, quite suddenly, there was a doorway surrounded
by the customarily numerous *Telefon* booths, and there, also,
was a very wide-mouthed gap in the wall—specially designed
for letters.

Having found what he had been seeking, Robert then
returned his attentions to the letter in his hand. Once he put
it inside the box he was committed. If discovered he could
consequently experience the full force of the law against him.
At present he was innocent and, although suspected by Ikmen,
there was nothing concrete that could connect him to the old
Jew's murder. If he posted this letter, however...

If he posted this letter and were discovered, some people,
including Ikmen, would see it as the act of a man who has
something to hide. The fraudulent aspect of the thing would
be almost as nothing to what the police might perceive as his
motive for doing it. If this man Smits had definitely had a hand
in Meyer's murder he could justify it, but...

But if he were to do what Natalia wanted he would have
to believe that, wouldn't he? And besides, who was to say that
it wasn't true? Unbidden, the image of Natalia running away
from him through the streets of Balat rose up large as life in his
mind. It made his hand and the letter that it held shake violently,

signalling that if he didn't act in some manner soon, he would be unable to do anything.

In order to spur himself forward to the act that he had known all along had to be done, he whispered under his breath what should be his belief—his personal catechism. 'Smits did do it! Smits killed Meyer! Smits killed Meyer!'

Like some sort of mantra he repeated and repeated these phrases, his eyes tight shut, aware only of moving forward ever so slightly, until...

The movement of someone behind him or perhaps even the noise of a car starting caused him to stop muttering. Now the letter was no longer in his hand and for a second or two he cast about wildly to see whether he had dropped it on the ground. But then, just as suddenly, he knew that he hadn't. The post-box wore far too satisfied a look upon its blank wide-mouthed face for that.

It was done. He had done it. Yet as he turned around to move away from the scene of his crime, he felt very suddenly, but also very certainly, that he was being watched. If this type of paranoia had not been such an old 'friend' he would have given it more thought. But, for once, he dismissed the feeling and then set his feet in the direction of the Bosporus and home.

Chapter Fourteen

THE DAY AFTER a sleepless night can seem interminable. Logic says that you should try and stay awake until the following night in order not to disrupt the normal sleep pattern. In practice, however, this is hard. Even when something interesting is happening, the hours seem to drip by. It's like having a terrible hangover without the riotous pleasure of the night before. The body screams for sleep and aches in protest when it is denied.

Robert Cornelius felt a wreck. After finally screwing up the courage to post the letter the previous evening he'd thought that he might feel better. But he hadn't. Nervous tension before the act had given way to anxiety after. He'd spent most of the night sitting on his bed, smoking and going over in his mind what he had done and the myriad possible results of his actions. None of them had a firm base in reality, of course. But then he had felt for some time that his hold upon that was becoming shaky.

He shuddered. The last time it had happened had been

after the divorce. He knew why, of course, but the lead-up was still a blur. Had it been weeks or months? The big incidents: finding that man in bed with Betty; the attack—they were clear. But the rest? Friends and family knew more than he did, they talked about it too. Bits of himself had been bandied about the stripped-pine living rooms of Socially Aware flats in Stoke Newington and Finsbury Park.

Somewhere in his head was a big black box with all this shit inside and it was locked. Robert liked it that way. When he'd come to Turkey, he'd left the key behind him. He'd left it back in Islington where it belonged, on its home territory.

Even now, and despite his current anxiety, he still didn't want to open it. But there was a bad feeling. He knew it wasn't external, it was too familiar for that. He couldn't put it into words however hard he tried. The nearest he could come didn't make sense. It was a darkening. Nothing about him was clear, even in the sharp brightness of the midday sun; things had blurred edges, smeared and broken lines. He was looking at the world through a dusty, tobacco-stained curtain that showed him shapes, lumps of flesh and concrete and metal, but no detail.

Although he wouldn't even acknowledge it to himself Robert knew that meeting Natalia had pushed him across some sort of unseen border. The subsequent journey had been a familiar one. A woman; a drawing away from friends; extravagance; acceptance of the unacceptable. It had been just over a year, a slow descent. But was it? The man, the lawyer, he'd found in Betty's—his—bed all those years ago was surely only the culmination and confirmation of what he had known all along. Betty had used him from day one. Five years he'd had of that. But he'd done it so willingly! He'd given her everything she wanted, turned not one but two blind eyes, even though it hurt like hell. He'd grown into a doormat, something pliant and comfortable for her to scrape the soles of her boots on.

He was doing it again. But this time he was aiding and abetting...No, he couldn't be certain about that even now. He had no real proof. The evidence of his eyes meant nothing. He had to try and remember that. And that day in Balat had been odd, climactically as well as other things. In retrospect it seemed like the darkening had deepened on that day. Of course it hadn't really, he knew that, but it was comfortable to think that it had. A new black box had been forming in his mind all night and he reminded himself to throw such musings into it. Natalia was in difficulty, that was all that mattered. That was the only fact.

Robert put his hand on the telephone, but he didn't lift the receiver. It was, by his reckoning, the eighth time he'd done that since dawn. He'd never used her telephone number before, but he wanted to. He knew she'd be pleased with his efforts on her behalf, she had to be, it was going to make everything OK again. Better than OK. She couldn't escape now because he had done this for her. Where he went she had to follow because he possessed knowledge. He couldn't form the words that damned her, but he knew.

Robert picked the receiver up and dialled her number. He didn't have to refer to anything, he'd already committed it to memory.

'Carelessness.'

Nicholas looked up from his paper and stared into the darkness that surrounded the great gilded bed. 'What?'

'I was careless, with talk. We think sometimes, quite wrongly, that people can cope with the truth when they cannot.'

He folded the newspaper up and rested it in his lap. 'To be fair, we never dreamt that your stories would have such an effect.'

She looked down her nose, contemptuously. 'You lace the word "story" with what I feel is an element of doubt.'

He sighed. 'I have always had doubts, Mama, you know that.'

'So you think that your own mother is a liar?'

'No.' He paused for a moment. 'No, I don't believe that. What I do believe, however, is that Uncle Leonid lied or rather elaborated—'

'You really believe that?' Her expression was one of pleading rather than anger now. The look of one who wants what is being said to be different.

Nicholas looked down at the floor. 'Yes, I do really believe it, Mama, and in the light of what has happened now I think that you must at least attempt to come to terms with it. For our sake and for your own peace of mind.'

'And how,' she said archly, 'do you think I might achieve this?'

'I think that we should go to the police and tell them everything that we know.'

Quite unexpectedly, but entirely without mirth, she laughed. 'With the odious Reinhold Smits placed fairly and squarely at Leonid's apartment on the day of the murder? Are you mad, Nicky?'

He leant forward, the better to see and, hopefully, persuade her. 'Ah, but we know that Mr Smits didn't kill Uncle Leonid, don't we?'

'We know nothing of the sort!'

'But we do!' Now he was losing his temper—a bad and possibly unwise thing to do with Maria, but he just couldn't help it. 'You're lying, Mama! Assuming that Mr Smits was at the apartment at all...'

'I neither want, nor need to hear it again, Nicky!'

'But—'

She held up her hand to silence him. 'Whatever happened and who, for whatever reason, perpetrated this crime is entirely irrelevant. We must, at all costs, protect who and what is of our own blood. That is, as you know—'

'More important than anything else?'

'Yes! Yes!' Her eyes blazed with a fire that was both angry and something else too—something not quite in control, something dangerous.

Nicholas had, of course, seen this before but, his own brief anger now spent, he returned her gaze with only a sad shake of the head. 'No, Mama, you are wrong. Our blood is the same as everybody else's.'

'So then why, my brave young son, have you lived this lie for so long?'

'Because,' he replied, 'when I was young, I knew no better, and by the time I grew old it had become a habit that I just couldn't break. I didn't want to hurt you, Mama, or the others. Sometimes when you have lived your whole life inside an illusion, it is better to stay there. But there are also times, like now, when it is expedient not to, which is why I am talking to you now.'

He went to take her hand, but she pulled it sharply away from him. 'When we go home—'

'We're not going "home", Mama! And the more preparations you make poor Anya perform for that "great day", the worse she becomes! Besides, all the rest of us *are* home. Even if the police hurl us all into prison for the rest of our lives, we are and always have been home!'

'You've lived as a Russian all your life!' She was mocking, scornful. 'You know as much about these Turks as you do about men from Mars. You dress like a Russian, speak like a Russian, think like a Russian.'

'My father was Turkish.'

Maria raised her eyebrows and a sneer clouded her features. 'That was an unfortunate expedient. If I could, I would have avoided—'

'Oh, yes,' he snapped, his voice now filled with bitterness, 'I know all about that, Mama! Your efforts to put that right included me, remember? The results of that led directly to where we are now!'

'No, no, that was right! I still stand by that decision! As I have said before, I was considering the condition of...I was far too loose with talk of an alarming and spiteful—'

The door to the apartment swung open and slammed

against the wall. Both Maria and Nicholas looked towards it. A tall slim figure stood silhouetted against the light from the hall. Something long and thin swung and creaked rustily in its left hand. Far away, three floors down in the dining room, the telephone started ringing.

Nicholas put his head in his hands and spoke with great patience and deliberation. 'What have you got there?'

For a moment there was silence, as if Nicholas's words had not been heard or had just disappeared into nothing. Maria squinted at the figure, forcing her failing eyesight to pierce the darkness. 'Is it a chain?'

She looked at Nicholas. His face was blank. 'Don't ask me, I—'

'Bicycle chain.'

It was a flat monotone of a voice. A man's but without vigour. Its tone was deep and rich, but its content was dead and dry as a piece of discarded bone.

Nicholas muttered something under his breath that only he could hear. The telephone stopped ringing. He looked at his mother accusingly, but his voice was directed to the figure in the doorway. 'Go and put it back in the cellar then.'

'Don't you...' The flat voice tailed off into a whine. It cut itself short.

'I will see it later!' The force of Nicholas's words made his head tremble on his neck, like a puppet's. His eyes left his mother's face and burnt through the darkness.

The figure in the doorway turned. The chain rattled slightly with the movement. Far away, down the stairs, a woman was laughing. Her voice sounded warm and humorous, as if she were pleased, overjoyed even.

Nicholas and Maria listened to the sound with interest. It was unusual, especially now.

Heavy boot-shod feet clumped noisily down the stairs. Although barely audible it was still possible to make out the sound of the attendant chain bumping and jingling against the banisters. If it carried on it would chip the paintwork. But neither Maria nor Nicholas moved or spoke to alert their recent guest. They both knew what a waste of energy it would be. Some things, even some unpleasant ones, were best left. This was one of them and so was their previous conversation.

Nicholas sighed. 'Sergei won't be up today, Mama, he's not so good.'

She laced her fingers together under her chin and cleared her throat. 'Accident?'

'No, no. I think—' He could hear running footsteps advancing up the stairs. He put his hand to his forehead and cringed. 'Sweet Christ! Back again!'

'What?' For a moment she couldn't hear it, but as soon as she did, she nodded her head and sighed deeply. 'Oh.'

Her son looked at her from between his fingers, his voice bitter. 'Yes, "oh", indeed, Mama! Well you might "oh"!' He sunk his head down deep into his shoulders and waited. His mother stared at his neck with black hatred.

The footsteps got louder. They bounced from step to step as if excited, as if they were anxious to get somewhere, tell someone something.

'What do you think, Nicky? Another artefact from the cellar? Another item of useless trivia?'

Nicholas's voice drawled into a sneer. 'Not all so useless, Mama.'

He knew she'd heard him, but she chose to ignore it. She often did. More often than he felt she should.

The running footsteps clattered into the room and Natalia, breathless but excited, stood before them, her thin cotton skirt billowing up around her legs like a sail.

The old woman and her son relaxed slightly. The girl looked bright and happy.

Maria reached under the covers for her cigarettes. 'Well?'

'Oh, Grandmama, Uncle Nicky, it's—' She walked over to the bed and sat down. She was fighting to breathe, but at the same time she so obviously wanted to tell them something. 'It's—'

'Well, come on!'

Nicholas snapped. 'Oh, for God's sake let her catch her breath, Mama!'

'It's, it's Robert—'

Nicholas frowned. 'Robert?'

'This English boyfriend Natalia has been...you know. The one she—'

'He's sorted out the police!' It came out in a rush, even breathless she couldn't contain it. 'There's a letter, he...he sent... It's...Look, it's all right now. They're going to think...'

At the back of Nicholas's mind a small warning light sprang into life. 'Letter?'

Natalia put her hand on her chest and took a deep calming breath. 'Yes.'

'What letter?'

The girl smiled, but her uncle didn't smile back. 'Robert wrote to the police, anonymously, but claiming to be some Nazi who knows and applauds Reinhold Smits. It's full of Nazi opinions and things and, well, it tells the police exactly what Smits is and gives reasons why he dismissed Uncle Leonid and hints at why he might have killed him. I told him all he needed to know myself and—'

'Is he mad!' Nicholas could feel a layer of darkness closing about him and he didn't like it. Where was it all going to end?

Natalia laughed. 'No, he's in love! He'd do anything for me. Anything.'

'Does anyone even remotely connected with this family ever tell the truth?' Nicholas got up from his chair and then threw it to the ground. 'Well, do they!'

His mother's voice was stern, a warning. 'Nicky!'

He looked from one woman's face to the other. His head pounded and he could feel sour tears of rage starting to sting the inside of his eyes. 'You are digging a hole, all of you! Unless you stop we are all going into it! Can't you see?' He pointed one long, trembling finger at Maria. 'You! You can stop this, Mama! The police can be here in five minutes—'

'And ruin my last chance! What is mine to—'

He screamed at her. 'Mama, when you get "home" they're going to put you in a padded room and throw away the key, if you're lucky!' He turned to the girl. 'Natalia, I order you—'

For an old woman Maria put a lot of force behind the hard-wood cigarette box that hit him in the face. Not only did it smart and bruise, it also broke the thin skin just below his eye. Red wetness dribbled slowly down his cheek. Nicholas put one shocked hand up to his face and touched his flowing blood. It stained the tips of his fingers, settled and crusted around the backs of his nails.

When he looked at them again, the two women appeared to him like witches, smiling, amused at what they saw as his weakness. The matriarchy. The family had always been one, despite everything. Even the old stories were full of it, what the wife did, the mother. The sainted, hallowed mother. He'd often wondered why they didn't just castrate their men after they'd had enough babies. All the power traditionally associated with manhood was obviously theirs.

Her cigarette lit up and coloured Maria's glittering eyes yellow. 'You can go now, Nicky. I will talk to Natalia alone.'

No apology, not even the slightest flicker of concern that she may have put out his eye. But then it was no surprise really. It was, had always been the girls, the women—

'Get out, Nicky!'

With four long strides he was out of the room. He'd made no attempt to staunch the bleeding from his cut. As he had passed those bitches, the blood had run down his face and into the collar of his tight red tunic. That was good. He wanted that because he knew that one of them would eventually have to wash it. Anya or Natalia, it didn't matter which.

As he started to descend the stairs he heard the sound of the women's laughter. They both had coarse laughs, Natalia and Maria. What they claimed be was one thing, but they laughed like alley cats. But then one of them really was an alley cat. He thought about Mr Robert, whatever his name was, and his letter.

He pitied him almost as much as he pitied himself.

The kitchen was not tidy, but as the only room in the house not currently infested with children it proved the perfect place for Ikmen to take Suleyman when the young man finally arrived. That Fatma had not been given the chance to do the washing up was, to him, neither here nor there.

Once the preliminaries of providing his guest with a glass of tea, asking after his health and getting him settled were over, Ikmen made a start.

'So, Suleyman,' he said, 'having followed Mr Cornelius over to Üsküdar and seen him post a letter, what then?'

Suleyman took a small sip from his glass and then put it down on the table. 'Then I had to make a decision about whether to follow him to wherever he was going next or wait around for a postman to arrive.'

'And so?'

'And so I did both. Or rather I instructed a local beat constable to wait around for the postman and then radio his findings to me later. I then followed Cornelius, who went back to his apartment for the night.'

Ikmen smiled. He'd trained this perfumed upper-class boy well. 'And so what did the beat cop find?'

This time, Suleyman smiled. 'The box contained five items, including two picture postcards. Two of the remaining three letters were addressed to people in the east and the third'—here he paused for what Ikmen could only imagine was dramatic effect—'the third was addressed, typewritten, to you at the station.'

'To me?' Ikmen frowned. 'Why to me?'

'I have no idea, but I suppose that when it arrives, all will be revealed.'

Ikmen sighed. 'And you say that he spent a lot of time outside Şeker Textiles?'

'Yes, once he'd found it. Not that he seemed to know its name. I spoke to several people he approached for directions and all he ever asked for was an unspecified textile plant.'

Ikmen shook his head as if trying to shake something loose inside there. 'This is all very odd. I mean I can't, as yet, see any real connection between Cornelius and Smits. But then to stand outside his plant for so long...Not, however, that he went to see Smits—or maybe he did and then...But then this letter, to me, from him in Üsküdar...'

'We should know more,' Suleyman said, 'when the letter arrives tomorrow.'

Ikmen scowled. 'It's a pity that constable couldn't have intercepted it then and there!'

'Now, sir,' Suleyman replied with a grin, 'you know as well as I do that he wouldn't have had the authority to do that.'

Ikmen threw him an acid glance. Suleyman's slavish adherence to 'good procedure' was sometimes really rather galling.

Noting his expression and knowing exactly what it meant, Suleyman quickly changed the subject. 'So, how did you get on at the university then, sir?'

Ikmen lit a cigarette and, as he exhaled, launched into his own exposition. 'Professor Mazmoulian was very well aware of the existence of Smits. Back in the 1960s he had actually interviewed him.'

'Oh?'

'Yes, for his 1968 book *Turkey and Germany: The Uneasy Marriage*. Although mainly about our alliance with the Germans in the 1914–18 war, there was a chapter at the end devoted to Nazi activity in Turkey during the 1939–45 conflict. It contained quotes from Smits and others like him. He was, apparently, quite proud of the fact that he'd dismissed all his Jewish workers. And, at least in 1968, he expressed absolutely no remorse with regard to this.'

'So he was definitely lying to us during his interview?'

'Oh, yes.' Ikmen cleared his throat of thick, morning-time

mucus. 'And I, for one, can see no other reason for this than to conceal his involvement with Meyer, can you?'

'No. Although…'

'Yes?'

'Well, sir, it's just that this anti-Semitic thing with regard to Smits hardly holds up if he and Meyer had been out of contact since 1940.'

'Ah, but they had been in contact, hadn't they? Meyer had few enough friends as it was without carrying about a completely defunct set of details in his address book.'

Suleyman nodded his assent. 'Yes, but I can't help feeling that if Smits were involved, there would have to be something more at work than just plain racism. Like Meyer had something on Smits, something recent and—'

'Oh, yes. I think that that is a real possibility which could also explain all the money that Meyer seemed to have.'

'Yes.'

For a few seconds afterwards the two men sat in silence as each attempted to absorb and evaluate what had just been discussed. On the face of it, Smits seemed to be digging a very deep and dangerous hole for himself—both with the police and, unaccountably, with Robert Cornelius.

When Ikmen finally spoke again, he had decided how to proceed. 'I think that we should pay Mr Smits another visit sometime tomorrow—or rather you should.'

'Me?'

'Yes.'

'Why?'

'Because I think we now need to confront Smits with all of this. Because I think you need the practice and because'—Ikmen lit a fresh cigarette from the dying embers of the old one—'I have another appointment at the university tomorrow lunchtime.'

'You're going to see the professor again?'

'No.' He smiled. 'No, I'm going to accompany Dr Ikmen to the European History section of the library.'

'Dr Ikmen is…'

'My father, yes, although if he heard me refer to him as doctor, he'd probably hit me. Timür says that only insecure people use titles which is why, of course, he is Timür and not "Father"—just in case you were interested.'

Suleyman smiled. Even from his scant knowledge of the old man, that sounded about right. 'So, might I ask why you are going to the library then?'

'I'm going to look for a name or names, if possible. With Timür's help I'm going to see what I can find out from actual Russian text-books about the Revolution.'

'This, I take it, is going back to Meyer's past involvement?'

'Just so. And from what Dr Sarkissian tells me, it seems that Meyer's involvement in Bolshevik killings may have been of an officially countenanced nature.'

'What do you mean?'

'Dr Sarkissian found some old wounds, or rather scars, on Meyer's hand and arm which Dr Ismail over at Ballistics thinks may indicate that he was part of a firing squad.'

'Oh?'

'Now,' Ikmen continued, 'I don't know how he came to that conclusion, but I think that it's a line of investigation worth pursuing. Right from the beginning, the Bolsheviks were very keen on keeping records of all these things and so if we can discover whom he killed we may be able to deduce something about his own death.'

Suleyman looked doubtful. 'You still think that this old crime may have some relevance?'

'Yes I do. The method by which he died was so illogical and bizarre that I can only think that someone was making a point. He was so old just stabbing him or smothering him would have finished him off in a second. So why the acid and why the swastika drawn in his own blood?'

'Oh, but surely the swastika indicates—'

Ikmen held up a warning finger. 'Not necessarily, Suleyman.

Symbols like the swastika are far older than you might think. I don't know anything about its origins, but perhaps the swastika could mean something other than "look at me, I'm a Nazi". And looked at in that context, the manner and motive for Meyer's death could take on an entirely different meaning.'

'Well, yes, I suppose so, but...'

'But, you're thinking, where does that now leave us in relation to Smits and Cornelius?'

Suleyman sighed. 'You have to admit that there is some evidence to connect both of them, in various ways, to Meyer.'

Ikmen smiled. 'And to Mrs Maria Gulcu too, remember? Lest we forget, she knew him during the Revolution and, despite her denials, there is a possibility that she witnessed Meyer's old crime. If I could find out what that was then I may be able to confront her yet again. The name under which our Gulcu friends rent their telephone may have been the old woman's maiden name and that could be significant, possibly.'

'Doesn't mean that she murdered Meyer though, does it?'

'No, it doesn't. But then just because Smits is a Nazi and Cornelius was in the vicinity of the apartment and also knows Natalia Gulcu doesn't mean that they are murderers either.'

Suleyman eyed his boss obliquely and then put his head down, sighing deeply. 'Despite all this evidence mounting up, we're still not really any further forward now, are we?'

'Oh, we are,' said Ikmen brightly. 'If you look upon this case as being like a shattered mirror, you'll see what I mean.'

'A shattered mirror?'

'Yes. When Meyer died the mirror was broken and all the pieces flew off in many different directions. What we've been doing since is collecting those pieces. It is my belief that we have all, or nearly all of them now. The problem that remains, however, is, without having any idea about its size or shape, we have to fit all those pieces back together again to produce one whole mirror.'

'Oh.'

Ikmen got up and, as he walked around Suleyman's chair in order to get to the cooker, or rather the kettle on top of the cooker, he patted the younger man on the back. 'Look upon it as a challenge, Suleyman. Some people would kill for the chance to do a job with a challenge.'

Chapter Fifteen

CHOOSING WHAT TO WEAR when she felt good was harder than trying to make a decision when she felt bad. The only option under the influence of depression was black. Not much black, only skimpy things. On even, balanced days she covered up; it was the extremes that made her court danger. But this morning her spirits were lighter and she required red. The black skirt and blouse she had worn in Yıldız Park on Saturday evening stared out at her, but she ignored them. Natalia didn't usually dwell on past triumphs for long—although that had been a particularly wicked little interlude. She smiled. One young soldier at least would have something to think about for a while. How stupid male pride was! She wondered how he'd twisted the story round when he told his friends. She wondered how much she had damaged him—at least mentally—and hoped that it was a great deal.

It had, of course, been a shame about the cancelled date with the silversmith, but then the events in Yıldız Park had given her so much more pleasure. However good the silver-smith might have been he certainly wouldn't have matched her anonymous soldier. What would he have put in her mouth—a bracelet? She'd catch up with him and his valuable trinkets another time, when she felt less sexy and more materially acquisitive.

She pulled a very short red lycra dress out of the wardrobe and held it up to her naked body. It was eye-catching; it would certainly attract looks at the very least. It would do. She put on a pair of white silk panties and slipped the dress over her head. Her hair crackled with electricity.

In retrospect she'd been right to keep Robert stringing along for all those dreary months. A regular boyfriend, if besotted, could be an asset. He would do anything to keep her. His puppy-dog devotion was, of course, intensely irritating, but it was also useful. He was acting on her behalf now, protecting her. That was good. It was going to work too. The police already half suspected that old Leonid's murder may have been racial. They'd actually told Robert. And even if the letter were traced back to him, it was nothing to do with her. It would look bad for Robert though. Not that that mattered much.

Natalia sat in front of her dressing table and rubbed foun-dation cream into her face. She was pleased with what she saw in the mirror, even before she applied the thick make-up of which she was so fond. It wasn't a nice face though. It was more hungry, sexual. But who wants to be nice!

Her mother and her Uncle Nicky were nice. Her uncle disapproved of her 'use' of Robert Cornelius. It was, he said, dangerous, and her mother had even used the word 'cruel'. It was her mother's opinion that Robert was in love with her, as if that changed anything. Anya was becoming nervous. She wanted everything to be right so that they could go as soon as possible, with no loose ends. Natalia thought about her mother sitting in front of her mirror talking to nobody and she felt sick. Her grandmama had understood, of course, but then she had to. She'd done a few things herself to get out of situations in the past. Grandmama knew that everyone and everything had its price. Nothing was so precious that it couldn't be bought in one way or another.

Natalia outlined her eyes with black kohl. Large, open eyes excited most men, they looked so innocent. Grand-mama always maintained that it was her big blue eyes that had really saved her. He'd been enchanted by them before, but, widened still further by terror, they must have been bewitching. The stupid vulnerability of men again. Even men with guns—*especially* men with guns.

She stroked some black mascara on her already thick lashes and then reddened her mouth with lipstick. Her big, fleshy mouth. Natalia smiled inside. She felt lucky. Work was going to be good today; poor, soft Robert had taken care of the police, so soon she could dispense with him, which was excellent. Life was good.

'Right.' Ikmen sat down and viewed Suleyman very seriously across the top of one of his file tower-blocks. 'What are you going to say to old Smits?'

'I'm going to confront him with the fact that documentary evidence exists which proves, beyond doubt, that he was a Nazi and that he was responsible for dismissing Jewish workers.'

Ikmen surveyed the small pile of post on his desk, took the top envelope, looked at it and then threw it straight into the bin. 'You'll have to be careful though,' he said. 'If you really go for him, he could have a coronary.'

'I will,' said Suleyman, in absolute seriousness, 'be my usual, controlled and polite self.'

'Good.' Ikmen opened the second envelope before depositing its contents into the bin. However, the third letter was quite a different story. 'Well, well,' he said, 'let it never be said that the Turkish postal service is not an efficient, well-organised machine.'

Suleyman looked up. 'Sir?'

'I think I've just received my little note from Robert Cornelius.'

'Oh!' Ignoring the usual niceties pertaining to others' personal mail, Suleyman stood up and scuttled quickly round to the rear of Ikmen's desk. 'Well, open it then!'

Ikmen shot him a look.

'Please, er, sir.'

Ikmen slid his finger under the gummed flap and pulled out a piece of paper which they both read simultaneously. When they had finished reading, they turned to look at one another, their faces bearing the same quizzical expression.

'I get the feeling, Suleyman,' said Ikmen once he had fully absorbed everything that was in the letter, 'that our Mr Cornelius has somewhat lost the plot.'

'Yes.'

Just at that moment, the door swung open and a very red-faced Commissioner Ardiç entered. As usual, he launched into his subject without any preliminary niceties. 'Well, Ikmen,' he boomed, 'how is it going with this Meyer thing?'

Now both standing in response to their superior's appearance, Ikmen and Suleyman looked at each other and then at the letter in Ikmen's hand.

'Ah...'

Ardiç, following their gaze, stabbed his fat Havana cigar in the direction of the letter. 'What have you got there?'

'Ah...'

Infuriated by their joint lack of response, Ardiç strode up to the two men and ripped the letter out of Ikmen's fingers. 'What's this?'

'It is a letter from someone,' Ikmen replied, 'who is obviously not thinking as clearly as he might, sir.'

Ardiç ignored entirely what had just been said and slowly, his lips moving throughout, read the letter for himself. As he came to the end of the missive, Ikmen whispered to Suleyman, 'I have a very bad feeling about this.'

Ardiç looked up when he had finished, his face uncharacteristically smiling. 'Well, there's some most fascinating information here about our man Smits! He and Meyer arguing over a woman and then Smits getting rid of Meyer from his job and—'

'With respect, sir...' Ikmen started.

'Yes?' Ardiç waved the letter at him like a weapon. 'What is it, Ikmen? What's the problem now?'

'With respect, sir, we know who wrote this letter and it was not an associate of Smits.'

'No?' He looked briefly at the letter again and shrugged. 'So?'

'The author is an Englishman, sir—the Englishman who was at the scene of the murder at—'

'Interesting! Go on, Ikmen, I like this!'

'Well, sir, as far as we know, this man has no connection with Smits, although I accept that he must have found out or been told some things about him. I mean we now know that it is true that he did dismiss Jewish workers—'

'Yes.' Ardiç's face darkened once again. 'And I told you to act on that some time ago!'

Ikmen looked down at the floor. 'Yes. Well. However, we are going to have to treat anything in here with extreme caution. This stuff about Meyer and Smits having a dispute over a woman is possible, but it's new and...'

'Yes?'

'Look, sir,' Ikmen continued, 'we've been looking for more concrete connections other than employer/employee between Smits and Meyer for some time now and for this to come along at this time and rather neatly...'

Ardiç, not uncharacteristically, grumbled dangerously under his breath. 'If I were you, Ikmen, I'd just be grateful that this has turned up when it has and to hell with who might be doing what for whatever reason.'

'Yes, but...'

Suddenly and explosively Ardiç's patience snapped. 'I don't

give a fuck about any of this! I want Smits in here and I want him in here today—do you understand?'

'Yes, sir. Suleyman was just actually going—'

'In here, Ikmen, today! Do I make myself clear!'

'Yes, sir, perfectly.'

Ardiç flung the note down on to Ikmen's desk. 'And this Englishman too!'

'Yes, sir.'

'And'—once again he stabbed his cigar in the air, this time right in Ikmen's face—'and next time do not attempt to hide evidence from me! You can work on any silly little theories you no doubt have about all this in your own time. But when you are here, you are mine, do you understand?'

'Yes, sir.'

'Good.'

He then turned, very quickly for such a large man, on his heel and stomped off back down the corridor. When the floor had finally finished shaking, Ikmen turned to Suleyman. 'The only reason I can think of for Cornelius writing that letter is to protect himself.'

Suleyman looked puzzled for a moment: Ikmen appeared to be ignoring the fact that Ardiç had ever been in the room. 'Eh?'

'Although where he got hold of these details, if they are true, and who indeed would have furnished him with them...'

'Unless it was the girl, Natalia Gulcu. After all, her family does know Smits.'

'True. And it is certainly a fact that Maria Gulcu was very keen for us to get on to Smits's case. And yet to do it via Cornelius in this strange and mawkish manner...I mean, why an associate of Smits would basically "give" him to us like this I cannot imagine. All I can think is that Cornelius must have been out of his mind on drugs or something when he wrote this.' He sighed a little, slightly defeated sigh. 'Oh, I don't know. I suppose you'd better go and bring old Smits in.'

'Yes.' Suleyman moved back round to his own desk once again. 'What about Cornelius?'

Ikmen lit a cigarette and then slowly slumped his chin into his hands. 'I'm going to have him watched—for now. Ardiç can fuck off if he thinks I'm going to pull him in before I've really got him in a state. Let him wonder what's been happening with his letter for a little while and, in the state of mind he's in, he could just tell us what we need to know anyway.'

'You think so?'

'He must be biting his fingernails down to the bone by this time. I know I would be. Now'—he stood up and rifled in his pocket for his car keys—'you go off and invite Smits out for a few hours while I go to the university library.'

'Oh, you are still going then? I...'

Ikmen visibly slumped under this, to him, obvious lack of understanding on Suleyman's part. 'I only ever do fifty per cent of what Ardiç wants, Suleyman. You know that! I can arrange for a man to watch Cornelius from this desk and then I'm out of here—which is what you'd better be if you don't want to get in trouble too.'

Robert walked into the staff room just in time to catch the start of the celebrations. At first he was utterly confused. Bottles of wine and glasses instead of coffee cups, red and gold streamers hanging from the ceiling, laughter, actual real, honest-to-goodness laughter. What the hell was going on? And why? Whatever was happening, no one had bothered to tell him about it.

Rosemary teetered over to him carrying a bottle of cheap white plonk and a glass. She was wearing a pale floral-print dress with a full skirt. It was very pretty, but even through the fog of his depression Robert realised that it was at least twenty years too young for her.

'Wet the baby's head, Bob?'

"What?'

She looked confused. 'Dieter and Hande. They've got a little boy, Bürgüz.'

'Eh?'

'Born at the German Hospital, eight o'clock last night.' She looked deep into his eyes and inclined her head to one side. 'You're not with us, are you, Bob?'

He pointed in the general direction of the corridor. 'I've been taking a conversation class, I...'

'Do you want a glass of plonk, or don't you?' His vagueness was irritating her. The world with its babies, its celebrations and its sorrows was going forward, but he wasn't. Somewhere he'd got caught like a fish in a keep net, neither free nor really caged.

Rosemary suddenly lost all patience with that blank face of his and moved on to the next new arrival. Yusuf, tall, dark, twenty-five and Turkish. When they came together, Robert heard Rosemary giggle girlishly. Yusuf was just her type.

Robert crept away into the corner of the room by the television and lit a cigarette. The rank smoke made his mouth taste dry and foul. He knew his breath stank. He needed to eat something, anything. If only his stomach didn't feel like an old walnut! Natalia had been pleased when he'd told her what he'd done. With that anxiety out of the way, surely this tightness, this sick feeling should lift!

But he knew that it wouldn't. There were others involved besides Natalia. He tried very hard to remember whether or not he had touched the paper with his fingers at any point, but he couldn't. He reached into his pocket for the security of that handkerchief. He'd left it at home. Not surprising really. Saturday's sleepless night had been followed by a fitful, uncomfortable slumber on Sunday. A doze punctuated and studded with images of tiny, filthy prison cells, dirt floors. His feet tied tightly together and hauled high up above his head; a young man in police uniform, his torso bare, wielding a heavy bastinado. 'Helping the police with their inquiries.'

But he wasn't! Robert looked down at his feet and tried not

to feel ashamed. Anyone in his situation would have done what he did! That was love, it was just like that!

He looked at the smiling faces around him. Normal, reasonably happy people. People who made the best of their jobs, allowed themselves to enjoy the good times without worrying about the future. People who got drunk in company, not alone.

Dieter, of course, was getting absolutely shit-faced. Well, his wife had just had his baby, he was entitled. Robert remembered Dieter's Turkish wife, Hande. She was nice, a gentle girl, she and Dieter got on without undue complications. Perhaps the fault lay in him, in Robert. Perhaps it was his Britishness that was the root of their difficulties? Maybe it was Natalia who was being reasonable?

Rosemary came over with that sickly-sweet Yusuf, that supposed administration assistant. That full-time gigolo!

'Perhaps you can get him to loosen up and have a little drink,' she said, nodding her head in Robert's direction. 'I think he should, don't you?'

Yusuf smiled, exposing enough teeth for a regiment. Robert cringed. 'Bob! Why you don't celebrate?'

Robert shrugged, smiling slightly. 'Bit of a dodgy stomach, actually.'

'Oh!' Yusuf's smile disappeared. Robert felt this was a shame. He had been hoping that the young man's head might fall in half at the mouth.

'Oh, but Robert, Turkish wine is very good for the stomach!'

Rosemary wound her hands around one of the young man's hairy arms. 'Turkish things in general are, I find, good for the body.'

They both exchanged a knowing look. Robert's disgust suddenly bubbled over. Rosemary was old enough to be Yusuf's mother, for Christ's sake! And the young man was just a tart anyway!

'Oh please!' he found himself saying. 'Please!'

Rosemary's face dropped into a frown. 'What's the matter? What is it?'

It was like working to a script. He didn't want to make a scene, but he knew that he had to. The words were already waiting in his head.

'For Christ's sake, Rosemary, you're old enough to be his mother! God, what are you doing, woman?'

'What?' Her voice was calm and low; it was obvious that she didn't want to shout. But her tone was dangerous and her eyes were fierce.

'Rosemary, it's almost prostitution! You feed him, take him out a bit, wash his smelly socks for a few months and he gives you the odd screw! He's probably got some Danish eighteen-year-old stashed at home! I'm sorry, but—'

'What he say, Rosemary?'

'I said—'

'I think you've said enough!' Now she had raised her voice. She didn't care who heard any more. Her face blazed with crimson blood. 'Just because your own love life is an utter shambles! You're probably a dismal failure at it too! How dare you! How dare you criticise me and the way I live my life!'

She didn't see, nor was she going to see.

'But, Rosemary, you'll get hurt again, you know you will!' He'd started shouting too, he could hear it.

Heads were starting to turn. Some people had ceased replenishing glasses in mid pour. They were bored language teachers, of course they enjoyed a good row.

'I don't believe you!' Rosemary shook her head, her blonde curls bounced against Yusuf's shoulder. 'I don't know what's got into you recently, you're like a, a...'

'Rosemary, I...' He touched his own face with stained and trembling hands. He'd started feeling bad. It had been a terrible, cruel thing to say.

'Just look at you! You're falling to bits!' She pulled a disgusted face and backed away. 'You've always been weird, but—You don't talk, you look like you don't sleep, the other day you didn't shave. God knows I've tried to help you, but quite honestly, I think you're beyond it!'

He looked into Rosemary's hurt middle-aged face and wondered: Why? Why had he said it? He hadn't had to! Like all that stuff with the confounded letter had been, it was optional. It occurred to Robert that perhaps in both these cases he'd done the wrong thing. In trying to do the best for someone, perhaps, just sometimes...

'I'll do what I want and when I want!' She shook her head angrily. 'Don't you dare tell me how to live, Robert Cornelius! And don't you dare come to my flat again, whining about your marriage fantasies! It's pathetic! You're pathetic!'

She turned and went back into the centre of the room. She pulled a confused Yusuf after her.

A few awkward seconds later the party started to come to life once more and Robert found himself alone. OK, so he'd done it, now what? Voices around him got louder again and he felt almost impossibly isolated. It hurt. He'd made a fool of himself. They'd all be thinking that he was jealous of Rosemary now, but was that a bad thing? His words had been there for a purpose surely? They had been! His life was changing and there was no going back. He smiled, but not out of happiness. Of course! Rosemary had to be hurt. It was essential she was kept at a distance. It had to be that way with people he cared about. His mind briefly touched against a vision of Natalia. He frowned.

Reinhold Smits surveyed his new surroundings with ill-disguised revulsion. And, in truth, there was little to admire in the hot, dingy little room in which he now found himself. Painted in the muddy shades of green and brown that seemed to characterise so many public buildings, police interview room number five was hardly a place of peace and repose. And, ever fastidious, Smits noticed the little things usually disregarded by the customary occupants of this place, like the fact that the old tin that served as an ashtray had not been emptied since the last 'suspect' left; like the fact that the young constable guarding the door had very bad acne.

After fiddling briefly with the tiny, almost useless fan on top of the table, the young Sergeant Suleyman sat down in front of him and smiled. Then, pressing a button on the large and antiquated tape recorder beside him, he spoke a few unintelligible words into the machine before addressing him.

'Could you please, sir, for the benefit of the tape, state your full name, age and occupation.'

Smits nodded first and then proceeded, his face taut and obviously strained. 'My name is Reinhold Smits, I am ninety years old and I own several major companies trading in textiles, coal and white goods.'

Suleyman nodded his acknowledgement. 'Thank you, sir. Now, before I ask you any further questions, I must inform you that we are now in possession of information which confirms both your past allegiance to Nazi principles and your actions based upon these which include the dismissal of several Jewish workers from your employ in the early 1940s. Do you understand what I am saying?'

He might have guessed. Indeed, subconsciously, he had probably already known that this would all come tumbling out at some stage. It was why he exhibited absolutely no surprise when it did come. 'Yes,' he replied simply, 'I understand.'

'Good.' Suleyman paused for a moment, probably—so Smits mused, collecting his thoughts—because the lack of shock and horror had quite thrown him. 'In view of what I have just told you, Mr Smits, why did you then plead ignorance of these facts during the course of our first interview with you?'

'Because you were asking me to recall a time in my life I would rather forget. Because if I owned up to such behaviour, you could make quite erroneous connections between myself and current events.'

'And yet, sir, I think I would be correct in saying that you did know and dismiss from your employ one Leonid Meyer?'

Smits drew in a deep breath and, during the pause between

drawing it in and exhaling, he came to a decision that he hoped was the right one. 'Yes, Sergeant, I did.'

The young man's eyes, although slightly averted, showed a little triumph. Smits suddenly started to feel sick. 'May I have a glass of water?' he said, holding on to the scraggy thinness that was his throat.

The sergeant nodded briefly at the constable who responded by walking out to the water fountain in the corridor and returning with a cracked cup full of oily grey liquid. Smits nodded in thanks.

The sergeant described what had just happened for the benefit of the tape before proceeding, which he did only when he felt that Smits was ready to start again.

'So,' he continued, 'what was the nature of your relationship with Leonid Meyer?'

'He was an employee of mine,' Smits replied.

'Was that all?'

'Yes.'

'You had no involvement with Meyer outside of work then?'

'No.'

It may possibly have ended there and later Smits would chastise himself for not leaving it at that point. But his own now-growing anxiety compelled him to ask: 'Why?'

'Well, sir,' the young man replied, 'because it has been suggested to us that Meyer and yourself may have been involved in a dispute over a woman.'

So that was it, was it? That was the game the old witch had decided to play with him! Smits felt his face blanch with anger, a reaction not lost upon his interrogator.

'I get the impression, sir,' the policeman said, 'that this information is not new to you.'

'No, you are right, it is not.'

'And so...?' The young man shrugged as if urging Smits onwards.

Well, if the old woman was going to play dirty then so was he! Smits cleared his throat before answering, the better to enunciate with perfect clarity. 'My dealings, Sergeant, with this woman never actually progressed beyond the acquaintance stage. I would suggest that if you want to know more about the machinations between her and Mr Meyer then you should ask the lady herself.'

'Who is she, sir?'

Smits sighed. 'Maria Gulcu,' he said, 'or rather Maria Demidova, as she was then.'

He fancied he saw something register in the young man's eyes.

'I met Leonid in 1919 when he came to work for my father and through him I met Maria.'

'I see.' Once again Suleyman paused, marshalling his thoughts for the next question. 'And did you, Mr Smits, ever vie with Leonid Meyer for the attentions of Maria?'

'Yes. Although not in the way you might think.'

'Oh? And what is that?'

'I found her interesting, as opposed to sexually attractive and...'

'And so you didn't dismiss Meyer from your employ because of her?'

Smits put his head down and murmured almost inaudibly, 'No.'

'So why did you dismiss Leonid Meyer then, Mr Smits?'

Smits continued looking at the floor. It was better to look truly contrite now. 'Things changed a lot in the Germany of the 1930s. With the rise of Adolf Hitler a new confidence gripped everybody—including those of us who resided abroad. There was no longer any place for those of inferior pedigree within our sphere of influence.'

'So you dismissed a man who had been your friend because he was a Jew?'

'Yes. But what you have to understand is that those were very different times. We—'

'And these are views that you still retain?'

Smits looked up and found himself confronted by a pair of eyes that were utterly without either mercy or pity.

'No.' Although smarting from the onslaught, he now attempted, if belatedly, to recapture some dignity. 'No, I came to my senses many years ago now, Sergeant. And if I could have made it up to Leonid, I would have, but...'

'You lost contact with Mr Meyer after his dismissal?'

To tell the truth was probably not that wise but then flying in the face of the evidence in Leonid's address book probably wasn't that wise either. 'I still used to see Leonid from time to time,' he said. 'I was sorry for what he became in later years.'

'You blame yourself for his alcoholism?'

'In part.'

The young man frowned. 'Only in part?'

What Smits said next came about via a conscious decision—a decision, furthermore, informed by his anger over this position he was in now: the one Maria had put him in. 'Leonid Meyer had a past, Sergeant. I don't know what it was, but I do know that even before he entered Turkey, he was already a broken man.'

'Do you know why that was?'

'No, I don't.'

'Do you know anything about how Leonid Meyer met Maria Gulcu?'

This was a question he had not, foolishly, anticipated. Smits felt, or fancied he felt, his heart flutter and, just briefly, he held his hand ready over the barrel of his chest. 'No, I know nothing,' he said, 'nothing at all.'

The young man eyed Smits narrowly. 'Are you sure?'

'Yes.' Smits's voice was small now, unsure and sadly so very like that of the old man he knew he was but so desperately didn't want to be.

And then, quite suddenly, the attack began in earnest. 'Did you kill Leonid Meyer, Mr Smits?'

'No! What reason would—'

'I don't know what reason you would have had for doing it, Mr Smits, that's what I'm asking you.'

'But...'

'It occurs to me that perhaps all this talk of your being a reformed character is as much a lie as all of the other falsehoods you have told us.'

Only now did Smits feel really afraid. Only now did the liberty that attended what was left of his life seem to be in real danger. It was an emotion that made Smits turn even more fiercely in the path of his own spite. 'If you want truth, Sergeant, then you might try speaking to one who knows what that is!'

'What do you mean?'

'I mean that you should speak to Mrs Maria Gulcu, very soon, and that your questioning of her should show as little mercy as you have shown me!'

'And why might that be, Mr Smits?'

'Because she had something on him, I—'

'What? What did she have on him?'

'I...'

'Where were you on the day that Leonid Meyer died, Mr Smits?'

'I was...I was at my home, it...'

The sergeant was leaning forward now, peering right into his face. 'A large black car, just like yours, was seen in the vicinity of the apartment. Was it yours, Mr Smits?'

'No!'

'You're lying. Now what is this thing that Mrs Gulcu had on Leonid Meyer? Where were you on the day of Meyer's murder?'

'I...'

'Come along, Mr Smits, I do not have all day! What are you talking about? You are making very little sense!'

He watched, and to him it seemed as if the act were in slow motion, the young man brought his fist down hard upon the table. The impact was loud and, as it reverberated through his head, Smits felt his hold upon events slip rapidly away—like water going down into a drain. And then suddenly there was nothing—just blackness. Like a little death.

The old man moved his finger slowly down the list of names as he read: 'Simonoff, Bagratid, Popov, Irimishvili.'

Ikmen raised one heavy, bored hand up in front of his face. 'Who killed...?'

'Does it matter if your man's name isn't here?'

'Not especially.' Then, seeing the tired look on his father's face as he turned to yet another tome, Ikmen softened his tone. 'I'm sorry, Timür, you must be bored too.'

The old man scowled. 'Yes, well...' He picked up another book from across the desk and gave it to his son. 'This one's in English, why don't you look through that while I carry on with the rest?'

Ikmen sighed. 'All right.'

The book, which was called *The Demise of the Tsarist Order,* was, in his opinion, rather thin when one considered the immensity of the subject area. Turning first to the index and discovering, unsurprisingly, that Meyer's name was not listed, he flicked randomly until he came to a chapter which, gruesomely he thought, was entitled 'Executions'.

Like the material his father had read out before, this consisted of lists of murders of various prominent people, plus the names of those responsible. The most comprehensively documented case was, naturally, that of the last Romanov Tsar Nicholas II and his family—the perpetrators of which the two men had already come across in the literature several times. Had Meyer been involved in that incident, they would have a real story on their hands. But that event had been so thoroughly documented, and everybody concerned had been investigated so minutely, that Meyer's involvement with it was totally impossible. Besides, as Timür had said some time before, a lot of the

killing that went on at the time was of very minor Tsarist offi-
cials and had been carried out by what amounted to roving
bands of vigilantes. An uneducated and, probably, politically
naïve little Jew like Meyer would, it had to be admitted, most
likely have been a member of one of those.

Ikmen turned the page and scanned once again for familiar
names. That the one which did finally catch his eye, which leapt
from the page at him as if self-propelled, was one that had only
been at the periphery of his consciousness made the experience, if anything, even more shocking. For here, suddenly, was
a connection that was real, a link between the present and a
past so dramatic and so violent that he hardly dared breathe,
much less think about what it signified. Demidova, a name
from a telephone directory; Demidova here again in this book,
the name of the Tsarina Alexandra's maid—the woman who
died in that long-ago hail of bullets with her imperial mistress.
One and the same, maybe, this name? It wasn't really possible,
was it?

But as he read on further and as he took in fully details
about how the last Russian monarchs had been killed, by firing
squad, Ikmen couldn't shake the image of Leonid Meyer the
Bolshevik from his mind. Could it be...? But then the names of
all the men involved in that action were listed here in this book,
as in so many others, and Meyer's was not amongst them. And
anyway the whole notion was absurd, just because this maid and
Maria Gulcu shared a surname...

But he would have to ask the old woman anyway. His
interest was piqued now and—

'Excuse me, but are you Dr Ikmen's son?' A small individual sporting an alarming pair of bottle-bottom glasses was
suddenly at his elbow.

'Yes, I am.'

'There's a telephone call for you,' he said softly, 'in the
office.'

Annoyed that his train of thought should be broken like
this, Ikmen replied tetchily, 'Who is it? What do they want?'

'It's someone called Suleyman. He says it's rather urgent.'

'Damn!' He turned and tapped his father on the shoulder. 'Keep all these books for me will you, Timür? I'll be back.'

'All right.'

Ikmen got up from his seat and followed the strange little man as he padded gently across the library.

Chapter Sixteen

T HE SUN HAD ONLY just risen when they arrived at Karadeniz Sokak. They were, however, both extremely wide awake and, in Ikmen's case, rather grave also.

As they entered her apartment, Maria Gulcu waved a greeting and then, smiling, added, 'So here you are again, Inspector. And your pretty friend.'

'Perhaps I just covet your fine ikons, Mrs Gulcu,' Ikmen replied.

She hauled herself painfully towards the headboard. 'You must excuse my nearly always being in this bed when you come, but age is so...limiting. Serge?'

She held her hand out to a small twisted man who sat in the chair beside her bed. Ikmen thought he looked about sixty, although it wasn't easy to tell. Whatever his condition was it had so warped his body that getting a clear view of his face was not easy. He took the old woman's hand in both of his and kissed it. 'Mama?'

'Serge, these two gentlemen are from the police. We will speak English while they are here and you will be nice.' She fixed him with a stern gaze and then turned to Ikmen. 'Gentlemen, my younger son, Sergei.'

Ikmen inclined his head. 'Mr Gulcu.'

He muttered something in reply, but Ikmen couldn't hear what it was.

She lit a cigarette. 'Please sit down, gentlemen.'

Ikmen smiled and lowered himself on to the edge of her bed. Suleyman, as usual, remained standing. He liked to have a clear view of the door in this house. It made him feel more comfortable.

'Well, Inspector, what can we do for you this time? I feel we are quite old friends, you and I.'

The door opened and the granddaughter Natalia tiptoed quietly across the room and then sank into one of the chairs over by the curtained window. No servant today. For a few seconds she shuffled, getting her long bare legs comfortable. She crossed one over the other in a movement that could only be described as pornographic. But once settled she was silent.

Ikmen knitted his fingers together under his chin and turned to the old woman. 'Just a couple more questions, Mrs Gulcu, nothing painful.'

She smiled and licked her dry lips. 'Good. Painless is good. I do not like pain, Inspector, I am too old for it.'

'It is not one of my particular pleasures either, madam.'

She laughed. 'I like you,' she said. 'You are little, you dress badly and you're ugly, but I like you.'

'A compliment policemen very rarely get, madam, thank you.'

The little cripple Sergei shifted painfully in his seat. His feet dangled uselessly before him, the toes turned inwards and back, a helix. Ikmen noticed that Suleyman could hardly take his eyes off them.

He cleared his throat. 'Mrs Gulcu, I need to ask you about your background.'

She narrowed her eyes. 'Why?'

'If you could just answer my questions, madam, I will make clear the reasons behind this later.'

She sniffed. 'If I must.'

'Good. Now.' Ikmen brought his hands up to his cheeks and pouted. 'I understand, Mrs Gulcu, that you also go under the name of Demidova, is that right?'

'My maiden name, yes.' Although she didn't flinch or register any discomfort, the little man beside her bed turned away. 'How did you discover that, Inspector?'

He smiled. 'We will talk of that later, if we may, Mrs Gulcu. What I am interested in at the moment is where the name Demidova comes from.'

'Well, my father—'

'No, no, let me rephrase that, madam. What I am looking for here is a specific Demidova; one in fact I discovered in a very interesting book about your country's history yesterday. One who was, I understand, a maid in the employ of the Tsarina Alexandra.'

'Oh.'

For a moment there was pure silence in that room. A silence, however, during which Ikmen felt all eyes present fall upon him.

The old woman cleared her throat before replying. 'No, Inspector, quite a different family, I can assure you.'

'Can you prove that?'

Her eyes narrowed and Ikmen felt she was just about to reply when the little cripple suddenly started laughing. 'Inspector, my mother you cannot expect to—'

'Serge!' Her voice was raised but quite cold, as if she were talking to a recalcitrant child. She turned her eyes on to Ikmen's face. He looked away and lit a cigarette.

'I may be missing something here, Inspector, but what bearing does this have upon your investigation?'

'It is of significance, or so I believe, madam,' he said. 'So can you prove whether or not you are related to this maid?'

'No, I cannot,' she replied and then looking up defiantly, 'but you can take my word for the fact that this lady's family and my own are not one and the same.'

Ikmen drew deeply on his cigarette. 'And why should I do that?'

She moved herself slightly in her bed, pulling her neck up to its full height. 'Because I give you my word and because the lady of whom you speak, Anna Demidova, did not have any relatives when she died.'

'You seem to know quite a bit about the subject, madam.'

'Most old Russians do, Inspector. But if you do not believe me about Anna Demidova, then look it up yourself. You seem to be possessed of numerous sources on this subject.'

'Oh, I am,' he smiled, 'and believe me I will, Mrs Gulcu; as soon as I get back to my car I will do just that. Thank you.'

'And when you do indeed discover that Anna Demi-dova and myself are not related, perhaps, Inspector,' she said archly, 'you will tell me what all this might be about.'

'I will tell you that now, madam.' He ground his half-finished cigarette out in her ashtray and then instantly lit another. 'Not, of course, that I am entirely sure about it myself, but…It seems to be becoming apparent that there is some sort of connection between what Leonid Meyer did back in Russia and what so recently happened here.'

'Oh?'

'Yes. By your own admission he was a Bolshevik and, for those who were damaged or persecuted by that faction, there may, it occurs to me, be some sort of satisfaction to be gained by the death of one of their number.'

She laughed. 'At this distance in time, Inspector, surely…'

'Without wishing to give offence, Mrs Gulcu, if I were dealing perhaps with my own people, I would say not. But it is well known that Russians have long memories and—'

'And you thought that if I were related to Anna Demidova I may have taken it into my head…' Here she paused, visibly scoffing at his suggestion. 'But Leonid was a friend, Inspector

Ikmen—a friend who, furthermore, helped to remove me from the horrors of that time.'

'And himself from his own rather more criminal situation?'

She moved awkwardly in her bed now, casting about impatiently as if imprisoned. 'Oh, I know nothing of that, Inspector! As I have told you. And with Leonid dead and gone I would suggest that your chances of ever discovering the truth behind that are most slim.'

'Maybe. Maybe. But from what my forensics experts tell me there is a possibility that our Mr Meyer was involved in the composition of a firing squad. Perhaps like the one that killed your late Tsar, madam?'

'Oh, really.' Her eyes were dead now, almost he fancied studiedly so.

'Yes, and if I find no evidence to suggest that Anna Demidova was indeed alone in the world I will come back and talk to you about this again.'

She shrugged. 'As you wish. If you want to spend your time chasing fanciful historical theories for the glory, no doubt, of your own career, that is up to you.'

'Very well.' He looked briefly across at Suleyman before continuing and noticed that the young man looked very strained. Ikmen knew how he felt—this was not proving either easy or pleasant. When he spoke again, he changed the subject. 'All right, Mrs Gulcu,' he said, 'so what about the illegal status of yourself and your relatives in this country?'

'Illegal status?'

'Yes. We discovered the name Demidova in connection with your telephone number when we were checking up on the background of Gulcu family members in this city. With the exception of your late husband, we found absolutely nothing. Can you explain that, please?'

She let a moment pass before replying and when she did she spoke in such a logical and ordered fashion that Ikmen could, had he not known better, have been led to believe that what she was saying was quite reasonable.

'When I first came to this country,' she said, 'nobody knew or even cared whether one had "papers" or not. It is like that after a war. Dear old Mehmet Gulcu looked after me and I, in return, gave him the children he so craved. But again nothing official happened—Christians and Moslems didn't marry back in those days, it was too complicated. And even when Mehmet died there was no trouble, he had no family and so his money and property became my own. It was like that then and it suited me and—'

'But your children? What about them—and your grand-daughter for that matter? They have right of Turkish citizenship through Mr Gulcu. Why were they not registered?'

She sighed. 'For you to understand, Inspector, you would have to be Russian and so what I am about to say will sound ludicrous to you. But'—she paused to light a cigarette and, as she exhaled, she continued—'when the sacred blood of Mother Russia flows through your veins, you are inclined to view the world rather differently. I was born a Russian and I have always wished to die a Russian too. As for my family?' She smiled. 'They do as I do. We live, inasmuch as we can, the lifestyle of Russians before the cataclysm in 1918. Mehmet understood and indulged all this and when he died he left me enough money to fund my eccentricities.'

Suleyman, who had been quietly listening and observing all of this, suddenly had to speak. 'But…but, I mean, do you all like to live like this?'

Maria Gulcu turned to her son and raised an eyebrow. 'Serge?'

'We have always lived like this,' he said simply. 'It is only Natalia who does not. She works for an old friend of my father's, but that is her choice.'

The old woman eyed Suleyman appreciatively. 'I am no jailer, young man. All are free to follow their own paths. Natalia works and my son Nicholas can and does leave this house on occasion.'

Ikmen cleared his throat, calling Maria Gulcu's attention back to him.

'Odd we may be and I am undoubtedly a breaker of your laws, but we are not wicked people. As I have told you before, Inspector,' she said, 'there are others out there in the world who have or had reason to want Leonid dead.'

Her great care in not actually naming anyone made him smile. 'Oh yes, your old pursuer Reinhold Smits.'

'Pursuer?'

'Yes,' said Ikmen. 'We have actually received information from another source which suggests that Meyer and Smits may have, at some time, argued over your favours.'

'Oh yes?'

'Yes.'

She smiled. 'And have you inquired of Reinhold...'

'Oh, Mr Smits has substantiated this story, yes. Although he did say a few other things of concern to us before he finally faltered under interrogation.'

It was here that her face changed and for the first time, Ikmen thought or fancied, he didn't know which—that he saw real fear in her eyes.

'But for the moment,' Ikmen continued, 'we cannot question Mr Smits because he is indisposed.'

She nodded, as if on automatic and then said, quietly, 'He has cancer.'

'Yes, he does,' Ikmen replied, 'although we, unfortunately, did not know that when we brought him in for questioning. Had I realised that you were aware of such recent developments in Mr Smits's life, I would have consulted you before.'

He thought, although he could hardly be certain because of the thickness of her make-up, that her face blanched.

'However, just before Mr Smits fell ill, he did tell my sergeant here that you, to use his own words, "had something" on Mr Meyer and further that you are the one who can provide us with the "truth" about him.'

'Reinhold Smits said that?'

'Yes.'

She cleared her throat and almost magically she also, or so

it seemed, cleared her previous unsure and frightened countenance too. 'Then,' she said, 'I would suggest that Reinhold Smits is lying.'

'Well,' Ikmen countered, 'while you are both accusing each other of, I must say, really rather vague "things", how can I possibly know whether he is lying or you?'

'Well, you can't, can—'

'No, I can't, Mrs Gulcu. Moreover, I get the distinct feeling that this impasse is exactly where you both want me to be right now.'

She laughed. 'Oh, Inspector!'

But Ikmen was not amused. He was extremely and almost furiously frustrated. But despite that he controlled that particular emotion now. He put his cigarette out in the ashtray, then leant forward and looked her straight in the eyes. 'You want to know what I think, madam? I think that all three of you "had things" on each other. Meyer had far too much money for an old derelict and I think that both you and Smits know exactly what happened in that stinking room in Balat and why. And furthermore, I think that you fed his guilt over his old "crime" in Russia for many, many years. After all, to have in your possession a broken-down, defeated old Bolshevik must have been quite exhilarating in a grim sort of way, especially in view of the fact that Leonid came from Perm, just a few kilometres from Ekaterinburg, where your Tsar was murdered.'

For almost a minute there was not so much as a breath in that room. Although none of those present so much as flickered recognition of what had just been said, the leadenness of the air spoke far more loudly than either words or expressions. Even Ikmen hardly dared to breathe until Maria Gulcu finally broke the silence.

'None of these things that you are saying make any sense to me at all, Inspector Ikmen. And I am therefore inevitably led to the conclusion that, given my admitted lack of knowledge, I am now of little further use to you.'

Ikmen first nodded his head, to indicate that he had

heard her words, and then looked down at the floor. 'Very well, madam. I will leave you be for the present...'

'Because you have nothing.' She was smirking again now, cool and triumphant. 'And because you know it.'

He spread his arms in a simple shrug. 'As you wish. But I will be back, madam, just as I will return to see Mr Smits again. And that, I assure you, will be very soon.'

She didn't respond except to wave one hand in the direction of the granddaughter whom she, in Russian, instructed to see the gentlemen out.

Ikmen stood up and joined his colleague, facing the exit.

'*Au revoir*, Mrs Gulcu,' he said and then, turning to the cripple, 'Mr Gulcu.'

'Goodbye, Inspector Ikmen,' she replied and for just a moment the tone of her voice quite caught him off his guard. Her words had been so final somehow. For one terrible pulse in time, Ikmen looked at the awful gap that could so easily open up in the investigation should she go. And yet she should have gone a long time ago, this monstrous cadaver. That fine mind trapped in an awful body of paper and wax—hell.

'Well, goodbye then,' he said and quickly grabbing Suleyman by the elbow, he led him across the room towards the door. Natalia Gulcu, like a voluptuous statue of Venus, held it open for them and followed the two policemen down the stairs. Nothing in her face save a vague bloom of red on her cheeks gave any clue as to her mood. She reminded Ikmen of those wax statues of the Virgin Mary in the old Italian church of St Anthony of Padua. And, as if on cue, a church bell from somewhere quite close, possibly even that very church, started ringing.

As the three of them descended the stairs their language reverted to Turkish. Behind Ikmen, Natalia Gulcu spoke to the back of his head. 'So I suppose we can expect a visit from the immigration people sometime soon?' she said.

'Oh yes. Just a formality in your case, I should imagine,' Ikmen replied brightly. Then turning to look at her, he said, 'That's all you really care about in all this, isn't it?'

She shrugged, her large breasts rising with her shoulders. 'I know nothing about any of the other stuff.'

Ikmen turned and continued after Suleyman. However, when they reached the front door of the house, Ikmen turned and looked into her sulky, passionless face once again. 'I find myself wondering what your boyfriend makes of all this business, Miss Gulcu. After all, he was in Balat at the time of the murder, wasn't he?'

This time she reddened up completely. 'That man is nothing to me and I know nothing of why he was in Balat!'

'I find that hard to believe.'

Her usually passive face broke into a mass of lined confusion. 'What?'

'In view of the fact,' Ikmen said, 'that you gave him information to be used to deflect attention away from himself.'

"What?'

He smiled. 'Mr Smits and your grandmother? How on earth do you think we came by that information unless somebody told us?'

She put her hands on her hips as if squaring up to him for a fight. 'Well, you didn't hear it via me!'

'Very well, Miss Gulcu, but if you don't shut this door very quickly I may very well lead you to tell me something you may later regret.'

Natalia Gulcu's face blackened. Then, without another word, she slammed the door behind them with such force that small pieces of paint flew from the lintel and on to Ikmen's jacket.

Chapter Seventeen

HE SAT IN A SIDE AISLE facing a huge circular candelabra. A few candles were burning, but not many. Two he had started himself for no particular reason. The rest had been lit by the few faithful who had wandered in during the course of the morning. He'd known them all of course, but only by sight. And they knew him—oh they knew him all right! They'd all looked at him, that way. He sniffed unpleasantly to himself.

He didn't often come to church; never had. Mama had said that it was inappropriate considering they were all of mixed blood. Nicholas smirked. Of course Mama would! Although the blood was only an excuse, he knew that. Neither she, in fact nor any of the others, for that matter, had ever had a place in any house of God.

Nicholas shook his head sadly. The lies! It made him wonder whether anybody anywhere ever really knew the truth about anything. But mainly he wondered whether his mother did. He wondered who she was. He thought about it often, he always had done. He touched the small cut beneath his eye delicately with his fingers. It was quite bad considering. The old woman had used a lot of force. She'd been protecting herself and her fragile cobweb world; of course she'd used power.

He looked at the candles again and tried to think. Doing what was right and doing what was for the best were often very different things. In spite of everything, he didn't want to hurt them. In a group they were terrible, himself included. But were they just terrible because they perpetuated her? Without her what would they be? Serge, he knew, would be better if he allowed himself to be taken to hospital. But then even if she died that was unlikely. Serge was hers completely, like the others. And Anya? He didn't even dare think about it. Not for the first time he felt himself wishing that they would all die. At least that way there would be an end and nobody would ever know. She would have failed.

Another old worshipper passed him and nodded gravely in his direction. Nicholas ignored him. He got no peace from being inside a church, no spiritual uplift. It made him sad because he'd always missed out on this aspect of existence. She had always been goddess to them all. God, the real one, didn't dare interfere. He just let her manipulate—or so it seemed. Let her distort nature for her own ends, write things, say things, change and manipulate as she went along. All the real evidence had gone, including his own father, the man he wished he had known better, questioned maybe. In the last few months he'd started to evolve this fantasy that she'd killed his father, her lover. In a way he hoped that she had so that he could hate her more.

The great double doors at the end of the narthex creaked open and a small priest in flowing black robes entered. Nicholas looked up. The man was familiar to him, but as usual he didn't know his name. As he recalled there were two priests attached to the church: a young one, tall and dark with fierce, fanatical eyes and this one, the little old one with the long white beard. Although he'd never spoken to him, Nicholas rather liked this elderly cleric; he had a kind, cheerful face, like a geriatric infant.

Nicholas sat and watched as he made his way towards the ikon of the Virgin and Child opposite. As he bustled forward, the old priest hummed a little tune. His voice was rich and dark as roasted coffee.

Nicholas looked down at the floor, but out of the corner of his eye he could still see the priest. He watched him cross himself in front of the sacred image and then get down on his knees and touch the ground with his forehead. An act of devotion and surrender. Odd that such a simple act aroused jealousy in Nicholas's mind, but it did. The priest was part of something that was good. All the worshippers who came to the church got something out of it: comfort, strength. It seemed that way to Nicholas anyway. Black and white. The church was life, love, safety; outside of that was the dark, the place he came from and to which he would soon have to return. He felt phoney and ashamed.

The priest sat up on his haunches and, smiling, regarded the dark Byzantine picture before him. The sad-eyed woman and her thin, hook-nosed infant were his friends. He spoke softly to them, not in prayer, but conversationally, as to a living person on the street. Because the old man's voice was so low, Nicholas couldn't catch any actual words, but the scene was enough.

He had a sudden, almost irresistible urge to reach out and touch this man who was speaking so casually to God. He stood up and opened his arms. They trembled as he held them aloft and he felt that if the priest would only turn and look at him he would see his pain and he would come to him. He longed for the feel of the old man's arms about his body; his mouth moved to make the first, dry syllables of his confession. His heart soared. Oh, that was it! The priest would listen, the priest would make it all right. 'Father, help me!'

But the priest didn't hear him because he never actually uttered the words he so wanted to say. Alone, silent and unworthy, he sat down behind the candles once again and looked at the world of the Divine through a veil of fire.

❀ ❀ ❀

Ikmen put his book down with an ill-tempered thud. 'Well, get into the car then, before somebody sees you!' he hissed out of the window.

Suleyman reached across the back of his seat and opened the door for a truly filthy-looking individual who slid into the rear of the old Mercedes.

'So, what's happening then, Ferhat?' said Ikmen as he minutely examined his own hands on the steering wheel.

'Not a lot,' the man in the back replied. 'He goes to the school, back to his home, back to the school again. Might as well be a eunuch for all the excitement there is in his life.'

'Not been near Karadeniz Sokak then?'

'Not even close.'

Suleyman put his hand up to his face and wrinkled his nose. 'You know you really do smell bad, Ferhat!'

Ikmen laughed. 'Ferhat just likes getting into character, don't you?' He viewed the unshaven, dishevelled heap in his rear-view mirror. 'Bit of an actor!'

Ferhat sniffed. 'I get the job done.'

'So,' Ikmen continued, 'nothing odd or strange...'

'Oh, he talks to himself quite a bit. But then he's always on his own so I suppose you could say that he is the only company he has.'

'No friends then? No idle chatter with colleagues on the way to the bus stop?'

'No.'

'It's all a bit sad really, isn't it, sir?' said Suleyman. 'I mean being on his own in a foreign country and—'

'Well,' cut in Ikmen, 'keep on him, Ferhat. You know what to do if anything happens.'

'OK.'

As quickly as he had slid in, Ferhat slid out again and

disappeared into the hot, bothered early afternoon crowds. To Suleyman's great relief, the smell also went with him.

Ikmen took out a handkerchief and mopped his sweat-sodden brow.

Suleyman, watching him, said, 'I wish it would rain.'

'You're full of pointless observations today, aren't you, Suleyman!' snapped his superior. 'First that pitying homily regarding Cornelius and now praying for the bastard rain!'

Stung, Suleyman retaliated immediately. 'Well, I'm sorry, sir, but I am just a little upset about Mr Smits almost dying on me! I mean—'

'You just have to get used to it I'm afraid, Suleyman!' Ikmen put his handkerchief back in his pocket and turned the key in the ignition of the car. 'Anyway, he didn't die, did he?' He took the brake off and the car started rolling forwards.

'No, but...'

'Well, there you are then!' As the car moved past the ornate front entrance of the Londra Language School, Ikmen stole a quick glance at the building—a slight sneer marring his features. 'In any event, we have far more pressing problems than Mr Smits's health right now. Every bit of evidence we have so far is purely circumstantial. Even that letter from Cornelius is useless—no prints.'

'We could always try and trace the typewriter that he used.'

'Oh, yes,' Ikmen agreed, 'we could do that but even if the machine could be traced to his place of work, how could we prove that he of all the people there had used it? Any decent lawyer could argue that that was circumstantial too! No, unless someone who witnessed something comes forward or we get hold of some real forensic evidence soon, I don't honestly know what we're going to do. While Mrs Gulcu and Mr Smits persist in attempting to take all their secrets to their respective graves, I don't see how we can move any further forward.'

As the car skirted the northern side of the Grand Bazaar, both men silently scanned the teeming streets—a habit, in both their cases, born of some hard time as beat constables amongst the pick-pockets, con-men and other assorted thieves who colourfully characterised this area.

'Do you really think that Mrs Gulcu is related to this Demidova woman, sir?' Although his question was serious and he did have his mind upon it, Suleyman's eyes were following what was happening on the street too. In this part of town there were a lot of familiar faces.

'Not now that I've read a bit more,' Ikmen said. 'Anna Demidova was, as Maria Gulcu said, quite without relatives. Although...'

'Although?'

'Although there is, rather oddly, another connection between the murder of the last Tsar and that of Leonid Meyer.'

'Oh?'

Ikmen took his hand off the steering wheel and searched his pockets for cigarettes. 'Both the Tsar and his family's bodies and that of Meyer were disfigured with sulphuric acid.'

Suleyman rolled down his window, preparatory to another onslaught of smoke. 'Bit tenuous, isn't it, sir?'

Ikmen lit up and exhaled contentedly. 'Meyer was a Bolshevik, he'd been involved in killing.'

'That is only really hearsay though, isn't it? And anyway there is no proof that he was involved in that killing. As you've said before, his name was not recorded or—'

'Unless he changed his name...' Ikmen put his head down for just a split second in an attitude Suleyman felt was one of defeat. 'No, you're right, how could he? All the people involved in that died years ago, all the books confirm it. We've got absolutely nothing beyond a few—I can't say coincidences—synchronicities. Stupid, useless, baseless synchronicities.'

Suleyman looked once again at the thick throng of variegated humanity beyond the car window and sighed. 'Have we really exhausted all other possibilities? His other associates, neighbours...'

Ikmen turned briefly to look at him and then fixed his eyes back upon the road again. 'Whoever went into that apartment did so when nobody else was about. Only the Englishman, Cornelius, was seen and he'd only just come from work and was not carrying anything according to our one witness at the scene, much less a large canister of sulphuric acid. And besides, if he had done it why would he have admitted to being there so easily? No, his appearance on the scene is the one thing in this whole Byzantine maze that I feel is truly coincidental. Through his association, maybe, with Natalia Gulcu he found himself involved in something that I don't suppose he understands either.'

Suleyman rested his head against the band of his seat-belt. What with the heat, plus the endless questions that were beginning to hurt both their minds, he felt tired and lethargic. 'Like the meaning of the swastika?'

'Oh, yes,' Ikmen replied, 'like the meaning of the swastika.'

They spent the rest of the journey back to the station in silence, both of them knowing that, the way things stood at the present time, there was nothing to be achieved by talking.

Night had finally come and with it total exhaustion. Çetin threw himself down on the sofa and pulled his thin sheet up to his neck. Best make certain he was covered in case any of the children wandered through to the bathroom. It was far too hot for pyjamas. He propped his head up on one arm and reached for his latest bottle of brandy. A new one, excellent! Full, pristine, laced with potential oblivion...

'Çetin?'

He put the bottle down again and looked up. She stood in the doorway; her nightie buttoned up to the neck, sweating heavily, her pregnant belly making her legs buckle. He was surprised to see her again. She'd gone to bed several hours before. 'Fatma?'

She staggered across the room like an agonised elephant

and flopped down on the arm of the sofa nearest his feet. He pulled them up towards his chest very quickly. 'What is it?' He looked up into her flushed face and felt his heart instantly leap into his mouth. Oh, no! Not now! Not with all the Meyer business going on. 'Fatma, it's not...!'

She smiled. 'Oh no.' She leant back and patted her belly gently. 'He's not coming out for a little while yet. You'll have to wait another three or four weeks...'

'Well, thanks be...'

'Oh Çetin, you are looking forward to it, aren't you?' His relief had been too quick and too obvious and now she was hurt.

He sat up and let the sheet drop down to his waist. He took one of her dry, puffy hands in his. 'Of course I am! I didn't mean...' He made a pointless gesture with his other hand. 'It's just this case! You know how it is! And this one's driving me mad!' He tapped his forehead with his fingers. 'I know it's all in here! I...'

'Come to bed, Çetin?'

He let go of her hand and leant forward, frowning. 'What?'

She looked down at the floor as if embarrassed by her own words. 'Come to bed? With me?'

'You mean...'

'Yes.'

Still hiding his nakedness under the sheet, Çetin swung his legs on to the floor and sat up. He looked at her lovely, rosy face. 'But, Fatma darling, you always say I take up too much space and make you hot when you're pregnant.'

'Don't you want to then?' She looked so sad.

'Well, yes, but...' Çetin shuffled over to make some more room for her and patted the seat beside him. 'Come and sit down.'

Like a dutiful wife she shuffled down on to the seat, her eyes modestly downcast. Çetin was worried. This wasn't his usual blood and thunder Fatma at all! He slipped one arm around her plump shoulders and put his other hand on her knee. 'What's the matter, darling?' Now she was close he could clearly see that she had been crying. 'What's happened?'

Her bottom lip trembled as she turned to face him and she blurted rather than spoke her words. 'Oh, Çetin, you do love me, don't you?'

'What!' He couldn't believe it! Fatma? Unsure of him? He kissed her trembling lips and smoothed her damp hair with his fingers. 'Sweetheart, you know I do! I've loved you since the first time I saw you!'

But her face was still agonised. 'You don't sometimes feel a younger and more attractive—'

'Fatma!' He still hugged her, but his back stiffened with shock. 'Younger women? Are you serious?' He slapped one of his knees loudly and shook his head. 'Women, younger, older or whatever, don't interest me. I've got you. You're my wife and my lover, you're the mother of my children and'—he pulled her chin around so that she had to look him right in the eyes—'I think you're the most beautiful thing I've ever seen!'

'Do you...'

'Well of course I do, you silly girl! I wouldn't say it otherwise, would I?' He didn't want to shout but he really was angry. How could she doubt him? 'What the hell is this about anyway, Fatma? This isn't like you!'

She cast her eyes downwards again. 'Oh...'

But then he knew. Attention—that was what this was all about. Sometimes when he was working on something particularly complicated he only turned up at home in order to sleep. That was happening now, but in her present condition that usually normal state of affairs had made Fatma nervous. 'Look, I'm really sorry I haven't been around much lately, but you know how it is. I love you all. I even love the bloody job on occasion...'

'Ah, but Çetin, don't you feel old sometimes?'

'Fatma, I've been old all my life! My brother and I had to run our house after Mother died! I was ten! I only know about responsibility! If I took off with some teenager and left all of you to fend for yourselves the worry would kill me!'

Fatma put her hand on his shoulder. 'So you still love me then?'

'Oh!' He threw his cigarette violently into an ashtray and kissed her full on the lips. Even though his breath was stale and his moustache tasted of tea, she opened her mouth to him. She wanted him to feel her passion. Even pregnant she desired her tired, smoke-dried little husband. He moved closer to her and she felt his kind hands massage the side of her neck.

After a few seconds he pulled away and smiled at her. 'Does that answer your question?'

For a moment she suppressed her rising smile, but then she gave in and laughed. 'I suppose so.'

He pursed his lips and tapped her lightly on the nose. 'Good!' He winked wickedly. 'Sexy girl!'

'Oh, Çetin!'

He leant against her and rested his head lightly against her belly. 'Well, you are! Red-hot lover you...'

'Çetin Ikmen!' She was laughing but she was shocked. His head rolled about wildly on her quaking stomach and he had to sit up.

'Trying to deafen me, Fatma!' But he was laughing too and she put out her hand to touch his face. Then her laughter died and she suddenly became serious.

'I love you so much, Çetin!'

'Well, somebody has to!' He could be so glib, but Fatma was used to it. That was Çetin, her man. It had been his humour, plus that wild wicked smile of his that had first attracted her to him. There had been plenty more attractive boys in Üsküdar at the time; boys with more money and decent prospects. But none of them were even half as intelligent and fun to be with as Çetin. Çetin knew things, he lived in a house full of books, he could speak foreign languages. He took her on the most daring and dangerous rides at the fair. Çetin understood a girl who liked to be thrilled. And when he kissed her...Fatma's mother had known Ayşe Ikmen before she died and like most of the women in the quarter she had believed that the statuesque Albanian had been, well, a bit of a sorceress. The first time Çetin kissed her, Fatma thought that she knew why. He had excited her so much!

And yet what had he been, the young Çetin? Thin, swarthy, no beauty even then!

'Is that all that was troubling you, Fatma?' His voice cut into her sweet memories and the old and treasured scenes dissolved.

'Er...'

He laughed. 'Where were you? The planet Jupiter?'

She smiled. 'No. Just back a few years. When things were a little simpler.'

He nuzzled his long nose affectionately against her cheek. 'Remember you, me, that old deserted house up by the Selimiye barracks?'

'When you seduced me, you mean!'

'Only a little bit.' He laughed. 'Only at the beginning.'

Fatma knew that what he was saying was true, but she pouted in mock disapproval anyway. She remembered the day he was talking about well. Although she would rather have died than admit it, she'd wanted him desperately. They had gone to that old house specifically to make love. Because it had been her first time, it had hurt a bit, but Çetin had been as gentle as he could. And after the pain had come a lot of pleasure. She'd conceived Sınan on that day, her very first time. She and Çetin had been just one month away from their wedding day. She pursed her lips and tried to look hard. 'Witch's child! You put a spell on me!'

He looked into her eyes and his hands came up to massage her breasts. 'Yes, nice, wasn't it?'

'Çetin!'

He put his mouth over hers and licked her closed lips with his tongue. A familiar excited fluttering tickled the inside of her chest and she felt her skin flush and sensitise. Fatma knew that were she not pregnant she would now be entirely at his mercy. He took his mouth away from hers and nibbled her hot, throbbing neck. Fatma closed her eyes and breathed his name.

Unfortunately neither of them heard the door creak open. The darkness curfew didn't apply to old men and Timür could not sleep. He saw what his son and daughter-in-law were up to straight away and simply couldn't suppress his laughter. Loud and dry, it hit Çetin's ears like a thunderbolt. He leapt backwards away from Fatma like a scalded cat.

'Timür! You disgusting old—'

'Sorry, son, I came back for my cigarettes.'

'There is no privacy in this place, is there!' He gathered his sheet tightly around his crotch and looked at Fatma. 'I'm so sorry, darling.'

'It's all right, Çetin.' She was smiling. It was all right really. They'd both got a bit carried away, but Fatma had known all along that sex probably wasn't a good idea in view of her advanced condition. She just felt sorry for Çetin. She knew how frustrated he could become during her pregnancies. She put her head against his shoulder and kissed his neck. 'I'd better get back to bed now or I'll be good for nothing in the morning.'

Çetin breathed deeply for a few seconds in an attempt to calm himself down. He took her chin between his fingers and kissed her lightly on the mouth. 'All right. I suppose it's for the best.'

The old man coughed. 'Oh, it is. When your mother was eight and a half months pregnant with Halil—'

'Shut up, Timür!'

Fatma eased herself slowly up from the sofa and rubbed the now permanently sore small of her back. If he hadn't been naked Çetin would have helped her, but the thought of revealing his body to his father was too much for him. Instead he scowled at the old man and hoped that he felt just a little ashamed of himself.

Fatma padded wearily towards the door. During her clinch with her husband, her nightie had got hitched up at the back and as she left the room, Çetin could see the small bunches of varicose veins that marred the otherwise smooth skin on her calves. He didn't understand why, but he knew that he even loved those ugly things. There was nothing he didn't love about Fatma. To him she would always be the pretty, plump little girl from whom he had stolen forbidden love in that old ramshackle house back in Üsküdar. The girl who hadn't been able to wait for their wedding night. The girl he'd had to cut his hand for, to smear his blood on to their marriage sheet. She closed the door behind her and he heard her footsteps disappear down the hall towards their bedroom.

As soon as she was out of earshot Çetin retaliated. 'Well done, Timür! Thanks!'

The old man coughed richly and lit a cigarette. 'No problem, son. Any time you want your sex life ruined…'

'Oh shut up, Timür!' Çetin rolled on to his back and looked up at the ceiling. The old man rarely angered him to distraction, but this time was an exception. He was nearly forty-six years old and still he had no privacy! Would he and his beautiful Fatma ever have a life together? Would the children ever grow up, the old man ever die? It was a nasty thought and Çetin felt very guilty about entertaining it, but it wouldn't go away. Perhaps he needed a holiday or a wild night out with the 'boys'? He thought it unlikely but he continued to stare at the ugly nicotine pools on the ceiling, divining for inspiration. But none came and he just remained angry. Timür was comfortable, the children were, with great difficulty, provided for. When was it going to be his turn?

Chapter Eighteen

NUR SULEYMAN LICKED a corner of her handkerchief and then scrubbed vigorously at the side of her son's face. There was an almost invisible patch of dirt marring his fine features and Nur was having none of it. Unfortunately she and her handkerchief came at the young man suddenly, with the result that he swerved violently and very nearly ran his new Renault off the road.

'Mother!' It was not his favourite word and he flung it at her through tightly gritted teeth. The car directly behind sounded its horn loudly and disapprovingly.

'Well if you washed your face properly I wouldn't have to!' she whined in reply. It was a sound that he hated and he scowled accordingly.

But then Mehmet Suleyman was not a happy man anyway. The previous night had brought him little in the way of sleep, due to a combination of the thick and sickening summer heat and a growing fear that he and Ikmen might never get to solve the Meyer case. For days they had been wandering down strange avenues; pursuing old people; talking to all manner of oddities; trying to make sense of the old man's past. But still they had nothing really! Just a bag of confusing, contradictory facts— although sorting out which facts were untrue was about as easy and reliable as placing a bet at the Casino. In the small hours of the morning, all had seemed utterly hopeless.

But then daylight had not proved to be a friend either. A furious altercation with a faulty electric razor had given way only to the greater horror of being bullied into taking Nur to the Eminönü Docks. It would have been nice just to go straight to work, but his mother wanted to catch the ferry to go and visit her sister and Mehmet had learnt many years before that resistance to her wishes was useless. He might have known that the queue of traffic waiting to cross the Golden Horn would be horrendous. Lane discipline was non-existent and he simply barged the car forward whenever the risk of an accident seemed minimal. Mehmet frequently wished that he lived somewhere 'civilised' like Holland where people learnt to drive properly *before* being let loose on the open road. Holland also had the added advantage of not being famous for arranged marriages. Although he'd successfully avoided dinner with his aunt and intended, the stupid marriage plans were still well and truly on course. And just to make sure that everyone was 'happy' about everything, Nur was now going to check on 'Auntie' and Zuleika for 'dear Mehmet' herself. He swung the car sharply to the left at the end of the Galata Bridge and fixed his mind firmly on to the practical considerations of his day.

'I'll drop you in front of the Yeni Cami, Mother,' he said. 'It's easier for me to carry on to the station from there and it's only a short walk across the road for you.'

'If it's simpler for you, darling.' His rough translation of this whine was that she was deeply disappointed he was putting his desire to get to work before her. He resolved not to give in.

'Good.' He glanced quickly at her and could see that she was crushed, but he just carried on concentrating on his driving and trying not to feel bitter. Knowing his mother, there could now be very little time left for him to indulge his fantasies about big, buxom blonde women. He wished he'd started sooner, wished he'd gone out, fallen in love with one and brought her home. Sadly, he realised that if he was ever to have the woman of his dreams she would have to be a prostitute or some transient, and possibly superior, foreign tourist.

He brought the car to a halt beside the massive square in front of the Yeni Cami. Of all the magnificent mosques in the 'old' city, this was his least favourite. Uniformly grey, it always seemed to lower unpleasantly at him. The interior wasn't much better either. Uninspiring. Perhaps it had something to do with the fact that it had been built by a Sultan's mother? He looked at his own mother and decided that this grim association probably didn't help.

Nur kissed her son on the cheek and ruffled her fingers through his beautiful hair one last time. 'I love you, Mehmet,' she said as she swung her slim legs out of the car and on to the pavement. 'I'll give Auntie Edibe and Zuleika your regards.'

He smiled weakly in reply and once she was clear of the car he lowered his foot down on the accelerator. But then he stopped. Over by the steps leading up to the mosque, something caught his attention. A uniformed officer was talking to what looked like a bundle of rags on the ground. He wasn't making much progress as the bundle, from Mehmet's point of view, appeared to be raving.

Of course he could have just driven away from the situation and forgotten all about it, but the uniformed man was very young and the bundle had very nasty, livid little eyes. With a sigh, Mehmet switched on his hazard warning lights and got out of the car. The heat hit him like a sledgehammer and as he walked towards the incident he put on his sunglasses and took his badge out of his pocket. A group of what were either English or American tourists crossed his path, including a very well-built blonde woman. She was about forty and she stared at him as he passed. Just the right age too! he thought, sadly. But he didn't stop, he could hear what the officer was saying now. He was in trouble. 'Look, Metin, nobody killed her, she just died!'

The bundle, which Suleyman could now see had no legs, was not easily convinced. 'She was a witch, they don't just die! Look at her!' He pointed one filth-encrusted finger at an even sorrier bundle of rags slumped against the wall opposite. 'Somebody killed her!'

Suleyman nudged the uniformed policeman with his el-bow and showed him his badge. 'What's going on?' he asked.

The noisy bundle keened pitifully and rubbed what was left of its legs with its hands.

'This man's friend has died. Sometime in the night. As far as I can see there's nothing suspicious about it. The old beggars die all the—'

'Oh, Sevin!' He wasn't an ancient man, like a lot of them, but he was old. Suleyman went down on one knee in front of him and looked at his face. It was wet with tears and his furious eyes were red as if he'd been drinking.

'Sevin was your friend?'

The old beggar paused for a long time before answering. Suleyman stole a glance at the other bundle balanced precariously between the wall and the step above him. If he hadn't overheard that the deceased was female he would never have known. The eyes were shut and the heavily lined jowls had already started to sag. Her beard and moustache were both luxuriant and very grey. Repelled, he stood up again, just as the beggar man started to speak.

'Last night, late, somebody came. I heard her talking.'

Suleyman bent down towards him again. 'Man or a woman?'

'Wasn't human.' He lowered his voice to a whisper. 'Azrael! He murdered her!'

Suleyman turned round to look at the young constable.

'The Angel of Death?'

The boy shrugged. 'Like so many of them, sir, away with the bloody djinn! Sir, I can manage here if you want to get off.'

Suleyman looked at the constable. The boy was attractive; he was very young too, just starting. He suddenly felt very jealous and very old, but he didn't show it. 'All right, Constable, you'll take care of, er...'

'Metin, sir. Yes.'

Suleyman half-heartedly saluted the constable and made his way back down the steps.

Sad, sad people. But Suleyman didn't dwell on Metin and his deceased friend for long. A big, ripe gypsy woman walked towards him carrying a large bundle of white linen on her head. Her strong face bore an expression of deep arrogance. He stopped and watched her, hands on hips. She didn't deviate one millimetre from her chosen course, but as she passed him she swished her long, filthy skirt against his leg. Noticing this, she turned just for an instant and looked at him, but then with a deep, throaty laugh she continued on her way.

Because it had been so unexpected, he couldn't get it out of his mind. He felt vaguely sick. To start the day like that...It seemed like an omen. One heavy blue body bag and the van from the morgue holding up all the traffic crossing the Galata Bridge. Everybody else on the bus had gawped out of the windows, pressed their faces up against the doors—except him. Some of them had even laughed when the skinny young policeman had dropped what was probably 'its' legs. But not Robert.

It was hot and he knew that the body, although safely encased in plastic, was already crawling with flies and infected with the hideous larvae of maggots. Death was like that. How the Victorians could ever have thought it glamorous was beyond him. Death through the eyes of someone like Rossetti was dignified, erotic and smelt of musk and sweet summer roses. A lie. He thought of Natalia and her death. He looked around his half-empty classroom and tried to imagine how her face would slacken and sag as soon as rigor mortis disappeared. Like that awful, ugly picture of Marilyn Monroe on the mortuary slab he'd once seen in a book. But then why should she die? Unless she had an accident or someone killed her, it was mad! Unless, of course, she had killed somebody herself and then...

He picked a sheet of paper up off his desk and held it aloft for the students to look at. It was a picture of Big Ben and the Houses of Parliament. Miraculously the sky behind the famous monument was blue. Even to himself, Robert's voice sounded as dead as his morbid thoughts. 'Who can tell me what this is?'

His question was answered by a small sea of open mouths and vacant faces. If the four Syrian boys and the Egyptian girl who made up his morning class knew, they weren't telling. Perhaps they'd all perform brilliantly when it came to the exams, but Robert didn't really think that was very likely. For the lads, at least, there were just too many distractions in sinful old Istanbul. 'Well?' he asked again. 'Anyone know? Any idea in which city you would find this building?'

The five teenagers looked hopelessly around the room for inspiration and, finding none, looked at Robert. He articulated slowly, as if to the inmates of an asylum, 'It's the Houses of Parliament and it's in London.'

He put the picture down and reached for another. Then, suddenly, and quite out of the blue, he wondered what Ikmen was doing. His heart jumped as his hand touched a small black and white photograph of Buckingham Palace. Natalia had rung and told him the policeman had been sniffing around again, talking about him and what he might have done behind his back. His poor darling had been so scared that at first she'd tried to bring their relationship to an end because of it. Robert had done well to persuade her not to do that to him—this time. But if Ikmen were to go there again...Was it perhaps going to be his last visit? Or was he perhaps coming for him now? On his way to the school right now? Robert shuddered and held the second picture up to the class. He hid his head behind it and scowled. He hadn't shaved again and his shirt smelt of old sweat. Rosemary had completely ignored him in the corridor. She wasn't alone either.

'What is this building?'

Again the silence from the class rose up and broke across him like a miserable, grey North Sea wave. His students' brains were as dead as that body the police had taken away from the Yeni Mosque. Useless things, fit only to be driven away to the morgue and subjected to undignified surgical procedures. He wondered whether Turkey was one of those countries that permitted compulsory dissection of executed criminals. He imagined some awful Dr Mengele-style surgeon touching her dead breasts with his cold, rubber-clad fingers.

It couldn't happen. It wasn't a loud voice that entered his head, but it was insistent. It couldn't happen, none of it. He was going to be OK, she was going to be OK, they were both going to be together, for ever. He'd do anything. He even looked up towards the ceiling and promised a God he didn't believe in that he'd do anything. Weird half-formed thoughts and ideas started crashing around him creating confusion. He knew this feeling. He hung on tight to the photograph of Buckingham Palace, but he felt sick and sweaty. He remembered that he hadn't eaten again, but knowledge did not make what he was experiencing any easier to bear. He felt so ill, so full up with the heat, the flies, the rich and meaty smell of death. He tried to hang on. 'What is this building?'

His head rolled. Underneath the photo he just caught a glimpse of his students' white, frightened faces as his chin descended towards the desk. His fear went and was replaced by a sort of donnish curiosity. Then everything went blank and silent.

'Look, if you don't want to marry this woman, then just say so!' To Ikmen it all seemed very straightforward. Suleyman's mother wanted to marry him off to his cousin. Suleyman was not impressed. All he had to do was put his foot down with his mother. End of story.

'I wish it were that simple.' The young man sounded morbid and self-pitying and Ikmen instinctively lashed out at him.

'It is! You tell your mother politely but firmly "no", and then you get out there!' He pointed towards the office window. 'You get yourself a big blonde bit who goes like a shit-house door during August and find true fucking love and a measure of happiness!'

'Sir—'

'Just do it, Suleyman! Like most aristocrats your family don't have so much as a *Kuruş* with which to feed themselves, so what do you have to lose?'

'I—'

'Your mother, you can't stand! Your henpecked father, you can't respect! Your brother's already made the break and married a Greek! Just follow his example!'

'But—'

'No!' He'd already wasted quite enough time on Suleyman's pathetic little problem. Sometimes people were so stupid and petty, Ikmen wanted to scream. Arranged marriages were easy—you just didn't. He hadn't! And besides, he was in a bad mood—he was sick of absolutely everything about the Meyer case. And he was especially sick of his total lack of progress. He changed the subject. 'I've decided to bring Robert Cornelius in again,' he said. 'I'm fed up with all this seeing what will happen nonsense.' He raised one hand in anticipation of any protest. 'And before you say anything, Suleyman, yes I do know that the notion of being easy on the Englishman was entirely my idea and was contrary to what the Commissioner wanted. However, unlike the Commissioner, I am always willing to admit my mistakes.'

Suleyman couldn't help smiling—ruefully—an expression not lost on Ikmen.

'And whatever you may think, Suleyman,' he continued, 'I am now going to do what my nasty old superior wants and become a total bastard. And after all the games we have been party to over the past few days, none of the players involved in this farce can complain that they are not getting what they richly deserve.'

Suleyman, his mind at least temporarily diverted from his own personal troubles, lifted his chin in assent. 'So what now, then?'

Ikmen sat down and, placing a pen between his teeth, began to 'smoke' it for a while. 'I want you to go to the Londra Language School and give Mr Cornelius the chance to clear his conscience of his own volition.'

'And if he refuses?'

'If he refuses then you tell him that we are going to check every typewriter in the school against the letter about Reinhold Smits. I think it would be instructive for him to know how fool-proof this method is.'

Suleyman smiled. 'Yes, sir.'

'Oh, and Suleyman, take Cohen with you too. I think that a little show of force, albeit of a shabby nature, may be advisable.'

Suleyman gathered together the various pieces of equipment that he might need: keys, notebook, pens, ID...

'What about Ferhat?' he said.

Ikmen took the pen out of his mouth and replaced it with a real cigarette. 'I'll deal with that, unless of course you see him. And if you do, get him to call in.'

'OK.'

As the younger man made to leave, Ikmen rose from his seat. 'Good luck, Suleyman,' he said. 'If we can get Cornelius to offer up whoever it was gave him the information about Smits, we might still get somewhere.'

'And if he doesn't offer up anyone?'

Ikmen pondered for a few seconds before answering. 'Well,' he sighed, 'if the typewriter business doesn't persuade him then I think that a full review of his work permit might be our next step. I mean, if that is not totally in order then it could be neces-sary for him to come and spend a little time with us.

Suleyman raised his eyes towards the ceiling and grinned just a little. 'I see.'

'Well, off you go then,' said Ikmen and, sitting down again, proceeded to light his cigarette.

The last person Robert had wanted to meet was the School Director. Unfortunately, however, Mr Edib wanted to speak to him quite urgently. There had been rumours, a couple of complaints and now this—fainting in class. Not that Edib would be heavy, that wasn't his way. No, a nice friendly chat in his office. He ushered Robert through the door and they both sat down.

Edib immediately assumed a professionally concerned expression. 'You are feeling better now?'

Robert mumbled. 'Yes. Nothing to eat this morning. Had a bad stomach for a while. You know how it is.'

Edib didn't but he agreed with a small, sympathetic grunt anyway. 'An unfortunate event, but one, I must say, of several over the past, I think, two weeks.'

Robert sighed heavily. 'Yes.'

'A very public argument with another member of staff, the matter of your appearance. I myself have noticed that in class you are less than—'

'Yes, I know. I'm sorry, Director.' Robert raised his head and looked at his employer. He could feel that his eyes were very red and watery. 'I've no excuse...'

'Perhaps.' Edib clasped his hands together underneath his plump chin. 'But I am bound to ask whether anything is wrong, Robert. If you have trouble maybe I can help. There is no question of disciplinary action at this time. Please do not be afraid.'

But Robert was, although for none of the reasons that were passing through Edib's mind. 'I suppose I'm a bit run down...'

'The curse of the dedicated disseminator of knowledge!' Edib smiled as pleasantly as his greedy, unpleasant face would allow. 'And the students are not always easy. I know.' He laughed. Trying to be one of the boys. 'But we must go on, Robert! These young people are placing their trust in us!'

And their parents' cash in your pocket! thought Robert spitefully. 'Yes, I know,' he said. 'I will try to—'

'Good!' Edib smiled again; it was horrible. 'I knew there was nothing serious. But really these things cannot happen again. You do understand?'

'Yes.' There wasn't much not to understand. Smarten up, stop having rows, toady to the horrible children and eat occasionally. It wasn't a massive agenda and Robert knew that he had to do it if he wanted to remain gainfully employed. If he did. Of course, the ideal scenario would be for himself and Natalia just to pack up and run away to England. But...

'You know,' Edib continued, 'we all have problems. I myself have a lot of difficulty in my life.' He took a cigarette out of his shirt pocket and lit up. 'Since that Inspector Ikmen came here with all his rude, arrogant policemen, I have had nothing but questions from the parents. Why were the police here? What did they want? On and on!' He held his arms up and shrugged. 'What I have done?'

But Robert's attention to Edib's words had switched off after the word 'Ikmen'. Then he thought about that stupid, stupid letter. The one he knew, but then again, didn't know whether he'd touched with his fingers. He'd written it right here. Used the information she had given him. Planned it.

'You look a little green again, my friend.' Edib had walked around the desk and placed his hand on Robert's shoulder. Odd he hadn't noticed him move. 'Perhaps you should take the rest of the day off. Get some food, some fresh air.'

'Er...'

'I really think that you should. Start fresh again tomorrow, eh?'

Tomorrow. Yes, if there were to be one, that is. Robert licked his parched lips and nodded his assent. Go home. Think. But then perhaps not, no. Perhaps it was best to go out now and divert his mind for a while. Possibly—or, more accurately, definitely—with the help of alcohol.

It was an impossible question to answer and even though it was one that a lot of his older patients frequently asked him, Dr Imad's necessarily oblique replies did not get any easier.

'The truth is,' he said as he replaced the old man's hand on top of the bed-covers, 'that I just can't give you any definite time frame.'

Reinhold Smits raised his red and rheumy eyes up to the doctor's face, his expression a mask of both wants and despair. 'I appreciate your difficulty, doctor,' he said, 'but am I looking at months or years or...'

'If you continue with the chemotherapy and restrict yourself to a quiet lifestyle there is no reason why you shouldn't experience quality of life for some time to come. So far, you seem to be responding positively.'

'But when the end does come, it will be both painful and undignified!'

Dr Imad sat down in the chair beside his patient's bed and then took hold of the old man's hand once again. 'Look, Reinhold, there are enough pain-controlling agents on the market these days to make me almost certain that you will not suffer an agonising death. You have more than enough money to allow you access to the most powerful and sophisticated drugs and besides, remission is, although unlikely, not an eventuality that can be entirely discounted.'

The old man laughed. 'You'd like that, wouldn't you!'

'To see you recover? Well, of course I would!'

'Yes.' Reinhold Smits looked down at what was left of his frail form under the bedsheets. 'Because dead men can't write cheques, can they doctor?'

The doctor did not raise his voice in reply. He was accustomed to goading of this type. 'That's rather unfair of you, Reinhold.'

'Yes, I know.' Now he looked sad, almost regretful. But

then that was the way of his moods now. 'The niceties of life somehow disappear when you stand upon God's doorstep.'

'Allah is, if nothing else, merciful, Reinhold.'

Smits laughed again. It was one of those days, grimly amusing. 'What Allah may or may not be is of no interest to me. In case you've forgotten, Doctor, I am a Calvinist like my father and believe me, my God will show little in the way of mercy to a person like myself.'

Dr Suleyman Imad had been Smits's personal physician for nearly forty years—plenty enough time to realise that there really was no answer to his last statement. Instead, he simply slipped his stethoscope off his neck and placed it back in his briefcase. Smits was as well as could be expected given his recent experiences and there was little to be gained by staying any longer.

Smits, seeing this activity, concurred. 'So, you had better be on your way then.'

'Yes.' Imad retrieved his jacket from the back of the chair and slipped it on. 'I would like you to think about what I said regarding the police though, Reinhold.'

The old man shrugged. 'I may. Although I can't imagine what it might achieve.'

'They had no right to harass a sick man like yourself, we can see the result of that strain in your condition now. I would be only too pleased to speak to your lawyer in those terms should you decide to take action.'

Smits closed his eyes and rested his head back against the pillows. 'We will see,' he said. 'Could you please send Wilkinson up here on your way out?'

'Of course.' Imad picked his briefcase up and then smiled at the closed and sightless face before him. 'I'll come by again tomorrow.'

'As you wish.'

'I'll see you then.'

As soon as he heard the bedroom door close behind the retreating doctor, Reinhold Smits opened his eyes again. God, but he was so awfully tired of it all! He had been tired even before all this Meyer business began, but with that now added in on top of the ghastliness of dying, the whole thing was utterly unbearable. Not least because the most terrible aspect of the whole affair was the one thing that he couldn't share with anyone.

The way Leonid's body and face had looked in death was, without doubt, the most frightening thing he had ever seen— that and the stench, the flies, the terror in blood that almost leapt upon him from that filthy wall. So horrifying, so barbaric and yet so awfully sacred too.

If only he hadn't mentioned the swastika to the old bitch. If only he hadn't been, wasn't still, so terribly vulnerable. A whole lifetime of being discreet, it now appeared, counted for nothing.

And just that one tiny bit of thoughtlessness meant that Maria Gulcu could, if she wanted, destroy him. Which was what he knew she would do. He almost laughed when he thought about it now. Leonid would have laughed himself sick.

A soft tap on his door was followed by the entrance of the butler.

Smits, as ever, pulled himself together for the benefit of the staff. 'Ah, Wilkinson,' he said, his voice once again a paragon of authority, 'I want you to gather some items together for me from the library and bring them up here.'

'Yes, sir.'

Using his fingers as markers for each item, Reinhold Smits listed those things that he needed. 'I would like all of my photograph albums, a book called *The Death of Russia* by Simon Danilov—it's in English and resides in the History section—plus my writing paper, envelopes and a pen.' He raised a finger in warning. 'Not a ballpoint, a proper pen. Do you understand?'

'Yes, sir.'

With a flick of his hand he waved the menial away. 'Off you go then.'

However, once the door closed behind the butler, Smits's mask of superior confidence fell. There is often a gap between knowing what is right and acting upon that knowledge and even though Reinhold Smits had now taken that step in his mind there were still niggling doubts. Once it was done, Madame Maria could place any sort of interpretation upon it that she wished. After all, even to the so-called dispassionate policemen, his actions could seem like guilt or spite or both.

But then did that matter? No. No, all that mattered now was that almost everything in the albums was destroyed. Then it would be just like none of it had ever happened and now, of course, without Leonid, it might as well have just been a dream anyway. But, oh, how he'd enjoyed it. Smits smiled again and this time the expression stayed on his features for some time.

Robert Cornelius's first thought after he had excused himself from Mr Edib's oily presence had been to get as far away from the Londra Language School as possible. This had, not of necessity but more as a reaction to a sort of internal dare he decided to have with himself, meant that he had to walk through the streets of Balat again. Although almost insanely confident at first, it wasn't until he came across that apartment block on that corner that it all, suddenly and with almost coronary-inducing power, became too real and unbearably horrifying. And that he then found himself running again only added to his sense of being inside a nightmarish and inescapable loop of time. At one point he almost fancied that he even saw Natalia running in front of him, her face scared and drawn and just that little bit too thin. And yet despite all this and despite his almost bursting chest he kept running until he was very far from Balat.

Finally stopping in order to catch his breath, he looked around him and, to his dismay, he discovered that he was in a part of the city that he didn't recognise. It was like he had got to wherever he was blindfolded and although he assumed that, since he had passed the old apartment block in the usual way, he was probably somewhere closer to the Sea of Marmara than to the Golden Horn, he couldn't be certain of that. But then given his current situation, did that really matter?

He looked first to his left and then right. It was a typical Istanbul street: a clutch of shops, a few broken paving stones, a selection of evil-eyed dogs and cats. For no other reason than it seemed like a good idea at the time, he started walking to the right. There had to be a bar or a hotel somewhere nearby and that was after all what he was here (wherever here was) for. With drink he might just be able to forget and that was all that he wanted—for the moment. To hell with letters and women and policemen and old, dead Jews. What he wanted was to be himself again, just for a bit, just before it all got going again, leading God alone knew where.

And then suddenly there was an enormous expanse of blue in front of his eyes—a great sea with its little boats and tankers and pleasure craft flying the familiar Turkish crescent and star flag. And then there was music too and bars and drink and happy, laughing voices. When they want to relax, people go down to be by the sea and have a few drinks. It's very benign and very normal. Robert Cornelius, unshaven, hurting and sick in all sorts of ways, moved to join in the fun.

Chapter Nineteen

LEONID. IT WAS STRANGE but looking back over the years it was almost as if she were thinking about two people. Leonid before and after middle age. He'd been young for so long! At forty he'd still been like a teenager, still coming round to the house with a smile and a jaunty spring in his step, his pockets always and forever full of Reinhold Smits's money. He'd made her feel quite old—then. She'd resented it. She remembered the feeling well.

But he'd paid in the end, of course. It had been almost as if his whole life had caught up with him at once. One day he was young, the next…Perhaps the enormity of it had come to him in a dream, perhaps like Lady Macbeth he'd finally realised that nothing he had done or could do would ever wash it away. But at that point they had ceased being friends and for a time she had felt sad. His new incarnation was an obligation, a mere mouth in which to pour alcohol and scraps of food. The last time she'd visited him in his foul Balat hovel, twenty, or maybe even thirty years ago, she'd been disgusted to discover that he was completely toothless. He'd tried to kiss her but she hadn't let him. She'd endured enough of his rough caresses coming across the mountains of Armenia and beneath the sparse trees on the central Anatolian plain. Although 'endured' she knew was not really the right word. Endurance implied lack of complicity.

Maria took a cigarette from the box beside her bed, lit it and then leant back heavily against her pillows. Leonid had been doubly excited during their journey out of Russia. Excited by her and also intoxicated by the situation. It had been a lot for a seventeen-year-old boy to take in. For days, although he'd been able to touch her, conversation with him had been impossible. It was almost as if his groping hands and searching tongue made up in some way for his inability to speak to her. But at the time, of course, she hadn't analysed it. All she'd known then was the blood. Three rivers: the one that poured from the wound on her face; the one that coursed painfully down her legs when he took her that first time; and the one she'd seen running down the wall just before they left. The one Leonid had slipped on as he tried to lift the woman's dead body up on to his shoulders. She could still see the look of horror on his face as, filtered through the mist of smoke that had seared her half-closed eyes, she'd seen him look into the woman's dead face. She'd wondered at the time what someone like him was doing there.

Not that she'd ever loved him. There had been gratitude and, just after they entered Turkey, a moment of great passion, probably brought about by relief, but not love. Leonid was a Jew, an animal, something 'other' and unpleasant—a killer of Christ.

She looked across to where Nicholas was leaning against the wall and squinted narrowly the better to see him. The first visitor she'd had after he was born had been Leonid. Even before Mehmet. Drunk, even then, Leonid had pinched the baby's cheek affectionately before sitting on her bed and trying to persuade her to one of his insane schemes. But she had, as she had always done, refused and rebuffed him then too. Besides pain and frustration, she had actually given him very little.

Perhaps even as he lay dying, looking up at that filthy smoke-stained ceiling, his stomach and his throat burning white hot, he'd thought his pain then was a present from her. Perhaps at the last he'd even cursed her. She felt cursed. When she'd first heard of his death, almost gagging at the horror of it, she'd felt cursed. And, in addition, Leonid's death had opened her own son's mouth against her and now there was no stopping it. Even from beyond the grave, Leonid still had her by the throat. Nicky's sullen eyes slid across her features in disgust and she looked away from them, down towards the picture of the pretty plump girl with chestnut hair that rested in her lap. The fat cheeks were unscarred, the eyes clear. She wished she knew where the original was, when and where it had been taken, but she couldn't remember. There had been so many photographs.

'Well, Mama?'

She sighed deeply and stubbed her cigarette out in a small terracotta ashtray. She looked at his face and was struck by the almost arrogant light she saw in his eyes. That was new. But then Nicky had done a lot of thinking and his conclusions were leading him down a new and exciting path. Nicky had nothing to fear, the world and all its unknown delights waited for him— the tall bearded man emerging from the shadows. Maria cleared her throat. 'I don't know, Nicky. I don't know.'

'Well, Mama, it is your decision ultimately, but unless we do something I cannot see that things are going to get any better. Natalia has, and with your blessing I might add, already involved one unfortunate outsider. I understand your views—'

'And I yours'—she shot him a look like a dagger—'now. But I've never lied to you, Nicky, whatever you may think. The fact that you have changed your mind, that events have caused you to question—'

'Events?' He moved across to the bed and sat down beside her. 'What we are talking about here, Mama, is murder! Two people from this family were present at Uncle Leonid's apartment on the day he died. And'—he held a finger up to silence her—'before you allude, yet again, to Reinhold Smits, let me remind you that we, in addition, have a confession here. If Smits says he was there—'

'Which he was!'

'Yes, admittedly. But the fact remains, Mama, that Natalia told us all about how Uncle Leonid looked in death some time before Smits contacted you and inadvertently confirmed some other descriptions—about the existence of the swastika, for instance. And with an admission of guilt and a detailed description of how it was done to poor Uncle Leonid originating from this house, I think that the chances of Smits being involved are rather slim.'

'Oh, but Nicky, Natalia could have been wrong. She could have got there just after Smits...'

Nicholas rubbed his eyes before replying. 'But then, Mama, you are forgetting, are you not, just whose hands Natalia—'

'She could be lying! You know what a wicked disgusting girl she can be!'

'Well, she's not lying about this, Mama. What on earth would be her reason for doing so? There really cannot be one, can there? You and I both know that.' He knew she wouldn't like this, but try as he might, he at least could not see any other way around the problem. 'Basically, such matters as this are for the police anyway. We must give them the information we have and let them make the decision. This has gone on far too long already!'

She cast her eyes downwards now and he had the distinct feeling that what she said next was really the principal area of concern. 'And what of the family?'

'What of it?'

She looked up quickly, the movement of her neck snapping her now furious face forwards once again. 'You say what of the family? You say this after a lifetime of belief and tradition? You say it in the face of what you know are our hopes and aspirations for the future?'

Nicholas sighed. And here they were again, back full circle with the family again—the wearisome and to him now completely irrelevant concept of the family. When he spoke he did so slowly and deliberately as if to a child. 'Mama, by the time the police and the immigration people have finished with us, we will be very fortunate if we are even able to lay claim to a couple of rented rooms.'

'No, no, no! I cannot and I will not let go of everything that I am, that I feel. That is asking things of me that are beyond my endurance!'

Nicholas looked his mother steadily in the eyes and saw in them the things, or rather the lack of things, that he had always known were there. 'And that is just about it, isn't it, Mama? The fact that you can't do what needs to be done is not because loved family members are involved. It's because of you and your delusions and your strange, crazy little world. It's never been about us and that is why you have allowed us to become the pitiful monsters that we are.' He stood up. 'Look at me, Mama! I'm an old man and yet I wear the uniform of a regiment of soldiers who all died before I was born! I am a freak! And what is more, I am your freak! Look at me, Mama!'

She didn't speak again and neither did he until he reached the door. But there he turned and, looking her full in the face, he said, 'I'll give you until tomorrow morning, Mama, and then I will do what has to be done myself. But if you have any honour at all, I suggest you make that move yourself. It will, if only in part, help to re-establish my respect for you.' And with one tiny bow he was gone.

Alone, bitter and frustrated, Maria Gulcu attempted to rip her bedclothes to shreds, but found that all her strength had deserted her.

The Bar Paris was not the sort of place to pop into for a quick drink. Unless the intention was to get wildly and outrageously drunk, it was the kind of establishment that was best given a wide berth. The regular clientele was generally noisy, frequently criminal and many of them were no strangers to violence.

Ikmen didn't go there often, but whenever he did he threw himself into the experience totally.

He held the grimy front door open for Suleyman and the young man watched as several highly painted prostitutes peered through the gloom in their direction.

The place reeked of old sweat and vomit. Suleyman didn't even attempt to hide his disgust. 'In here!'

'Yes,' Ikmen replied simply, his face as innocent as that of a guide showing a tourist round a mosque.

'You want me to go in here!'

Ikmen shrugged. 'The drinks are cheap.' He let go of the door and stepped into the smoky gloom.

Suleyman watched the door close on him and sighed. The choice was simple really. Either he joined Ikmen in the alcoholic hell of the Bar Paris and risked life and limb at the hands of the various undesirables beyond its grim door or he went home to his mother. He pushed the door boldly aside and drifted towards the bar on a sea of smoke.

He saw Ikmen immediately, sitting on a barstool, holding up a glass and shouting something he couldn't make out at the barman. Even amongst such bizarre company as the Bar Paris provided, Ikmen stood out as something especially shabby and unkempt.

Just before he reached Ikmen, however, Suleyman saw an extremely tall woman in a green sequinned dress rush in front of him and grab the barstool he'd been heading for. As soon as she sat down the woman flung her arms around Ikmen's neck and kissed him affectionately on the cheek. To Suleyman's surprise, rather than pull away from this unlooked-for advance, Ikmen the devoted father and husband kissed the woman back—on the lips.

To say that he was shocked was an understatement. For a few moments he just stood and stared with his mouth open like a goldfish.

Ikmen laughed. 'Come over then, Suleyman. Come and meet Samsun.'

He looked at the woman with her long hooked nose and grimy teeth and attempted a smile. Ikmen placed a large glass of something that smelt dangerously close to petrol in his hand and made the formal introductions.

'Samsun, this is Suleyman my sergeant. Suleyman, this is Samsun, a divine lady of dubious profession who also happens to be my cousin.' He grabbed a sequin-clad knee between his fingers and squeezed. The woman giggled girlishly, her large Adam's apple bobbing up and down against her blue and red pearl necklace.

'Çetin, you always know how to treat a girl!' The voice was very deep and contained just the slightest trace of a foreign accent, but it was unmistakably male. The creature put one hand on the bar and Suleyman noticed the thick mats of hair that grew on the knuckles just below the painted fingernails.

Suleyman tried not to freeze. 'Hello,' he said and quickly took a gulp from his glass. The nearest he could come to describing the effect the liquor had upon him was to liken it to being smashed in the face by a tank.

Samsun, seeing his distress, patted him gently on the back and looked concerned. 'The brandy's a little violent here unless you're used to it.'

'But worth cultivating, if only from a financial point of view,' said Ikmen, pulling his cousin's heavy claw away from Suleyman's back. He winked, slyly. 'Now, now, Samsun, no touching!'

'What, with a policeman? Are you mad!'

Ikmen shrugged his shoulders. 'You're Albanian.'

'Which makes me crazy?' Samsun pursed her lips in mock affront. 'Anyway, I prefer gold-dealers, they're very generous and they like to play *femme* in bed.' She pouted the last word lasciviously at Suleyman.

The young man forced himself to make headway with his drink. The only consolation he had was that he could see Ikmen was fully aware of his discomfort. He wouldn't have to endure this for long.

Samsun put her hand on Ikmen's shoulder and caressed his neck. 'So what are you doing in this dump then, Inspector?'

'Same as you, I suspect, minus the sex.'

'Just wrecked or falling down drunk?'

Ikmen looked into his glass and rubbed his chin. 'I don't know yet, haven't made up my mind.'

Samsun laughed and took a small gold cigarette case out of her handbag. 'I always favour falling down if I'm not having sex, and you're not, so...'

Ikmen leant forward and stared into Samsun's eyes. 'You going to be here later, gorgeous?'

'Why?' Samsun narrowed her eyes. 'Want a reading?'

'I might,' replied Ikmen archly.

'Well, it's the real reason you came.' Samsun lit a cigarette and breathed the smoke out into his face. 'Want it now?'

'No.' Ikmen inclined his head towards Suleyman. 'When you've turned a few tricks.'

'Like a girl with money in her handbag, do you?'

'I find an enhanced ability to pay for my drinks endears a person to me.' Ikmen drained his glass and motioned to the barman to fill him up again.

Samsun screamed once again and Suleyman found himself wondering whether her jiggling breasts were the result of hormone treatment or some sort of clever prosthetic device.

'Anyway.' Ikmen slapped his knee with his hand and then stood up. He looked across at Suleyman. 'The sergeant and I have things to discuss, so I'm going to take him to one of the tables. Away from flapping ears.'

Samsun pouted. 'Well, no fiddling under the table then, Çetin. Not unless you let me watch.'

Ikmen held up one hand as if taking an oath. 'Promise.' He took Suleyman by the elbow.

Samsun noticed this and tutted furiously. 'You're a married man, Çetin! Remember!'

Ikmen leant back towards Samsun and kissed her on the cheek. 'I've got eight children for an *aide-mémoire!*'

They smiled at each other and Samsun pinched Çetin's cheek. 'I'll see you later then, little cousin.'

'You will.'

Ikmen steered Suleyman towards a rough beer-stained table in a particularly dark corner of the Bar Paris. All the action seemed to be concentrated around the bar itself and by the front door. This one corner, however, was empty.

'Perfect,' said Ikmen as he sat down on a small stool covered with biscuit crumbs. 'Sorry about all that, Suleyman.' He pointed back towards where Samsun could still be seen languishing across the bar. 'Family.'

'Er, yes.' Suleyman sat down opposite and cradled what was left of his drink in nervous hands. 'Samsun as a name is, er...'

'His real name's Mustapha, but that sits a bit uncomfortably with the handbag.' Ikmen leant across the table and whispered, 'Rumour has it that he chose the name Samsun because he has a particular penchant for men from that city.'

There really was no reply to that and so Suleyman just smiled.

Ikmen changed the subject. 'Anyway, on the work front, a day of unrelieved ill fortune, I think you'll agree.'

'Yes.' Suleyman lowered his head and looked into the depths of his glass. The horrid brew seemed almost to leer back at him. Like an evil omen.

'Of course,' Ikmen continued wearily, 'if I hadn't ordered Ferhat back we wouldn't be in this situation now.'

'You weren't to know that Cornelius would go off sick.'

Ikmen sighed. 'No. But if only the swine had gone back to his apartment! I mean what is he doing out there wandering about if he's supposed to be ill!'

'I don't know.'

They sat in silence for a few moments, both men pondering upon what might have been had fate not placed yet another obstacle in their path.

It was Suleyman who came out of this grim reverie first. 'But still,' he said, 'at least we now know that Cornelius and Natalia Gulcu are definitely more than just friends.'

Ikmen laughed. 'Well we always knew that—at least I did.'

'Oh, yes, but the *kapıcı* was very graphic about it all: the fights, the loud sex'—he wrinkled his nose up just very slightly—'the shamelessness of that girl.'

'Yes, well…' Ikmen paused for just a moment to light a cigarette. 'You asked at the Gulcu house, I take it?'

'Yes, but he wasn't there. The old man with the beard answered the door and was, it must be said, really very emphatic on that point.'

'Mmm.' Ikmen narrowed his eyes, his suspicions instantly aroused.

'But then what could I do?' Suleyman continued. 'As you said yourself, we don't have enough proper evidence to arrest Cornelius and I had no authorisation to search the Gulcu property.'

'Then perhaps that's the next step,' Ikmen said.

'What, you mean search the house for Cornelius now?'

'No. No, he isn't there, I'm pretty certain of that. But…'

Suleyman used this pause in order to push his foul drink to one side. 'But what, sir?'

'But that canister, or whatever, that held the acid has to be somewhere, doesn't it?'

'Yes.'

'And if one of them did kill Meyer then it's likely that it's still in the Gulcus' house.'

Suleyman looked doubtful. 'Yes, but they'd have to be mad to still have it now, surely!'

Ikmen smiled. 'Ah, but then they are mad, aren't they, Suleyman? You've seen how they dress, how they live. The Gulcus are not quite of this world and I suspect they don't really appreciate the rules of the world as the rest of us do.'

'Granted, but…'

'But what?'

He shrugged. 'Well, I still don't see why they would have killed Meyer. I still don't get the motive.'

Ikmen tipped what was left of his drink down his throat

and then banged the glass back down upon the table. 'Well, you're not alone there! And until Mrs Gulcu, Mr Smits or both of them give up some of their secrets we can only guess about that I'm afraid. I do, however, believe that Meyer's supposed involvement in an execution all those years ago does have something to do with it. I mean, if you do away with people, I imagine that after such a great passage of time as we are dealing with here the memory or hurt, or whatever, goes away. But not so for Meyer. Not even the drink could keep his guilt at bay. It's like it was on his mind all the time, informing every self-destructive thing that he did. And, as I've said before, it is my belief that someone kept it well in his mind too.'

'Yes, but why? I mean particularly with regard to Smits, why keep Meyer guilty for all that time and to what end?'

'I can only assume,' said Ikmen, 'for reasons we do not yet understand. It is, I believe, all to do with the three of them having "things" on each other.'

'Like what?'

Ikmen shrugged. 'I don't know. Meyer's old crime, Smits's guilty Nazi past. Mrs Gulcu? Well...'

'Her illegal status?' Suleyman offered.

Ikmen took another pull from his glass. 'Oh, no, I don't think so,' he said. 'You and I both saw how bothered she was when that subject came up in conversation and it wasn't very much. Whatever else she may be, Mrs Gulcu is not a respecter of bureaucracy.'

'But...' Suleyman noticed that Ikmen was looking down at his empty glass now and thought that perhaps he should give him a chance to replenish it. Ikmen, however, had other ideas.

'But what, Suleyman?' he urged.

'But why would either Smits or Mrs Gulcu kill Meyer now? I mean what is the connection?'

Ikmen threw his cigarette end down on to the floor and then ground it out with his foot. 'That I don't know,' he said, 'but unless something either concrete or of a forensic nature turns up soon, I'm really afraid we're going to lose this one.'

Suleyman let out a long, weary breath. 'This is a nightmare. And like you I'm beginning to wonder if we'll ever find out what's going on, what has gone on, who is telling the truth...'

'Well, if I have anything to do with it we will.' Ikmen smiled suddenly and brilliantly—it was typical of him, this sudden switch from deep despair to over-confident optimism, in almost less than a heartbeat. He pointed to Suleyman's nearly full glass. 'Can I get you something else? Something that won't make you go blind?'

As he watched the last glorious, cherubic countenance curl up amongst the flames and turn to ashes, Reinhold Smits wiped one small tear from his eye. It had been a long, long time since he'd actually felt the pressure of a little girl's skin against his own and yet had he been asked to name any of those children he could have done so. But it had to be better this way and with the poor, tattered examples that Leonid had held over his head for all these years now also consigned to a fiery grave, there was finally an end to the matter. Now he was where he had always, in reality, resided, totally and completely alone—all the crutches removed, all the self-delusory stories told.

A sharp rap on his door announced the arrival of Wilkinson. Smits, wearily, got up from his place in front of the fire and started to make his way back to his bed.

'Come,' he said as he moved, so painfully, across the room. As the butler entered, Smits could tell by the expression on his face that he looked even more ghastly than usual. But then it had been a long day. As usual, however, he did not allude to anything of a personal nature with his staff.

'You can take that book back down to the library now,' he said, pointing to the volume that rested on his writing table. 'Lay it out at the page indicated on my desk, if you will.'

'Yes, sir.' The butler glided soundlessly across to the table and took the book lovingly between his gloved fingers.

'Oh and there's a letter you might deliver for me also, beside the book.'

The servant picked up the pink perfumed envelope and looked at the information on the front. 'Do you wish me to do this now or in the morning?'

'Now, if you please.' Smits eased himself painfully back into his bed. 'Tell Muhammed he's to take you in the car.'

'Very well, sir.' He made to leave but Smits momentarily prevented him.

'Oh, Wilkinson...'

'Sir?'

'Just one more thing.' He moved his pillows slightly in order to be more comfortable. 'Have you ever wondered, having worked for me for so many years, what it must be like to be as wealthy as I am?'

For a moment, the butler looked totally nonplussed, but then, regaining his customary *savoir-faire*, he replied, 'Well, yes, it has crossed my mind, sir.'

Smits smiled. 'And?'

'I think that in some ways, it must be really rather nice, sir.'

Smits nodded. 'Yes, I thought so.'

The butler put the book under his arm and slipped the letter into the pocket of his tailcoat. 'Well, sir, if that will be all...'

'That will be all, Wilkinson, thank you.'

He bowed before he left. 'I'll see you in the morning then, sir.'

'Goodnight, Wilkinson.'

'Goodnight, sir.'

Smits didn't move again until he heard the engine of his car start up in the drive outside. Then, with one uncharacteristically swift movement, he opened the drawer of his bedside cabinet and took out what had been waiting in there for him all that day. He knew that he would need to move quickly now or his nerve would desert him.

Chapter Twenty

IT IS SAID THAT A CRIMINAL will always return to the scene of his crime. It is the sort of cliché that causes those too sophisticated actually to work in the law-enforcement profession themselves to laugh. But it didn't have that effect upon Robert Cornelius. As he watched the moon rise above the dark bulk of the Kariye Museum, mirth was the last emotion that motivated his thoughts.

He had returned to Balat almost unconsciously. It had all started innocently enough with the simple desire he'd had earlier that afternoon to get drunk. One drink in the first bar had led to others in other bars and it wasn't until he was on his seventh or eighth gin and tonic that he'd realised where his seemingly random wanderings were leading him. At first the sight of Meyer's grim apartment block had come as a shock: how and when had he got back there? But as he looked from it to the Kariye and then back again he realised that somehow it was meant. He didn't know why, perhaps it was simply the way the alcohol was acting upon his brain. By the light of the round, bright moon he fancied he saw her again, pressed close up against the wall, ready to run. But he blinked and saw that it wasn't her, it was a policeman, complete with submachine-gun, looking bored and leaning against the entrance to the stairwell. He'd seen a lot of them since he entered the quarter, but none that he recognised and certainly not Ikmen. Their presence did, however, bring home the fact that for him to be wandering around Balat at night was probably not a good idea. If Ikmen were to find out it could lead him to certain damaging but understandable conclusions. There was, however, another bar just around the corner, he'd seen it once before when he'd worked late at the school, and Robert desperately needed another drink.

The police guard outside Meyer's apartment appeared to look straight at him and cleared his throat as if making ready to speak. Robert put one unsteady foot in front of the other and moved very carefully in the direction of the bar. The policeman took a step back at this point and to Robert's relief seemed to melt into the shadow beneath one of the first-floor balconies. Perhaps he too felt that slightly eerie sensation that had come over Robert when he'd first looked around and discovered where he was a few minutes earlier. The quarter was certainly quiet, but then it always was—the Jews didn't seem to share the Turks' love of blaring radios and maximum-volume televisions. But wasn't there something else?

He turned into the little alleyway where he remembered seeing the bar and peered ahead of him. Here, because of the height of the buildings on either side, the clean white rays of the moon couldn't penetrate and where balconies overhung the street even the night sky was blotted out. The intense darkness was similar to that experienced when a tube train stops in a tunnel and the lights go out. Robert hated that feeling too. But if he wanted a drink he'd have to go forward into the blackness and just take his chances. Either that or he'd have to turn away and leave the quarter altogether and he didn't want to do that. Not yet.

As he staggered forward he experienced a sharp rush of sour bile entering his throat and he gagged noisily. Too much booze already—as if that mattered. But then not much did any more. He was a bad teacher; he'd never really been cut out for the job, never really liked it. He'd just sort of drifted into it, like most of the things he'd done, except of course his relationships. That was what was so galling. Conscious or unconscious, he always seemed to make a mess of everything. Perhaps it all came down to lack of self-esteem, his anticipation that everything was always going to go wrong affecting actual events.

Just ahead of him a door opened and a hand threw a squawking cat out into the sultry night. For a moment a tiny part of the street was illuminated, giving him a depressing view of the piles of rubbish heaped high against the edge of the pavement. The door closed and Robert knew that he was alone with the cat, wherever it was.

It was when he was about halfway down the unnamed and unknowable street that he heard the music. At first he thought it was Turkish, but as his ears became accustomed to the sound he realised that the singer, a woman, was performing in a language that was completely unknown to him. Perhaps it was Ladino, the queer Hebrew/Spanish dialect native to the district. Whatever it was was clearly oriental. Even after all this time the half-tones still jarred uneasily against his ordered European ears. It was good though because the advent of music probably meant that he was on the right track for the bar. He hoped so, he was having odd thoughts and no longer wanted to be alone. It wasn't like him, this irrational rage against a poor old dead Jew he'd never known. Logically he knew whom he should be angry with and it wasn't Leonid Meyer. But the anger persisted. Everything had been all right up until the point he'd seen Natalia running away from Meyer's apartment. Progress with her had not been either fast or easy, but...

Another policeman stepped suddenly out of a doorway and pushed roughly past him. Robert turned and watched him strut arrogantly on his way towards the Kariye. For a second he wondered why the officer hadn't challenged him, they often did late at night, but then he remembered the invisibility of drunks. People always gave them a wide berth, even sometimes policemen. It was less hassle to leave them where they were than to bring them in. It saved on cell space and nine times out of ten it was the more pleasant option. Robert turned back and noticed a small string of red and green Christmas lights strung across the top of a doorway to his left. That was where the music was coming from, and as he drew closer he could smell the sharp, oily aroma of cheap raki.

It was an odd notion, a Jews' bar. Years before, when he was still at university, Robert had been to a Jewish wedding in a place called Forte Hall, just to the north of London. It had been a peculiar affair and had been almost entirely devoted to the consumption of large amounts of food. Of course there had been alcohol, lots of it, but nobody had bothered much with it. He reached the dark and, as he could see even by the meagre light of the Christmas bulbs, filthy door, and pushed it gently with his foot. It wasn't locked and creaked open easily. Light the colour of thin rosé wine spilt out into the street and across Robert's shoes, closely followed by a puff of dense greenish smoke. There was noise inside, the woman still singing and the sound of deep masculine voices conversing in a tongue that sounded both hard and liberally laced with thick mucus.

Emboldened by his need for alcohol, Robert stepped forward and pushed the door wide open. Twenty or thirty dark, bearded faces looked up from their liquor-filled glasses and stared. One nose shaped like a scythe and surmounted by a tall faded Homburg sniffed loudly as if in disgust. The only woman in the place, the fat gold-spangled singer, kept up her mournful rendition of whatever the song was, but she had seen Robert and she was staring too. None of them looked in the least bit kind, in fact most of the eyes that met his were openly hostile. It wasn't something to which the Englishman was accustomed and for a moment it rendered him totally incapable of all movement. It reminded him of the time he had inadvertently stepped into a

Kurdish coffee house in the east, out near Mardin and experienced the open, rather dangerous hostility in the people's faces,
that creeping feeling that if he crossed the threshold he might
live, or not, to regret it.

And yet these were only Jews! These were only people like
Marion and Martin from Hornsey, the Charles family who
used to live next door when he was at primary school! None of
the eyes before him so much as flickered as they hardened. As
he stared back Robert realised that he couldn't even begin to
wonder what they were thinking and nor really did he care. He
meant them no harm and he wanted a drink for which he was
willing to pay. The cold black eyes made him angry again and
he staggered forward across to the shabby, poorly stocked bar.

It was then that the woman stopped singing.

Samsun breathed in deeply and looked down into the bowl of
water on the table. Apart from herself, Çetin and a few quiet
stragglers, the Bar Paris was empty now. Of course the staff
would still serve anyone who was capable of buying a drink, but
with each passing minute that was becoming less and less likely.

Samsun closed her eyes for a second and tried to cut out all
external distractions. She listened to the sound of her own bron-
chitic breathing and mentally washed the far corners of her mind
in a stream of crystal pure water. Çetin had come specifically
to her for this reading and he only did that when it was important. Samsun's 'sight', though so often devastatingly correct, was
not an easy gift to be around. It could be frustratingly random
in character and frightening. Samsun rarely saw good in her
scrying bowl, which led many to believe that she was beholden to
some sort of devil or djinn. The way her life had progressed thus
far, Samsun sometimes wondered about that herself.

Still breathing deeply she opened her eyes and stared into
and beyond the thin meniscus that covered the surface of the
water. All was gone now: the bar, Çetin sitting opposite, the faint

sounds of the grieving alcoholics. There was just water where Samsun was, completely still like the lens of a camera, giving her access to, at the beginning, strange jumbled images.

As if printed on rags the edges of these images were feathered and frayed. Without noticeable movement one gave into the other, melding like soft clay from shape to shining shape. For just an instant she saw Çetin's face, his eyes clamped tightly shut, his brows knitted as if in great distress or pain. But then it was gone, replaced by a small group of children running down the road which leads from Aya Sofia to the Eminönü Docks. Samsun saw her own young face amongst their number, a sharp-tongued boy of twelve.

High up. She didn't know where but above the roofs of the city, the sun burning on the back of her neck like a torch and beneath her feet…beneath her feet was hot too. It hurt, just like the pavement had done against her bare feet when she was a child. The image didn't go and although she knew she didn't want to Samsun looked down. Below was a street, very narrow and winding like a twisted vein on the back of an old man's hand. There were people down there and a car. They were all looking up, but she couldn't really see their faces clearly. Some were quite still, but a few, including one in a fine grey suit, were waving up at her and shouting. Although she tried very hard she couldn't say what they were shouting, but they were afraid.

And then she wasn't alone in her high place any more. Turning her head to the side she saw a young man. He was dark and quite beautiful in a feminine, beardless sort of way and she was gripped by the most horrible feeling of dread. Something red spread out across her feet and lapped against the legs of the young man and he smiled. His mouth was like a door and through it she saw the picture of a woman falling down a wall, her blood searing and staining the plaster behind her, for ever.

Then with one short bound the young man was gone, flying through the air like a rocket, hovering for just a second and then descending. Down there. And a beautiful sight it was too. The young man was so graceful as he swooped and dived on to and away from the currents of air that blew to and fro between the gaps in the buildings. For an instant the sight quite bewitched Samsun's mind until she saw where the falling and suddenly now limp body was plummeting. Down below, on the ground, another young man, grey-suited, familiar, rushed forward, right into the path of the other's descent. Samsun wanted to call out to warn him but she knew he wouldn't hear her. It wasn't real. It was just waiting, that was all—preparing to be real.

Samsun's eyes flew open. She licked her lips. 'It's tomorrow.'

Çetin's hand shook as he took a cigarette out of his packet and put it between his dry, cracked lips. He averted his eyes from Samsun's. 'And?'

'You'll be all right, little cousin.'

Çetin turned back to face her and she looked him straight in the eyes. 'But only if you're alone. You mustn't under any circumstances take that young sergeant with you. Do you understand?'

It wasn't that Rabbi Isak didn't enjoy these occasional meetings he was obliged to attend together with other members of the local clergy, it was just that there were problems. The priests, both Roman Catholic and Orthodox, liked to accompany the proceedings with a convivial glass of wine or two. Of course the wine wasn't kosher, which meant that he and his colleagues had to bring their own if they wanted to indulge. However, the Imams were not comfortable with it and he had always felt that it created a barrier between them and the rest of the party. Rabbi Şimon said that it didn't matter and the Imams understood and were quite happy with the arrangement but then he was a foreigner. Rabbi Şimon, although well meaning, didn't understand the Middle East any more than he understood old age. Accompanying him through the streets indeed! Who did the young puppy think he was! These were his streets, even if he were blind he couldn't get lost in them, but then the man was a Pole and therefore couldn't possibly understand. Rabbi Isak knew his way home and if he was attacked, well, it was God's will. Europeans didn't understand that; if something was written it was written and there was nothing he or the whole Turkish army could do that would change it.

But the meeting had gone well. As usual the Moslems had been the least forthcoming and the Christians the most, but then that was just life. Islam disliked change as much as Orthodox Judaism, mainly because neither faith really needed it. The synagogues and the mosques were always full, unlike the churches. So he supposed the priests had to do something: build more orphanages; try to persuade the Pope to visit again. Turkey was such an outpost of the Christian world he had often thought that it could not be easy. But then was it easy for anyone? Strange fierce-eyed men with beards had been seen on the streets for some time now. Many of them came from the east and the doctrine they preached had little to do with the traditional tolerance the natives of Balat had come to expect. All over the world, it seemed, people were embracing extreme ideologies again, willingly. War in Yugoslavia; Fundamentalist violence in Egypt; the resurgence of Fascism in Germany. Manifestation of this last phenomenon had even appeared on their own doorstep. That old Russian tortured, his wall daubed with a swastika not two minutes away! Şimon for one was very worried, but then his parents had been in the camps. He didn't understand Turkish Judaism and was fearful that old Meyer's death was only the beginning. Isak smiled and turned slowly into the tiny back alley that ran behind the houses of the street on which he lived. Şimon was, in his opinion, taking one isolated, if insane, incident and blowing it out of all proportion. Vile though the act undoubtedly was, it meant little as far as Isak could see, beyond the fact that somewhere in the city a lunatic was at large. Things such as this had and always would happen where a lot of people lived in close proximity to each other. The real issues didn't involve old alcoholics being done to death in filthy apartments, they involved Governments and the manipulation of nationalist or religious fervour by Governments. There was nothing of that nature happening in Turkey, at least overtly, apart from the situation with the Kurds of course. But then, rightly or wrongly, that was their affair and so long as their admittedly sad situation did not impinge upon his own community, Rabbi Isak was content simply to forget about the Kurds, poor souls! But...but most countries had situations of that sort with which to contend.

He passed along behind the back yard of Mr Zarifi's garden and glanced briefly at the wide-spreading branches of his lemon tree. It had taken a lot to get that thing to grow in the rough and exhausted soil of the inner city, but Zarifi had done it.

It was as he was taking his leave of Zarifi's lemon tree that Isak heard the singing. Although instantly recognising it as a drunken lament he was incapable of saying what the tune was or even which language it was being sung in. That it was even one song was also impossible to deduce as the singer periodically stopped and mumbled angrily before continuing. The only thing he could be sure of was that it was coming from that part of the alleyway directly in front of him, the bit he had to travel down in order to reach his home.

Isak didn't like drunks but he didn't actively dislike them either. In his long life he'd seen too much poverty and suffering not to understand the sweet oblivion and even relief a full bottle of raki could bring. Sometimes he'd even resorted to it himself, although he'd never actually been blind drunk. That was a terrible state to get into. Drunks were a nuisance, they pissed into gutters and vomited on buses. Poor creatures.

With a sigh Rabbi Isak set his feet in the direction of his house. The singing was louder now and as he peered into the thick darkness he fancied he saw a figure, its long limbs swaying close to the ground like an ape, lurching past the outhouse at the bottom of the Cohens' yard. But he couldn't be sure. Maybe he was alone in the alley, but maybe he wasn't. In reality it made little difference, he still had to get home and if he was obliged to pass some stinking drunk along the way then so be it. From the sound of the singing, the person, whoever he was, was almost certainly too inebriated to do him any harm. Rabbi Isak took his keys out of his pocket and whistled a little tune to himself. The old songs from his youth were always a comfort when he was alone. Suddenly, however, the status quo changed very quickly and with deadly intent. A limp hand flew out from nowhere and touched him lightly on the chest.

Isak gasped, but more out of shock than fear. It had happened so suddenly that it made his heart jump and for a second he felt quite breathless. The hand slid down his coat and as he bent towards it he could clearly smell the sharp reek of cheap raki-laden breath. Although he couldn't see him Rabbi Isak knew that his singing drunk was lying just in front of him, stretched out across his path like a human carpet. A sad state to be in and one that required him as a member of the clergy to assist. He bent his old back low and as he descended he became aware of a pair of small but glittering eyes staring bewildered into his.

Rabbi Isak put his hand out towards the creature and lowered his voice to a gentle whisper. 'Oh dear, you poor thing. Let me help you.'

'What the hell are you doing out of bed?'

As usual when he was in one of these states he wasn't so much angry at her as he was at himself. Çetin Ikmen drank but actual drunkenness was a rare occurrence. It usually meant that he was very depressed or worried about something, although even those excuses cut little ice with Fatma. It was gone two o'clock in the morning and he was drunk. Her eyes cold, she snapped back at him.

'I'm out of bed, Cetin, because I found your performance of "looking for my key" at the front door just too absorbing to miss.'

He peered at her through blurry half-closed eyes and stabbed the air in her direction with his finger. 'Very good, Fatma, a reply worthy of a born Ikmen.'

She turned her head away from him and muttered, 'Well if you're going to be insulting...'

'Oh, I didn't mean anything, Fatma! It's'—he took off his jacket and flung it across the back of a nearby chair—'it's because I'm having a bad life. First this case, then bloody Suleyman—'

'Mehmet?' She turned back to face him again, her brows knitted. 'What's he done?'

'Oh, it's not what he's done.' He moved one hand awkwardly to emphasise his point and then sat down. 'I went to see Samsun for a—you know, and he said—'

'I don't believe you!' Fatma moved forward, hands on hips, and stood furious in front of him. 'Samsun! A great authority that is! Honestly, Çetin, I thought you'd done with all that occult nonsense. If our friends knew—'

'I know! I know!' He put his head in his hands and rubbed his brow vigorously with his fingers. 'It's just that it's all been so terrible recently.'

'And you think that peering into bowls of oil or shuffling cards is going to make any difference? And Samsun too! The man is unglued, Çetin, not to mention immoral!'

'Oh, I—'

'And Samsun of course means the Bar Paris, doesn't it! Lovely! My husband down among the pimps and the prostitutes! My husband the police inspector no less!'

He took his hands away from his face and looked at her. He had to make her understand—somehow. It was late and he was drunk but what Samsun had told him hadn't lost its awful power during his long and tiring walk home. 'Something's going to happen and I can't take Suleyman with me. It's too dangerous and—'

'Rubbish!' Her burning eyes as well as her voice shouted at him and he cringed. 'Some ridiculous member of your family says that something is going to happen, but it isn't! Honestly, Çetin, for an educated man you can sometimes be so stupid! You'll believe anything these weird people tell you! As long as they are mad or they're filthy dirty or known to be a "witch" or—'

'I've solved cases before with the help of—'

'Yes, you have, or rather think you have!' She pursed her lips and regarded him silently with deep distaste.

The telephone started to ring. The shrill, almost ghostly sound hurt Çetin's ears and he groaned. This time of night it could only mean one thing and, judging by the exasperated expression on her face, Fatma knew that too. He reached across to the coffee table and picked up the offending instrument.

'Ikmen.' The word was said with such a heart-rending and despairing tone that for a second the caller didn't reply. He or she must have wondered what awful event or disaster the call had interrupted.

'Inspector?' It was Cohen's thick, phlegmy voice, which, although it came as no surprise to Çetin, did not fill him with joy either.

'What is it, Cohen? What do you want?'

'There's been another murder, sir, in Balat. Just behind my Uncle Zavi's house actually, a—'

'Oh no.' Çetin could already hear the recriminations that Ardiç would throw at him, the fierce sound of his cigary voice beating and raging against the white walls of his office. 'Jewish?'

He could almost hear Cohen shrug in that distinctly Jewish way of his. 'It's Balat.'

'Know who the victim is?'

'It's actually Uncle Zavi's rabbi, sir. Rabbi Isak, seventy-eight years old, native Balat.'

Another old man! Younger than the last and a different type of Jew to Meyer—as if that mattered. Çetin looked morbidly into the telephone receiver and wondered where the murder of Rabbi Isak would leave his arcane and convoluted theories about Meyer and Smits and the Gulcu family and old, old crimes. He didn't know and for the time being he couldn't even think about that. What he had to do now was sober up fast and get down there.

'All right, Cohen,' he said. 'Get a car over here to pick me up and I'll be with you.'

'Haven't you got your own—'

'Cohen, I've been out half the night, I haven't been to sleep yet and I'm drunk! Just get me a driver and a car—'

Cohen giggled. Ikmen knew they all secretly sniggered about his love for the bottle, but to have it done openly like this enraged him. It wasn't on and he snapped, 'Just get the car laid on, Cohen, you disgusting animal!'

He heard the still giggling reply 'Yes, sir' as he replaced the receiver with a bang. He could feel the muscles in his face were very strained and taut and for a few moments he neither spoke nor moved. Through the alcohol-soaked haze in his head he tried to think. Of course this killing might not be connected with Meyer's at all, but he feared that it was. The victim was a rabbi! How the man had died he wouldn't be able to tell until he got to the scene, but he had a bad feeling. It was like the first time, late, late at night. There were differences, of course; this time he was drunk and this time it was not Suleyman who had called him but Cohen. For that and that alone he was grateful.

If it had been Suleyman he would have felt bad. But Suleyman was safely, he hoped, tucked up in his bed at home and if Çetin had anything to do with it that was where he would stay. He had, somehow, to give Suleyman the day off, but then he knew his sergeant wouldn't wear that. Suleyman, like Fatma, couldn't believe. They'd both worked hard at being 'modern' people, they both had the kind of religious belief that refuses to admit even the possibility of other kinds of forces in the universe. Blinkered. It wasn't a nice thing to think about two people for whom he cared but they were. Fatma particularly. No evidence, however watertight, was good enough for her.

He got to his feet and retrieved his jacket from the back of the chair. 'I've got to go out, Fatma, I'm—'

'Yes, I know.' She looked tired, resigned and frighteningly pregnant. 'I try to understand, Çetin.'

'Will you be all right if I leave you?'

'I always have been before.'

He put his hand in his pocket to make sure he really had

replaced his keys. His fingers found them immediately. So he was drunk? But he obviously wasn't that drunk, which was a relief. He got legless so seldom it was sometimes difficult to remember how he was with it, the kind of things he was liable to do.

He put his hand down to Fatma, offering to help raise her to her feet. 'You should get back to bed, darling.'

She pushed his hand away, but she did it gently and without malice. 'No, I'll stay here now, Çetin. It makes little difference anyway now. Bed, chair, they're all the same—painful. The baby's resting on my back this time and it's like having a permanent slipped disc.' She looked up at him and managed a half-smile. He looked so pathetic in his dirty, rumpled suit, his face thin and ghastly with tiredness. 'You need some time off, Çetin Ikmen. You look older than your father lately.'

Çetin let a little laugh escape from the back of his throat and he took one of her hands in his. 'Timür will outlive us all, especially me. But I know what you're saying and one way or another I'll finish this case and then I'll take some time off. A long time.'

'You will?' She gave him a look of such sweet tenderness that he bent rather unsteadily over her and kissed the top of her head.

'I promise. It will all work out, you'll see. The case will close, the baby will come. I might even take you out, who knows?'

Through her tears she laughed. 'I'd like to see that!'

He patted her hand before he let it go and walked towards the door. 'I'd better wait downstairs. If any of my men come up here they'll wake the whole block.'

'All right.' She raised one swollen hand up and gave him a tired little wave. 'I love you.'

He felt the tears start in his own eyes and turned his head away from her. Silly, sentimental old fool! 'I love you too, Fatma,' he murmured as he disappeared into the hall. 'I just wish I had the time to show you a bit more often, that's all.'

Chapter Twenty-one

THE BODY WASN'T that unpleasant to look at, but Cohen tried to avoid it if he possibly could. Dr Sarkissian reckoned that death had probably been caused by a single blow to the head. Certainly there was no evidence of the terrible mutilation that had, apparently, been present on Meyer's body. But it still wasn't nice. The thin blood of old age was still dripping from the gaping wound in the Rabbi's head and Dr Sarkissian had said as soon as he touched it that the flesh was still warm. Cohen turned away from the corpse and took two very large gulps of air. Who the hell would want to beat up a poor defenceless old rabbi, and why? It wasn't often that he thought about being Jewish. For most of the time Cohen saw himself as no different to the rest of his colleagues. But not this time. Whereas all the rest of the lads could quite happily stand around chatting and smoking while the doctor went about his grim task, Cohen couldn't. Mercifully he'd never seen Meyer's body, he'd been busy that night interviewing neighbours and had felt fine. But Rabbi Isak was something different; he was his, he had found him.

That it had happened by accident was creepy too. He wasn't even supposed to have been in that alleyway anyway. But he'd been thirsty, desperate for a glass of tea, a little beer, anything. Uncle Zavi, like a lot of old people, rarely slept and besides he'd just wanted to talk to someone.

He remembered the dull thudding sound as his foot met dead flesh, the horrible moment when he shone his torch down into a face that was not ghastly but surprised. As first he hadn't even thought he was dead and had even asked him to get up, get sober and get home. Until, that is, he'd noticed the blood seeping out of the back of his head. Probably wrongly he hadn't tried to revive him, not that that would have done much good. But it might have made him feel better. In retrospect there was no difference between administering first aid to a rabbi than to anyone else. Cohen hadn't been able to touch him though, it had seemed wrong, sacrilegious somehow. He regretted that now, he also regretted blurting out about what he had found to Uncle Zavi. The poor old soul had nearly died himself when he told him and there hadn't even been so much as a drop of brandy in the house to help him over the shock. People like Zavi shouldn't have to deal with such things at their age.

'All right, Cohen?' Ikmen was directly in front of him and was looking, for him, strangely concerned.

Cohen tried to laugh. It was expected of him: sharp, randy little Cohen who doesn't give a shit. But he failed. 'Oh, Inspector, you're...'

His voice trailed off, he didn't know where; it left him high and dry, just staring at Ikmen like a fool.

Ikmen put his hand on Cohen's shoulder and eyed him carefully. 'You're in shock, lad. Sit down.'

Cohen knew that he was and, uncharacteristically, sat down without protest.

Ikmen moved towards a crowd of late-night, slovenly-looking constables who parted to allow him through and for

the first time he saw the body. It lay on the ground horizon-
tally across the narrow alleyway and from even quite close it
looked remarkably like a bundle of old clothes. But there was
a face there, an old and leathery one, and the eyes were still
open, just like Meyer's had been. But the expression in these
eyes was different. There was no horror, there wasn't even any
shock, there was surprise. The sort of pre-delight expression one
sees on the faces of children when they have been given their
birthday presents but haven't yet unwrapped them. Behind the
head, apparently pulling at something Ikmen preferred not to
think about, was Arto, his plump features illuminated by the
thin light from a police arc lamp.

'Ah, Inspector, good.'

'Morning, Arto.' Ikmen took out his cigarettes and lighter
and started working. His head was beginning to clear rapidly
now, he was just entering the jumpy alert phase that often
follows intense alcohol consumption and lack of sleep. 'What
have we got?'

Arto finished whatever it was he had been doing and stood
up. 'What we have is a very heavy blow, just one I think, inflicted
by this piece of metal.' He pointed to a strange-shaped, shiny
lump near his feet. 'It cracked the skull causing the massive
hemorrhage which killed him. Death would have occurred more
or less instantaneously.'

Ikmen lit his cigarette and puffed on it determinedly.
'Time?'

'An hour, maybe two hours ago. Some of the men are out
doing house-to-house already.'

Ikmen crouched down and peered closely at the body. The
small hands were curled inwards in front of it like cats' paws.
There was something so innocent and touching about this sight
that for a moment Ikmen felt quite overwhelmed by sadness. 'He
was a rabbi, wasn't he?'

Arto took off his surgical gloves and wiped his sweaty
hands on a towel. 'Yes. Rabbi Isak. According to Mr Cohen who
lives over the back there he was very popular around here.'

'And now he's dead.' Ikmen stood up again and gazed around him at the pathetic collection of rude dwellings that passed for houses in this quarter. 'Where's forensic?'

'On their way, as is the van from the morgue.'

'Good.' Ikmen sighed deeply. He knew that it was self-indulgent but he couldn't help thinking that he might have done more. And yet this was different. Whoever had killed Meyer had planned and gone prepared for what had to be done. But the Rabbi's murder was another matter. He looked at the wide selection of stones, pieces of wood and lumps of metal that littered the alleyway, all potential murder weapons. The twisted, blood-stained hunk that sat at Arto's feet had been chosen at random. An impulsive if crazed act that had caused instantaneous death. 'Has the body been mutilated in any way?' He had to check.

'Not as far as I can see yet. I would think it unlikely. Out in the open, albeit in a quiet place like this, the risk of discovery usually puts them off even if the desire to do so is strong.'

Ikmen raised his chin upwards in agreement.

'Sir! Inspector Ikmen!' The voice was young and he remembered vaguely hearing it somewhere before, although he couldn't quite place it. Ikmen turned and saw the young, soft face of Avcı directly behind him. He was with someone, a very short, heavily bearded man, the whites of whose eyes were scarred and cracked by heavy red veins. Ikmen raised one eyebrow. 'Yes?'

'Sir.' Avcı was breathless with excitement; he'd found something. Ikmen could just remember being like that—once. 'This man, Mr, er...'

The man waved one unwashed hand across Avcı's face and grinned. The expression made him look like some sort of medieval demonic spirit. Ikmen didn't need the evidence of the reeking smell of whisky that came from his mouth to realise that he was very drunk. 'Not Mr,' he said, 'just Nat. Everyone, all misters, they call me Nat.'

'Ah well,' said Ikmen. 'Mr, er, Nat, you, er...'

Avcı could contain himself no longer. 'Mr Nat saw a stranger drinking in his bar, which is just around the corner, earlier this evening. The man was a foreigner, couldn't speak Ladino, and he was very drunk.'

'He was shout, make some trouble, you know.' Nat swayed slightly and smiled stupidly. 'Rosa throw him out, too drunk.'

It did cross Ikmen's mind to ask why Rosa, whoever she was, hadn't thrown Mr Nat out also, but he decided not to. 'What did he look like, this man?'

'Oh!' Nat's torso lurched backwards a little from his legs and he hiccuped loudly. 'Very big, tall. Hair was white, you know, like American or German, I don't know. Too much drink, start to cry, make lot of noise.'

It was August and the city was full of tourists from all over the world, but Ikmen couldn't help wondering. A tall, fair, foreign man in the right place at the wrong time? 'When was this?'

'Couple hours ago.'

'You didn't see where he went when he left, I suppose?'

Nat shrugged. 'I'm busy, you know.'

It was not difficult to imagine what with. This wasn't like Meyer's murder, because this time they had clues. The murder weapon, especially if the assailant had been drunk, could yield fingerprints. Analysis of the victim's clothes could be useful too. This had been a sloppy job, poorly executed in an open space. The surrounding area could hold untold treasures. And if Mr Nat had seen the tall blond stranger then other people must have done too. Maybe even sober people more able to give detailed and reliable descriptions. Ikmen felt strongly that that must be so and dismissed Avcı and the roaring Mr Nat for the time being.

'Can I move the body when the mortuary attendants and forensic get here, Çetin?'

He'd almost forgotten about Arto. Ikmen turned towards him and pursed his lips thoughtfully. 'Yes, I think so, although I want the whole area searched thoroughly, centimetre by centimetre. And I want the body and its clothing to have the same treatment too. I want to know everything about this one, right down to what his clothes are made of, what he had for dinner. He was native Balat, I understand.'

'Yes.'

'Mmm.' One victim native Balat, the other a Jew from else-where. There could always be connections through friends or friends of friends, but on the face of it it seemed unlikely. And Ikmen wasn't even sure whether it was really necessary to his theory. Perhaps in a way it was more necessary that there was no connection. But what he needed before he could even think about that was a break. 'Arto, I want you to get going with this one as soon as you can and I want anything unusual reported directly to me immediately.'

'OK.'

A van pulled up at the far end of the alleyway and two suit-ably sepulchral-looking individuals got out. 'Ah,' said Ikmen with a smile. 'Your ghouls from the morgue, I believe, Dr Sarkissian.'

'Yes.' Sarkissian looked down at the body and put his hands in his pockets. 'Time to go.'

Ikmen moved out of the way and leant his back up against one of the nearby wooden fences. Now all that he could do was wait. Wait for witnesses, wait for more information on the blond man in Mr Nat's bar, wait for Arto and forensic to contact him. Being sure was absolutely essential, even though that deep part of him already knew. He leant his head back against the fence and took in some deep, revitalising breaths. Oh he felt rough! But he had to keep going. He was close now. Two hands, two crimes but a cord connected their perpetrators. The roots if not the branches joined, known to one another. Now speed was vital. But before that there was just one more thing he had to do and it filled him with sadness. But do it he must because some-times seeming cruelty is the only course of action left open. All he could hope was that in time he would be forgiven.

He was woken by a stray ray of sunlight touching his nose and the area just beneath his eyes. It wasn't a rude awakening as it was still very early and the sun was not yet either very hot or particularly bright. But it was enough to rouse him and even before he opened his eyes he knew that he was in trouble.

The nausea, although not fierce, kept coming across him in waves and his mouth and throat felt tight, dry and scarred. He turned to one side in an effort to assuage the rising sickness and discovered to his horror that his mattress was not below him. His slim gangly limbs clunked painfully against something much harder than that. He opened half an eye and found himself looking at a lot of gravel and one of those tall, thin Turkish gravestones.

Inside his head blocks of information started to shift and grind up against one another, like small children's wooden bricks in a box. Obviously he'd had such a skinful that he hadn't managed to make it home and had just flopped down into the first available space, which just happened to be a graveyard. He didn't dare move his head. Instinct told him that if he did he would discover a headache too and it would not be one of those that responds to paracetamol.

Robert tested out various unamusing descriptions for the state he had been in the previous night. Wrecked, arse'oled, pissed, shit-faced, whammed, bombed, legless, rat-arsed. All very jolly and laddishly amusing if one conveniently forgot about the hangover that always followed these expletives. But what had he done and where had he been? He opened his eyes fully, and, although the light hurt them, he made himself check his own body for damage. The sight of the crusted and dried blood on his shirtsleeves provoked an immediate reaction and he was sick all down his chest and on to the gravel.

As Ikmen's eyes travelled down the second page of Reinhold Smits's nauseatingly perfumed little missive he found that his reaction to its contents was not what he thought it would be. Instead of anger, he felt only sadness—sadness for another life, irrespective of its owner, gone. Another totally unique individual completely and utterly wiped off the face of the earth. Beside such an enormity his little questions regarding the seemingly endless Leonid Meyer conundrum suddenly seemed really rather paltry.

As he picked up the telephone, preparatory to doing what he knew had to be done, Ikmen caught sight of young Avcı in the corridor just outside his office. In his present revolting condition, he would need, at the very least, someone to drive him and so he called him over.

As Avcı entered the room, he smiled, one of his big, silly bovine smiles. 'Yes, Inspector Ikmen, sir?'

'I need someone to drive me over to Bebek,' Ikmen replied. 'Are you up to it?'

'Yes.'

'Oh, for the strength and fortitude of youth!'

'You what?'

Ikmen allowed himself the luxury of flopping back into his chair again. 'Oh, nothing, just go and get my car ready for me.'

'Sir.'

As Avcı left, Ikmen readdressed himself to the telephone and, once again, with a deep sigh, he began dialling.

Mehmet Suleyman sprinkled a little Monsieur Dior cologne on to his comb and dragged it lazily through his hair. He felt fine, but he had his doubts about Ikmen. The 'Old Man' had been absolutely roaring when he left him and his strange cousin, whose 'tricks' had taken a remarkably short time to perform, had just ordered another round of drinks. Really he should have dragged Ikmen away then or at least stayed around until he was finished and seen him home. But the Bar Paris wasn't his sort of place and the time he had spent there had depressed him enough already. The constant hassling by prostitutes of uncertain gender hadn't helped either. It seemed odd to him that a husband and father like Ikmen could feel comfortable in such a setting. But then Ikmen was odd all round. He didn't seem to have the same values or beliefs as other people. He was uncompromising, he did things his way or not at all. It was a miracle he still had a job.

Downstairs the telephone rang and somebody picked it up. Mehmet briefly tidied up his new grey suit with a soft camel-hair brush and then spent a few moments inspecting teeth he knew already were perfectly clean. But then, with a totally unwanted breakfast and his mother's endless inane chatter to look forward to, going downstairs did not hold much appeal for him. His mother was not a bad woman, but, like his boss, the world either conformed to her or she wasn't interested.

However, it had to be done and so, leaving his teeth to their own devices, he made his way downstairs and out on to the terrace. As usual the table groaned beneath the weight of his mother's spread of breakfast food: bread, cheese, olives, tomatoes, home-made rose jam, the ridiculously ornate silver coffee pot. It looked beautiful but he wanted none of it. Ikmen had taught him many things over the past five years and probably the greatest of these was the benefit of skipping breakfast in favour of a chocolate pastry at around midday. He'd wanted to make it a habit, but it wasn't easy with his mother.

He sat himself down beside the silent outstretched newspaper that was his father and poured himself a coffee. The swishing sound of clean skirts rustling around slim legs and the click-click of high heels on concrete signalled the arrival of his mother. Mehmet looked up and smiled. His father didn't move.

His mother beamed. 'I've just had your boss on the telephone, Mehmet, he's given you the day off. Isn't that nice?'

'The day off?' It didn't make any sense! Suddenly? For no reason? 'Are you sure, Mother?'

'Well, he was quite specific, Mehmet.'

Why did she always take offence so easily! His father put down his paper and looked confused. 'What?'

His mother tutted impatiently. His father's increasing

vagueness never failed to irritate her. 'Mehmet has been given the rest of the day off, Muhammed.' She shouted at him too, like he was deaf. He wasn't but it had never occurred to him to mention this fact—it seemed like too much trouble.

'Oh.' He lifted the paper once again and turned to the sports pages.

Nur Suleyman removed her son's unused plate from in front of him and replaced it with another even cleaner version. Her son winced. She was such a mistress of the pointless that it almost hurt.

She put her hand on his shoulder and squeezed affectionately. 'We can go shopping if you like.'

The implication that he had a choice was almost laughable. He couldn't bear it. 'I think I'll just go and check.'

As he got up her hand fell from his shoulder and her eyes took on a hurt expression. 'Oh, but Mehmet, I—'

'It's all right, Mother.' Although he didn't want to he made himself bend low to kiss her cheek briefly. 'I do believe you, but there are a few things I have to check up on.'

'Oh.' It was a distracted little exclamation, the sort of sound people make when they've just been told something so awful that they can barely take it in. It was the sort of overreaction he was accustomed to.

He walked back into the house but even before he reached the telephone he'd made up his mind. Whatever Ikmen said he was going into work and that was that.

Just before she left the house that morning, Natalia Gulcu went up to the top apartment to see her grandmother. As she had hoped, the old woman was still asleep as she entered and for a brief few moments Natalia merely looked at her, rather as one would view a vaguely interesting exhibit in a museum. She'd caused so much trouble for all of them, this old, old woman. Because of her, Natalia had both seen and done the most awful, unthinkable things. And yet still, unlike everyone else in her life, she loved her. Why? Well, it was obvious really. Without her and what she represented, who was she or any of them? If it hadn't been for her, they would all be ordinary, boring—all the things that she had never wanted, or been instructed to be.

Natalia looked down at her watch and, noting that precious and precarious amounts of time were passing, blew one last kiss across the room at her grandmother and then shut the door behind her. She would attempt, inasmuch as she could, to put recent events behind her today. She was, after all, a gold merchant's assistant and it was therefore her job to persuade, charm and cajole people to buy Mr Avedissian's fine jewellery. And anyway, who knows whom she might meet in the course of her work? She often met interesting and exciting men and, subsequently, had said men. Perhaps, especially in view of the fact that Mr Avedissian was now on holiday and she was alone in the shop, she would get lucky today and lose herself in some nice, rich man's excesses. Provided, of course, Robert Cornelius didn't make an appearance. She frowned. Acceding to his request to continue their affair had been, she now felt, a mistake. She just hoped that it wasn't a mistake she was one day going to have to pay for.

'He shot himself through the mouth with a pistol.' The doctor was still shaking his head in disbelief, just as he had been when Ikmen had first walked through the door. 'He had enough drugs in his possession to annihilate half the district and yet Reinhold chose to shoot himself through the mouth.' He looked up and then, flinging his arms wide in a gesture of helplessness, asked, 'Why?'

Ikmen sighed. 'I don't know, I'm afraid, Dr Imad. All that he put in his note to me was notice of his intention to kill himself plus some details about this case we are, or were, pursuing with his assistance.'

Imad's features darkened at this, his eyes taking on an accusatory tint. 'Yes, your case,' he said, 'and your men who, in my opinion, have quite a lot to answer for with regard to what has happened here.'

Ikmen, who was now almost delirious with both the heat and the lack of sleep and his ever-present hangover, snapped back rather more sharply than he would have done under normal circumstances. 'Yes, well, doctor, if you have a complaint against us, you know what to do.'

The doctor stood up and, needlessly straightening his perfect jacket, said, 'And be assured, sir, that I will do it!'

Ikmen, ably shadowed by the lumbering form of Avcı, waved the medic on his way. 'Well, off you go then!'

'I will!'

Rather unprofessionally, or so Ikmen thought, Dr Imad slammed the door of the library behind him, causing several of the books near to the entrance to fall off the shelves.

Swearing copiously, if gently, under his breath, Ikmen made his way back over to Smits's desk and looked again at the assorted items assembled upon it. Just as Smits had written in his letter there were three things: two photographs and a book, *The Death of Russia*, which lay open at page 325. The page, which like the rest of the book was written in English, was marked up about halfway down: a line in red had been drawn under a phrase. It said: 'This night Balthazar was murdered by his slaves' and it was, apparently, something that had been found scratched upon the wall of the house where the unfortunate Romanov family had died in 1918. A reference, seemingly, to the justifiable demise of an autocratic despot—a concept which, to Ikmen, sat uncomfortably with his own vision of Nicholas II, which consisted of a rather beleaguered, weak and misguided soul. Not that that particular aspect was what interested Ikmen. That the quote had been written, so the author presumed, by one of the Romanov family's captors was what had his attention now. The guards whose names he had seen many times before were here also, all present and correct. Except that they weren't.

As he read onwards he discovered what he hadn't known before: that the guards were changed shortly before the executions and that a group of unknown and now probably unknowable guards had taken over from several of the more minor players in that awful drama. Ikmen put his hand up to his forehead, which was now sweating profusely. He had a bad, bad feeling about all this.

He shifted his attention to the photograph which lay beside the book—black and white—of three people wearing clothes that placed them almost certainly in the 1920s. The woman, who was laughing, wore a large cloche hat which, although pulled down quite far across her forehead, nevertheless clearly revealed her features beneath. They were, Ikmen could clearly see, despite her apparent merriment, just as sharp and snake-like as the older version of them he had seen in the Gulcu house. Young Maria. She'd been quite striking—as if she could ever be anything else.

In the picture she had her arms around the shoulders of two young men. Both of them wore the wide-lapelled suits of the period and the one that was so unmistakably Reinhold Smits smoked a long, thin cheroot. The second man, who was much shorter and darker than Smits and whose eyes had a vaguely closed, hooded appearance was, Ikmen assumed, Leonid Meyer. Was it just Ikmen's imagination, or had Meyer looked troubled even then? Gently, he stroked the old print with his fingertips before he turned to the second photograph.

Stuck on to a plain brown backing board in order, Ikmen imagined, to help preserve its ancient delicateness, this was a picture of a young girl—a young girl long ago, at the end of the last century. She had long, thick hair hanging in ringlets across her shoulders, which were covered by what looked like a printed shawl. Her face, though trying to be serious, had just been breaking into a smile when the picture was taken.

You could, so Ikmen imagined, almost see her breaking down into giggles as soon as the seriousness of the photographic session was over. Happy then, and young. He sighed. But what was written beneath the face was not so cheerful. In English, yet again, it simply said 'Belshazzar's Daughter' which, when put together with the quote from the book, probably meant that this lovely young girl had been one of the last Tsar's doomed daughters. Or maybe it didn't. Belshazzar, Balthazar...He looked back at the book. The phrase was, so the book stated, a quote from the German—by Heine—so perhaps the spelling was different, or...

He stared briefly at Smits's letter which, cryptically, had exhorted him to 'work it out, Inspector'. And then slowly as his eyes skimmed from item to item across the desk, all the disparate blocks of evidence he had accumulated over the weeks started to come together. Meyer's crime; the name Demidova; that unknown 'thing' he had theorised Smits and Meyer 'had' over Maria; those weird and wild thoughts of his own—the ones he'd dismissed but now suddenly couldn't. He couldn't! Not now that he could see that the faces of the smart 1920s woman and the young girl in the shawl were one and the same.

For reasons that he didn't even begin to understand, Robert stuck to the back roads when he left the confines of the Old Imperial cemetery on Divan Yolu. Although he had no actual destination in mind, for want of any better idea he started making for Eminönü Docks and the Galata Bridge. They were, after all, on his route back to his apartment, which was a place that, if he wanted, he could go to. Not, of course, that he would feel safe there. Not that he would feel safe anywhere. Covered in blood and aching from head to foot, his body felt as tense and assaulted as if he had been mugged which, until he found his wallet and credit cards safe and intact in his pockets, is exactly what he thought had happened to him. But then perhaps, and most likely, he had just been beaten up. People did that to drunk and unstable-looking folk. He remembered that from his time in the hospital. How, if you were a very ill patient, you could suffer a thousand indignities a day and nobody would so much as turn a hair. It had only been his iron resolve to not appear as totally paranoid and mad as he really had been that had saved him—until now.

As he passed by the entrance to a commercial garage, he saw that several of the mechanics turned to look at him. He tried to smile normally but then gave up as the awareness of the blood all over him and what that might signify to them hit him. If only he could remember—something, anything—then perhaps he could make some sense of it all! But try as he might, nothing would come. As far as he knew he had gone drinking down by the Sea of Marmara and then next he had woken up in the graveyard. True, he had gone to wherever it was by the Sea of Marmara in order to try and blot out or exorcise some of the devils that were currently haunting him, but...

As he crested the top of one of Istanbul's many famous hills, he looked down upon the two great waterways that bisected this massive city: the Golden Horn and the mighty, sparkling Bosporus. Straight ahead of him, across the Golden Horn, he could see, as well as numerous banks and other assorted mercantile buildings, the Galata Tower, that strange, almost rocket-ship-shaped article where he and Natalia had once had a meal—long ago and far away in time. Just the thought of her made him want to cry. He hadn't seen her for what seemed like such a long time and he had to acknowledge that, still fuddled with drink as he was, he couldn't exactly picture her face any more. In spite of the directness of the hot sunlight above his head, he then sat down upon the pavement and put his head between his hands. Despite everything that he had done for her, despite persuading her not to give him the Big E, he knew within that instant that he had lost her. How could he not have? He was a drunken madman who had smashed some poor old fellow...

And then it began. Robert, his heart now beating like the clack of an old Gatling gun, suddenly, fully and horribly knew. The old man, the large piece of rock or whatever it had been, the absolute terror that it had all evoked—the being in Balat again. The blood that was not his own. The blood that belonged to a Jew!

His eyes now almost blinded by tears, Robert lifted his head and looked, or rather tried to look around him. Large, mobile, multicoloured shapes loomed out at him from the all-encompassing white glare. Were they people or devils from inside his own mind? He didn't know anything except that they were threatening, except that they kept on saying 'Jew-killer! Jew-killer!' over and over and over again in his head.

With a speed and agility he never knew he possessed, Robert Cornelius suddenly sprang to his feet and, screaming his denial to the wind, flung himself down the hill towards the Golden Horn.

Chapter Twenty-two

AVCI SLOTTED HIMSELF rather uncomfortably behind the steering wheel of the car and turned to Ikmen. 'So where now then?' he said to what looked remarkably like a pile of old junk.

Ikmen lifted his face from his shoulder and with a wave of one totally exhausted hand said, 'Beyoğlu, Karadeniz Sokak.'

Avcı turned the key in the ignition and, as the car's engine sprang into life, he asked, 'So what are we going to do there then, sir?'

'I think,' Ikmen replied slowly, which was the only speed at which his mind would work now, 'that we are going to find out something really quite extraordinary.'

The telephone rang. He put his hand on the receiver and closed his eyes. Oh, please, please, please let it be Ikmen! This waiting, this being kept in the dark, was killing him. He lifted the handset and spoke. 'Suleyman.'

'Is that you, Mehmet?' It was a woman's voice and he recognised it, but he couldn't think from where.

'Yes, this is Mehmet,' he replied, then added tentatively, 'Who is this please?'

'It's Fatma Ikmen.' Of course it was! 'The girl on the switchboard told me that my husband is out so I thought I'd better speak to you. You don't know where he is, do you?'

Suleyman sighed. 'I wish I did. I know he was out all night in Balat, but where he is now I just couldn't say. One of the men thought he saw him getting into one of the squad cars, but he isn't in any of those as far as I can discover now.' He stopped. He was making it sound like Ikmen was a missing person and probably frightening the man's poor wife to death. That wasn't very professional. 'I'm sure he's all right, Mrs Ikmen,' he added limply.

'Oh so am I, it's just that—' She paused in a way that made him think she'd suddenly been grabbed by someone or something.

'Mrs Ikmen?'

'It seems like I'm going to have my baby very soon.'

'Oh.' As far as Suleyman could remember the Ikmens' baby wasn't due for about another month—not, of course, that he could ask Mrs Ikmen about that.

'One of my sons has called the doctor. But it's my husband I really want.'

'Yes I expect you do.' Although he couldn't think why, she wouldn't even see him. Ikmen would be with the other men: his father, sons and his wife's brothers in the kitchen, smoking. Wouldn't he?

'So if you see him or hear from him will you tell him, Mehmet?'

'Of course I will.'

'Thank you.' She sounded tired. He wondered how long she had been in labour. 'Goodbye, Mehmet.' She put the phone down.

Suleyman rubbed his face with his hand, replaced the receiver and wondered what on earth had possessed him to sound so confident. He didn't know where Ikmen was! Nobody seemed to! All he knew was what he'd learnt from the switchboard girl: that there had been another murder in Balat the previous night and that Ikmen had gone off somewhere with Avcı. But where? Based upon their previous conversations, Cornelius's apartment in Beşiktaş was a possibility, although, not knowing where or if this latest murder fitted in with what had gone before...If anyone, Dr Sarkissian would surely know... but...

The door banged open and the edge crashed into the side of his desk. For half a second he hoped, but the man who entered, although short and dark, was in uniform and his heart sank. 'Oh, it's you, Cohen.'

Cohen jumped and swung round quickly. 'Mehmet? What are you doing here?'

'I work here, remember?'

'Ah yes, I know. But didn't old Ikmen give you the day off?'

Suleyman pulled a sheet of paper out of one of the drawers underneath his desk and scanned down it for Sarkissian's name and extension number. 'He did, but I ignored him. I don't understand what's happening today, Cohen, I really don't. Do you know anything about this latest murder in Balat?'

Cohen leant against the side of Ikmen's desk and lit a cigarette. 'Well I should do, I found the body.'

Suleyman looked up sharply. 'You?'

'Yes, me. He was an old rabbi, the victim. My Uncle Zavi's rabbi actually. Been cracked over the head with a lump of metal. I felt sick, I can tell you! Just walking along and you trip over something like that! I called the station, I called Ikmen. It was late, can't remember the time, I was a bit upset. Mind you, I was sane enough to realise that the Old Man was drunk!'

Suleyman frowned. 'So why didn't he call me?'

Cohen shrugged. 'I don't know. Said nothing about it until this morning when he told me that he'd given you the day off.

He was excited though, said he thought he might be close. What to, I—'

'So he's close and he blows me out!' Suleyman rarely got angry, but when he did it was no half-hearted affair. He banged his fist down hard upon the top of the desk and gritted his teeth furiously. 'Well, screw him! I would never have believed it! He doesn't want to share the limelight, that's it! How could he after all the work I've put in on this!'

Cohen moved behind Ikmen's desk and sat down. Mehmet, he knew of old, needed space when he raved. 'You don't know it's like that, Mehmet.'

'Can you think of another reason?' This was less of a question and more of a challenge.

'Well, not off the top—'

'Precisely!' Suleyman got up from his seat and paced the room like a caged cat. 'He's egotistical, everybody's always said so and I like a fool have always defended him, but he is!'

Ikmen's telephone rang and Suleyman threw himself across his desk and picked it up. 'Suleyman.'

'Hello, Suleyman, Dr Sarkissian here. Can I speak to the boss-man, please?'

'He's not here I'm afraid, Doctor, can I help?'

'Yes, all right. Look, could you tell the Inspector this. I've found a hair on the collar of the dead Rabbi's coat. It definitely doesn't come from the victim because it's blond and fine. I would say it's European. You can also tell him that the lab have found good prints all over the murder weapon. If he wants comparisons done with his English suspect it's going to be very easy.'

Suleyman's mind raced. Of course! At the scene during the first murder, friend and lover of the Gulcus, a blond European hair...Why on earth hadn't Ikmen really grilled him after the first killing? He'd been there all the time. Of course he, Suleyman, was as much to blame, but—

'Are you still there, Sergeant?'

'Oh, er, yes, Dr Sarkissian, and thank you.'

Suleyman was much calmer and milder now. He put the telephone down and looked at Cohen. He smiled. 'I think I know where Ikmen is now. I don't know how he's getting there, but I know where. Get yourself ready, Cohen, you're coming with me.'

When he reached the far end of the Galata Bridge, Robert Cornelius looked first up the great looming hill in front of him and then down the wide, sweeping coast road. There were advantages and disadvantages associated with each route. If he chose the coastal route he could go home, get cleaned up…And what? And possibly be arrested at the airport, that is if he could even get a ticket out of this confounded hot as hell country.

But what of up the hill? The going would be hard and with all the millions that lived up there up and about and going to work he would be seen for sure…But she was up there, Natalia, up there—high in the sky so far above him now, so perfect, so free…so wicked and evil and murderous! And if she hadn't— yes, he could say it now, not out loud but in his mind—if she hadn't killed old Meyer then none of this would have happened or would be happening now.

If only that were true…

If only he wasn't entirely and absolutely of his own volition a murderer himself now. A man, furthermore, who would now have to go to the police. To do anything else would not be right, would not be him.

And for a few moments he stood outside his own mind and considered all of this. It calmed him. It was funny really; mild-mannered teacher, ex-public schoolboy…Some of his class-mates were actors, writers, captains of industry now. Doing well but unmemorable. He'd never been the captain of the rugby team, nor had a straight run of 'A's in the sixth form, but soon everyone would know who he was. Robert Cornelius, the sadistic Jew-murderer, the man the Foreign Office didn't bother to save. But people would talk, for years. Hanratty, Edith

Thompson, Timothy Evans—they'd even made a film about Ruth Ellis. If you were hanged by the neck until you were dead it almost guaranteed your immortality. Perhaps that had been what he had been looking for all the time. What a dreadful conceit! He laughed. It was funny; he was funny. The desperate trier for whom nothing ever worked out, the boy who wanted so much to ride horses but couldn't conquer his fear. It hadn't been the speed, but the unpredictability of the animals. Perhaps there'd been a lesson somewhere in that early experience which he should have applied to the women in his life. A kind of backward echo.

He looked up at the Galata hill again and smiled. One more time wouldn't hurt. Of course he wouldn't be able to have her, not that that bothered him. In fact it would be interesting to see what was left when the sex was stripped away. It would be almost gratifying if there was nothing and the great thing was that he knew that was precisely the case. She didn't love him and yet he still wouldn't give her to the police for her part in this débâcle. They could torture him if they liked—and they would. The perfection of the futility must be maintained. If his life had any meaning at all it had to be that. One day some author might even write a pitying book, trace it all back to the seeds of loneliness and inadequacy he'd felt at school. Well, it was extraordinary. How many other boys had cut up their arms just because of one poor examination result? He could still remember the look on Matron's face as she applied the iodine, without kindness, to his weeping wrist. She'd been disgusted, not by the wound, but by the state of mind that had inflicted it. And that was just about it really. Nothing he had ever done had been of itself bad—until now—it was the desperation behind these acts that disgusted people. Love affairs were fine provided there was no desire to become the loved object's slave. Teaching too was good as long as it wasn't a substitute for something better, some great and mythical career more worthy of him and his intellect. But then perhaps he would have failed if he'd done whatever it was he'd originally wanted to do. Whatever that had been.

Yes, going to see her one more time would be good. She'd pretend to be sickened but she would be relieved. In years to come she may even, when alone, laugh. Until and unless she found the pure, round perfection inherent in his failure, the one he knew was there. Perhaps when she learnt about his history she would know, although maybe that in itself was wrong, perhaps even that marred the perfection. The perfectly farmed and nurtured pointlessness. Perhaps even future generations knowing his name was an abomination?

Slowly now, because he was so tired, he started to trudge his way towards the Galata hill and the front door of number 12, Karadeniz Sokak.

Suleyman sat down heavily on the bed and sighed. He picked the small colour photograph up again and looked at it. It was a good likeness, very sharp, taken with a decent camera. A portrait, head and bare shoulders. He wondered, idly, if she had been naked when it was taken. It was possible, knowing how she was. Strange, though, that her face was so sombre. But then again didn't models in dirty magazines have that look? That worn-out, desperately sad light about the eyes? Whatever Cornelius may feel for her, Natalia Gulcu was a being in whom there was little of any great value left.

'So what now then, Mehmet?'

He'd almost forgotten that Cohen was there. Suleyman got up from the bed and looked around the room. Apart from the photograph it was disturbingly anonymous. In his experience foreigners who lived abroad were usually more sentimental than this. But Cornelius? Not a letter, not a card, not even some old snapshot of his baby self grinning on his mother's knee. Nothing and no one to remind him of England. Perhaps he'd cleaned everything else out of his life in order to get her in? A curious thought.

On what seemed to Cohen like a whim, but was really a

very considered act, Suleyman said, 'I think we should get over to Beyoğlu now.'

'You think that's where the Old Man's gone, do you, Mehmet?'

'If Cornelius is there, which is possible, then maybe Ikmen is too. It's where the girl in that picture lives.' He passed the photograph of Natalia Gulcu over to his deputy.

Cohen's face lit up. The picture seemed, character-istically, for just a moment, to excite him. Then, however, and for seemingly no logical reason, his expression changed to one of creased seriousness. 'Mehmet, this girl, I think I might...'

But Suleyman, intent on what had to be done, wasn't listening any more.

'Come on,' he said and led the way back through the bedroom and into Cornelius's white, white lounge. It struck him as odd that such a bright place should be so depressing, but again it was because there was nothing personal about the place. It reminded him of a hotel room, a place for someone in transit.

Suleyman then stopped and, thoughtfully, put his hands on his hips. 'OK. I don't want to radio for back-up yet, if at all. I do however want your pistol, Constable, if you'll be so kind.' He extended his hand for the weapon.

Cohen, still a little dazed from the impact of the photograph, looked confused. 'My pistol?'

Suleyman didn't want to explain. He didn't want to have to say that he didn't trust Cohen and would not, indeed, have trusted any of the junior officers enough to let any of them anywhere near a foreign national, even a possibly deranged one, with a firearm. Although no really high-profile offences had been committed in Turkey by foreign nationals since the 1970s, Suleyman was only too aware of what magnitude of international wrath a dead or injured foreign national could cause. He didn't know that he trusted himself entirely either, but as the senior officer in this instance, it was his duty both to control and protect those beneath his command. 'Just give it to me, Cohen, all right?'

The constable took the weapon out of the holster on his hip and put it into Suleyman's outstretched hand. Suleyman made sure that the safety catch was on and then placed the firearm in the empty holster underneath his armpit.

'Are you armed then, Mehmet?'

Suleyman forced a smile. 'I am now, Cohen.'

'Oh.'

Chapter Twenty-three

THE ONLY TIME ROBERT had ever seen anything like it was in films. Nasty, rather frightening films about people who had been wicked and were just about to die. Of course he couldn't actually see much because his eyes still had to adjust to the weak light from the oil-lamp, the pungent sting of the incense. But they were all there—well, nearly all. He couldn't see Natalia yet, unless of course that was her in the big chair over by the window, separate from the main group. But whoever it was was turned away from him and he couldn't tell. It would be like her not to want to look at him.

The other bodies spread out and away from the huge lilac and gold structure in the middle of the room and he felt one of Nicholas's hands upon his shoulder. 'Mama would like you to sit down on her bed, Mr Cornelius.'

The cripple Sergei scuttled out of his way. Robert stepped forward and found himself at the foot of a golden prow. It curled towards him like a gilt wave. He looked at it closely and decided that in a full light it would look like what it really was. Something cheap and tastelessly ornate. He wasn't afraid, that feeling had disappeared some time ago, but he did wish that they would show him Natalia. He didn't want these theatrics; the sweet but stale-smelling air made him feel nauseous. He looked away from the prow and along what was obviously a bed. He stopped when he reached her face. The wrinkles parted and what were left of her painted lips smiled. All the sounds in the room including his own breathing seemed to stop.

'So you are Robert Cornelius, are you?' The English, both in content and accent, was perfect. Robert took a deep breath to steady his nerves and nodded dumbly. 'My, my, but you are covered in a lot of somebody else's blood, aren't you?' He didn't answer. The eyes of all the Gulcus and of the portraits that lined the room fixed upon him.

The red mouth opened again. 'I think we owe you an explanation, Mr Cornelius, regarding the death of Leonid Meyer.'

'You did it?' It just came out! Even though he knew that such a brittle thing as her couldn't possibly have done it, it came out.

She smiled and patted the space on the bed beside her. 'Indirectly. Please sit.'

Robert took a step forward and lowered himself slowly on to the dusty, moth-eaten bed. She gathered her long thin arms about her flat chest as if symbolically holding him close to her like a spider with its prey.

'Do you like stories, Mr Cornelius?'

He watched mesmerised as her red-tipped fingers massaged her own dry shoulders. He didn't answer.

A tiny laugh drifted up from the back of her throat. 'I know you do.' He noticed that her eyes were a very deep blue and was surprised. Old people's eyes usually lost their colour, watered down by time. 'This story, however, is different in that it is based upon a premise that only some of us in this room believe to be true.'

A woman, Natalia's mother, started crying softly.

'To start I must go back in time to 1918, Mr Cornelius. As

you must be able to tell from my appearance, it is a year that I can clearly remember.'

With a normal person he would have made at least some small sounds of protest, but this wasn't someone to whom the normal rules of anything, including politeness, applied.

'I do not I think need to waste any time talking about my nationality. In 1918, Mr Cornelius, I lived in a town called Ekaterinburg in the Urals. Before the Bolsheviks my family... they, they had been powerful and we...' She sighed. 'Some people, including myself, were shot.' She looked behind him at her son Nicholas. 'Before we were shot, Mr Cornelius, and some of my family, I know, struggle to understand this too, I remember very little.' She paused and bowed her head.

Sergei muttered something hard and bitter that Robert could not understand.

Nicholas coughed to attract her attention. 'Go on, Mama.'

She smiled at him, but without love. A heartless mother spider. 'My earliest real, complete memory is of lying on a filthy floor covered with blood. I looked, I should imagine, not unlike you do now. Not the same as remembering the kiss of a beloved father or sister, but there it is. Other people were on the floor too, but they were all dead. Men in uniform who I knew to be Bolsheviks were walking about amongst the corpses finishing them off with bayonets and pistols. The room was full of gunsmoke, I could taste it in my mouth. I still can sometimes.' Her eyes met his and held them. 'I feel the incident has a familiar ring to you, Mr Cornelius.'

'No.' But he wasn't sure.

'No matter. Anyway, they thought I was dead. They loaded us on to a truck. They threw me on top. I found myself pressed between the body of a boy and a leg almost severed by bullets. When the truck moved this limb fell against my mouth and I tasted its blood. If I had ever had a name I had forgotten what it was. Can you understand that?'

But a kind of numbness had filled his body and he just continued to stare into that awful face without moving.

'Time passed, I don't know how much, and then the truck stopped. I held my breath because I knew that if they heard me they would kill me. The boy beside me moaned. He still lived but because he was now a danger to me I didn't want him to. I heard voices. I put my hands hard around the boy's neck and I squeezed. You have to believe that there was no other way. I closed my eyes but he gurgled and his arms came up to push me away. A thick rope of blood rose from his mouth and sludged against my face. And they heard him. A youth with a little sharp face like a fox jumped up amongst the bodies and looked into my eyes. Two other men followed and I took my hands off the boy's throat.'

Natalia's mother said something and the old woman smiled.

'The truth, if you want to know, Anya, is that I don't know. I strangled the boy to kill him because he was a danger to me, but whether I succeeded or not, I cannot say. I told Leonid and the other two that he was still alive.' She turned away from her daughter and faced Robert. 'The man with the sharp face was Leonid Meyer, Mr Cornelius. He and the other two guards took myself and the boy off the truck and hid us in some woods. He saved my life. Unfortunately I was never able to repay the debt, as you know.' She cleared her throat. 'To explain: the boy and I were taken off the truck while the Bolshevik commanders were reconnoitering the road ahead. When they rejoined the vehicle the truck moved on. The rest of the bodies were apparently beaten and then burnt with fire and sulphuric acid at an old mine a few versts down the road. If it helps you at all, Mr Cornelius, they had to do this in order to disguise the identities of the victims.'

Oh it helped all right, but it didn't make any sense. The story was now all too familiar, almost laughably so. 'You're talking about the murder of the last Tsar, aren't you?'

She offered him a short black cigarette, which he declined. 'I might be.' She shot her son Nicholas the kind of look that silences dissent. 'Anyway, the boy, the one I'd tried to strangle, was dead when I next looked at him. I didn't attempt to bury him and just lay on the ground waiting for something to happen. And a while later it did. Leonid returned. He gave me a little bread and while he soaked the boy's body in petrol and set it alight, he told me things.'

She paused obviously for effect. Robert lost some pa-tience with those deep blue eyes and shrugged. 'What things?'

'Leonid told me who the boy was and I was shocked.' She looked down at her hands and her voice became quiet. 'He was my brother. His name was Alexei.'

Robert's patience suddenly snapped. Here he was in the midst of the most terrible situation that had ever occurred to him and this hag was coming out with a fairy-tale almost as old as the century. And where was Natalia? He preloaded his voice with irony. 'So you're Princess Anastasia of Russia, are you?'

Her head snapped upwards again and those eyes of hers silenced him immediately.

'Leonid told me my name was Maria Nicolaeva Romanova, the Tsar's third daughter and the only survivor. It meant little to me at the time, Mr Cornelius. At the time my only feelings on the matter were that everybody I had ever known was now dead. I was totally alone.'

'So what happens then,' said Cohen, looking away, as was so irritatingly his custom, from the road and at the person he was talking to.

Suleyman grabbed wildly at the steering wheel and shouted, 'Will you watch the road, or—'

'OK! OK!' Cohen turned his attention back on to the thick morning traffic and then returned once again to his original subject. 'But what happens if this Cornelius person is at Karadeniz Sokak and old Ikmen isn't?'

'Then we will bring Mr Cornelius in,' replied Suleyman with some determination.

'And it'll be our kill, so to speak?'

'Yes,' said Suleyman with, it had to be admitted, some satisfaction. 'Yes, it will.'

Cohen laughed. 'That'll show him, won't it!'

'Yes it will,' the young man said through his teeth. 'Yes it
will.'

Her story was hard to follow, not because it was complicated, but
because she herself, at times, appeared to be unsure about the
facts that lay behind it. Leonid Meyer had taken her out of the
country via Armenia. Until they reached the comparative safety
of Constantinople, they both worked as casual labourers in a
circus. Maria took the money at the entrance to the freak show.
This memory amused her greatly. At the time she had difficulty
coming to terms with who Meyer told her she was. She couldn't
necessarily trust the man, for a start. She had only vague
memories of events before the execution. Events that could have
happened to numerous aristocratic girls of her age. The bullet
graze on her face didn't help either and she frequently felt that
her true place should be behind those filthy curtains that hid the
three-legged man, the bearded lady and the Siamese twins from
non-paying public gaze.

But Meyer was insistent about her identity. It seemed to
excite him sexually and he took her often and without tenderness during their long and arduous journey.

'Then, just before Constantinople, something happened.'
She looked him straight in the eyes and stared hard without
blinking. Robert knew it was all so much twaddle, it had to be,
but he was mesmerised. 'One day I woke up, not with regained
memories, but with the perfect certainty that Leonid was right.
All the way across Anatolia he had browbeaten me with it—how
I as the only surviving member of the family was now heiress to
a fortune. He said someone had once told him how the Tsar had
managed to get much of his private fortune transferred abroad

just before the Revolution. His plan was for us to find our way across to Western Europe and claim it. I agreed at first, what else could I do? But then that day came and with it came fear. I was the Tsar's only surviving child, a person Russia's new rulers had hated enough to want to kill. Under the Tsar, the old Imperial Secret Service, the Okrana, had agents all over the world, even I knew that. It was unlikely that the Bolsheviks would operate in a different fashion. And as you know, history has proved me right in this case. I became afraid for my life.'

Nicholas walked up to the head of the bed and took his mother's hand. She had been talking for some time and was beginning to look tired. But Robert was tired too: of her and her stupid story; of the irrelevancy of everything she was telling him; of not being able to see Natalia. Also the desire to tell the police was going. Perhaps it was all the talk of death. 'I still don't understand what Meyer's murder has to do with all this.'

'You will.' She squeezed her son's hand and smiled at him. 'Anyway, I refused to go along with Leonid's plan and at Üsküdar I left him. He was very angry and threatened to expose me anyway, but I knew that he wouldn't. You see Leonid was implicated too. It was Leonid who shot my brother, little more than a child at the time. Even then the guilt crucified his soul. So I was alone. But not for long. I met an old man, Mehmet Gulcu. Then I met Leonid again and I told him about Mehmet. Mehmet was rich and Leonid approved. We didn't marry, but I bore him three children. The second one, Sergei'—she looked across, Robert fancied in disgust, at the cripple—'confirmed my belief in my identity. Serge is as he is because he has haemophilia, just like my brother the Tsarevich Alexei.' She stared at the wall behind Robert's head. 'Strange his blood was so thick, really.'

She didn't speak again for a while. Nicholas took up the story. 'When Papa died, Mama had little to think of except her past. She read, you know. It grew. This room she painted violet, just like the boudoir of the Tsarina Alexandra. She collected pictures of "herself" and others. Sometimes she thinks maybe she remembers something...Shut in this house, so afraid, the blood becomes very important to her. Romanov blood, so she tells us. At twenty years old I want to marry some girl, but Mama says no. The blood—'

Anya screamed. Robert turned to look at her. What he saw was a trembling white ghost, its mouth twisted like a Möbius strip. Strangely, Nicholas smiled. 'Mr Cornelius, my sister Anya is also the mother of my two children. Mama was most specific about preserving Romanov blood.'

For the first time in his life Robert really felt his skin crawl. Not because of what Natalia and her sibling, brother, sister, whatever it was, were. That wasn't their fault, but the mind behind it...A young male voice interjected. It came from over by the shuttered window. The person Robert had hoped might be Natalia, but wasn't. The old woman cooed at him in dark, liquid Russian. Robert remembered that most of the 'Anastasias' hadn't actually been able to speak their 'own' language.

'Cruel, isn't it?' Maria Gulcu turned her attention to him once again. 'But it was necessary and Leonid, who had by this time taken to drink, approved.' She smiled. 'All my family loved Leonid; he had saved me. If Uncle Leonid said a thing they knew that thing must be right. The grandchildren particularly, idolised him—until that is, some of us older people, well, myself, really, became a little careless with our talk. When one day, just prior to that fateful Monday of yours, I became sick of the endless paean of praise that always surrounded mention of my poor old Jewish friend. When, out of jealousy, I told a dear young person a truth that shattered each and every heroic Meyer illusion.'

She looked around the room at her almost complete family, her face set and impassive. Robert followed her eyes with his, but they came to rest nowhere. 'You see, sadly, Mr Cornelius, when secrets do come out, some people find it very hard to come to terms with them.' She called out towards the chair by the window in Russian.

Two pale hands braced themselves against the arms of the chair and a very familiar profile leant into view.

❀ ❀ ❀

'Do you have any idea what would happen if a stray cigarette end or spark landed in the back of your rig?'

The pop-eyed driver crossed his arms on top of the half-open cab window and nodded his head aggressively. "What?"

Of course he could be genuinely stupid, although Ikmen, in his present state of mind, preferred to think of the man as criminally negligent. After all his accursed truck had just rendered his back bumper into the shape of a tormented letter 'S'.

He shouted, 'You drive around with a fucking great waxed bag full of gasoline, exposed to every element going, and you want me to tell you what happens if that little lot meets a flame!'

The driver paused for a second before spitting his reply. 'Yeah.'

'Well it catches fire of course, you dull cunt! What do you think it's going to do? Run to the doctor for a bandage?'

He took his notebook and pen out of his pocket. 'What's your licence-plate number and whom do you work for?'

The driver puffed indignantly and folded his arms. 'You're not in the traffic division. I don't have—'

'Don't fuck with me, you little shit! One more smart word from you and you'll find yourself in a very small room sharing toilet facilities with a homosexual rapist for the rest of the week!'

Several hundred horns at the back of the accident all sounded in unison. The truck driver's mouth turned down at the corners and he mumbled: '34 KV7 99 and I work for my brother.'

Ikmen wrote it down. 'Who is?'

'Adnan Kemal.'

Avcı tapped Ikmen on the shoulder once again. 'Sir, there's a traffic cop coming over from the cigarette kiosk.'

'Good,' Ikmen snapped back to the driver of the truck. 'And where does Mr Kemal live?'

'Iskender.'

The traffic cop drew level with Ikmen's disgruntled little party. Ikmen tore a page out of his notebook and thrust it into the traffic policeman's hand. 'Here. There's his licence-plate number and the name of the man he works for. I'm busy, I've had it with this bastard, you do it!'

He'd only been on duty for ten minutes. He'd only been a policeman for six months. 'Oh,' he said ineffectually.

It wasn't Natalia. But then, thinking about it, she had to be at work now, didn't she? Robert peered, his eyes watering, through the smoke-encrusted gloom and felt his breath stop. It was a young man and he was crying. His voice broke as he spoke in their language. He pleaded with her, his hands stretched out trembling before him, but her face was stone. Like her soul, Robert thought. The pleading continued like a soft dirge. She spoke over the top of it, drowning its dark, melodious lower registers.

'This is Misha, Mr Cornelius, Natalia's twin brother. We don't show him to many people because he's not quite right. Sometimes people mistake him for his sister, which is very convenient. When, on the very rare occasions he leaves this house, and people who know us see him they just assume it is Natalia. It takes their minds off his bizarre behaviour. It is a mistake, I believe, you once made yourself.'

But he'd already made that connection. Misha's body was thin, all of it. 'So what's wrong with him?' Robert kept his eyes firmly fixed on to what looked like a carnival mask of his lover's face.

The old woman sighed. 'He is inbred. What more do I need to say? They can be more stupid than the rest of us, Mr Cornelius, and Misha is very stupid.'

Robert hated the malice in her voice. If Misha was stupid it was hardly his fault. 'Well, you created him.'

'Yes, God forgive me.' She paused and lit another cigarette. 'However, stupid though he may be, my poor grandson knew full well after I had done my business what Uncle Leonid had done to his great-grandfather the Tsar and his family and he decided that the old Jew was going to have to pay for that.'

'So it was Misha who killed Leonid Meyer?'

'Yes. You saw the boy, I believe, on your way home from your work.'

Robert looked across at the sad, slack-jawed but sickeningly familiar face. It all made sense now, or at least that part of it did. The thin shoulder, the unfashionable clothes...

'But then, if you knew...'

'Oh but I didn't even for a second dream that he would act upon his new knowledge,' she replied. 'I stupidly thought him far too dull and passive even to think about doing such a thing. However, when Misha went missing just after lunch on the Monday, I did become alarmed. He rarely left the house and had never done so on his own and then when Nicholas found that part of Mr Gulcu's old car had been tampered with...'

'Car?' Robert frowned. 'What car?'

She smiled. 'When Mehmet died he left, amongst other things, a car in the cellar, which is also a garage, beneath this house. Because none of us could or wanted to drive we let Misha play with it, which he did. And as Nicky explained to the boy, provided he didn't tamper with the battery, which contained a powerful, corrosive acid, no harm could come to him. He obeyed this dictate about the battery until that Monday when he removed it for precisely its devastating destructive powers.'

'Acid?' Robert felt his mind reel and spin with information that was coming both too rapidly and too late.

Quite inappropriately, he thought, she smiled. 'If you had been listening to me as you should, Mr Cornelius, you would know that after the Bolsheviks shot the Romanovs they attempted to destroy their bodies with sulphuric acid. Our little Misha here has lived and breathed that story all of his life, and so when it came to selecting a weapon with which to kill Leonid, a hated Bolshevik murderer, sulphuric battery acid seemed to offer him the kind of poetic justice he was seeking.'

Robert paused for a moment before speaking. The notion of using acid as a murder weapon was proving rather too much to take in. After all, hadn't the police said that Meyer had been battered to death? 'So what you are saying, Mrs Gulcu...'

'What I am saying, Mr Cornelius, is that Misha went to Leonid's apartment that afternoon, hit him over the head with either the battery or something else, I don't know, and then emptied the acid down his throat and over his body.'

'But the police...'

'The police did not make the more dreadful aspects of this crime known to the public, Mr Cornelius, fearing as they always do that demented people may copy it. I know of these things only because Misha and Natalia told me about them.'

'Natalia?' His heart jerked. 'Where does she come into all this?'

'When Nicky told me that Misha had gone, taking with him something of potential destructiveness, I called Natalia at her place of work and told her to get over to Leonid's apartment. I was hysterical by this time and bitterly regretful of what I had said to the boy. As soon as Nicky had told me about the battery, I knew what Misha was about to do. Knowing little else besides Romanov history in his poor blighted little life and, in the light of what I had so recently told him about Leonid, it seemed obvious to me. But when Natalia reached the apartment, the deed had already been done and Misha had gone. Left with only Leonid's dreadful body, which reduced the poor girl to violent sickness, she then had very quickly to decide what to do. Fearing that when the police did finally arrive they would find her brother's fingerprints on the old battery she took it away with her when she went and then deposited it on some waste ground on the way home. She was there very soon after her brother and you may even have seen her as you chased Misha down the road. Not that you would have recognised her. She always covered her head and face with a shawl when she went to visit her uncle in Balat—she didn't like the way the Jews stared at her. Odd, don't you think, given her usual outlandish behaviour? But then the shawl did allow her to get that battery out unseen and so...'

'And so,' put in Nicholas Gulcu, 'we have decided now to go to police and tell them what we tell you.'

Robert Cornelius felt the skin around his forehead pull upwards as his eyes widened in shock. 'You are going to give your own flesh and blood, however dreadful, to the police?'

'We have no option,' the old woman replied. 'I must, as I have always done, put the reputation of myself and the family as a group first.'

'But...'

'I did what I could—via yourself, unfortunately—but when that didn't work...' She shrugged.

Robert Cornelius looked puzzled at this point. 'You did what you could via me?'

'Yes, I told Natalia to get you to implicate the odious Reinhold Smits, which you did because you were so pitifully besotted. We were fortunate however in having the swastika—'

'What? What?' He held his hands aloft to stop her. She was moving too fast again and he was getting confused. 'What is this about a swastika? Can you tell me that, please?'

Nicholas Gulcu whispered something into his mother's ear and she nodded. 'When Misha had finished killing Leonid, he daubed a large swastika on the wall above the dead man's head. This was, as it were, a sort of calling card. The Empress Alexandra loved the swastika. In 1918, it did not possess the vile associations that it does now. In whatever house the family lived, she always drew one on the wall. It was as much a part of her soul as her love of the colour lilac. I have them myself, swastikas, in this room, drawn in pencil underneath my lilac wallpaper. Not that the police made that connection. They came to the obvious conclusion and with my, and your help, they soon found Reinhold Smits.'

'Who is, I understand, a Nazi, and...'

'Reinhold Smits, or rather his father, became Leonid's employer soon after he arrived in this country. Time passed and despite the obvious disparity in their social positions, Leonid and Reinhold eventually became acquainted via a rather revolting sexual preference they both shared for very young girls. In Leonid's defence I must say that nothing illegal ever occurred on his part, but Reinhold was of a rather different order. The older he got, the younger his lovers became—a fact that he would boast about openly to his "poor little pet Jew" Leonid.' She sighed, sadly so Robert Cornelius thought. 'And it was at this time, during the 1920s, that I re-established my own association with Leonid once again. I was with Mehmet by this time and therefore secure in myself. So sometimes I would go and meet Leonid from work for a coffee or just a talk and... It was at one such meeting that he introduced me to Reinhold Smits who was, I thought at the time, rather more pleased to see me, a complete stranger, than he should have been.'

'Why?'

'For two reasons. Firstly, and less importantly, "elderly" as I was then, he found me attractive and secondly, Leonid had told him who I really was.'

'And so he was impressed by the fact that you said you were royal?'

She smiled at the Englishman's use of his own doubts about her when framing his question. 'No, Mr Cornelius, Reinhold was interested in me because he had plans for the person that I was. Even in the 1920s the seeds of fascism were well planted in the soil of Germany. In addition, they hated the new Bolshevik government in Russia—the young Adolf Hitler and his friends saw it as an almost pure embodiment of evil. And so did Reinhold Smits, who also when he met me started to dream about some sort of Christian crusade against the Soviet Union—preferably with this pure little Russian princess and all her Tsarist gold as a figurehead. Leonid, being the simple-minded soul that he was, saw it as a great opportunity but, as ever afraid of discovery and fearful for my life, I wanted none of it. As soon as Reinhold had gone I flew at Leonid in a fury. I told him to put a stop to this rich, powerful and arrogant German's plans, which of course he did.'

'How? How did he do that?'

'Reinhold Smits was, by that time, a fully practising pedophile. He showed and even gave photographs of his conquests to Leonid—so proud he was of it all, so safe he felt behind all his money.' Her face fell. 'Some of the little girls were as young as six. I don't think I have to spell out how Leonid managed to stop Reinhold putting his plan for me into action.'

Robert shuddered visibly with disgust. 'Blackmail?'

'Yes. And even though Reinhold hated him passionately afterwards—it informed, amongst other things, his later, even more florid, anti-Semitism—he kept on paying Leonid for the rest of his life. He was, in fact, and quite coincidentally, at Leonid's apartment making payment on the day that Leonid died.'

Robert shook his head in disbelief. 'What?'

'Oh, he got there after the deed had been done and was most horribly shocked. I know that because of a very grave error he made when he phoned to console me. However, even though I knew inside that he couldn't possibly have killed Leonid himself—apart from anything else he, such a wealthy man, had no motive—I never told Reinhold that. I just let him sweat and worry and helped the police to find him.' She sighed. 'Such a dreadful shame they did not appear to be too interested.'

'Oh yes what a dreadful shame that is!'

Maria Gulcu physically bowed her head momentarily to his anger. 'I can understand—'

'No you can't! You can't even begin to!' Robert touched one shaking hand up to his puffy, livid face and for a moment it looked as if he was about to cry. But then he collected himself 'I have, I think, done something truly terrible and, and...all right, indirectly, I think I may have done it because of this—this business. I was ill, some years ago, mentally ill, and even now when I become agitated I find that I can get out of control. And'—he looked down at the floor now—'I have been so agitated about Natalia. Because...because I think that I knew all along, Mrs Gulcu—not all about this bloody Byzantine Russian stuff—but because I knew that she was at Meyer's apartment and even though you say that she hasn't killed anyone, she might just as well have. Hiding her brother's evidence and leading me...' And then he looked up at her, his eyes shining. 'But I loved her, you see.'

The old woman nodded her head in recognition. 'I know. Just as Mr Gulcu loved me. He was a good man too and had I been someone other than who I am, a fact he both protected and respected, I could have had a very good life with him. But I chose to continue to consort with people like Leonid. I chose to be different and distance myself from poor Mehmet's world. And when he died, leaving me all of his money and his property, I chose to bring our children up as Russians—to make them wear the clothes of those long since dead—to try, through them, to rebuild the blood-line I had contaminated with Mehmet.'

Robert, his teeth now gritted in anger, said, 'You're a very evil woman, Mrs Gulcu—princess or no princess!'

She shrugged. 'I should have been more careful with regard to what I said in front of poor Misha. I let my desire to be always first in everybody's affections get the better of me. And spite, of course, too. Knowing what Leonid really was and hearing the boy endlessly praise the man was, on this occasion, just a little too much. But then as you can see, the boy always looks as if he doesn't have a thought in his head. But there. If only I had listened to Leonid long ago I—I would have been more careful.'

'Meaning?'

'I mean, Mr Cornelius, that the one and only reason why poor Leonid drank to excess, as he did almost all of his life, was because he didn't trust me. Rescue or no rescue, he had killed my family, my very special, *divine* family, and he knew that one day I would come for him. I didn't believe it and indeed I used to laugh when he said such things, but when one of my little ones killed Leonid it was in a way my hand that was reaching out for him. Indirectly, if you will, but I killed Leonid. I have even, during the last few days, wondered whether I said the things that I did in front of Misha to obtain just that result.'

Silence, with the exception of the sobbing that was now coming from Natalia's mother, sat like a stone between all the occupants of the room—an absence waiting to be filled. Characteristically, it was Maria Gulcu who finally obliged.

'And so now we must go to the police,' she said. 'I do not want to but—'

She was interrupted by her daughter who, still sobbing, flung herself across her mother's bed, shouting out words that Robert Cornelius could not understand. The old woman stroked her hair and attempted to calm her even though, and to Robert's open disgust, her face was still as hard as granite.

'My daughter is upset, Mr Cornelius,' she explained, 'because the plan has always been that one day we all return to Russia in triumph. With the collapse of the old Soviet Union, that even looked possible—until now. God alone knows what will happen to us now.'

Returning suddenly to the reason why he was there in the first place, Robert Cornelius shook his head and then said, 'But what of Natalia? I mean, I presume she is at her work?'

'Yes,' the old woman replied, 'and she will be found there by the police once I have spoken to them.'

And then Misha spoke again. Maria's reply was bellowed sharply at him. 'In English please, Misha! Mr Cornelius cannot understand!'

Robert forced himself to look at him. The identical features on the boy's face made him flinch. He'd done things he hadn't even dreamt about before for that face.

In hideously halting English he cried, 'I not want to go to prison, Grandmama! Police they even kill me for it!'

'Ah, Misha!' She sighed deeply and looked at Robert. 'What can I say? You hear he knows what will happen to him and I cannot deny it. He will confess to them as he did eventually to me. I know this. But what can I do?'

Misha screamed. It was a high, piercing, womanly sound. 'I am Romanov, you cannot!'

Every eye in the room was upon him. His agitation made

him hop from foot to foot, his arms wound protectively round his body. Robert had a sudden and terrible feeling that the boy was about to go seriously out of control. He had seen people like him before—psychotics winding themselves higher and higher up into panic until the only way to bring them down was via a needle or a straitjacket. All the old fears returned in a huge, heavy rush. The boy's eyes were on him, narrowed, and he knew what he was thinking. It was his fault, this foreigner had messed it all up, and Robert knew that it was only a matter of time before he either raged insanely or attacked. He had to remain calm, even though he could feel his fear mounting at an alarming rate. He had to make some gesture towards him that the boy would understand.

Nobody else in the room saw the danger. Maria leant back against her pillows and just said 'Sssh!' very softly under her breath. She knew that Misha wasn't really a bad boy, he wouldn't do anything to harm anyone.

'Misha…' Robert reached towards the boy, his hand open in a classic gesture of giving and friendship.

But the boy pulled away as if scalded. His long arm wheeled backwards through the air. As it descended it just caught the edge of the glass shade that enclosed the big oil-lamp on the table beside him. It fell to the floor with a crash and flames, at first very small and tender, licked and fed from the bottom of the curtain.

Chapter Twenty-four

'NO, DON'T PUSH, Mrs Ikmen, pant instead!'

Fatma screwed up her face and small painful gasping sounds came from her mouth.

The eldest of her daughters, a wide-eyed twenty-year-old called Çiçek, looked on in horror. 'But Mummy wants to push,' she told the doctor. 'It's hurting her!'

'Well, she can't yet!' She was young, she didn't like attending confinements and most of all she didn't like to be questioned by people who didn't understand anatomy. 'Your mother's cervix isn't dilated enough yet. If she pushes now she'll tear and I don't think any of us want that, do we!'

'No!' But her mother was in such pain! Her face was red and covered with sweat and her legs were already parted, they quivered on top of the plastic sheet below her, aching for delivery. Çiçek looked at the large puddle of water and blood that had gathered down by Fatma's feet and wondered whether or not she should be thinking about clearing it up.

The doctor placed her fingers on Fatma's wrist and took her pulse. She didn't comment.

'Is she all right?'

'Your mother's doing very well,' replied the doctor, 'for a woman of her age.'

Fatma opened her eyes and looked up at her daughter.

'Where is your father? Where's Çetin!'

'He's on his way, Mummy.'

Fatma scowled. 'You don't have to humour me, you know!'

'He is!' But Çiçek couldn't give it much conviction.

The doctor leant over the bed. 'Your contractions are coming every three minutes now, Mrs Ikmen. You're still not fully dilated, but I can give you some pain relief which might help. Do you want that?'

'Yes!'

She walked over to her attaché case and took out a syringe. For a second she placed it beside the bed while she rubbed a small ball of cotton wool on Fatma's arm. It contained a wet substance that was very cold. She then retrieved the syringe and knocking the clear liquid up into the needle she injected it into Fatma's arm. 'That should ease things a little for you.'

After all the agony she had already experienced Fatma hardly noticed the pain of the needle. She just lay like a great fat fish, panting in the heat, waiting for the next contraction. 'Dr Koç, could you telephone my husband, please. I want him to be here.'

The doctor looked confused. 'But—'

'My husband is a policeman, Doctor! He needs to be shouted at to get him home!'

Her face dissolved into a mask of agony as another pain gripped her. The doorbell rang and Çiçek flew towards the bedroom door. 'That must be Dad now!'

Why he or nobody else moved immediately to stop the flames

spreading Robert would never know. Perhaps it was the speed with which they climbed up the curtains, like skinny children, hand over hand. If only someone, anyone had had the presence of mind to pull them down and smother them with a blanket. There were plenty of blankets on her bed.

But they all just watched instead. It was so unusual to see a bright light in that room. It harshly illuminated the old woman's face and for the first time Robert saw the long, lopsided scar that ran down the side of her face. Had she got it there, in that cramped Ekaterinburg cellar? Had perhaps that old Jew, in whose death all these terrible, frightening people had had a hand, inflicted that wound? Why had he saved her anyway?

A loud, splintering, cracking noise alerted Robert to the fact that part of the bone-dry wooden wall had ignited and he moved. 'Somebody get some water, for Christ's sake!'

But still they didn't move. A strange sort of calm seemed to have come over them, even Misha. They looked at the fire as if they were watching television. It was an unreal image from which they were removed in both time and location. It was then that Robert's instinct for self-preservation kicked in.

Cohen swung the car into the steep, narrow alleyway beside the Pera Palas Hotel and was struck immediately by an appalling stench that hit him like a brick wall. It was a very acidic smell that actually hurt the inside of his nostrils. He pulled a face and looked across at Suleyman. 'What the fuck is that, Mehmet?'

Suleyman, by the disgusted expression on his face, had obviously noticed it too. He took a deep sniff and nearly choked on the contents of the air drawn in. 'Oh, I don't know! It's almost like burning, although'—he put his head through the wide-open car window and looked up at the sky—'I can't see anything...'

Cohen pulled a face and paused the car at the top of the alleyway before proceeding across Meşrutiyet Caddesi. He saw the hotel doorman run across the road and up into the little road opposite.

'Is that Karadeniz where that man's just gone?'

'Yes.'

A few other men and a young woman dressed entirely in black followed after the doorman, also running. For some reason Suleyman looked up again and saw a thick curl of black smoke rise above the grim buildings towards Istiklal Caddesi.

He snapped at Cohen. 'Stop the car!'

With one clean bound he was through the door and running across Meşrutiyet Caddesi in the direction of Karadeniz Sokak. The tiny street was full of people all looking up towards the top of a house about halfway down. For a second Suleyman looked wildly about him for signs of Ikmen's presence, but when he found none he looked up too. The whole top floor of number 12, Karadeniz Sokak was on fire.

Panting heavily in the wake of his headlong dash out of the old woman's apartment, Robert looked up through the ocean of woodsmoke rolling towards him from the stairwell he had just descended. They, the family, were moving about now, he could hear their feet running above him, their voices. His break for the door had woken them. Nicholas had followed him as far as the bathroom and had gathered some water in a bucket.

Robert looked at the telephone on the hall table and wondered whether he should use it. But there were people outside now, lots of people, one of them surely must have called the fire brigade.

He stared up into the stairwell again. A six-foot gobbet of smoke rolled down towards him and the walls of the house creaked and splintered as they expanded in the intense heat. To go up again would be insane, but none of them were coming down to him and if the brigade didn't arrive soon they would all be incinerated or overcome by smoke. Not, of course, that they would understand that. Although why he should care...

But he did. Whatever the Gulcus claimed to be it was beyond doubt that they were human, if unworldly. If someone didn't organise them they would all die. They would try to fight the flames with what little water they had without even thinking about getting themselves downstairs and into the street. They would do that because she, by virtue of her age, was going to be so difficult to move. And they wouldn't leave her. Leaving her was pointless because without her they had nothing. Whatever flimsy proof had ever existed about them was contained within her. They either all came or they all didn't.

Robert put one foot on to the first stair and took a deep breath. Of course for him it wasn't about them and who they were at all. He didn't really know the Gulcus and what he did understand about them painted a very ugly picture in his mind. No, it was guilt that was going to make him act. The guilt of a man who knows he has done something unforgivable—the subsequent pathetic attempt to make amends that sometimes overwhelms the most logical of minds. That old Jew he hit might be dead but if he could just save even one of the people upstairs...

The smoke was thicker now and was beginning to make his eyes smart. If he didn't go soon, he would never go. Then the opportunity would be lost and he would be just like every other man of violence who had ever lived. Cruel and thoughtless—not like the self he knew he had really always been at all.

Robert took another deep breath, put his hand over his mouth and ran up towards the black, curling smoke. The house sighed around him.

❀ ❀ ❀

Dr Koç took hold of Fatma's sweaty hand and smiled. 'It's all right, Mrs Ikmen, you can push this time.'

'I won't tear?' There were tears running down her cheeks. She wiped them gently away with the back of her hand.

'No, you won't tear. You've been very brave and you're going to be fine.'

She gripped her hand hard and for a second Dr Koç thought that she was starting another contraction, but she only wanted to attract her attention. 'Was that my husband at the door just now?'

How could she tell her when she was in the heat of heavy labour? But her expression had already given everything away.

'I'm afraid it wasn't, no. Just your father-in-law.'

She wanted to give vent to her anger, but the pain in her pelvis gripped like a vice and she took in a deep, rasping breath. Dr Koç let go of her hand and ordered Çiçek, who was sitting behind her mother, to grip Fatma's shoulders very tightly. She moved over and peered between Fatma's wide-open legs.

Fatma let her breath out with a loud bellow and bore down hard with every atom of her strength. There was a movement inside her followed by the slight feeling of relief obtained when the baby's head crowns the cervix.

The old Mercedes rolled down the street just in front of two fire appliances, their sirens wailing like agonised muezzins. Avcı banged his fist down hard on the horn and left it there. So many people were crowded into the street it was almost impossible to drive. Ikmen looked at them with disgust. The ghouls, the sickos, the watchers of accidents and other natural and unnatural disasters.

He'd seen the smoke as soon as they reached Taksim. And he'd known. A high place. He looked up at the burning roof of number 12, Karadeniz Sokak, the whole top storey and half of the next one down were violently ablaze. Naturally. That was the problem with the old wooden houses, especially in summer. All it needed was a spark.

Avcı pulled the car over by a small grocery shop and stopped. The two fire appliances moved into position and men began unravelling hoses.

Ikmen got out of the car and shook his head in disbelief. A little old man shuffled towards him, away from the scene. Ikmen hailed him. 'Hey, Uncle!'

'What's that?' He walked with a limp and wore his War of Independence medals pinned to a very holey green cardigan. He peered at Ikmen. 'What do you want, boy?'

'The burning house—do you know if anyone's in there?'

'Oh yes. Couple of minutes ago one smashed a window. There's several of them, all screaming, they have been. If Allah wills it the fire brigade will get them out. If not...' He shrugged.

Ikmen looked back at the fire again and the old man shuffled off. If the Gulcus died, he would never get to ask her that question, confront her with old Smits's photograph. Of that he was certain. But there was nothing he could do apart from what everybody else was doing—just let the firemen do their job. His only consolation was that Suleyman wasn't around.

He put his hand in his pocket and pulled out his cigarettes. People around him, including Avcı, looked at him as if he were mad.

The firemen lined their hoses up and switched on the water. As the water poured down the rubber tubing the hoses bucked and thrashed. People tried to get out of the way, but one woman got her ankle caught and fell over. Avcı immediately went to her aid. She was, Ikmen noted vaguely, young and pretty. He felt a movement behind his back as that section of the crowd parted. He took no notice and shouted to Avcı to make their presence known to the fire officers. A long, slim hand landed on his shoulder. 'Sir?'

It felt like going to sleep again in the full knowledge that a hideous nightmare was about to return. He looked around and up and there were tears in his eyes. 'Suleyman.'

Now that the floor was alight their only hope lay with the firemen in the street below. If they could swing their ladders up to the window he'd broken they could get out that way. Except perhaps for her. She still hadn't moved from the bed and now her daughter had joined her. Robert could see them through the flames. The daughter was screaming. Her hair was on fire, it made her look like an agonised saint, a halo of red and gold tongues around her head. The old woman, by contrast, was quite calm. The agony of burning hadn't yet started for her. But even when it did Robert had the oddest feeling that it wouldn't elicit so much as a single murmur. In her mind she'd already gone elsewhere. Back to Ekaterinburg maybe? Perhaps it had happened while he'd tried to escape downstairs. While Nicholas desperately tried to put out the flames with buckets of water. That had been a useless exercise.

For some reason at this point Robert remembered the old Jew, the way he had looked down at him with kindness and concern, the way he, Robert, had reacted with violence. Notwithstanding the bad associations he had built up against Balat, it was still extraordinary that he had done what he did. Mistrust, the instinctive lashing out at the unknown other, the barely restrained prejudices of nearly two thousand years. And how easy it had been! How simple to look into a sharp, pointed face and see, actually *see* the eyes of a demon. He looked down at the floor and saw Sergei's twisted body stretched out before him like a broken mannequin. He knew that if he touched him he would find no sign of life. He had gone to join the old Jew and Meyer and all the other dead people whose lives his mother Maria had touched.

The smoke was so thick now that he could hardly see anything any more and his lungs felt heavy and painful. Misha alone stood by the window and if Robert knew what was good for him he should join the boy. Robert moved slowly through the darkening smoke. There was a smell like roasting meat and he ducked down closer to the floor to avoid it. Oxygen always gathered at floor level and if he was to survive he had to get some into his clogged lungs soon. He bent low and scampered quickly across the smouldering carpet towards the light. As he ran he fancied he passed another body moving in the opposite direction, back into the room, but he couldn't be sure. Things shifted in the smoke. Shapes loomed and then subsided, like figures in fog.

Misha was still at the window when he got there, trembling. He and Robert looked at each other, but nothing passed between them. The young man was almost totally blank, Natalia's cunning face rendered passionless and insensible. It was an obscene travesty. It taunted Robert. On the one hand he wanted to kiss her thick red lips one more time but on the other...

A noise like the creaking of a large boat groaned agonisingly from the centre of the room. The two men at the window looked round. But there was nothing to see. All that had been in the room: the great bed, the golden ikons, the sad mock-empire furniture, the people—all were covered in red and yellow and the eerie green that signifies the presence of gas. Evil green, Natalia's favourite type of gold.

A gulp of air, big, like a wind, funnelled in through the open window. Sucked up by the house. The flames rejoiced and lengthened their bodies in celebration. It was like watching some sort of joyous tribal dance. Joyous because the fire loved it so, because the bigger it got the more beautiful it became. Natalia had been a flame.

Illusions live in fire. In cold countries like Britain people gather round their fires in the winter and look for pictures amongst the liquid, shifting fingers of brightly pulsating and impermanent colour. Robert's grandmother, Millie, had seen the Devil once, or so she had claimed. He'd had a thin blue chin like a stiletto. Robert had always been good at seeing pictures too. His family had commented on it. But as he saw the side walls of the house puff outwards like old, dry cheeks he wondered, as he had done when he'd seen Misha in Balat that day, whether it was not just his mind deceiving his eyes. What sounded like a clap of thunder from beneath his feet punched its way into the body of the room. The sound hit what remained of the ceiling and for just a fraction of a second everything was still. As the flames subsided he saw three burning heads. Features, if that is what they once were, slid down their faces and gave their static forms the appearance of waxworks. Sad, defunct waxworks.

Misha saw it too and with a scream climbed out of the

window and on to the roof. But Robert didn't follow him. What the boy was doing was without point. There was nothing left to do now but wait.

The floor gave way beneath the weight of her bed and all the other accumulated gewgaws of self-delusion. Robert gripped tightly on to the burning window-frame and felt the sickening sensation of fat and blood boiling in his hands. The three waxworks plunged down into the white-hot pit and were replaced by a massive, muscular tongue of thick red fire. It seemed to turn and look at him and Robert knew that it had both sense and intent. His feet scrabbled backwards as he tried to maintain some sort of hold on the thin ledge of floor that remained. The huge flame breathed in sensuously and let its swollen belly billow towards him. It kissed him, open mouthed, about the cheek and on the tip of his nose.

One of Robert's wrecked hands moved up to push the flame away. But as it wheeled forward it overbalanced and plunged into the pit with the waxworks taking the rest of his silent body with it. Other, smaller flames took him and consumed him.

Chapter Twenty-five

THE WHOLE CROWD as one body saw the man pull himself through the open window and stagger out on to the roof. Everything around him was burning and if the fire brigade didn't get someone up to him soon he was going to die very horribly and publicly. The men holding the hoses shouted at those operating the pump to switch the water off. They'd only just started spraying the building but it was too risky to continue with someone stuck precariously on the roof. One glancing touch of just the spray from such powerful jets could have him overbalancing and tumbling into the street.

One particularly nimble fireman jumped up on to the hydraulic ladder and signalled to others to winch him up. He pointed towards the man and the rest of the crew started to ease the ladder round, positioning it ready for extension.

Ikmen placed his hand very heavily and obviously on Suleyman's shoulder. It wouldn't be long. The man was already up on the roof and very soon it would occur to him that his safest course of action was to jump. That was natural enough given Homo sapiens's innate fear of fire. All Ikmen wondered was how long it would take him to fall. He thought about ordering Suleyman to the back of the crowd, but by that time it was too late.

'He's going to jump!'

They all shouted it, the stupid bastards! It was almost as if they were encouraging him. The fireman on the end of the ladder urged his comrades to get him in position now. There was a flurry of frenzied activity around the tender. Ikmen only moved his eyes for a millisecond to look at this action, but it broke his concentration.

Suleyman darted forward. 'Stay where you are! Don't move!'

Ikmen reacted immediately, but however fast he ran he couldn't match the young man's long athletic strides. I've fucked it up! he thought to himself. I've come all this way and I've fucked it up! He felt himself start to cry and brushed the tears roughly away from his eyes with the back of his hand.

'He's going to jump!' They shouted it again! The poor fireman on the end of the ladder screamed at them to stop, but his voice got lost in the general sound of mayhem and panic that roared up from the crowd. Everyone was so afraid and yet no one could stop looking.

The man on the roof bent his knees and flung his arms out to the sides as if preparing to launch himself like a bird. Suleyman had stopped now and was waving and shouting up at him. If only Ikmen's winded body could get there in time to pull him back. He urged himself forward through the pain and put one arm out in front of him. Suleyman was directly below the man now.

Oh, it was a long way down! The people looked like some toys he'd once had, little wooden people whose heads and arms moved when twisted sharply. They'd always ended up in odd, jerky poses, those figures, even when he had wanted them to be relaxed and calm.

One of the figures below was closer than the others and seemed to be shouting at him, but he couldn't make out any words. Perhaps he was trying to tell him that he was forgiven and that everything would now be all right. But it wouldn't. If you killed someone, even someone as wicked as Uncle Leonid, nothing could ever make that better ever again. Uncle Nicky had said so and therefore it had to be true.

The roof was very hot now. Under his feet things that were usually solid bubbled like liquid. Nobody else had come out on to the roof after him. He liked to think that somehow they'd managed to make it back down the stairs, but he knew that wasn't so. They were all dead, which was perhaps where they should always have been. If Grandmama had died in Ekaterinburg none of it would have happened. He wouldn't have happened—the dynasty would have just died when it was supposed to. Perhaps there really were proper times for things. Maybe by keeping the Romanovs alive Grandmama had committed some kind of sin. That Uncle Nicky was his father had sounded odd, but whether that was wrong or not was beyond him.

Another man was running towards the one who continued to shout at him. This looked peculiar because surely if the second man wanted the first to stop shouting all he had to do was say so. Turks were different like that, he'd watched them. They weren't a logical people, which explained why he didn't like them very much. Russians were better, Grandmama had always said so. He felt a little sad when he thought about Russia. He'd always wanted to go 'home', but now it was too late.

Somebody on the end of a ladder was coming towards him but he remained calm. He wouldn't reach him and even if he did it wouldn't matter. He had his own plans. He looked down at the ground again. It was a very long way and he had no doubt that it would hurt. The family would never have credited him with such perception, but he'd always known that he possessed that quality. He could reason and think like the rest of them. Perhaps at a different rate and along, to them, different lines, but he had always been able to do it. Duty, that was what it had been about. And he fully understood duty—that was very important. Grandmama had often said that people had criticised the Tsar for being too rigid in his sense of duty to the dynasty, he'd died because of it. So it had to be a good thing, didn't it?

But then not even that mattered any more. His feet felt boiling hot and even without looking he knew that his shoes were burning. He hurt all over. Strangely, though, he wasn't hot. The feeling was one of being stabbed many times. Not that that sensation would last for long. He was out in the open, the smoke couldn't possibly overcome him as it had done Uncle Serge. But that wasn't important now. The important thing was to get off the roof away from the flames. If that could be done then at least he could retain some dignity. The others hadn't, which meant that it was now up to him. Was it the right thing to do? He thought he'd done the right thing before...

Best to do it before too much thought got in the way! Misha spread his arms out wide and closed his eyes. Until he hit the ground it would be quite pleasurable, like flying. He let his knees go limp and toppled forwards.

Ikmen thought his lungs would burst as he lurched forward and grabbed Suleyman with both hands and pulled him backwards.

The most sickening sound that either of them had ever heard followed as the living body of the man smashed into the pavement before them and expired. It was a damp, dark, purple noise like the sound a fishmonger makes when he slaps squid down on his wooden chopping board. For a moment both men stayed absolutely still. Ikmen's ear pressed hard against Suleyman's back rejoiced in the sound of his strong, heavy breathing. Whatever horror lay on the ground before them, at least he was alive and for that Ikmen thanked the God in which he did not believe. There was no other being he could thank, certainly not himself. It had been too close for that.

Ikmen pulled himself out from underneath Suleyman's body and looked around. Two firemen were running towards them, their faces darkened by what looked like terror. Suleyman sank backwards on to the ground and Ikmen bent across him. Suleyman was covered with blood. He lay on his back trembling, looking at his gore-stained hands, trying not to touch them to his body.

Ikmen took him gently by the shoulders and tried to pull him into a sitting position. The blood was unpleasant to the touch as it was still warm, but Ikmen had to try. Suleyman was starting to cry and if he stayed on his back he'd choke on his own tears. But it wasn't easy. Suleyman didn't want to move. He turned his head to one side and pressed his shoulders hard into the ground in order to keep his body where it was. Ikmen looked down towards Suleyman's feet and saw why. The body of the man had landed on its stomach, which had burst on impact. Blood and offal were spattered in pools all around, although it was Suleyman himself who had taken the brunt of the mess. It had splashed and slopped up at him; the blood into his face and eyes, more unpleasant and happily unidentifiable things clung like bloody leeches to his legs and feet. The face of the dead man was familiar to Ikmen and not for the first time he felt sorry for the boy. What his place had been in the peculiar drama that had surrounded the Gulcus, Ikmen realised he would probably never know. In fact everything that had passed since the death of Leonid Meyer was suddenly feeling very alien to him. The Gulcu house was burning, there was still no sign of Cornelius and now this boy, this dead boy.

'Are you all right?'

Ikmen looked round and saw the two firemen bending over Suleyman's weeping body. He knew he should have answered the firefighters, it was always important to ascertain who was injured and who was not. But he couldn't speak. That Suleyman was alive was enough for the moment because he knew that it could all have been so different. Ikmen touched his sergeant's face and felt his mouth move beneath his hand. It was a miracle.

A pair of strong arms pulled him away from Suleyman and set him unsteadily on his feet. Ikmen became aware of the crowd again. The noise of their crying and screaming filtered through the temporary stop his mind had put inside his ears. They'd come to see a drama and had found themselves inside a horror. They were seeing just the edge of the blackness that had tortured his soul since the beginning of the Meyer affair: the past crashing bloodily into the present.

The second of the two firemen lifted Suleyman to his feet and led him away from the scene in front of Ikmen. Behind them the house burnt on in spite of the hoses pouring thousands of litres of water at its white-hot heart. All sorts of substances were playing their part: wood, gas, oil, the complicated biochemistry of the human body.

Around the back of the largest fire tender an ambulance was waiting. At its open back door, beside the paramedics, was a very shaken Constable Cohen. The paramedics took Suleyman from the arms of the fireman and loaded him silently into the vehicle. He didn't look at Cohen, or even appear to be aware that he existed. Shock. At least if Suleyman was in shock it meant that he would be blank and therefore without anguish for a few hours, Ikmen thought grimly.

As for himself? Even though Ikmen knew that he should go to hospital himself and let a doctor just check him out, he had already decided that he wouldn't. When the fire was out there would be time enough for that. That he was just as helpless as all the other spectators was not sufficient excuse. He'd found the Gulcus, he couldn't leave them now.

Ikmen disengaged himself from his fireman escort and walked across to Cohen. He opened his mouth to speak, but only found one word. 'What…?'

Cohen clasped one hand across his eyes and sighed. He replied in kind. 'What?'

Ikmen breathed rapidly and shallowly as if panicking. 'What...what...were you doing here?'

Cohen looked at Ikmen somewhat askance. He didn't tend to trust people in shock. 'We came to find you, sir. And to look for this Englishman who might have done for—'

'But I told Suleyman to take the day off! I told him because I...' His head hurt and he put his hand up to it gently. He must have banged it on the ground when he fell, not that he could remember.

Cohen took him by the arm and led him away from the ambulance. He too knew Ikmen should go to hospital, but he also knew that the Old Man would resist if forced. 'Hasn't anyone told you yet then, sir?'

'Told me what?' There was smoke everywhere and it made him cough, but he lit a cigarette anyway.

Cohen sat him down on a bollard. 'Your wife went into labour this morning.'

'Oh.' It was a very flat and uninterested response from a man just about to become a father. But then both of them were in the middle of a scene that looked like something from Dante's *Inferno*. The smoke was so thick that even the faces of some of the spectators were smudged and smutted with soot. There was also a smell of burning meat on the air now. Cohen knew what that was, but he didn't point it out to Ikmen. Ikmen sighed. 'Fatma will kill me.'

'Well, I can drive you there now, sir, if—'

'Where's Avcı?'

'Oh, er, I don't know.' Cohen looked about him but the boy was nowhere to be seen.

'Well, look for him, will you, Cohen?' It was a panicky request. Ikmen needed to know that everyone was safe now. It was important.

'All right, yes, um...'

'Tell him to go to my apartment and inquire after my wife.'

'You don't want to go yourself?'

Ikmen scowled. 'Just do it.'

With some reluctance Cohen left his boss and went to look for Avcı. Considering the gruesomeness of the occasion he fully expected to find him hiding somewhere.

The ambulance carrying Suleyman sped off down the narrow street and was almost immediately replaced by another, empty vehicle. There were three paramedics attached to this one and they all looked very grim. One of their number, a short, stocky, Armenian-looking man, opened the back of the ambulance and took out a folded blue bag. Ikmen looked inside the vehicle and noticed that none of the patient stretchers had either pillows or mattresses. The Armenian unfolded the thick blue body bag. This wasn't transport for the living.

Ikmen stared straight ahead of him at the back of one of the fire tenders. Out of the corner of his eye he could see that at last the men of the fire brigade were getting the flames under control. Strange really that wood should give them so many problems. If Ikmen hadn't known better he might have said that the building actually wanted to burn. He laughed grimly to himself. Prophecy was one thing, but ascribing intelligence to fire? Sometimes he felt like the old fool Fatma always said he was. All he could do now was live in hope that at least some of them had survived the inferno—not that there was much chance of that. And with them had gone all the answers to those questions he had come to ask. Questions about Cornelius and the letter he had typed to the police, questions about who the Gulcus were and why they had killed Leonid Meyer, because now he knew that they had. They had killed him for that old crime, the one in Ekaterinburg all those lifetimes ago, the one the premise for which lay between those two old photographs that had belonged to Smits—the ones that rested in his pocket now. He knew all that. But what he had really wanted to know was now irrevocably lost. Who was Maria Gulcu really, because despite everything he still wouldn't believe those photographs. He just couldn't. And why had she waited seventy-four years before taking her revenge?

The realisation that he would now never know suddenly made him want to cry.

❁ ❁ ❁

'Are you Inspector Ikmen?'

He looked up and saw a tall thin man of about his own age wearing a fireman's uniform. He was covered with soot and filth and looked exhausted.

Ikmen knew how he felt. It had been hours since they had put the fire out, even the crowd had dispersed now, but he was still there. 'Yes, I'm Ikmen. What is it?'

The fireman took his helmet off and wiped his forehead with the back of his hand. 'One of your men told me I should let you know when we start bringing the bodies out.'

So here it was. Ikmen sighed and lit yet another cigarette. 'Yes, thanks. How many bodies have you found?' Maria Gulcu's last 'Goodbye' flashed into his mind. That had sounded very final. Had she known?

The fireman took a small cigar from his tunic pocket and joined Ikmen in a smoke. 'Three so far. Do you have any idea as to how many persons might have been in the house?'

Ikmen looked at faces in his mind and counted. Maria Gulcu (perhaps she had been beautiful once with those hypnotic blue eyes?), Nicholas, Sergei, crippled Sergei, Natalia and...poor old Robert Cornelius. Had he been there? Where else could he have been? Ikmen took a stab at it.

'Five, I think,' he said. Then he remembered. 'Oh no, six. There was a servant boy too. But I think that was the one who jumped from the roof.'

The fireman smiled. 'Ah yes. The one that nearly killed your colleague. That was you who dragged him back, wasn't it?'

'Yes.' Ikmen turned away. He had no desire to discuss that matter any further. If people wanted to ascribe heroics he wanted none of it. The last thing he felt was courageous.

The fireman must have understood and he left. Ikmen got to his feet and followed him towards what was left of the Gulcu house. There wasn't much. All the upper storeys had crashed through into the basement. The only thing that remained standing was the great black front door and its frame. It swung to and fro on its hinges, creaking in the dry, hot breeze blowing in from the waters of the Golden Horn. Behind it lay heaps of smoking rubble. What had once been window-frames, joists and brackets stuck up and away from the blackened mess like agonised limbs.

The fireman who had just spoken to him cleared a small pile of rubble away from something that looked like a carbonised tree. A thing struck by lightning. Ikmen's stomach lurched and he turned away. Too tired for bodies like that.

'Sir?'

Cohen was standing right in front of him and he hadn't even noticed. He'd looked straight through the man as if he were a window. But then Cohen always had been shallow. Ikmen giggled stupidly at his own joke. 'What is it, Cohen?'

'Avcı just radioed in.' He smiled. It wasn't easy because Ikmen looked like he was going out of his mind. 'Your wife is fine, sir, and you have a son, who is also fine.'

'Oh.'

Cohen carried on smiling through Ikmen's vagueness. There was little else he could do. 'And Dr Sarkissian's at the morgue now, getting ready for the bodies to arrive.'

Babies and bodies. Ikmen looked into Cohen's large, sensual eyes. 'They've found three bodies, four if you include the jumper.'

'Yes, I know. It started on the top floor, you know, the fire.' Out of the corner of his eye Cohen could see things that looked like wooden statues being loaded on to stretchers. He cleared his throat and changed the subject. 'Commissioner Ardiç would like to see you when you return to the station, sir.'

'What a pity I don't want to see him.'

It was his usual cynical style, which relieved Cohen some-what, but without his customary light touch. Cohen sighed. He'd never really understood this case. 'What now then, sir?'

Ikmen chanced one glance towards the firemen and then

looked quickly back at Cohen. Even his ugly face was preferable to what they were digging out of the rubble. 'Sit here and try to make some sense of it all for a bit. Then see Ardiç, I suppose. Wrap this thing up.'

'What, you mean the whole Balat thing?'

'Yes, I think so, Cohen.' He pointed behind him towards the remains of the house. 'One day I'll explain all that to you, as far as I understand it myself. The curtain's fallen on this one.' He lowered his voice to a whisper. 'Pity it fell before the denouement.'

Chapter Twenty-six

FATMA LOOKED DOWN at the baby in her arms and brushed his tiny face with her finger. He opened his mouth and screwed his eyes up tight. 'Now then, don't scream,' she said, 'you'll wake that horrible daddy.'

But it was only a joke. Fatma knew that it would take a lot more than a crying baby to wake her husband at the moment. She was glad that most of the other children had gone out, however. It was the clouds that had sent them whooping down into the street, the promise of rain. Fatma welcomed it too. She looked out of the window at the darkening sky and felt a tremendous relief course through her body. The city hadn't seen so much as a spot of rain for nearly two months. If only it had come a day earlier perhaps all those poor people wouldn't have died in that terrible house-fire. And maybe then Çetin would have got some answers to those questions that had been torturing him. He had finally got to bed at about midnight, after nearly forty-eight hours without sleep. He'd barely looked at his new son, he'd been so tired. Fatma hoped and prayed that his case was closed now. If it was he could take some annual leave. He had enough owing. But then with Çetin she never really knew. Where other people would just give up and move on to other things, Çetin would continue until he was satisfied, which was frequently a very tall order indeed. His desire to root out the truth at all costs was not one of those qualities that endeared him to her. His mother had always wanted to know things too. The Albanian witch had spent her short life dabbling in things best left undisturbed.

It was so quiet in the apartment without the children, but Fatma liked it. Çetin and Timür were asleep, the younger man in his bed, the older one snoring gently in his chair opposite her. Çiçek was somewhere around, but she was being very quiet too. Ever since the baby had been born she'd been thoughtful. Fatma wondered whether perhaps the arrival of a new life had made her stop and consider her own existence. Birth could do that to a person. She remembered how she herself had been affected the first time she'd witnessed a human birth. Fatma smiled at the memory. She had been disgusted. That her lovely Aunt Mihri could be party to something that messy and undignified had shocked her. The eleven-year-old Fatma had resolved on the spot never to do 'that' herself. Nine children down the line she had a somewhat different view.

The front-door buzzer rang and luckily woke Timür from his light slumber. Fatma had not relished the thought of trying to open the door with her arms full of, at the moment, quiet and contented baby. The old man rose stiffly to his feet and wandered slowly past her, chucking the baby lightly under the chin as he went. Timür could drive Fatma mad, especially when he was in wild, irreligious mode, but she couldn't fault him when it came to doing things for her when the babies were tiny. He would fetch, carry, sort out the other children—sometimes he would even cook. Only plain spaghetti and courgette, but it was a meal. Fatma sometimes wondered how often he had served that food up to Çetin and Halil after their mother died.

She heard the sound of the front door opening followed by several deep male voices. Then Arto Sarkissian walked into her living room followed by her own husband's handsome partner. She was surprised to see Suleyman as Çetin had told her that he was in hospital.

Arto bent low and looked carefully at the baby. 'Perfect.'

Fatma smiled.

Timür came back into the room and offered both men seats.

Fatma looked at Suleyman's white, drawn face. 'I'm surprised to see you, Mehmet. Çetin told me you were in hospital.'

'I was discharged this morning, Mrs Ikmen.' He smiled weakly. 'I think they needed the bed for someone who was really ill.'

'You don't look exactly fit to me!' said Timür. He had strong views about the public health service and its duty to the public, which he gave vent to frequently.

Arto smiled. 'I met the Sergeant as I was leaving to come here. He wanted to see Çetin, and of course the rest of you, as much as I did.'

Fatma shifted the now sleeping baby in her arms in order to get a little more comfortable. 'Çetin's still asleep, I'm afraid, but—'

Before she could finish, an extremely crumpled individual entered the room, its eyes misted with sleep. 'Hello everyone,' said Çetin. 'Anyone care for a case conference?'

The three men waited until Fatma and the old man had left of their own accord before they actually started their deliberations. Çetin poured large brandies for himself and Arto and got a Coke from the kitchen for Suleyman.

Arto was the first to speak. 'I found what was left of a British passport on one of those bodies. It's unreadable, but they are quite distinct, you know. Hard cover, gold lettering.'

Çetin sighed. 'I expect you'll find it belonged to a man called Robert Cornelius.'

'I intend to notify the Consulate.'

Suleyman looked deeply into his can of drink. 'What about the other bodies?'

'Two women and three men.'

Çetin smiled sadly. 'Maria, Natalia, Sergei, Nicholas and the servant boy. I wonder which one of them killed Leonid Meyer? Because one of them did. If you want I'll tell you the story as I see it. I told Ardiç yesterday.'

'What was his reaction, sir?'

'Well, Suleyman, he didn't believe me, but then I never really expected him to. That it conveniently wraps up the case he liked, but, as he said, my reasons for pointing the finger at the Gulcus will have to be "reassessed". A picture of him lying to all the big nobs, the Israeli Consul and the Mayor et cetera, passed through my mind at the time and I thought how much he was going to enjoy it. Ardiç is good at lying. By the time he's finished I will probably discover that I actually caught Reinhold Smits red-handed as he tried to knock off the poor old Rabbi and that that was the reason for his suicide.'

'So what's the truth of it then, Çetin?' Arto leant forward in his seat and stared hard into his friend's face.

Çetin lit a cigarette. 'Well, it's wild, Arto, and it revolves around these two women'—he placed the two photographs he had discovered on Smits's desk down in front of his colleagues— 'who may or may not be one and the same.'

'Who are they, sir?' Suleyman asked.

'The woman with the two men is Maria Gulcu. Incidentally, that's Reinhold Smits and the dark one is Leonid Meyer.'

Suleyman looked closely at the face of Meyer particularly. It seemed to fascinate him, possibly, Ikmen thought, because the last time the younger man had seen Meyer had been under such appalling circumstances. But, at length, he pointed to the other photograph. 'And this one?'

Çetin smiled. 'Ah, this one. Yes. This is a photograph, I

have since discovered, of Tsar Nicholas II's third daughter, the Grand Duchess Maria. The words below it refer to an inscription that was discovered on one of the walls in the Ipatiev House where the family died. They were written by Smits. If you look at the photograph of Maria Gulcu and then at this one, you can see the similarities.'

Suleyman's eyes widened. 'You don't mean...'

'Now then, hold on,' said the good doctor, picking up both pictures and holding each in turn up close to his eyes. 'We all, I hope, know how easy it is to see similarities where they do not really exist.'

Çetin grinned.

'For instance,' the doctor continued, 'something that is absolutely unalterable is the width of a person's face. If you look closely you can see that the Gulcu woman's bone structure is narrow while this one is wide and, if I were called to make a judgement, I would say that the lovely Grand Duchess has a far more typically Russian shape to her countenance. The eyes, I admit, are very similar in character, but the noses, which are quite different types, do not, I feel, bear close examination.' He looked up in order to gauge the reactions of those around him. 'I may be wrong, I mean I am no expert with photographic evidence...'

'Oh, I don't think that you are wrong, Arto.' Çetin smiled again, if a little sadly. 'I, although I must say that I didn't to begin with, share your opinion. Unfortunately Reinhold Smits, who left these on his desk for me to discover after his death, did believe that they were one and the same.'

'Meaning what exactly, sir?'

Çetin sighed heavily. 'Meaning, in the absence of all of the protagonists in this story that I can only, at best, theorise about things like meanings.'

'Well, tell us anyway,' said Arto as he replenished both his and Çetin's drinks.

'All right.' Çetin took a deep breath and, despite his still debilitating tiredness, launched enthusiastically into his story.

'On or around 16 July 1918, Leonid Meyer, a young Bolshevik soldier, for want of a better term, found himself assigned to guard duty at the Ipatiev House in Ekaterinburg which is where the ill-fated Romanov family were held at the time. Under the command of another Jew, Yacob Yurovsky, this posting was both dangerous—because of the large numbers of Royalist White Russian forces which were advancing into the area—and prestigious because he was going to kill the Tsar. And on 17 July 1918 Leonid Meyer and his comrades did just that. Shot the Romanovs, chopped up their bodies, destroyed them with sulphuric acid—poetic?—felt very pleased with themselves. With, that is, one exception.'

'Meyer?'

'Yes, Arto, Meyer. I mean, why else would he rave and cry and carry on about it over seventy years later and why would he have stolen this lovely picture here—which from its age and condition would seem to be quite genuine?'

'He could have taken it as a trophy of "battle",' said the doctor. 'People do do things like that.'

'I accept that,' Çetin replied, 'but bear with me. Now, I don't know whether Meyer met the girl who was to become Maria Gulcu before or after the events at the Ipatiev House, but whatever, somehow he came across this girl and somehow he convinced himself and her that she was the Grand Duchess Maria.'

Suleyman, who had been silently deliberating his superior's rather shocking words for some minutes now felt that he had to speak. 'Oh, look, hang on a minute, sir! I thought you dismissed all that Romanov stuff some time ago?'

Ikmen smiled. 'I did. When I discovered that there couldn't possibly be a link between the spinster Anna Demidova and Mrs Gulcu, any Romanov connection with Meyer's old crime, plus his gunpowder wounds, seemed to fall down around my ears. But in light of the history Smits instructed me to read, plus these photos, it all fitted that little bit too snugly.'

'History? What history?'

'He left me a book open at the page where that Belshazzar line was quoted. Apparently, just to enlighten you, it had been written on a wall of the Ipatiev House by one of the guards—oddly in the original German. However, that page also told me that just before the execution, some of the guards were changed and that nobody now knows who they were. Only the major players, like the commandant, Yurovsky, were ever listed—a point frequently glossed over by most other commentators because, on the face of it, it is a very minor detail. And who, after all, would have bothered with a little nobody like Meyer?'

Suleyman still looked doubtful. 'But then why and how would Meyer take some unknown girl and convince her that she was this Grand Duchess person?'

'Perhaps he did it in order to assuage his own guilt. If this lovely girl were still alive, he could convince himself that his own part in the proceedings had never happened—it would seem to fit with what we know of his character. Perhaps he was actually the one who was solely responsible for her death—hence his obsession with her. But then again, maybe he simply saw her as somebody he could perhaps make money out of some day. Who knows? As to how? Well, maybe Maria Gulcu had herself been through some sort of trauma at around that time. It is more than possible; as we know she was from a wealthy family and her face was also covered with old scars. If indeed her whole family had been murdered, as she always claimed, it could be that she was sufficiently traumatised to accept almost anything that he told her then.' He paused in order to light another cigarette. 'Anyway, at some point after these events, Meyer took the decision to take this girl, who may or may not have been his lover, out of the country.'

'Yes, but if the White armies were advancing...'

'If they had found out what he had done, they would have killed him. And in addition, they would have discovered that his "new" Grand Duchess Maria was a fraud and would therefore have completely destroyed his delusion.' He looked around at his companions and smiled. 'Because that's where I believe we now are, gentlemen—in the world of delusion. And, in fact, everything that happened in both Maria and Leonid's lives from here on was circumscribed and informed by that delusion. It was very intricate. Even her "cover" name, Demidova, the same name as the Tsarina's maid, was connected, albeit in a not immediately obvious way.'

'You mean,' said Suleyman who was now struggling a little with the psychological intricacies, 'that they both started actually to believe...'

'Oh, yes. I think that, in order to understand why Meyer later died, basically because he had once been involved in an ultimately unforgivable crime against this family, we have to accept that they must both have become convinced. Yes, they believed and when Meyer came to this country and started working for Reinhold Smits, with whom he became acquainted, Smits believed also. In fact poor old Smits, it would seem, became infatuated with Maria Gulcu for a while. Whether Meyer or Maria or both of them gave him that old photograph of Grand Duchess Maria and for what reason, I don't know. But I do feel that Smits knew about and was fascinated by this great secret that the little Jew and the young woman shared.'

'So why did he dismiss Meyer from his job? If he was, as you say, so fascinated by this pair?'

Ikmen sighed. 'That I don't know either—unless of course it was as Smits said it was—he had become a Nazi and there was no longer a place for a Jew in his sphere of influence. After all, Maria Gulcu was settled with her children by this time and was perhaps no longer in contact with Smits. Who knows? I do, however, believe that Meyer later blackmailed Smits about his old Nazi past. It is the only explanation I can see for his continued association with the German, plus the large amounts of money in his apartment. Allegiances like that have not been popular for some time—a fact which may have given Meyer the excuse he needed to take some sort of financial revenge upon Smits.'

'And so who killed Meyer and why?'

'Maria Gulcu, or rather some other more capable member of her family killed Meyer.'

'But why?'

Çetin's face took on a grave aspect. 'You saw how that family lived, Suleyman. How far do you think you would have to retreat into a delusion like this to arrive at the conclusion that your "father's" murderer must die?'

'But why now?'

'I don't know.'

'And why couldn't it have been Smits?'

Çetin sighed. 'Because the swastika, as it did, would have led us right to him and what did he, a dying man, want with trouble like that? Don't forget that he killed himself because of all this—he knew everything, the lot.'

'So why,' put in Arto, 'didn't he tell you all this and get himself off the hook?'

'I can only assume,' Çetin answered, 'that even at the end he didn't want to give the lovely Maria away. Remember that if you follow the line of the delusion to its logical conclusion and if Maria Gulcu were indeed the Grand Duchess Maria, she must have been at considerable risk for much of her life. Had she truly been genuine then the old Soviet Government would have wanted her dead.'

'But they're all gone now,' said Suleyman, 'so what was the point?'

'The point is, Suleyman, that old men and women do not change. Smits had harboured this "great secret" for most of his life and he wasn't going to let go of it now. Perhaps he even, deep down, feared that it was an illusion too and maybe he just couldn't face that.'

'So,' Arto mused, 'the swastika was daubed there to implicate Smits?'

'I assume so,' Çetin replied, 'although as I think I've said before, it does have other, older meanings.'

'Strange then,' Arto continued, 'that he should continue to

keep Maria's secret when she, obviously, had no regard for him whatsoever.'

'He had wanted her once. He and Meyer had argued over her. Infatuation like that, particularly for a princess, dies a hard death. Although I must say that I think he was getting close to revealing something just before he died. He told us Maria "had" something on Meyer. He was almost ready, but not quite.'

'And this Robert Cornelius, where does he feature?'

'Robert Cornelius was totally ignorant of the events I have outlined. He had, for him, the double misfortune of being in love with Natalia Gulcu and being in the wrong place, i.e. Balat, at the wrong time. Having said that, however, I do believe he had some knowledge about who may or may not have killed Meyer. My personal opinion is that it was probably his girlfriend.'

Suleyman frowned. 'How so?'

'Remember when he asked us about penalties and sentences during that last interview we had with him?'

'Yes?'

'Remember how he went on about the death penalty and about people who might be excepted from it?'

'Mmm?'

'Well,' Çetin continued, 'if he didn't have anybody in mind then why ask? I think that he had at least a vague notion of who might be involved in his mind. Perhaps he thought that if one of the more elderly members of the family were involved age might preclude execution.'

'Yes, but...'

'But then that's only a theory too. Like everything else to do with this case, including the definite identity of the person who killed Rabbi Isak, we can only theorise.'

'Even though,' Suleyman put in, 'we know that it had to be Robert Cornelius.'

'Even though we think we know that, yes. With his body in the condition that it is, quite where we start with regard to forensics, I don't know.' Çetin smiled. 'And why he, poor soul, would have done such a thing, I cannot imagine.'

All three men sat in silence for a while after that and until Suleyman altered the subject slightly there didn't appear to be anything more to be said.

'So,' Suleyman began, 'why, out of interest, did you give me the day off yesterday, sir?'

Çetin and Arto briefly exchanged a knowing glance. The good doctor knew all about Çetin's family and their little peculiarities. Therefore, rather gallantly, so Çetin later thought, he answered for his old friend. 'Çetin's reasons for doing that centred on certain beliefs he then had about what was about to take place. He feared for your life.'

Suleyman, who didn't know his superior as well as the doctor, did nevertheless understand that this referred to Ikmen's rather unconventional belief in precognition. Not sharing such views he responded rather sourly, 'I see.' He could not help it.

Arto, who had anticipated a reaction of this type, went on to say, 'And, as you are only too painfully aware, Suleyman, my old friend's intuitions were, in part, rather borne out—don't you think?'

'Yes.' It was said slightly sulkily, but just accepting enough to indicate to all present that the subject was now closed.

'Well, it's been absolutely fascinating,' said Arto as he rose, rather stiffly, from his chair, 'but I really must go now, I'm afraid, Çetin. Those bodies of yours won't formally identify themselves, will they, and after all the trouble and confusion there has been over this case, I want to make sure that everyone is who we believe them to be.'

'Oh, yes, please. I don't think that I can stand any more mystery with regard to this one.'

'No.' The two men embraced warmly.

After the doctor had gone and Çetin was alone with Suleyman, however, his earlier, almost jovial mood disappeared. 'You know,' he said as he went out to retrieve another soft drink for his colleague from the kitchen, 'this case has been the nastiest one I have ever worked on.'

"Why's that?"

'Because there was absolutely nothing to like about any of the people involved in it. For one reason or another they were all absolutely selfish.'

Suleyman shrugged. 'I suppose you—'

'Yes, they were,' Ikmen concluded, 'even in the wildest reaches of their delusions.'

It was late and all the children were in bed. Fatma was sleeping too. Mercifully, the baby had gorged himself into a deep, open-mouthed slumber. Only Çetin and Timür remained in the living room, drinking and watching the wonderful rain wash down the window-panes. The air seemed so much clearer now, as if a great thick blanket had been lifted from the city and flung into the sea.

'So why did you try and get rid of that boy yesterday then?'

'What, Suleyman?'

'Yes, Suleyman. Well?'

Çetin pulled a miserable face and stared down into his drink. He hated explaining these things to Timür. 'Samsun did a reading for me. She saw it. The boy falling from the window, the fire. Suleyman standing in the path of the falling body—the lot.'

The old man grunted. 'Coincidence. Anyway, what was Samsun doing in town, I thought that Ahmet and his terrible tribe had moved away.'

Çetin shrugged. 'Uncle Ahmet moved to Izmir, but Samsun stayed behind. Istanbul's better for people like her.'

'Him.' Timür spat the word out contemptuously. 'Your mother's family are weird. You should stay away from them, Çetin.'

'You married her and I'm like her!'

'Yes, you are, cursed witch-boy!' Timür paused for a second, wishing he hadn't said it, knowing that it was too late. 'But you're also like me too, Çetin. Your mother wasn't clever. She was artful, but she was no intellectual.'

Çetin lit a cigarette and looked at the reflection of its glowing tip on the window-pane. 'I know. But they are my family and they are the only people I can talk to about...' He changed the subject. 'Anyway, Suleyman is safe, that's all that matters. How is not important. Now his mother can marry him off to his boring cousin and watch helplessly as he has affairs, just like Cohen.'

'Cohen?'

'One of my constables. Jewish. His hobby is chasing young Swedish tourists. I despair.'

The old man took a cigarette from his son's packet and lit up. 'I never did that to either of you.'

'I'm grateful, OK?' He was still smarting from being called a witch-boy. Only Fatma could do that and expect to get away with it. Timür always claimed to understand Çetin's 'gift' but he couldn't, not really.

The old man realised that the time had come to change the subject. 'You know I heard all of your explanation of the Meyer murder, don't you? I listened at the door before I came in.'

'I guessed you were probably there.'

Oh, they knew each other so well! Timür laughed. 'It was good, Çetin, but there was one possibility that you didn't consider.'

Çetin raised a tired eyebrow. 'Oh? And what was that?'

'Well, remember you said that you didn't know what Maria Gulcu was doing in Ekaterinburg?'

'Yes.'

'Well, did it never occur to you that perhaps she was supposed to be there?'

It was very late for this cryptic kind of talk. Çetin rubbed his eyes and yawned. 'What are you talking about?'

Old eyes gleamed mischievously at him. 'That she was one of the prisoners! That she was shot at too and that somehow Meyer managed to save her.'

Çetin groaned. 'And her real name was Anastasia, right?'

'No, Maria like you said, as in the photograph.' He leant

forward and rested one shoulder against his son's side. 'It's not that crazy, Çetin. I was reading the English newspaper *The Times* not so long ago and a report in there said that although most of the royal remains have now been found in a wood near Ekaterinburg, two bodies are still missing. The Tsarevich and one of the girls, they think.'

'But Maria Gulcu and the Grand Duchess looked nothing like each other—really. We've established that, I thought.'

'In your and Arto's opinion, yes. But what about getting some expert advice?'

Çetin was really too tired for all this. 'I don't know. What about it?'

'Well, isn't it worth pursuing it?'

'Look, they all died, Timür. It was just a delusion, a dangerous one, but a delusion and—'

'Ah, but what if it wasn't!' The old man's eyes were shining now as slowly he leant forward and picked up the picture of the Grand Duchess Maria from the table. 'What if this Gulcu woman was Belshazzar's Daughter?'

Çetin smiled. He had to under the circumstances. 'You're a bit of a secret royalist beneath all your republicanism, aren't you, Timür?'

'No, no.' But as he looked down at the picture, his usual scowling expression changed. 'But I do come from that era, Çetin, and even I have to admit that it was a more gracious time. Sultan Vahideddin still ruled over what was left of our Empire when I was born.' He sighed, 'We were Ottomans then as we had been for hundreds of years. What are we now?'

'We're Turks,' said his son, yawning as he spoke, 'and we're a great deal better for it.'

The old man smiled. 'Yes. Yes, you are right. No more veiled women, no more wars fought on the whim of one man.'

'That's just about right.' Çetin stood up and stretched, only suddenly and quite unexpectedly to be grabbed from behind.

'What if I were to be right about Belshazzar's Daughter, what if...'

Gently, but firmly, Çetin removed his father's hand from his waist and smiled. 'I've got to get to bed. I am a dead man.'

'Oh, but Çetin, if it were true! If Maria Gulcu had been the Tsar's daughter! The miracle of it! Think!'

'But she's dead now anyway, Dad.' It wasn't often that Çetin called Timür 'Dad', but here it seemed appropriate somehow.

The old man persisted. 'But if she was then you met history, my son. You touched a great mystery. You know that?'

Çetin humoured the old man as he knew he should. 'Yes, I know that, Dad. Don't stay up too long. Goodnight.'

The old man didn't answer until he heard his son enter his bedroom. Then, looking at the two photographs laid together once again, he said, 'Goodnight, my son. My poor blind soul.'

Epilogue

*30 September 1992, Side, a popular resort on the Southern
Mediterranean Coast*

EVEN THOUGH IT WAS the end of the season it was still
hot. The beach was quite crowded too, although mostly with
locals now. The foreigners had gone, which was good in one way
because so many of them were irritating and ignorant. Their
passing did leave her feeling somewhat exposed though.

She chewed thoughtfully on the vegetable, relishing its
sweetness, and then picked up the newspaper yet again. It
was, even now that she'd read about it three times over, almost
impossible to believe. That Turkey's latest millionaire, the one
time English butler, John Wilkinson, could have done such
a thing was both amazing and really quite despicable. To tell
the world about the depraved proclivities of a man who had

bequeathed one so much money smacked of base lower-class ingratitude. Not, of course, that she didn't have other, more personal concerns on her mind...

She drank deeply from her blue water bottle and scanned the beach for Anwar. He'd said he wouldn't be long. He'd only gone to the garage to make sure that the car was ready. She hoped that it was because that meant they could leave immediately if they wanted to. She wanted to.

She pushed her hair behind her ears and put on her sunglasses. Touching her hair wasn't nice as the dye had made it very dry and brittle. Anwar loved the colour, but she sometimes wondered how he felt about its texture, especially when they were making love. He liked to hold her hair when he rode her, he used it as a handle when he thrust himself inside her body. Anwar was very rough, which was good, especially in view of the fact that she might have to be with him for some time. She put the paper down again, taking care to avoid reading the very good description of herself on page five. Someone had taken great care to identify all those poor bodies very accurately. Someone, she felt, she didn't much like.

'The car's fixed.' He'd come up behind her which was why she hadn't seen him. His Turkish was so perfect, but then so many of the big Egyptian families were originally Turkish. The old Ottoman civil-service class. It reminded her of the flawless way in which her grandmother had spoken English. But that was for another reason.

He sat behind her, spreading his legs on either side of her body, pressing his groin into her plump, rounded bottom.

'We can go whenever you like, Maria,' he said, winding his arms around her shoulders and touching her breasts with his fingers.

She smiled. She was so used to the name now it was almost second nature. The way she had adapted in such a short space of time pleased her. It also meant that at least something lived on, even though she was the only one who could ever appreciate it.

'I'd like to go today.' She didn't turn to look at him. She knew he was there, she knew how handsome he was too. Not that his looks had ever been a consideration. The Rolls-Royce, the Sudanese manservant and the finest hotel suite in town were the things that had persuaded her to give him everything on that first date. Times were hard and a girl had to live. If the man was handsome it was a bonus, but not essential.

'Then we should go and pack now,' he replied.

Yes, she thought, I will pack all the things you've bought for me. I've little else.

She put one of her hands on his arm. 'You go first. I'd like just a few more minutes here.' She turned and looked into his young, innocent face. 'I'll join you soon.'

He kissed her. 'Promise?'

'I promise.'

Oh, he was so keen to keep her! How much he reminded her of that other man. But Anwar would keep her, of course. The wedding was scheduled for December, after her conversion to Islam. She knew his parents weren't happy, but then what could they do? She knew about powerful families.

He disengaged himself from her and ran up the beach towards the hotel. Twenty-four and fit as an athlete!

She thought about her hair again and wondered whether she should soak it in olive oil again before they started the journey. Not that it made much difference. Her hair wasn't supposed to be the colour of sand, it was rebelling.

She looked along the beach to where a group of young Turkish boys were playing football on the waterline. For just a moment an old evil thought crossed her mind. She knew that was impossible now. The things a person had to do to survive! But then wasn't that what it was all about? Wasn't that the reason why she had despised those sainted dead so much? No woman had to die at the hands of a man—ever. Quite the reverse. And one day, perhaps when Anwar was not quite so young and she had grown tired of playing consort to a member of the *nouveau riche,* he might have to learn what that reverse meant.

Natalia popped another plump bottled beetroot into her mouth and smiled again. When your family have ruled half the world you can do what you like.